George Vandenhoff, Henry Seymour Carleton

Dramatic reminiscences

Actors and actresses in England and America

George Vandenhoff, Henry Seymour Carleton

Dramatic reminiscences
Actors and actresses in England and America

ISBN/EAN: 9783337303655

Printed in Europe, USA, Canada, Australia, Japan

Cover: Foto ©Andreas Hilbeck / pixelio.de

More available books at **www.hansebooks.com**

DRAMATIC REMINISCENCES:

OR,

ACTORS AND ACTRESSES

IN

ENGLAND AND AMERICA.

BY

GEORGE VANDENHOFF.

EDITED, WITH PREFACE,

BY

HENRY SEYMOUR CARLETON.

LONDON:

THOMAS W. COOPER & CO., 36, PATERNOSTER ROW;

JOHN CAMDEN HOTTEN, 151ᴮ, PICCADILLY.

——

1860.

PREFACE.

DESPITE the weak whinings of a certain class of unhappy souls who are constantly growling about the "decline of the drama," and calling from the mouldy past phantom ideals of actors and acting as they should be, there is luckily a much larger class always anxious for the welfare of "things theatrical" at home and abroad; in fact, to the British public generally there is something fascinating in the origin and history of histrionic productions. Authors, Actors, and all artists honestly devoting their time and talents to the support and improvement of our British Drama, will ever

find a large and interested audience to whom
they can appeal for encouragement : while to
that audience their silent struggles and trembling triumphs will be sources of anxiety, sympathy, and admiration ; and were the public
better informed of the constant dangers, great
hardships, and sad depressions of hopes long
cherished and toiled for by the greater part
of the dramatic profession, I am convinced
that there would be a still more general
expression of sympathetic interest for the
comfort and happiness of those who live for
the amusement of the public, and who constantly study its taste and pleasure.

John M. Vandenhoff (the father of our
Author) was the founder of that dramatic
reputation which seems inseparable from the
very name; for nearly half a century did he
study and work to support in proud pre-
eminence the classic school of acting which
the matchless talents of the Kembles had
rendered so famous, to vindicate and illus-

trate the supremacy of intellect over buffoonery, and, through the medium of amusement, to instruct the mind and develope
the "nobler attributes of man;" for such
honourable labour he has won golden opinions,
kind thoughts, and rich blessings, with which
enviable dower he has left the "mimic scene"
and retired into private life, leaving behind
the most worthy character as actor, scholar,
and gentleman.

Of Mr. George Vandenhoff I have little
to narrate, beyond the fact that his easy
entrance and rapid success upon the stage were
chiefly owing to the high reputation of his
honoured father; and having thus introduced
the author, I leave his character to be revealed
in the following pages—by HIMSELF.

Sheridan Knowles asserts that "the stage
has suffered more from the incapacity of its
professors, than from the unjust prejudices of
its opponents." This is most ably illustrated in
the present work. Certainly Mr. George Van-

denhoff should have left in the silent shades of
the past many of the reminiscences of weaker
and less fortunate fellow artists, who have long
since gone to their last account. It cannot be
considered kind or noble to rake up foul
rumours and vile inuendoes that darken the
memory of one who now sins no more, and to
whom the grave should, at least, have proved
a refuge secure from the intrusion of rude
curiosity or sacrilegious malice.

Poor Vestris !

" Owning her weakness and evil behaviour,"

still it is a pleasure to record in this Preface
that many good acts and helping kindnesses to
her co-workers will long be sunny memories to
a large circle. It would have been better had
Mr. Vandenhoff refrained from perpetuating the
petty scandals against the woman who gave him
the helping hand on to the stage, and to whose
advice and assistance he owed the first lessons
in his art. If authors would only write upon
subjects they know something of, it would pre-

vent errors from becoming so popular; thus, if Mr. Vandenhoff had only written his own experiences it would have been well; but when he narrates anecdotes of his contemporaries, or slyly seeks an opportunity to give an opinion upon any actor or actress, he is so signally unhappy in his statements of circumstances and personages that I almost blush to let the errors pass through my hands. But my province being merely to introduce the volume to an English audience, I cannot presume to interfere with the principal part of its contents, yet, to appease my conscience must just point out one or two glaring mistakes, and beg the reader to accept the cream of the anecdotes regardless of digesting the hard facts :—

" Mrs. Jordan did not die at Boulogne, but at St. Cloud."

" Mr. Harley did not die in Harley-street, but Gower-street, Bedford-square."

" Mrs. Glover played Mrs. Malaprop at her last benefit, not Mrs. Heidelberg," &c. &c.

Notwithstanding these drawbacks, the book
is well worth a careful reading. There are
many capital gems of stage chit-chat charmingly told—there is some queer French and
puzzling Latin, capable of the freest translation,
combined with descriptive pictures of English
and American scenery, painted with the glowing colours of an enthusiast inspired by a keen
perception and poetic appreciation of the beautiful in Nature.   There are some true accounts of
the Yankee World, unveiling tender points in
the strange character of over-cute "Jonathan;"
a faithful history of all the "fretful hours"
that the Author strutted upon the stage; with
descriptions of the leading dramatic artists of
England and America for twenty years, from
1839 down to the retirement of Mr. Charles
Kean from the Princess's Theatre ; and,
above all, there is an episode from real
life, entitled "Coralie Walton," a sad and
sorrowful page from life's solemn tragedy—
a tale poor Tom Hood would have wept over,

and which brings vividly to memory his un-
dying "Bridge of Sighs." Still, it is the
history of a pure and loveable being, a flower
that

"wasted its fragrance on the desert air;"

a tale well told of one who "loved not wisely
but too well;" and I am sure this narrative
alone will win a favourable reception for the
volume from many admirers.

Mr. Vandenhoff, regretting the step he took
in 1839, when he quitted the Bar for the
Boards, and set aside Sugden to study Shakspere, has now retraced that step, and leaving
Beaumont claims a new hearing for Blackstone : has bidden the stage a long adieu, and
resumed a practice which, I hope, will make
his comforts perfect.

From his new home in America he sends
forth these remembrances as a farewell tribute
to the dramatic world; therefore I trust they
will meet with a general welcome, and be
received in the same frank, honest spirit in

which they are written.   That all is kindly
meant I fully believe, for

> " Time to me this truth hath taught,
> It is a truth that's worth revealing,
> More offend from want of thought
> Than from any want of feeling."

HENRY SEYMOUR CARLETON.

7, *Coleman-street, Arlington-square,*
Islington, N.

CONTENTS.

REMINISCENCES OF ACTORS.

I.

SOME men, under trouble, disappointment, or rack of mind, take to drinking; a base resource! Some lull their griefs by opium,—just as bad a one! Some seek distraction and oblivion in the excitement of the gaming table,—a worse one still! Some blow their brains out,—the worst of all! *I* took to the stage; it saved me from any, and all of the others.

The necessity of bending all my energies to a new study and a new pursuit; the excitement of a new struggle in a new field, with new difficulties, new motives, new associations, caused a diversion of my thoughts, and, by degrees, restored my mind to a healthy tone. The remedy was, indeed, a desperate one; but, as Hotspur says,

" Out of that *nettle*, danger, I plucked this *flower*, safety."

No matter what my troubles were (they were not pecuniary difficulties; they were nearer the heart

B

than the pocket); they were sufficient to unhinge my mind, and to render me incapable of pursuing my then profession of the law with undivided attention. So I went upon the stage; diverted my thoughts into a fresh channel; and, I do verily believe, by that means, saved myself from insanity—perhaps from a drunkard's fate.

I vow I had no particular predilection for the stage. My father was an actor, it is true, and an eminent and prosperous one; but I was anything but stage-struck. I had been carefully educated to the law, and had fortunately attained, at a very early age, a secure position, and a handsome income in that profession. If there had been a war at the time, or any chance of one, I might probably have entered the army, as a change and a diversion; I recollect debating such a step in my mind at church one Sunday (by way of relief to a very dull sermon), and seriously thinking of enlisting in a cavalry regiment (I had great example for it; Coleridge did so, you know): but there was no Italy on fire for liberty yet, no Crimean war, and little chance of distinction or preferment by fighting: so, instead of entering a cavalry *corps*, I entered myself in MADAME VESTRIS's *corps dramatique*, then being organized for active service at Covent Garden Theatre, London.

VESTRIS had previously managed with great success the little Olympic Theatre in Wych Street, —quite a band-box of a place—where CHARLES MATHEWS made his *début*. Charles was brought up an architect, and held the situation of surveyor to the parish of Bow; but Bow-bells had no music for his ears; and, as he was far from being " monarch of all he surveyed," he took to the stage, came out at the Olympic, under the wing of old LISTON, and yoked his fortunes, in a lover's knot, with those of "the widow." (Vestris was the widow of Vestris the French dancer,—Vestris *fils*, of course; her father was an Italian, Bartolozzi, a sculptor.) PRICE, the old Park Theatre manager, had them—Vestris and Mathews I mean—married, as a necessary, preliminary sort of *purification* before their being admitted to the rarified atmosphere of New York; and, after that ceremony, brought them out,

"In linked sweetness,"

to this country. Here, from a variety of causes, they failed, returned to England in a huff, and became lessees of Covent Garden Theatre; that is, Charles Mathews, *lessee*, Madame Vestris, *manager*; for, in management, Charley was a cipher by the side of

" Her humorous ladyship,"

whose temper (*comme son haleine, selon ce que l'on disait*) was none of the sweetest, but whose taste, tact, and judgment were almost equal to her fickleness, luxury, and extravagance.

She was, when Mathews married her (1837-8) already in the " sere," with a good deal of the " yellow leaf" visible; that is, when the *blanc* and *rouge* were off, and allowed

" The native hue and colour"

of her cheeks to be seen. She had run through a great variety of fortunes; principally those of foolish young lords, fast young guardsmen, and some hoary old sinners; she was the *Ninon de l'Enclos* of her day, less the piquancy and *delicatesse d'esprit* of the

B 2

French *Laïs*; she was accomplished, though ignorant
(a duplex "effect defective" by no means uncommon
on the stage, or off it either); she had commenced her
theatrical career with *eclât*, as an Italian opera-singer;
she had afterwards played at Paris in French comedy;
and had latterly, for many years, been a standing
favourite in the English theatres, in characters requiring a certain *espiéglerie*, nearly allied to effrontery,
together with fair musical capabilities,—the *soubrette
chantante*, in fine.   Her speciality had been what are
technically called *breeches parts*, from their requiring
a lady to invest herself in mannish integuments.   Peg
Woffington, a century before, had been great in these
assumptions, and her Sir Harry Wildair turned the
heads of the *beaux*, by its easy abandon, and graceful
étourderie, to say nothing of the display of her *tour-
nure*, which completed the witchery.

Now, Vestris was admirably gifted, cut out, and
framed to shine *en pétit maitre*; she was remarkable
for the symmetry of her limbs, especially of those
principally called on to fill these parts; she had a
fearless off-hand manner, and a fine *mezzo soprano*
voice, the full *contralto* notes of which did her good
service in "Don Giovanni" (a sort of burlesque on
the opera), Captain Macheath, Carlos in the
"Duenna," Apollo in "Midas," and other epicenes.
For purity of intonation and simple truth of expression, her singing of

"Had I a heart for falsehood framed,"

n the "Duenna," and

"In infancy our hopes and fears,"

in "Artaxerxes," have seldom, if ever, been surpassed. She was the best *soubrette chantante* of her day ; self-possession, archness, grace, *coquéterie*, seemed natural to her ; these, with her charming voice, excellent taste in music, fine eyes, and exquisite form, made her the most fascinating and (joined to her *esprit d'intrigue*) the most dangerous actress of her time. Believe it, reader, no actress that we have now can give you an idea of the attractions, the fascinations, the witcheries of Madame Vestris in the heyday of her charms.

That day, with its triumphs, its intrigues, its conquests, its " Handsome Jacks," its " Lord Edwards," and " Honourable Horatios," was nearly past ; the setting sun was tinging it with its long slanting beams, and charms and popularity were fast fading away. Changing the name of *Chloris* to *Vestris*, the lines of the old French poet, Chaulieu, exactly fitted her :—

> "Chloris par mille cosmetiques,
> Veut couvrir ses rides antiques,
> Et resusciter ses attraits ;
> Mais c'est en vain qu'elle s'abuse,
> Ni le carmin, ni la ceruse
> Ne la rejeuniront jamais !"

Something was necessary for, at least, a temporary revival ; and her last throw of the dice was Covent Garden Theatre, with a husband to bear the liabilities. This last, by the bye, was an important *rider to the bill ;* for it had, not unfrequently, happened to her, in her protracted widowhood, to be suddenly arrested, of an evening, on suspicion of debt, on her way to the theatre. Now this was doubly inconvenient, for it also arrested the performance for the night, until the assistance of " a friend," or the

pledge of her diamonds released her from Moses
Levi, or Abraham Isaacs, representatives of the
Sheriff of Middlesex in his executive capacity. But
now she had one on whom she could repose the
burthen of her responsibilities—one compelled to
bear them, too—and so she could pursue the even
tenor of her way from Kilburn to Covent Garden,
regardless, like Don Cæsar de Bazan, of "a whole
legion of Alguazils;" or, what is more terrible to
modern Signoras and Signors, of sheriffs' officers
armed with *Ca. Sas.* Poor Eliza Lucy!—as one of
her old flames, a veteran himself, always calls her,—
she died at a respectable old age, after much suffering.
Requiescat in pace!

But at the time of which I am speaking, she was
manageress of Covent Garden Theatre; lessee, Mr.
Charles Mathews. He, about thirty-five; she, about
forty-three years of age; and they were just on the
point of commencing their first season at the great
National Theatre, which has since been converted
into an Italian Opera House. It was the theatre which
had been the scene of the triumphs of John Kemble
and Mrs. Siddons. My father made his first *entrée*
on the London Stage (1819) in the same theatre;
Mr. Macready also commenced his London career
there (1816), and had conducted the theatre with
great *éclât* as its lessee and manager, the preceding
season.

As for myself, as I have said, I was brought up to
the law, and very shortly after my admission to practice, I had obtained, and now held the important and
lucrative office of " Solicitor to the Trustees of the
Liverpool Docks," the second legal office in the gift of

the corporation of the borough. The highest office, the " Town Clerkship " (Attorney to the Corporation) was in the hands of a very able lawyer, who, poor fellow ! at the maturity of his years and reputation, fell into the first category I have mentioned at the beginning of this chapter, and, fatally for his health, drank deeply of the cup that " steals away the brains ; " his deputy, a young man of steady habits and good promise, became, probably from over-work and anxiety, the inmate of a lunatic asylum. *My* exit from legal toils was, at least, happier than either of these.

I made my resolution one sleepless night ; rose early, took the express train to London, called on Madame Vestris, was graciously received, stated my wishes, and after expressions of astonishment on her part, and a consultation with Mr. George Bartley, her acting manager, I was duly engaged for the sea-son about to commence, at a salary of £8 per week, and the character was settled in which I was to *debûter* three weeks after that day. The whole affair did not take half an hour to arrange ; with almost any one of our present theatrical managers it would have occupied a fortnight. Slow coaches ! myste-rious diplomatists about an egg-shell !

You must understand that I was utterly unpre-pared in any part ; I had not studied any : I had only made up my mind to quit Blackstone, Coke, Sugden, Chitty, *et hoc genus omne*, for Shakspere, Beaumont and Fletcher, and the worthies of the Drama. I had seen a good many plays, and the performances of most of the principal actors of the day. I had seen old Kean as a boy, and sat on the knees of John Kemble, as a

baby; but acting is not to be acquired by contact or
by imposition of hands; nor can one (as Jacques says
of melancholy) "suck in ' genius' as a weazle sucks
eggs." Some preparation was necessary; for I was,
practically, as complete a novice as if my father had
been a parson; he had never given me an hour's instruction in elocution in his life; and the stage was
forbidden ground to my steps. I had little more than
a fortnight's time to prepare myself for the ordeal of
a first appearance before a London audience at the
principal metropolitan theatre—an ordeal not without terrors to an old stager; how awful then to a
novice !

I hurried back to Liverpool by express, resigned
my public situation, sold off my movables, broke up
my establishment, and set about studying my part,—
LEON, in Beaumont and Fletcher's comedy of " Rule a
Wife and have a Wife." This comedy had been laid
on the shelf for several years, and justly so; for the
nature of the plot and the license of the language are
little adapted to modern taste and refinement. Looking back, I have frequently regretted that it was reproduced on my account; but its long absence from
the London stage was the motive for its revival;
and though the same cause put me under the disadvantage of never having seen it played myself, yet I
thought that more than counterbalanced by my
escaping comparison with living actors of eminence—
a comparison always dangerous, oftentimes fatal to a
young aspirant. Leon had been a great character
with John Kemble and the elder Kean; they had
departed from the scene years since, and it was probable that the beauties and *points* of their perform-

ance did not live in the general memory ; so Leon was fixed upon as my *coup d'essai.*

Great was the wonder of the *quid-nuncs* of Liverpool, on my resignation of my public office, for which on the instant a hundred candidates appeared. I kept my own secret, nor was the riddle explained till the London *Times* announced my coming *début* at Covent Garden Theatre. Then the murder was out ; and divers were the comments and prophecies

> " In accents terrible,
> Of dire combustion and confused events,"

to attach themselves to me henceforth and for ever. The mildest judgment passed on me was that I was *mad ;* the gentlest sentence, that I was *ruined.* But, thank heaven ! I have never yet worn a strait jacket, and I have continued to "hold my own" up to the present writing, June, 1859.

Well, I made my first appearance at Covent Garden Theatre on Monday, 14th October, 1839 (20 years ago !

> Eheu ! fugaces Posthume, Posthume
> Labuntur anni !)

and had the satisfaction of disappointing friends and enemies by obtaining a unanimous verdict of success from press and public. At one of my rehearsals, I well recollect Mrs. GLOVER—the last representative of that great school of acting in which she had been born and brought up, a great *Estifania* too in her day—being present ; she gave me much encouragement, saying aloud in her *brusque,* semi-Johnsonian infallibility of style,—" Well, he's sure to be heard, at all events ; and has plenty of confidence ; voice enough, and face enough ; he'll do !"

B 5

I confess I was not overwhelmed with terror at appearing before the much-dreaded tribunal of a London audience, though it was my first essay in arms, and much depended on the result. I made, I remember, a very hearty dinner about three o'clock, went calmly down to the theatre at six, dressed, and "made up" my face in quite a business-like manner (I wore, by the bye, for my first dress the very same costume that John Kemble had worn for the part ; think of that for a novice ! "Shade of Kemble," I internally exclaimed, "let thy mantle fall on me !") and entered the Green-Room cool and self-possessed. There was Charles Mathews, dressed for Michael Perez, and also Madame Vestris. On my replying to their inquiries that I felt perfectly at ease, Mathews, placing his hand on my left breast, said,—"Let's see ; *let's feel !*" He kept his hand there a moment, then withdrawing it, exclaimed to Vestris,—"By Jove, Liz, its as calm as a child's !"

"Now, then," said I, "let me feel how *yours* goes."

"O, no !" said he, "I'm as nervous as I can be !"

And so he was. It was his first time of playing the Copper Captain, and he was naturally anxious about his success in a style of character beyond his usual flight. His nervousness was the result of experience, bringing a sense of responsibility ; my coolness, of *in*experience :

"Fools rush in where angels," &c.

And I can safely say that I do not recollect ever to have walked on to the stage, on any important occasion during my subsequent career, with as perfect a self-possession as on that night of my first attempt. I believe this is not unfrequently the case, too. The novice is not fully conscious of the difficulties of the task that he has undertaken, and of the thousand and one chances that may balk his success ; he is, consequently, if his nerves are good, frequently self-possessed and tolerably calm. The old actor, on the other hand, who has made a name, has his reputation to support, is conscious of the responsibility, and anxious for the result, so that he is generally what is called *nervous* on the first night of a new play, or a new part. The great comedian, WILLIAM FARREN, was proverbially so, to such an extent, in spite of his fifty years' experience and continued practice on the stage, that authors trembled with apprehension on their " first nights," lest Farren should unexpectedly break down in the words of his part. I once, myself, prompted him on the stage, through a whole scene in Bourcicault's comedy of West End (Irish Heiress), the words escaping his memory from nervousness, and I luckily having retained them from the repeated rehearsals we had had of the play. He thanked me at the end of the scene, and complimented me on my self-possession. Mr. MACREADY was always nervous. The least casualty would throw him out. He said to me once :

" I don't know how it is with you, but on the days in which I act at night I can think of nothing else ;" and it was so. On those days he allowed himself no pleasure, no distraction ; nothing that could excite him or divert him from the business of the night.

To resume :—The cast of the play " Rule a Wife," &c, was a very good one; though, of course, the critics,

" laudatores temporis acti "

called it weak, and groaned over " the lights of other

days." Still (setting my own untried name out of the question), I think a cast that embraced the names of George Bartley, Charles Mathews, Frank Matthews, Meadows, Diddear, Mrs. Nisbett (poor Nisbett!)

"Where be your gibes now, your gambols" ("songs" she had none), "your flashes of merriment that were wont to set the theatre in a roar?"

and Mrs. Brougham, then in full bloom,—I say such a cast was not to be sneezed at! It is needless to add that, at Covent Garden Theatre, with Madame Vestris at the helm, the *mise en scène* was perfect.

As to the merits of the performance generally, the papers of the next day exhibited their wonted *acumen,* and accustomed diversity of opinion; one praising to the echo what the other denounced, and leaving the inquiring reader, as usual, in a happy state of bewilderment as to whether the actors were the greatest idiots or the greatest geniuses that the stage had ever produced! I know not whether it is a source of greater consolation or confusion to the mind of an *artiste* of any pretensions, to observe that if he extract passages of *praise* only from the different journals, he may establish himself, by the accretion of these culled selections, perfect in every point, " factus ad ungem,"—a piece of Carrara marble, free from bias, flaw, or blemish; while, on the other hand, if he collect the censure in detail, he may find himself a conglomerate incarnation of faults, defects, over doings, underdoings, misfeasances and malfeasances.

For myself, looking back to that my " maiden effort," I willingly acknowledge the extreme indulgence of the London press in my regard. *Times*, *Herald*, *Post*, *Chronicle*, *Sun*, all spoke most favourably of my *début*, and all were very lenient to the faults and deficiencies inseparable from a first attempt. There was a great house : the box-price at that time was seven shillings sterling, and the prices of other parts of the house were in proportion. The audiences were really worth playing to, representing the rank, taste, and elegance of the metropolis. I received frequent applause, and had the honour of a loud and prolonged "call" (calls were not so *dirt-common* then as now !) at the close of the performance, which was announced for repetition by Mr. Bartley, the stage manager, for the next night ; and it was repeated cn alternate evenings for a fortnight.

The curtain had barely touched the ground, when that hearty creature, Mrs. Nisbett, the queen of comedy, Thalia in her most frolic mood, turned to me with one of her most radiant smiles, and shook me warmly by both hands, exclaiming in her off-hand way,—

"*You're* all right !" adding, "You've got into a hornet's nest, though !"—a pleasant illustration of her idea of "the whips and spurns" I had to look forward to. She meant to tell me, I suppose, that, like a young bear, all my troubles were to come !

Madame Vestris, who was dressed for Gertrude in the afterpiece of the Loan of a Lover, was my next congratulatrix ; and her good opinion was most important to me in her managerial capacity. She was good enough to say, in that winning way which she knew so well to assume, and in that tone of affable *bonhommie*, so gratifying in the mouth of a king to a courtier, a president to a place-hunter, or of a manager to a young actor,—

" I intended to have been the first person to wish you joy ; but I see one of my ladies has anticipated me !"

" *One of my ladies!*" The expression amused me : there was a sort of burlesque semi-royalty, the royalty of the theatre about it ; as if Queen Victoria were speaking of one of her *dames d' honneur.*

Nearly every person engaged in the play " followed on the same side," as the lawyers say, with kind expressions and encouraging compliments. Among the rest, Anderson (J. R., I mean) came round to my dressing-room, having seen the performance from the front, and in the frankest manner offered his congratulations ; he was a member of the Covent Garden Company.

Tom Greene, as he was called, a comedian whose *legs* were said to have twice made his fortune in a matrimonial way, added to his compliments, that " it was refreshing to see an actor who could *speak naturally, and did not imitate Macready !*"

Altogether, I felt that I had made a fair start, and might be well placed in the long run.

Apropos of Tom Greene's *mot*, whether I merited the exceptional eulogium or not, it is certain that, in it, he hit exactly the two great blots and vices of the acting of the day,—an unnatural and inflated style of delivery, and a servile imitation of Mr. Macready. It seemed to be forgotten that acting is, or ought to be, a copy of nature ; and that the tragic style is only an elevation of the simply natural one ; just as blank verse is more elevated than ordinary prose. But this elevation is not to be on stilts.

"Speak the speech as I pronounced it to you, *trippingly on the tongue;* but if you *mouth it,* as many of our players do, I had as lief the town-crier had spoke my lines !"

Now the actors have grown utterly to ignore this teaching of the master ; the great rivalry seems to be who shall *mouth the most ;* and the vulgar audience, always misled by extravagance, and dazzled by the showy and the glaring, mistake rant for force, lose the sense of elegant simplicity, and, on the principle of *omne ignotum pro magnifico,* deem that man the finest actor whose style is the furthest removed from nature and truth. Thus the worthy citizen of Leeds thought lightly of John Kemble, "because *he didn't shout out* like Cummings," a local ranter; and Old Partridge in Tom Jones preferred the man who played the king in Hamlet, to Garrick, because Garrick "only acted just as any one would have done under the circumstances ; while the other *spoke out so loud* that any one could see he was a great actor !" And this is a fair satire on the judgment of common auditors.

The slavish copying of Macready revealed the Theatre's barrenness of original genius, and was, at the same time, a cause of its decay. It was pushed to such an extent at Macready's own theatre, that the very *supers* who carried a banner adopted "the *eminent* tragedian's " (such was the epithet he particularly affected to monopolize) rolling walk; and the man who delivered a message gave it out with " the eminent's" extra-syllabification of utterance. It was really a singularly strange thing to see, in

the tragedy of Gisippus, for example (which Mr.
Macready brought out at Drury Lane with great care
and taste), at one view, a whole company surrender-
ing their own identities with plastic subservience, and
melting themselves down into the Macready mould.
There was Anderson in Fulvius, who had caught the
master's tones, slides and angularities, sway and action, till they seemed almost his own : the assumption
was so complete, that some people would have it he
was Mac's son.   Then came Hudson as Chræmes, who
had been indoctrinated into the same routine, only on
a higher pitch, with a dash of flippancy thrown in,
like an acid, to give effervescence to the mixture:
then came Helen Faucit, as Sophronia, who, having
commenced her career under " the eminent's " management, was entirely made up of his mannerisms,

"Subdued even to the very quality of her lord,"

redeemed only by the charms of her own feminine
sweetness ;—and last, George Bennett as Lycias, a
violent exaggeration of every singularity, angularity,
and formality of the Macreadian method. These were
the principal characters.   Then came the subordinates
and *supers*, all formed on the same model, crying in
the same tune, and rolling with the same swinging
gait ! It was a perfect Babel of confusion to the
mind, on an *inverse principle*, from a puzzling general
communion of identity—one could scarcely separate
the interests and positions of people who were so
much alike.   When they came together, it was a
great organ, and you had to watch the mouths of the
speakers ·to see which *stop* was playing ; nor could
you always keep your mind clear as to how all these
people could be engaged in plots and counterplots for

intermarrying with, or destroying each other, when it seemed evident that they were all members of the same family, and so ought to be barred, by ties of consanguinity, from schemes of love or intrigue.

Macready's style was an amalgam of John Kemble and Edmund Kean. He tried to blend the classic art of the one with the impulsive intensity of the other ; and he overlaid both with an outer plating of his own, highly artificial and elaborately formal. He had, too, a mania for inoculating every one from his own system : he was a Narcissus in love with his own form-alities ; and he compelled, as far as he could, all within his influence to pay him the worship of imitation. It was, I believe, Mrs. W. Clifford, mother-in-law of Harrison the singer, who well rebuked this tyrannic egoism. He had been remorselessly hammering a speech into her ears at rehearsal, in his *staccato*, extra-syllabic manner, when she very coolly, but very decidedly, told him that she much preferred her own stylé, and declined to change it for his ; adding, as she opened her eyes and expanded her hands and mouth, with a strong *crescendo* ◁ emphasis on the word *all* :—

" If this goes on, we shall be ALL Macreadys !"
The " eminent's " battery was silenced at once.

Servile imitation is the grave of genius. To be great, an artist must study his kind, not an individual ; Nature, not any single type of her. No surer sign and cause of decay could befal any art and its professors, than that they should all form themselves on one model. To put any man's livery on our mind is the lowest of self-abasement, and must surely destroy in us all sense of the true, the beautiful, the great.

II.

HAVING made a successful *début*, I now set myself
diligently to the study of my new profession ; got perfect in the text of, and privately rehearsed, new parts ;
took lessons from Angelo, and also from Roland, in
fencing ; put myself under a drill-sergeant to throw
off the legal bend of body (all bent of mind for the
law being gone) and to replace it by a manly, erect
carriage ; in fine, I conscientiously devoted myself to
attaining the position of a " well-graced actor." And
believe me, reader, in spite of the common cant about
" spontaneous genius," study, cultivation, observation,
reflection, labour, are the talismans to success.

Genius is a high, a special gift of God ; but it must
be wrought out by man. It is the diamond in the
mine : patient effort must bring it to the sun, cut and
polish it, and shape it to prismatic perfection, or it
may sleep in its silent bed, unvalued and unseen.
That genius has the most power which has the most
instruction, and is the best regulated ; which is the

most rhythmically true, the most harmoniously proportioned. The heaven-born lightning's flash was only
a dazzling, blinding, destructive fire, till science conducted, regulated, guided it, and made it an instru-
ment of far-spreading light and intelligence.

The distinguishing feature, the mark and the test
of genius is, that it strikes out a novelty which it es-
tablishes as a truth; that is, it originates, it creates a
new truth, a new law, whether in science or art.
Talent makes the best application possible of the inventions of genius: genius makes the discovery, and
talent works the patent.

It is not stage-struck enthusiasm that carries a
youth to the top of the tree; *that* usually evaporates
before its owner has got half way up; or the weak
flame is put out by the rubs and hard knocks it re-
ceives. Stage-struck heroes are only good at the
start: they want bottom for a long race, and

> " Like horses hot at hand
> Make gallant show and promise of their mettle,
> But when they should endure the bloody spur
> They fall their crests, and like deceitful jades
> Sink in the trial."

The great honours of the buskin (I do not speak of
mere transient, ephemeral, spasmodic *éclâts* of success) have been won by men who earnestly devoted
themselves to the study of their art, conscientiously
and perseveringly mastering its principles, sounding
its depths, and drawing out its harmonies with nature
and humanity, and its bearing on the philosophy of
life; and, to that end, have sharpened and brightened
the special faculties with which God may have endowed them,—fancy, imagination, sensibility, mimic

power, physical grace, and sympathy with the beautiful and the true.   For truth should be the artist's
Egeria; when he ceases to seek her in her silent cell
and secret groves, he will insensibly lose dignity, self-
reliance, conscious power, and become vapid, common-
place, hollow, superficial; he will not be an actor, but
a mummer; he will cease to be an artist, he will be
a quack, a mountebank, a buffoon.

I know the name of the elder (Edmund) KEAN will be
objected to me, as an exception to this rule of study and
self-accomplishment : but he was not so negligent of
form and method as is commonly supposed ; a judgment
to which his irregular and reckless life seemed to give
countenance. Kean (*the* Kean, of course, I mean) was
as nearly an actor born—a *nascitur*, not a *fit*—as such
a thing is possible ; he was marked for an actor, as
was Burns for a poet, and Opie for a painter, by
sovereign Nature in the cradle ; and he was gifted with
peculiar aptitudes, special powers, and a temperament
highly mercurial and sensitive to the extremes of passion, with a face and eye capable of the strongest
expression and of the quickest transitions of expression,—all peculiarly fitting him for an actor's work.
And this natural fitness was seconded and strengthened
by his earliest impressions.   Education, properly so
called, he had none.   He was truly "to the manner
born ;" he was on, " and *of*," the stage from infancy, if
he did not actually first see light behind the scenes of
a theatre (such light as he *could* see there !) and made
his first recorded essay on the boards, as one of a corps
of young imps, or other juvenile supernaturals, in
John Kemble's production of " Macbeth ;" on which
occasion, he carried his keen love of mischief to the

extent of causing a general downfall of his brother imps by a *faux pas*, an intentional slip of his own, sweeping the entire set with him,—as the middle pin, well struck, will topple down the whole ten,—dis- arranging the gravity of the audience, and incurring his own dismissal by the " classical tragedian" whom he was, in after years, to rival and supersede.

Poor Kean ! I was but a boy when I saw him in his *décadence*,—worn out in constitution, not by years, —but I shall never forget him. I can never hear of Richard III., Othello, Sir Giles, Bertram, Sir Edward Mortimer, Shylock, without thinking of *him*, and bringing him before my mind's eye. His style was impulsive, fitful, flashing, abounding in quick transi- tions ; scarcely giving you time to think, but ravishing your wonder, and carrying you along with his im- petuous rush and change of expression. But this seeming spontaneity was not *chance-work ;* much of it, most of it, was carefully premeditated and prepared. You might hear the same soft flutelike tones, the same waves of melody, the same cadence, night after night, in his delivery of the lines in Richard,—

> " But soft, my love appears : look where she shines,
> Darting pale lustre like the silver moon
> Through her dark veil of rainy sorrow !"

So, his delivery of Othello's " Farewell " ran on the same tones and semitones, had the same rests and breaks, the same *forte* and *piano*, the same *crescendo* and *diminuendo*, night after night, as if he spoke it from a musical score. And what beautiful, what thrilling music it was ! the music of a broken heart— the cry of a despairing soul !

So, all his most striking attitudes,—and he was

the most picturesque of players,—all his most effective
points, and abrupt transitions of voice and manner,
were reproduced in oft-repeated performances of any
particular character ; so that his admirers were ready
with their applause almost by anticipation, before the
well-known *coup* was made : it was a certainty ; it
lay on the balls and he was *sure* to make it.   Did this
detract from his genius ?   No : it proved that he was
an *artist ;* and there is no art without *method* and
design.   What then was Kean's peculiar merit ? in
what did his genius especially assert itself?   In intensity, in the power of abstraction, and of identifying
himself with a passion.   In the words of John
Kemble's tribute of involuntary praise,—" he was
terribly in earnest."   This was his master-quality ;
his next—which, indeed, followed from, if it was not
included in the former—was his natural, and unforced,
yet striking delivery of simple phrases, or passages of
a familiar, conversational style.   In these he threw
away the tragic stilts entirely, and was easy, conversational, *un-stagey*.   Thus, in Othello, his

> " Were it my cue to fight, I should have known it
>   Without a prompter,"

always brought down the house, from the natural, yet
pointed expression, conversational, yet full of meaning,
with which he gave it ; it conveyed a wonderful
mixture of sarcasm and courtesy, if such a duplex
effect can be imagined.   So, in Shylock, his

> " I am a Jew !"

in the passage :

> " He hath disgraced me, and hindered me of half a million, laughed
> at my losses, mocked at my gains, scorned my nation, thwarted my
> bargains, cooled my friends, heated mine enemies : and what's his
> reason ?   *I am a Jew !*"

This was always a cue for the most intense applause : it was the natural simplicity with which he gave it, the sort of patient appeal his tone seemed to make to your sympathy against undeserved oppression, that touched the heart and the intellect at once. He hurried you on through the catalogue of Antonio's atrocities and unprovoked injuries to him, enforcing them with a strong accentuation, a rapid utterance, and a high pitch of voice ; and when he had reached the *climax*, he came down by a sudden transition to a gentle, suffering tone of simple representation of his oppressor's manifest un-reason and injustice, on the words—

"I am a Jew !"—

and the effect was instantaneous.

I might go on multiplying instances of this power of his, of sudden transition from the height of passionate expression, to the familiar key of conversational earnestness, but it is unnecessary. I have said enough to indicate its working. His enemies—and every man, especially every public man, who is worth any thing, *has* enemies—his enemies called it a *trick ;* it was so ; but it was a trick which he gathered from nature, a trick which he transplanted into *art.*

In *intensity* of passion I have never seen any actor or actress that could approach him, except the Italian, Ristori, of whom I shall speak more fully hereafter.

Kean's general method was probably built on Cooke's (George Frederick) ; surpassing his predecessor, perhaps (I speak now only from tradition, of course I never saw Cooke), in fervour and poetic feeling, as well as in grace of action. Those, however, who

remember the Richard III. of both these actors, do
not hesitate to award to Cooke the palm for sustained
power, and intense, enduring energy of passion; Kean
excelled him probably in light and shade of expression.
Kean was a brilliant swordsman, and his early practice
as *Harlequin*, in which he had excelled,—for he had
begun at the very lowest round of the ladder, and
climbed his way upwards till he could

> " build in the cedar's top
> And dally with the wind and scorn the sun,"—

his early practice as Harlequin gave him extraordinary
agility and grace of action, and these physical accomplishments told with amazing effect in the last act of
Richard III.; his fight and death were the perfection
of melodramatic action.

Kean's admiration of Cooke was well known; he
testified it by raising a monument, or rather a tablet,
to his memory in St. Paul's church-yard in the city
of New York, for Cooke died and was buried there,
as is well-known; and

> " No stone marked the spot "

till Kean, on his last visit, about thirty years ago,
erected one.   This reminds me of a singular *cut*—a
" reply churlish "—that was given to Kean, a very
unfair wound to his vanity,—but too *keen* a jest not
to be remembered,—on his return to England, in
connection with this monument to Cooke.

Kean was at a supper-party of friends at Liverpool, after having played Richard, that same evening,
to an audience most enthusiastic in their applause.
Elated, and in the very best of spirits, the actor was
full of chat, and the wine passed freely round.   The

conversation naturally turned on his recent visit to America, thence to Cooke's death, the place of his burial, and the stone that Kean had raised above his head.

" All that is wanting, now," said Kean, " is an epitaph, worthy of the man ; and I should be infi nitely obliged to any one who would furnish me with an appropriate line or two."

Several quotations from Shakespere were offered from various points of the table, but nothing that was suggested seemed entirely satisfactory. Among the company at supper was an eccentric, and somewhat sarcastic fellow, named Taylor, noted for his clever ness and ready wit. To him Kean at last appealed :

" Come, Taylor," said he, " you can do the thing in a minute if you like : come, give us an epitaph for George Frederick Cooke !"

Taylor, thus appealed to, smiled, took a pencil, wrote something on a scrap of paper—the back of a letter—and passed it up to Kean at the head of the table. The tragedian, smiling graciously, in anticipa tion probably of some well-turned compliment to himself coupled with the name of Cooke, proceeded to read aloud what was handed to him : thus—

> " Beneath this stone lies COOKE interr'd ;
> And *with* him—

Kean paused with a darkening brow ; but he was in for it ; there was no help ; and with ill-subdued vexation he read on,—thus :—

> " And *with* him,—*Shakespere's Dick the Third !*"

I leave you to imagine the blank silence that ensued, and " the clouds that lower'd " on Richard's brow,—

a face peculiarly strong in its expression of scorn and
hate.   The wicked Taylor had " stol'n, like a guilty
thing, in haste away," and the rest of the company
shortly followed.   It was a "foul blow" of Taylor's;
but some men would rather lose their friend than
their joke ; and this fellow was one of them.   " Pour
moi,"—as the Frenchwoman said, under very trying
circumstances,—"*Je déteste les mauvaises plaisan-
téries.*"

I have mentioned Kean's early initiation, almost
ab ovo, into the mysteries of the histrionic craft ;
Mrs. SIDDONS' commencement appears to have been
almost as early, and even more strictly elementary, if
what we learn from Rogers's Table-talk be true, that
the embryo Lady Macbeth was seen, when a girl,
standing at the wing of her father's stage, and
knocking a pair of snuffers against a candlestick, to
imitate the sound of a windmill during the representation of some Harlequin piece.   Ye Gods!   The
future Queen of Tragedy a mechanical succeda-
neum! the hidden voice, the *falsetto* of a creaking
windmill! the secret agent of a pantomimic sham!
" To what base uses " may not genius be turned !
Who dreamt, then, that that candlestick-rapping
girl would, in after years, prove such a spirit-rapper!
and that her candlestick-scene in " Macbeth " would
one day knock so terribly at many throbbing hearts,
as she muttered in her tortured sleep,

" To bed! to bed! to bed ! "

She herself, perhaps, felt, within, a foreshadowing
of the

" All hail, *hereafter !*"

for genius is self-prophetic, and heaven vouchsafes it

glimpses, through present darkness, of the future glory that shall environ it, and thus makes it " strong to hope and patient to endure : " so she stood at the wing, and hammered away at the snuffers and candlestick.

We have seen that Kean (Edmund) was almost born upon the stage, certainly in the purlieus of the theatre ; and his son Charles,—the late manager of the Princess's Theatre, from which he has just re-tired with great éclât, loaded with honours, and, I trust and believe, with an ample fortune to crown them. CHARLES KEAN, educated at Eton, and destined by his father for the army, donned the buskin at about eighteen years of age, and followed in his father's walk (*haud passibus æquis*, perhaps), if not with his father's genius as an actor, yet with a much higher position and character as a man.

Mrs. Siddons's father, Roger Kemble, the father of JOHN and CHARLES KEMBLE, and consequently the grandfather of Mrs. FANNY KEMBLE, was also an actor, and the manager of a provincial theatre. So was Mr. Macready's father actor and manager, before him ; he himself was destined originally for the bar, and commenced his education at Rugby, I believe with the intention of finishing it at Oxford ; but. as he told me himself, pecuniary difficulties preventing his father from carrying out his intentions in as full a manner as the youth had expected, he adopted the stage as a profession, and came out at Birmingham under the fostering care of the paternal management.

It is a fact that the children of actors usually take to their fathers' profession, spite of all the well-laid plans of the parent to prevent it: as Prince Hal

C 2

reminds the fat knight,—"Wisdom cries out in the street, and no man regards it." Actors, in general, especially those who have attained eminence, have a dread, amounting almost to horror, of their young ones following in the same career. I recollect, as a boy with my father, meeting old BRAHAM in Covent Garden market, London; and *ápropos* of my future destination, the law, my "governor" asked Braham, then a rich and prosperous gentleman, living *en prince* almost, if either of his boys would be on the stage; to which the great tenor, with emphatic earnestness replied,—"God forbid! One is for the church, the other for the army." Yet both of them ultimately followed in the paternal footsteps, and are public singers. It might be some consolation to the veteran that his daughter became, by marriage, the COUNTESS WALDEGRAVE, one of the stars of the stage of high life, and whose name figures conspicuously in Court Play bills, among the noblest of the land.

In our case, my father was the first of the name of Vandenhoff who ever braved the dazzling glare of the footlights. Our origin, is of course, Dutch; an ancestral Dutchman came over to England in the train of William of Orange, and was, by that prince, so far distinguished, after his landing at Torbay on the 5th November, 1688, as to be allowed to use armorial bearings, with the crest a mailed hand and sword, with the motto " *En avant*." The legend in our family is that these words " En avant" (Forward!) were the exclamation made, and the order given by a Vandenhoff to his company, on leaping ashore at Torbay, suiting the action to the word with his sword in his mailed hand.

My father, John M. Vandenhoff, was educated at Stonyhurst College, Lancashire, England, and his original destination was the Church : his bent for the stage, I have heard him say, was awakened at College, where he got up a play (Sothern's "Oronooko"), in the large play-room, or Truck-house, as it was called, from the old game of Truck being played in it. Leaving College about 1807, I imagine the *res angusta domi* prevented his carrying out his views either for church or law ; and after having, for about a year, submitted to the drudgery of a classical teacher in a large academy in the South of England (he is to this day an excellent Latin scholar), his thoughts reverted to his boyish triumphs on the rude, extemporised boards, or rather flags, of the College, which encouraged him with the idea of trying his fortune in a more public and extended arena. Accordingly, at little more than eighteen years of age, he made his first appearance in the Salisbury Theatre (11 May, 1808) in the character of Osmond, in Monk Lewis's then highly popular, now forgotten, play of the "Castle Spectre !" a *mélange* of melodramatic mysteries and spectral terrors, such as Lewis delighted in, presented in not inelegant, though high-flown language, which seemed to suit the dramatic palate of that day. Osmond is a Scottish earl, the lord of a castle, where he dwells surrounded by slaves obedient to his will ; which will is a very diabolical one, delighting in deeds of blood and crime ; he is a hero of the *Conrad* species:

"Lone, wild and strange, he stood alike exempt
From all affection and from all contempt :
A man of loneliness and mystery,
Scarce seen to smile, and seldom heard to sigh :
And where his frown of hatred darkly fell,
Hope withering fled, and Mercy sighed farewell!"

The general tone and spirit of the language and
the design may be gathered from Osmond's description of his dream, which will be new to most of my
readers, and is curious as a specimen of what pleased
our forefathers.   It is one of the strong passages of
the play, and gave the actor an opportunity of depict-
ing the satanic pride of guilt shaken and torn by·the
agonies of remorse :

> Hark, fellows ! instruments of my guilt, listen to my punish-
> ment !   Methought I wandered through the low-bred caverns
> where repose the relics of my ancestors.   Suddenly a female form
> glided along the vault ; it was Angela !   She smiled upon me, and
> beckoned to me to advance.   I flew towards her ; my arms were
> already enclosed to clasp her, when suddenly her figure changed,
> her face grew pale, a stream of blood gushed from her bosom !
> Hassan, 'twas Evelina !

[Osmond has murdered Evelina, and now wishes
to marry Angela.]

> *Saib and Hassan.*   Evelina !
> *Osmond.*   Such as when she sank at my feet expiring, while my
> hand grasped the dagger still crimsoned with her blood !   "We
> meet again this night !" murmured her hollow voice.   " Now, rush
> to my arms,—but first see what you have made me !   Embrace me,
> my bridegroom !   We must never part again !"   While speaking,
> her form withered away ; the flesh fell from her bones ; her eyes
> burst from their sockets ; a skeleton, loathsome and meagre, clasped
> me in her mouldering arms ?
> *Saib.*   Most horrible ?

[Decidedly unpleasant, I should say.]

> *Osmond.*   And now, blue dismal flames gleamed along the walls ;
> the tombs were rent asunder ; bands of fierce spectres rushed around
> me in frantic dance ;

[A by no means attractive *corps de ballét* these
corpses.]

> furiously they gnashed their teeth while they gazed on me and
> shrieked, in loud yell, " Welcome, thou fratricide ! welcome, thou

lost for ever !" Horror burst the bands of sleep; distracted I flew
thither. But my feelings—words are too weak, too powerless to
describe them !

[Very probably ; but that is a shabby way of getting out of the difficulty. " A most lame and impotent conclusion !"]

Such was the rôle my father chose for his first appearance ; very different from the characters on which
he afterwards built his reputation,—Hamlet, Othello,
Lear, Shylock, Brutus, Iago, Cato, Coriolanus, Virginius, Master Walter, &c., and by which he stamped
himself as *the* classical tragedian of his day. After
an apprenticeship of seven or eight years in various
country theatres, playing all sorts of business, tragedy,
comedy, and farce, — and even sometimes English
opera,—(he and Edmund Kean, I have heard him
say, sang together the celebrated duet of " All's
Well," in the operetta of the " English Fleet,") he
was engaged to " lead the business" at the Liverpool
Theatre in 1815, opened in Rolla, stamped himself
at once a favourite, and during a long acquaintance
with that public, secured their almost affectionate
regard to such an extent, that it was said, ironically,
yet with a spice of truth, that the children there were
taught to bring his name into their prayers, thus :—
" Pray, God bless my father and mother, sister
and brother, and—Mr. Vandenhoff !"
The jest has a point in it, by no means to the dis-
credit of the subject of it. From Liverpool, he went
to Manchester, Dublin, Edinburgh, making periodical
visits to all the principal theatrical cities and towns,
and everywhere winning golden opinions, till, in 1819,

he was engaged to appear at Covent Garden Theatre, London, and opened there in King Lear, Charles Kemble playing Edgar ; the Cordelia was, I believe, Miss Foote, afterwards Countess, now Dowager-Countess of Harrington.

I need not enter into the further particulars of my father's theatrical career, except to allude to these facts.

That, in 1835-'36, he " led the business " at both the Theatres Royal Covent Garden and Drury·Lane, playing on alternate nights at each theatre (the other nights being filled with opera), with a company of which Miss Ellen Tree (Mrs. C. Kean) was a member : that on Charles Kemble's retirement from the stage (1836), my father and Mr. Macready appeared together with Mr. Kemble to houses crowded to overflowing, several nights at Covent Garden Theatre, in the two Shaksperean plays, Othello and Julius Cæsar, with this cast :—

Othello, Mr. Macready ; *Iago*, Mr. Vandenhoff ; *Cassio*, Mr. C. Kemble :

Brutus, Mr. Macready ; *Cassius*, Mr. Vandenhoff; *M. Antony*, Mr. C. Kemble.

That, in the season of 1836-37, he played the part of Eleazar, in the " Jewess," at Drury Lane Theatre, eighty-nine nights in succession, Ellen Tree playing his daughter : that, the season following he visited the United States, for the first time, and was engaged by Mr. Wallack to open at the National Theatre, in Leonard-street (burnt the season after) ; that, in his particular line,—the characters I have specified above,—he obtained a reputation and popularity in this country never surpassed by that of any English actor :

That, on his return to England, his assistance was

eagerly sought by Mr. Macready in his enterprise at Covent Garden Theatre : that his performance of Adrastus, in Ion, was allowed by Talfourd himself, the author, to have raised Adrastus to the dignity of the principal part in the play ; as the *Times* observed, " With the death of Adrastus the interest of the play was over :"

That his rendering of the Chorus in Henry V., was pronounced to be the great feature of the whole performance, and that Mr. Macready himself declared his delivery of the magnificent language to be " the perfection of musical elocution :"—

Finally, that after more than a half century's work " in harness," he has taken off his armour and retired from the field in his seventy-first year, without a blot on his escutcheon, or a blemish on his name ; and that it was only a few months since he was honoured, in Liverpool, with a magnificent testimonial from old friends and admirers ; the Mayor, who presided on the occasion, being seated in the (well authenticated) chair in which Robert Burns wrote the " Cotter's Saturday Night," and the whole company present pledging their guest in a cup that belonged to Garrick.

(Pardon me, reader, if I have dwelt too long on this sketch ; it is a son's passing tribute to a father's name : I may say, with a slight alteration, with the poet,—for it has not come to *desiderium* yet ; he still lives :—

> Quis desiderio sit pudor aut modus
> Tam cari capitis !)

Well, as to myself, I was sent away from home to school at a very early age, and afterwards to the same college at which my father had been educated ;

where, however, I was expressly forbidden to take
any part in the plays that were acted at Christmas
time, with " scenery, dresses, and decorations," in
the large hall or lecture-room of the college elegantly
fitted up as a theatre; and, on emerging from the
precincts of Alma Mater, I was forthwith set to the
study of the law, and in due course duly admitted
and sworn of " Her Majesty's Courts at Westminster ;" and yet—(" Heaven save the mark !")

" for all his prayers, the fool (*ego met ipse videlicet*) was drowned,"

that is, fell into the very pond the parental care had
been so desirous to save me from !   But the fault
was entirely my own.

The result of my experience is, that the Stage is
the last occupation a young man of spirit and ambition should think of following, for this one reason,
if for no other : that it seems to cut him off from the
business of life, and from the great movements and
practical working of the world—the objects of a
worthy and legitimate ambition.

The actor's individuality, as a citizen, seems lost
in the fictitious world in which he lives and moves
and has his being. He is king, governor, general,
statesman, hero of a fantastic realm, but from the
practical interests of this work-a-day world he seems
to be segregated and apart. His ambition, if he have
it, must be confined to the narrow circle and the un-
substantial honours of the mimic scene : from those
nobler ones of the great stage of life, its civic laurels
and political triumphs, he is silently shut out. Who
ever heard of an actor being sent to Parliament or to

congress, being made an alderman or a justice of the peace, or even a "gentleman of the select Westry?"

Besides, the novice's career is one of continual humiliations and wounds to self-love; great uncertainty of employment; and, if employed, hard work and small pay. As he advances into the position of a regular actor, the amount of study piled upon him, of fresh parts to be "up in" at short notice, is brain-splitting: in some cases over-study has produced brain-fever. Therefore, let no rash youth, "with a soul above buttons," adopt the stage as a means of elegant idleness; if he do, he will be wofully mistaken, when he finds that, after a hard week's work, even Sunday is not always a day of rest to his study-wearied brain, worn out with

"Words, words, words!"

I have it from an eminent living actor, that in the early part of his career in England, he has, on one and the same night, played Hamlet, sung a comic song between play and farce, and wound up with Jeremy Diddler in the after-piece; all for the splendid reward of the applause and broad grins of a set of country rustics, with a very sparse sprinkling of intelligence and gentility amongst them, and the magnificent salary of *one guinea* per week; and he was expected on this to "wear clean linen and live like a gentleman!"

"Think of that, Master Brooke!"

III.

HAVING repeated my opening part of Leon five times
at Covent Garden, I asked, and was allowed a *congé*
of a week, to accept a very advantageous offer of five
nights at the Theatre Royal, Liverpool, then under
the management of Mr. Lewis, son of the celebrated
comedian, and a man of independent means and fortune. His acting manager was Mr. R. Clarke; and
the Liverpool Theatre was, at that time, the most
profitable theatrical property in England, second only
to London. I played my five nights with considerable
éclât, received great attentions from the very best
quarters, my audiences comprised the fashion and
wealth of the town, and I pocketed, for my share of
the proceeds, £211. This sum, however, was
almost entirely exhausted in providing myself with
costumes for the Duke Aranza, Julian St. Pierre,
and Faulconbridge, which, with two performances
of Leon, took me through the week. When it is
recollected that I had not belonged to the profession
a month, it will be admitted that I had not been idle
to get "up" even in so small a list, in that limited

time. But my "study," as the actors call the habit of swallowing words, was always quick; and there was an excellent and experienced prompter at the Liverpool Theatre, Lloyds, who did me good service in putting me up to the "business," or conventional action of the scenes in which I was engaged. I owe Lloyds thanks for that; his assistance was valuable to a novice, and I willingly acknowledge it. The actors, too, and actresses were, with very few exceptions, kind and considerate; and the Liverpool press more than confirmed the favourable opinion passed on me in London. So I had reason to congratulate myself on my first engagement in Liverpool, where, from old associations in a different sphere, the ordeal was a trying one.

One incident that happened to me on the stage at Liverpool was amusing, though rather trying to the nerves of a novice, or indeed of an old stager. I was blessed at that time with a luxuriant crop of light, curly hair, which, in the heat of my young ambition and æsthetic determination to have my stage-wigs set as closely and naturally as possible at night, I had sacrificed to the razor; wearing, during the day, a *toupée*, made from my own shorn locks. Of course, there was no necessity for this: it was simply an ambitious novice's martyr-like desire for artistic perfection. The result was certainly gratifying. I had wigs made by *Truefit*, of Burlington Arcade celebrity : they were worthy of his name; they fitted my shaven crown like wax ; and, with their more-than-natural artificial parting at the side, it was impossible to detect the *sham*, at a yard's distance. In Julian St. Pierre I wore one of these triumphs of capillary

perfection — an elegant dark brown, with tints of
auburn cunningly interwoven in it, glossy, and grace-
fully wavy in effect.   I made up my face in harmony
with its crown, was dressed in picturesque costume,
new for the occasion, and presented myself, on the
change from my beggar's garb, in the third act, with
perfect confidence in the general completeness of my
appointments.   The audience flattered me with a
gracious reception, and all went on admirably till the
last scene of the fifth act. Here a dreadful *contretemps*
befell me.

To carry out the idea of a secret flight from
Mantua, at the end of the fourth act, after the great
dagger-scene with the duke, in which St. Pierre com-
pels him to sign the confession, and then leaves him
locked up in the chamber in which he himself had
been confined,—to aid the effect of St. Pierre's entrance and discovery in the fifth act, I had enveloped
myself in an ample disguise-cloak, and had covered
my head with a large black *sombrero*.   The hat was,
like all my appointments, quite new, had never been
worn, even, and consequently was very stiff and tight
to the head.   The result was that when, intending
to make a tremendous assertion, I rushed down to
the lights, confronting the slanderous duke in his
calumny of Mariana, with the words—

"Liar ! she is as true as thou art false !"

and throwing of hat and cloak to reveal myself to his
astonished eyes, the unlucky hat, on which I relied so
much, unfortunately sticking rather tightly, brought
off my wig with it ! and there I stood, the foremost
figure of the group : all the honours of my head van-

ished ; and my crown, as bald as the back of my hand, for it had been clean shaven that very morning ! There was a dead silence in the house ;

> "Big drops of sweat stood on my brow,"
> "Tremor occupat artus ;"

but I stood firm. The actors behaved with great steadiness,—in fact, I believe they were " horror-stricken,. and moved not." The scene went on, I spoke my words, the duke stabbed me, I died with my sister's arms round her long-lost brother's neck,

> " Our father's cottage, Mariana,"

swimming before my death-glazed eyes ; and not a soul in the house even laughed, or testified any sense of the ludicrousness of the mischance. Nay, more ; at the fall of the curtain I was honoured.with a loud and general call ; put on my wig, reappeared, and made my obeisance to applauding friends. The actors generally complimented me on my self-possession, which they declared had alone prevented the curtain from falling amid shouts of laughter. It was a narrow escape ! I never repeated the effect afterwards. you may well believe.

Miss (Harriet) FAUCIT, afterwards known in this country as Mrs. Bland, was the Mariana of the evening : her horror at the fall of the wig was breathless ; she stood statue-like, a stone-struck Niobe !

Let me pay this slight tribute to her memory (she died in Boston some six or eight years ago) ; she was an excellent actress, both in tragedy and comedy ; with natural talents for the stage, quite equal to those of her more fortunate sister Helen, and without her affectation and mannerisms learnt from Macready ;

but Helen was brought out in London under Mr.
Farren's protecting care, and under Macready's
schooling, and .

"So father'd and so husbanded,"—

manager'd I mean,—soon rose to distinction. She
was the original Pauline, in Bulwer's " Lady of
Lyons ;" that one part alone was enough to make
any actress ; and the position she thus acquired was
confirmed by several other original parts in new
plays—Clara Douglas in " Money," Nina Sforza,
&c.—in all of which she had the advantage of Mr.
Macready's tuition, and the disadvantage of his manner being, by example and contagion, ingrafted on
her style, which, in other respects, is refined, highly
intelligent, and marked with a winning feminine softness.   I have played with her in later years, at
Manchester and Dublin ; and, though she is perhaps
somewhat exacting, yet I have always felt it a great
pleasure to act with her.   Her expression of love is
the most beautifully confiding, trustful, self-abandon-
ing in its tone, that I have ever witnessed in any
actress ; it is intensely fascinating.   The great Miss
O'NEILL (now Lady Beecher) is celebrated tradition-
ally for her exquisite *abandon*, and yet feminine
delicacy of passion in love-scenes, but I cannot conceive that she could surpass Helen Faucit in this
one excellence, however she may have gone beyond
her in others.   And this is an excellence of the highest consequence to a tragic actress ; without it, she
may be powerful in passages of great force, and strong
passionate energy, but she cannot be winning, charming, crowned with the graces of a woman.

This was Rachel's great want ; *she had no love in her* ; I mean love properly so-called : of the baser passion, its bastard brother, she had more than enough ; but of the pure, unselfish, self-sacrificing love of a virtuous woman, she knew nothing ; it was out of her dictionary ; she had no expression for it ; it did not seem to enter into the catalogue of her received sensations. She had scorn, irony, rage, despair, passion, but no love ; unless the heat of a tigress be love. Such was her Phædre ; but what would she have done with Imogen or Juliet ? Bah ! she would have degraded them to mere impersonations of animal passion, or voluptuous *cynisme.* This is the point, too, in which Ristori, the Italian *tragédienne*, so far surpasses the French one ; in loving sweetness, the outgushing of a trustful, unselfish woman's heart. Rachel might make you wonder at her energy, her force, her demoniacal intensity, Ristori makes you weep with her, and love her by her nobleness, the depth of her feeling, and its feminine expression. Even in Medea, the character which Rachel refused to play, Ristori is a woman ; outraged, injured, revengeful, maddened with her wrongs, but still a woman : Rachel would have made her a tigress, or a fiend !

Ellen Tree had a great gift of this woman's winning softness. She was an elegant, graceful, delicate actress ; refined, well studied ; playful, lively, sarcastic, in comedy : her Rosalind, Mrs. Oakley, Lady Teazle, Beatrice, were all charming performances. In a certain line of tragedy, too, she displayed great concentration of passion, a subdued intensity, a suppressed fire, that seemed to burn her up and gnaw her heart ; as in the Countess in " Love," Ginevra in the

" Legend of Florence," and others ; the woman spoke out in all of these.   Her Mrs. Haller was the most naturally touching performance of that character which I ever witnessed.   She is a noble creature, too, in face and form ; not unlike Ristori in many of her personal traits ; but in the highest walks of tragedy, as Lady Macbeth, Lady Constance, in " King John," and such parts, she is deficient in massive power of execution ; a defect which her intelligence, great as it was, and her conscientious study of her author, are inadequate to supply.   She is a charming *artiste*, and a high-souled woman.   Would the stage had many such !

Ristori is the tragic actress of the day ; and that, not by the decease of Rachel, but by her own preeminent and surpassing genius, which places her on the throne, to

" wear without co-rival all its dignities."

On my return to London, after my five nights at Liverpool, I was not called upon to play for some weeks, in consequence of the run of " Love," at Covent Garden Theatre.   Ellen Tree had just returned from the United States, where she had made herself a universal favourite, the admired, almost the beloved of all ; and this new play of Knowles' was produced to display her talents worthily in the Countess.   The part was admirably suited to her ; and she did it full justice. She was well supported by Anderson (J. R.) in Huon, the first original part of importance which had been entrusted to him on the London stage ; he acted it with great spirit ; and, with Madame Vestris in Catherine, and Cooper in the Duke, the play ran

ten successive weeks, and put money into the treasury
of the theatre.

During this time I was necessarily idle. I employed
myself in adding to my list of characters; and gave
at least an hour every day to Hamlet; which practice
I continued for six months, before I ventured to offer
myself to an audience in the part; going regularly
every day through an act, aloud, as I conceived and
intended to present it, with action; until I felt myself easy and confident enough in the text, purpose,
and working of the whole play, and particularly in
the execution of Hamlet, to venture before an audience,
as the representative of this wonderful incongruity,
this harmonious discord, this paragon of imperfections,
adorned with every grace and accomplishment of
person and of mind; capable of "enterprises of
great pith and moment," yet "sicklied o'er with the
pale cast of thought," and thus losing the time of
action in philosophical speculations and metaphysical
abstractions.

Such was the spirit in which I undertook the study
of Hamlet; but, previous to venturing on its representation, I assured myself of the compactnesss of my
design and general conception, as well as of my ability
to execute what I intended, by giving a discourse on
the play, with readings of the principal scenes and
soliloquies before the Westminster Literary and Scien-
tific Institution. This was the first Shakesperian
Reading I ever gave, and the applause I received on
that occasion, from a very large, overcrowded, audience of more than average intelligence, was a great
encouragement to me, and first turned my thoughts
towards public reading.

And here, apropos to studying new parts, let me impress upon young actors beginning their career, the high importance of a strict, conscientious, exact study of the text of the author, to start with. Negligence or slovenliness in this respect is fatal to success; if our first study of a part be careless and inexact, after-study will seldom secure perfectness, and we shall always have a painful feeling of insecurity, in playing the character. The young actor should habituate himself at the outset to great correctness of text, and he will be amply rewarded by the confidence and case which it will give him. An ambitious aspirant, with just pride in himself and his art, will scorn to look to the prompter for help; who is, besides, a very uncertain reed to lean upon; for it is a well known anomaly in prompters (who are seldom prompt—*quasi lucus a non*), that they are usually a page or two behind the actual *locus standi*, or sticking-place in a performance; so that, if a hitch occur, the prompter has generally to inquire " where they are," and to turn over two or three pages to get to the line where they are at fault. This is, of course, awkward for the defaulter.

Thus, it is told of Old Barry, as he was called, formerly prompter in the Dublin Theatre (no relation to him of " the Boston ") that he was so entirely independent of, and abstracted from the portion of the text actually going on, that on an actor's " sticking " one night, and looking anxiously towards Barry at the wing, for the "word" (as it is called), Barry, who was, of course, engaged in some other business at the time, and his thoughts far away, took not the slightest notice of the appeal ; till the actor at last, in despair,

called out,—" Barry, give me the word, will you?"
To which Barry, with the imperturbability of a
prompter, and the exquisite unconsciousness of an
Irishman, replied, loud enough for the audience to
hear,—" What word, my boy?" and coolly wetting
his thumb, began turning over the leaves to get up
with the unfortunate defaulter, who, wanting the
word, was asked " what word he wanted !"

This same Barry, by the bye—as good-natured a
soul as ever tossed off a tumbler of whiskey punch
without winking—(dead, now, poor fellow,) was an
eccentric old humorist; and, having been years an
actor in Dublin, was on most familiar terms with that
most easy, impudent, and familiar audience. The
colloquies they held together,—the actors from the
stage, and the *habitués* of the shilling gallery, from
their

" Nook and coigne of vantage,'

were, in themselves, " as good as a play," and frequently stopped the play itself, and kept the whole
house, actors included, in a roar.

Thus Barry, who had a well-known *penchant* for
the "matayrials" nicely blended, came rolling on to
the stage, one night, under an unusual press of poteen,
when he was immediately saluted by a voice of one
of the *upper ten* in the gallery, with

" Barry, you tief o' the woruld! how many
tumblers o' whiskey-punch did you take to night?"

To which Barry, looking up with a scornful leer,
replied—

" None, ye blackgyard, at *your* expense !" and not
the least abashed, went on with his business. In this
case the laugh was against his assailant.

Not so always. During the run of Tom and Jerry, which was played in Dublin some fifty or more nights successively, Barry's originally white Russia-duck pants, which he continued to wear, night after night,

Unwashed, unbleached, and *unrenewed,*
With all their imperfections *on their front,*

began to assume rather a dusky shade, indicating their innocence of soap and water. At last, when these long-enduring pants (Russia-duck) made their appearance about the twentieth night, encasing Barry's legs as if they grew there, and were never to "undergo a change" ("*sea-change,*" fresh-water or other), one of Barry's persecutors cried out to him, from the gallery—

"Whisht! Barry, you divil!" thus arresting the attention of the house for his *coup.*

"What do ye want, you blackgyard?" said Barry, nothing moved by a style of address with which he was familiar.

"Wait till I whisper you," said the voice. (All were silent.) "When did your *ducks* take the *water* last?

The house was uproarious with laughter for several minutes; and Barry, for the first time in his life, was left without a retort to the gallery-boy. The next night, however, a change was evident; and his Russia-ducks were white as Russia's snows.

IV

THE GREEN-ROOM of Covent Garden Theatre—Its Regulations—
Queen's Visits—DOLLY FITZ—MRS. JORDAN and the DUKE of
CLARENCE—Reading of New Plays—LEIGH HUNT—SHERIDAN
KNOWLES—Casting a New Play—The Plausible Manager.

LET it be recorded, to Vestris's honour, that she was
not only scrupulously careful not to offend propriety
by word or action, but she knew very well how to re-
press any attempt at *double-entendre* or doubtful in-
sinuation, in others. The Green-Room in Covent
Garden Theatre was a most agreeable lounging-place,
a divan adorned with beauties, where one could pass
a pleasant hour in the society of charming women
and men of gentlemanly manners, and from which
was banished every word or allusion that would not
be tolerated in a drawing-room. A man must be
hard to please who was not agreeably entertained,
with such gratification to ear and eye, as could be
found in the elegant society and ladylike conversation
of Ellen Tree, the sprightliness of Mrs. Nisbett, the
quaint humour of Mrs. Humby, besides the attractions
of a bevy of lesser beauties, the "jesting spirit" of
Harley, the amusing egotism of Farren, and the jokes,
repartees, anecdotes, and reminiscences of others ; and
this, with the addition of a popular artist, or of one
or more dramatic authors. Such was the fare we
enjoyed in the first Green-Room.

It must be understood that in Covent Garden and Drury Lane Theatres, there were a *first* and *second* Green-Room : the first, exclusively set apart for the *corps dramatique* proper,—the actors and actresses of a certain position ; the second, belonging to the *corps de ballét*, the pantomimists, and all engaged in that line of business—what are called the *little people*—except the principal male and female dancer (at that time, at Covent Garden, Mr. and Mrs. Gilbert), who had the privilege of the first Green-Room.

The term Green-Room arose originally from the fact of that room being carpetted in green (baize, probably), and the covering of the divans being green—*stuff*. But the first Green-Room in Covent Garden Theatre was a withdrawing room, carpeted and papered elegantly ; with a handsome chandelier in the centre, several globe lights at the sides, a comfortable divan, covered in figured damask, running round the whole room, large pier and mantel-glasses on the walls, and a full-length moveable swing-glass ; so that, on entering from his dressing-room, an actor could see himself from head to foot at one view, and get back, front, and side views by reflection, all round. This is the first point to attend to on entering the Green-Room, to see if one's dress is in perfect order, well put on by the dresser, hanging well, and perfectly *comme il faut*. Having satisfied him or herself on these interesting points, even to the graceful drooping of a feather, the actor or actress sits down, and enters into conversation with those around, which is interrupted every now and then by the shrill voice of the *call-boy* " making his calls." The call-boy is a most important " remembrancer ;"—he may be named the prompter's devil, as the boy in a printing office who calls for copy is yclept the printer's devil. His business is to give the actors and actresses notice, by calling at the door of the Green-Room (he is not allowed to enter those sacred precincts in a London theatre) the names of the persons whose presence is required on the stage. This he does by direction of the prompter, who about five minutes, or three lengths (120 lines) before a character has to enter on the stage, finds marked in his prompt-book of the play a number thus [3]. He then says to his attendant imp, who has a list in his hand (a call-list—very different from a New Year's call-list), " Call *three;*"—the boy looks at his list, walks to the Green-Room door, and calls the character marked [3] in that act ; or the prompter orders him to call 4, 5, 6, 7 : he consults his list for the act, finds these numbers, and at the Green-Room door calls the characters they represent, thus :—

> HAMLET,
> HORATIO,
> MARCELLUS,
> GHOST.

The gentlemen who represent these characters, on being thus called, rise, leave the Green-Room, and go and stand at the wing—the side-scene—at which they are presently to enter. All the calls are made at the Green-Room door, and it is at an actor's peril to take notice of them ; it is only on a change of dress that he is entitled to be called at his dressing-room, except *stars*, and they insist on being always called there, as well as in the Green-Room ; and the point is conceded to them.

D

In many theatres the calls are made by the name
of the actor or actress representing the character
called. It was so, if I recollect, at Covent Garden ; at
the Haymarket it is otherwise ; and generally throughout the theatres of the United States, the calls are
made by the names of the characters ; and it is the
safer plan, and less liable to mistakes on the part of
the call-boys : each way has its own advantages and
disadvantages.

The Green-Room was exceedingly comfortable
during the Mathews and Vestris management. Indeed I must pay them the compliment of saying that
their arrangements generally for the convenience of
their company, the courtesy of their behaviour to the
actors, and consideration for their comforts, formed
an example well worthy to be followed by managers
in general ; who are not, I am sorry to say, usually remarkable for those qualities. In fact, the reign of
Vestris and her husband might be distinguished as
the *drawing-room management.* On special occasions—the opening night of the season, for example,
or a " Queen's visit,"—tea and coffee were served in
the Green-Room ; and frequently between the acts,
some of the officers of the guard, or gentlemen in attendance on the royal party, would be introduced,
which led, of course, to agreeable and sometimes
advantageous acquaintances.

I remember, on one occasion of the Queen's visiting
the theatre, the late Lord Adolphus Fitz-Clarence
(Dolly Fitz, as he was familiarly called), was one of
the royal party, who, at the end of an act, came behind
the scenes. Lord Adolphus was, as all the world
knows, the son of the late King William IV., when

Duke of Clarence, and the celebrated *comédienne*, the most *enjouée* and fascinating actress of her day, Mrs. JORDAN. The royal duke, in his youth, had been devotedly attached to this lady, and they had lived many years together (the law did not allow of their marriage —that is, she could not be made Duchess of Clarence), and the result of their union was several children. State reasons, and the command of George III., separated them, to the royal duke's great grief; and Mrs. Jordan died at Boulogne, in France, in an obscure lodging, and in indigent circumstances. This, it must be confessed, was not to the honour of the royal duke, to whom she had been faithfully devoted, and had given her best years, when he could do nothing to advance her interest or her future (for he was strictly and scantily allowanced by his rigid old father, George III.,) and had lavished on his pleasures and in his society the treasures of her charms and the large earnings of her genius. But so it was? The duke married Adelaide of Mechlenberg Strelitz, afterwards Queen Adelaide ; and the poor actress perished forgotten, abandoned, and in distress, on a foreign shore !

The Duke of Clarence, on the death of his royal brother, George IV., "the finest gentleman," and greatest—not to use too strong a word—*roué* of his day, succeeded to the throne. The Queen of Comedy was, alas, no more !—she lay in a country churchyard in France. But her memory rose up before her former lover's eyes ; and such reparation as he could, he made. The two sons had been educated in a suitable manner; the eldest of them was now created, by his royal father, Earl of Munster, and the other, an officer in the navy, was made Lord Adolphus

Fitz-Clarence ; a daughter was also ennobled, and married, I believe, to an earl. The Earl of Munster, unfortunately, died by his own hand, a victim of melancholy gloom ! On the accession of the present Queen, by the demise of William IV., she appointed her cousin (*de la main gauche*) Lord Adolphus, to the command of her yacht ; which many of my readers may have seen, and been aboard of, off Cowes, perhaps.

Well, Dolly Fitz-Clarence was a Green-Room visitor, on the night in question. Now, Covent Garden Theatre had been the scene of some of Mrs. Jordan's greatest triumphs in comedy. Some early memory was awakened in his heart, and he requested to be shown to *his mother's dressing-room.* He was conducted thither by Madame Vestris, I believe, herself. He entered the room that had, some twenty or thirty years before, been his mother's, in silence : stood there, looked round a moment, as if recalling old recollections, and noting changes in the room, then, shading his eyes with his hands, exclaimed, in trembling accents, " My poor mother ! "

Vestris told me this incident herself, and I relate it, as honourable to the heart of the man, in whom courts and royal favour had not obliterated the holiest feeling of humanity ; and who, ennobled by fortune, did not blush to shed a tear to the memory of his actress-mother.

Poor Lord Adolphus ! he had not a strong head, but a good heart. He died about a year ago.

*　　*　　*　　*　　*

The Green-Room, too, is the place where new plays,

that have been accepted by the management, are read by the author, to the ladies and gentlemen who are to be engaged in their performance. Here, I heard LEIGH HUNT read his elegant and poetical play of the "Legend of Florence," which was admirably played, as he himself delighted to acknowledge—Miss Tree, a gentleman named Moore (a new man), Anderson, and myself, were in the cast; and here, also, I heard SHERIDAN KNOWLES read his play of "Old Maids," the season after, in which Mrs. Nisbett, Madame Vestris, Charles Mathews, and myself, played.

Leigh Hunt was a charming, genial, kind-hearted, simple-mannered, old gentleman,

"Soft as summer,"

with rather long hair, tinged with gray (now white as snow, I am told), with something of a Lorenzo de Medici look, softened; and he read clearly and pleasingly, with just emphasis, but without any aim at effect.*

Sheridan Knowles, on the contrary, was a hearty, rather boisterous, old fellow; of strong, rather coarse features; reminding one of the traditionary portraits of Ben Jonson; and he read his play in a loud, rollicking style, with marked emphasis, a theatrical effect, and strong dashes of the brogue.

Leigh Hunt looked like a poet of the gentle elegiac school; you could well conceive him as the teller of the tale of the *Rimini* in such sweet words; and you would not doubt that he wept over them himself.

Knowles, on the contrary, looking anything but

---

* Leigh Hunt has lately closed his course, in his 75th year.

poetical: *brusque* in manner, slovenly in dress, absent in mind, quick and rapid in utterance, he gave you rather the idea of an Irish schoolmaster. But he had great power as a dramatist; deep poetic feeling; and a nervous, energetic diction, when he was not misled by the affectation of imitating the old dramatists, into an involved and inverted style, most painful to the actor to learn, unpleasing in the delivery, and difficult for an audience to follow. In reading a play, he could produce strong effects by his earnest intensity; and though you might sometimes laugh at his abruptness, and his brogue, that would peep out, you would not unfrequently catch yourself weeping at his touches of natural pathos, and the deep feeling he knew how to throw into his tenderest passages. The stage owes him much for what he *has* done *for* it, in spite of what he *is* doing *against* it, by his pulpit denunciations.

Some authors, new to the *coulisses*, are terribly embarrassed on being presented to the Green-Room, to read their play, under the battery of so many sparkling eyes, and the criticism of so many captious ears. The actors are usually courteous in attention, if not always encouraging in applause; and they sit, silently watchful, and picking out, by degrees, the part that each thinks will be allotted to him. The reading being closed, the parts are then and there distributed in manuscript; and then is made manifest the disappointment of some who find they have not got the parts they expected, and the disgust of others, who have got just the very parts that they dreaded and detested in the reading. It is then the acting manager's business—no easy one, sometimes — to

smoothe these difficulties, and to soothe their discon-
tented spirits. His is the task to persuade Miss
Jenkins that her part will *act* much better than it
reads; and that it is ("really now") a much more
effective part than Mrs. Timkins's; and,

" Consider, my dear, two changes of dress; besides
breeches in the last act."

(I have explained what breeches-parts are, in a preceding page.)

Then, the leading actor is to be reconciled to his
part, which he thinks very much below his abilities.

" My dear sir," says the manager, " it's just the
thing for you, you will produce a great effect in the
third act."

" But," objects the actor, " it falls off so confound-
edly in the fifth act; the lady has it all to herself."

" Well, well," says the ready manager, " we'll get
the author to write you up in the fifth act; and we'll
give you the tag to speak (the *tag* is the closing
lines of the play). And so the great man is smoothed
down.

Then comes up an actor, third or fourth-rate, but
thinking a great deal more of himself than audience
or manager can be brought to do, with a very scanty
manuscript in his hand, which he opens, to show how
little writing there is in it, exclaiming in a voice of
suffering innocence—

" Why, Mr. Bartley, my part is all *cues;* there
are only ten lines to speak, and I am on in every
scene, in every act."

" It's not a long part, my boy, I know" (replies
the plausible manager), "but it's a very responsible
one; and you'll be splendidly dressed!"

That last consideration reconciles the youth to his bad part, with the consolation that he will, at all events, have an opportunity of exhibiting his own good parts to advantage : and he is smoothed over.

Then Mrs. Shady thinks that "she really ought not to be called on to play *old women*."

"Old women, my dear," says he, "what do you mean? Your part's not an old woman; she's a young dashing widow, my dear; that's the reason I cast *you* for it."

"Young!" exclaims Mrs. Shady, "she must be fifty, at least; she has a daughter married."

"Nonsense, my dear," says the manager, "fifty! she's not more than thirty. She was married young, of course; and so was her daughter. In the period of this play, and in Spain, girls married at thirteen : so did you and your daughter. *Play* it young, my dear; as young as you like; I've no objection!"

And Mrs. Shady collapses, out-answered, and feeling herself the victim of oppression and managerial injustice (to say nothing of that odious Mrs. Middleton, who will triumph over her) ; has a good cry, and goes home and studies her part.

V.

I HAVE a very agreeable reminiscence of the production of "Romeo and Juliet," with Shakespere's text,
at Covent Garden, showing the kindness of a great
comedian, now no more, and the interest he took in
the advancement of his art.   I allude to Mr. CHARLES
KEMBLE.

Every one knows how fine he was in *Mercutio*,
what a gallant, courtly, soldierlike, high gentleman
he was in it ; overflowing with animal spirits, and
elegant *badinage*, and playful humour.   Mr. Kemble
was always very kind to me ; and therefore I was
not much surprised, though highly gratified, the
morning after I first appeared in this character
(which for only a two-months' stager was somewhat
of an undertaking), by Mr. Kemble's saying to me—

" Vandenhoff, they tell me you played Mercutio
capitally last night."   (I bowed.)   " I didn't see you

myself; so come; come into the second Green-Room,
and speak Queen Mab for me."

Here was a proposition! To speak Queen Mab,
in plain clothes, and in cold blood, at high-noon, in
the second Green-Room, to the great Mercutio of his
day. I never felt more inclined to bolt in my life.
However, he allowed me no time to hesitate, but led
the way to the designated spot. There was not a
soul there; I could not escape. Down sat Mr.
Kemble, saying, " Come, begin."

I knew I should botch it: how could it be otherwise? What was any audience that any theatre
could bring together, to this one, knowing, experienced, sure, critical, undeceivable eye that was now
fixed upon me; this one ear so well acquainted with
the text, its delicacies, and every nicety of tone and
expression required to bring them out, that now
waited for my crude and unfinished recitation! But
I scorned to take refuge in excuses, which I knew,
too, that he would despise as signs of imbecility or
affectation; so to work I went, and delivered that
wonderful overflowing of Shakspere's teeming fancy
in the most stupid, lame, impotent and matter-of-fact
manner possible; I know I did!

The kind old actor, and courteous gentleman,
listened with a pleased smile, clapped his hands at
the end, and cried " Bravo! bravo!" in that high,
animating pitch of voice, which his admirers so well
remember.

I bowed, and looked foolish, afraid that he would
fancy I really believed that I merited his applause.
Then jumping up, he said: " Now, then, I'll speak it
for *you!* And he placed me in the seat he had

quitted, and, in his overcoat—for it was winter—
stood up and recited, or rather, impersonated Mercutio's brilliant inspiration, with a grace, a point, a
buoyancy, an *abandon*, that made me laugh and
applaud, involuntarily. "There," said he, "I don't
know how you'll like my style, but perhaps you may
find a hint or two in it." I thanked him sincerely;
he shook hands, and left me with all sorts of encouraging expressions.—Need I say that I treasured
the lesson ?

Cibber's comedy of the "Double Gallant" was
revived this season with a strong cast, except in the
principal part. Mr. C. Mathews' Atall was a very
water-colour sketch; it wanted breadth, force, stamina.
Mathews had not *physique* for that audacious rollicking rake; he was evidently all brag; he could not
stand the test, if put to it. C. Mathews is perfect
in little finical, man-milliner parts; cool, easy men
about town; *chevaliers d'industrie*, or genteel Jeremy
Diddlers; but he is lost when he has a manly part to
deliver, or a gallant bearing to assume. Trust me,
heart goes for a good deal in acting! Farren's Sir
Solomon, however, and Mrs. Nisbett's Lady Sadlife,
made ample amends; Madame Vestris was Clarinda;
Mrs. W. Lacy was Lady Dainty; Mrs. Humby,
Wishwell; and Mrs. Orger, Situp; I played Careless. This revival ran thirteen nights.

The most brilliant production of the season, presenting the most classical, and perfectly artistic *ensemble*, of all the spectacle-pieces brought out under
the Vestris and Mathews management, was that of
Milton's "Comus." It was an honour to the theatre,
the representation of this beautiful masque, breathing

the divine philosophy of virtue in tones of highest
poetry, with all the luxury of scenic display, with
the accompaniments of music sung by syren lips, and
every aid that art could bring to delight the senses,
and to realize the great poet's picture—a dream of
Paradise, broken in upon by Comus and his satyr rout,
and rebuked by the chaste lady, " pure, spotless, and
serene," in the midst of their midnight orgies and
incantations.　The groupings and arrangement of the
tableaux were admirable, and some of the mechanical
effects were almost magical ; especially that exquisite
scene in which Madame Vestris, as Sabrina, appeared
at the head of the waterfall, immersed in the cup of a
lily up to the shoulders, and in this fairy skiff floated
over the fall and descended to the stage !　Mrs. W.
Lacy was the Lady ; Miss Rainforth sang the spirit-
music charmingly ; while Mr. and Mrs. Gilbert and
an immense *corps de ballet*, gave effect to the revels
of Comus and his crew.　There were forest scenes of
the greatest pictorial beauty, equal in effect to the
finest efforts of Moreland or Gainsborough, filled
with mythological and fabulous beings, bacchanals,
satyrs,—a herd of anomalies, half human, half
bestial, intermingled with wood-nymphs and strange
and grotesque monsters, forming a wild medley, and
abandoning themselves to the frenzy of wine-inspired
mirth, with the superadded intoxication of a maddening dance.　All this was fully and picturesquely
carried out.　J. Cooper (" the judicious ") was not
a very magical Sorcerer, it is true ; but, if he did
not seem to enter fully into the spirit of " the son of
Circe," or the poetry of the language, yet he spoke
Milton's text with that accuracy and good sense

which always distinguished him. This production of Comus was a thing to see, as a work of art, and to remember; it was truly a poetic realization of a poet's creation, and did great credit to the taste and fancy of the management, as well as to the artistic resources of the theatre. Yet, successful as it was, I have been informed that it did little more than re-pay·its outlay !

The second part I was called on to play at Covent Garden Theatre was Lovewell, in the " Clandestine Marriage "—one of the finest comedies in the language —with this cast :

Mrs. Heidelberg Mrs. GLOVER.	*Betsy,* Mrs. ORGER.
Fanny, Mrs. WALTER LACY,	*Sir John,* Mr. COOPER.
(the Original Helen in the	*Mr. Sterling,* Mr. GEORGE
Hunchback, then Miss TAY-	BARTLEY.
LOR,)	*Lord Ogleby,* Mr. FARREN.
Miss Sterling, Mrs. NISBETT.	*Brush,* TOM GREENE ;

and every other character well and worthily filled. What would the play-going public think of such a cast nowadays, when we read in large letters of

EXTRAORDINARY CASTS !

AND

WONDERFUL COMBINATIONS!!

with frequently only one name in the bill perfectly competent to do full justice to his part. Why, now-a-days, a second-rate actress would decline to play Miss Sterling, as unworthy of her talents (Heaven save the mark!), which Mrs. Nisbett, the Queen of Comedy, did not think beneath her. But the present is the reign of pretentious mediocrity on the stage.

Men and women rush into the profession without any
special natural gifts, and without previous education
for the task; as soon as they have arrived at the
power of speaking a sentence without a blunder, think
themselves accomplished actors; and when the favour
of the audience flatters them with a round of applause
they are so elated as to set up for *stars*, and insist on
their names appearing in large capitals !   •

In the cast I have given above, where nearly every
person *was* a star, not one of the names was distinguished by any prominent type, or peculiarity of
announcement: nor was there any trumpet-blowing
about the *wonderful combination of dramatic talent.*
There was no need; it spoke for itself.

MR. WILLIAM FARREN.

Setting aside the other great names, Farren's Lord
Ogleby alone was worth the price of a ticket : it is a
character that has left the stage with William Farren.
In addition to his expression of the ludicrous, this
great comedian had a particular grace of manner,
which, assisted by his fine person and elegant figure,
admirably qualified him for the representative of Lord
Ogleby, the dilapidated beau of the old school; a
rake and a coxcomb, it is true; yet with a man's
heart beating in his worn-out old body, and with the
honourable feelings, and the scorn of meanness that
should distinguish a noblemen, and a gentleman.
Farren's acting of the scene with the charming
Fanny, when she confided to him her affection for
Lovewell, which the vain old fellow mistakes for a
covert declaration of her passion for himself,—his

devoted gallantry, highbred courtesy, and senile delight, were really beautiful to behold. His after disappointment on discovering his error, and that " the adorable Fanny " is actually married to the humble Lovewell, was so truthfully expressed, that though we laughed at, we pitied him ; and our sympathy was entirely won, when Mr. Sterling, the purse-proud old cit, threatening to turn the young couple, his daughter and her husband, out of his house, Farren, as Lord Ogleby, exclaimed, with remarkable dignity, and an *épanchement de cœur* that atoned for a thousand coxcombries,—

" Then I will receive them into mine."

The effect was magical, and never failed to be rewarded with instantaneous applause ; a tribute paid to the actor's manner and execution, as much as to the situation and the sentiment.

Farren's Sir Peter Teazle was equally excellent ; I have never seen any representative of Sir Peter that could compare with him for a moment, in animation, ease, naturalness of manner, and piquancy of effect. His opening soliloquy commencing,—

" When an old bachelor marries a young wife, what is he to expect ?"

and his enumeration of the matrimonial troubles that beset him from the very moment of his marriage— nay, even before it, for he says,

" We tiffed a little, going to church ; and fairly quarrelled before the bells had done ringing,"—

his alternate quarrels and *badinage* with Lady Teazle,

his uxoriousness, his gentlemanly tone, and his extreme irritation and provocation when he swears,

"He will make an example of himself for the benefit of all old bachelors;"—

his exquisite sense of the joke against Joseph, with his blank expression of amazement on the turning of that joke against himself by the falling of the screen,—made up, altogether, a highly elaborate, yet naturally coloured picture, not to be surpassed for justness and *vis comica*, undefiled by grossness or exaggeration.

The performance of the Clandestine Marriage was the first occasion of my encountering this great artist on the stage; and, on entering to him as Lovewell in the fourth act, I was a little annoyed to find that he did not turn towards me, or even look at me, during the scene; but stood with face turned full on the audience, making his observations *at* me, but *to* them. Most, at least many eminent actors, have some particular trick for engrossing attention to themselves, sometimes even to the detriment of the general effect of the scene, which is thus made one-sided and inharmonious. Now, this was Farren's trick; which, whenever he thought he could, with impunity, he put into play, for monopolizing the attention of the house: he ignored, as it were, the actor in the scene, and addressed himself to the audience alone. In the present instance I was a novice, and he indulged his full-front, foot-light acting to the height. Of course, I felt the impertinence of this proceeding; and when we repeated the comedy the night but one after, I resolved to pay the old-stager in his own coin, and see how he liked it. Accordingly, when it came to my cue in the fourth act, I entered hastily, as the stage-direction orders, and addressed his lordship without looking at him, rather turned away from him, with my face full upon the audience : thus I stood on the right hand : in the same way, on the left hand, with several yards between us, stood Lord Ogleby, in a state of exaltation at his recent interview with Fanny; and the dialogue went on between two people who seemed not to be aware of the presence of each other.

Lovewell. (Not looking at him.) I beg your lordship's pardon ; are you alone, my lord ?

Lord Ogle. (Elated.) No, my lord, I am not alone; I am in company, the best company.

Lovewell. My lord !

Lord Ogle. I never was in such exquisite enchanting company since my heart first conceived, or my senses tasted pleasure.

Lovewell. Where are they, my lord ?

Lord Ogle. In my mind, sir.

Lovewell. What company have you there, my lord ?

Lord Ogle. My own ideas, sir, which so crowd upon my imagination, and kindle in it such a delirium of ecstacy, that wine, music, poetry, all combined, and each in perfection, are but mere mental shadows of my felicity.

Still, neither character looked at the other, but addressed himself to the front of the house. Consequently, the dialogue thus independently and divergently given, in spite of Farren's animation, and exaltation of manner, fell flat upon the audience, who were puzzled, and whose attention was distracted by the apparent anomaly. Farren, finding his usual points fall pointless, began to be uneasy, and to sidle towards me, in a fidgetty and nervous manner. On we went again on the same plan of mutual aversion ; the scene grew flatter and flatter ; and Farren, always covetous of applause, grew more and more nervous, till he began, at last, to trip and falter in the words of his part. As his irritability increased, he turned towards me, as if to inquire by a look, what was the meaning of the insensibility of the audience ; then, for the first time, he became aware of the fact that my face was turned entirely away from him, and that, after his own fashion, I had been delivering my share of the dialogue to the front of the house, without any notice of him at all. This put the *comble* to his annoyance ; I heard his ominous *sniff* (a trick he had), I heard his gradually approaching step, I felt his hand on my arm as he turned me towards him, with the words of the text which seemed peculiarly appropriate,—

"What's the matter, Lovewell ? thou seemest to have lost thy faculties ;"

and for the rest of the scene he never turned away from me, but, as a gentleman should do, kept his eyes on the person to whom he was speaking. I did the same, the *vraisemblance* of the scene was restored, and all went right.

But Farren was boiling, within ; and the moment we were past the wing, and off the stage, he broke out,

" Good heavens ! Mr. Vandenhoff, I never saw such a thing in my life ; you entirely ruined my scene, spoilt every point."

" Indeed ?" I replied, very coolly, " how so, Mr. Farren ? I spoke the text, and gave you every cue !"

, " Good gracious, yes ; but you turned away from me, sir ; you never looked at me ; you spoke entirely to the audience ! "

" Why, so did you, Mr. Farren ! I only copied you. You know I am a novice, and I thought I could not do better than form myself on the model of the greatest comedian of the day ?"

A grunt was his only reply, but the retort had its effect ; he never gave me his side-front after that night, and we always got on very well together.

He was the greatest comedian in his line I ever saw ; but his egotism was equal to his talent. It was really sublime in its self-exaltation. In the profession, he had the *sobriquet* of the Cock Salmon. It was said that having demanded—of Bunn, I think—£60 per week salary, on the manager's remonstrating on the largeness of the demand, Farren replied,—

" If there's only one cock-salmon in the market, you must pay the price for it. *I* am the cock-salmon."

So, when some one asked him in the Green-Room, if he had been to see the celebrated French comedian, Bouffé, at the St. James's Theatre, many of whose characters Farren played in translation, and played admirably—

" No, sir," said the Salmon, " let him come and see me ! Let Bouffé come and see William Farren."

He was, in truth, a finished artist, well studied, and perfect in all the details of his profession. Not so ready in conception as happy in execution, his first reading of a new part was generally unsatisfactory, and imperfectly developed. He was, as I have said elsewhere, always very nervous on the first night or

two of a new play, and dared not give himself free
scope, till he was quite easy in the words and the
action of every scene ; and then he, as it were, grew
to the character, and elaborated the creation to the
highest point of excellence.   Those who have ever seen
him play Sir Harcourt in "London Assurance," know
to what a high pitch of ease and polish he could carry
his execution.   It was the perfection of art.

Mr. Farren still lives, retired from the profession.
The last time I saw him, three years ago, he was
walking in Regent-street, not certainly as erect as a
few years ago ; but a fine, handsome, white-haired,
clear-complexioned old gentleman—a fine *échantillon*
of the *ancien regimé*,—a beautiful picture of age—
looking like an old nobleman more than an old actor.

MRS. GLOVER,

whose name appears in the above cast, was an actress
of Farren's day ; they had flourished and run their
course together.   She was the daughter of a Better-
ton ; she trod the boards with almost infant feet ; her
earliest recollections must have arisen in a theatre,
and almost her last hour of consciousness was on the
stage.   She was a great actress : good in every thing,
but greatest in a certain line of characters,—the
dashing, volatile widow (Racket or Widow Green),
the affectedly good-natured, but truly malignant ditto,
Mrs. Candour ; or the vulgar and ignorant ditto, as
Mrs. Malaprop and Mrs. Heidelberg.   In her youth,
she had played with applause all the principal
characters in comedy, and some in tragedy (but she
was weak in tragedy), with John and Charles Kem-

ble, Cooke, Lewis, Elliston ;—she had been associated
with all the great lights of the stage in the early part
of this century, and she was one of them herself.
She had had a long career of popularity at Drury
Lane, Covent Garden, and the Haymarket Theatres,
always being engaged at one or other of them. She
was essentially of, and bound up with, the stage ; her
manner in daily life smacked of her profession : it
was large, autocratic, oracular. She took her final
leave of the stage at upwards of seventy years of age,
in the character of Mrs. Heidelberg, at a farewell
benefit given to her at Drury Lane Theatre in 1851.
Farewell, indeed ! She had been failing some time ;
and the excitement was too much for her weak state.
How she ever got through the five acts was mira-
culous. She was almost unconscious as the curtain
fell ; and, I believe, never spoke intelligibly after she
was borne from the theatre !

In private, she was a broad, hearty-mannered
woman, quick-tempered, and not unfrequently indulg-
ing in strokes of sarcastic bitterness ; so that, in the
Green-Room, her tongue was held by young members
of the profession in some dread, and was not entirely
devoid of terror even to old-stagers.

A conversation is reported between Mrs. Glover,
Mrs. Orger, and Mrs. Humby, the two latter younger
women than the former, but experienced, and *rusées*
as well as *passées*,—a conversation characteristic of
the *trio*. The subject was Charles Mathews' then
recent marriage with Madame Vestris :—

" They say," said Humby, with her quaint air of
assumed simplicity, " that before accepting him,
Vestris made a full confession to him of all her

lovers!   What touching confidence !" she added, archly.

" What needless trouble ! !" said Orger, drily.

" What a wonderful memory ! ! !" wound up, Glover, triumphantly.

MRS. NISBETT (Lady Boothby),

who lent the aid of her brilliant talents to the above cast of the " Clandestine Marriage," merits a special tribute of admiration and regret : for she, too, is no more. So are the lights of the stage extinguished, one by one, and darkness gathers o'er the fading scene !

> " The wine of life is drawn, and the mere lees
> Is left this vault to brag of."

Mrs. Nisbett's real name was Macnamara ; she assumed that of Mordaunt as a *nom de théâtre*, and, under that name, two sisters of hers were also candidates for dramatic honours, but with scant success.

Miss Mordaunt commenced her theatrical career at a very early age. It has been said that she was the original from whom Thackeray drew his Miss Fotheringay, the daughter of old Costigan, in Pendennis ; and there are some traits and incidents that seem to give confirmation to the idea. Be that as it may, she herself told me, walking on the parade at St. Leonard's, on the south coast of England—where she retired, and lived in a very elegant *cottage orné* during the latter years of her life,—she herself told me that she never had six weeks' schooling in her life, and that she played Lady Constance in " King John," in a country theatre, at thirteen years of age !

She first appeared on the London stage in 1828, at Covent Garden Theatre, in the character of the Widow Cheerly in the " Soldier's Daughter :" her success was instantaneous, and was sealed by subsequent performances. Her beauty, elegance, gaiety, gushing spirits, and talents, very soon surrounded her with admirers; among whom Captain Nisbett, of the Guards, a gentleman of good family, fortune, and distinguished position in the fashionable world, carried off the palm, was accepted as her husband, and immediately on his marriage withdrew his fascinating wife from the theatre. Captain Nisbett was a fine, young, dashing fellow, of great animal spirits, passionately fond, and justly proud, of the lovely creature he had made his own. He was happy only in her society; in her he found not only all the attractions that could secure his heart and grace his home, but a congenial spirit, sympathizing in all his tastes, and falling into all his pleasures and amusements. He was never weary of parading her to his friends ; to his idea, no company was attractive, no party was complete—not even the dinners which he gave to his brother officers and military associates—unless she presided, or, at least, adorned it with her presence. Thus she was thrown a great deal into men's society by her husband's fondness ; and so, perhaps, contracted some freedoms of manner and frankness of expression, not exactly vulgar, but *mannish*, which always remained with her in after life, and gave rise sometimes to a more unfavourable construction than they or she really merited ; so that people sometimes set her down as indiscreet, when she was only thoughtless. She was a gay, volatile, impulsive creature that everybody

liked, and who was easily carried away by her love
for her husband to take up his style of manner and
conversation. They were devoted to each other. I
have heard her say, with tears in her eyes, drawing
Captain Nisbett's miniature from her bosom,—"I
never *loved* but *once ;* now I can only *like !"* She
lost him when their happiness was at its height, their
harmony most perfect. He was thrown from his
phaeton, the wheel passed over his thigh, and amputation and death were the fatal results.

On his death, the young and fascinating widow
found that his affairs were not in such a state as to
allow her to continue her then style of living; and
though she ultimately, some years after, came into
possession of, I believe, £10,000 or £15,000 sterling,
yet she found herself, at the moment, thrown upon
her own resources for her future maintenance, unless
she chose to accept some one of the many aspirants
for her hand. This, with her wound still fresh and
bleeding, she shrank from doing; and nothing remained for her, therefore, but to return, however
unwillingly, to that profession which opened its arms
to receive her; in the practice of which she would
find immediate distraction from her grief, and occupation for her mind, and of which she was destined
to be a living ornament.

O, glorious prerogative of genius ! all-sufficient for
itself; a kingdom to its possessor, a crown, an *independence !*—setting its heaven-gifted owner beyond
the patronage of titled arrogance, or purse-proud
wealth ?

This was Mrs. Nisbett's *dower ;* she needed no
other from her husband or his family; the public

opened their arms, hearts, and purses to her; she reappeared with increased *éclât* as the Widow Cheerly; and the position was soon conceded to her of the first *comédienne* on the English stage. It was at this time, 1835, that I first saw her playing a starring engagement at the Liverpool Theatre; and (as Burke said of a much higher actress, in a much loftier and more tragic scene) " Surely, never lighted on this orb, which she hardly seemed to touch, a more delightful vision."

She was, at that time, slight and fragile, yet graceful in figure; all life, sparkle, and animation—

> " as if *Joy* itself
> Were made a living thing, and wore *her* shape."

Her laugh was a peal of music; it came from her heart, and went direct to yours: nothing could resist it; it was contagious as a fever, catching as a fire, flashing as the lightning! An anchorite would have joined in it, without asking why; St. Anthony himself would have chuckled in accord with her, had he heard its silver echo in the wilderness! It was as merry as joy-bells for a wedding; as exciting to the nerves as sleigh-bells on a frosty morning, when the bright sun glitters on the crisp snow which crackles beneath the horse's feet! It would " create a soul in the ribs of death!" At its sound the hypochondriac forgot his griefs; and thick-blooded, lymphatic dullards, impregnable in Bœotian inertness,—

> "that will not smile,
> Though Nestor swear the jest be laughable,"

would be roused to a spasmodic action of the cacchi-

E

natory muscles, by the electric battery of Nisbett's thrilling mirth !

I have seen her set a whole theatre, when the audience seemed unusually immovable, in a delirium of gaiety, by the mere contagion of her ringing laugh ; *gurgling*, at first, like the throat of a canary-bird, swelling with unuttered song—anon, growing into full, firm tones like the blackbird's notes,—anon, clear and sparkling like the trill of the lark,—then gradually subsiding to a muffled cadence, only to burst out again into stronger, louder, but still *musical* gushings of irrepressible melody ; running through the whole diatonic scale of *Ha-ha-has !* till every soul in the house felt the spell, gave themselves up to its influence, and joined in a universal laughing chorus !

This it was, this mirth-inspiring power, that crowned her triumphs in Constance in the " Love Chase," and Lady Gay Spanker in " London Assurance." They were both written for her, and she *topped* them both. I have seen many actresses try and *try hard* at them ; to her, alone, it was no effort : *they* wore their mirth as part of the costume for the character ; Nisbett came fashioned thus from nature's hand, and THALIA dropped her mantle on her favourite's shoulders !

Yet, singularly enough, she had a weakness for tragedy, a *penchant* for sentimental parts, and a decided conviction that she shone in them.

Like the Fotheringay, she delighted in the sorrows of Mrs. Haller ; the distresses of Pauline were *nuts* to her; and the more tears she could be called on to shed, the more satisfied she was. As Tony Lumpkin says of Miss Neville's affection for heart-rending romances, " The more she cried, the more she liked them !"

This taste for the pathetic she could only indulge in the country, where, as a *star*, she could shine as she pleased, and be a *watery planet*, if she chose. In London, she was not allowed so to pervert herself ; the manager would not be a party to the transformation of Euphrosyne into a weeping statue—

" A Niobe, all tears"—

and so she was compelled to maintain her empire over hearts by lighter chains. She always, however, at heart believed that her *forte* lay in sentimental tragedy, and that she was a very ill-used woman, in not being permitted to indulge her inclination !

Though Mrs. Nisbett was engaged at a large salary, by Madame Vestris, at Covent Garden Theatre, it must not be imagined that there was any particular *love* between them. It is true, they kissed when they met, and called each other " My dear," — but, as Crabtree says, " That's neither here nor there." Vestris probably detested Nisbett for her superior good fortune and superior position in life ; and Nisbett, without being naturally more malicious than ladies in general, instinctively felt an aversion where she knew no good feelings were felt towards her. Occasionally, these little secret fires—the

" animorum cœlestium iræ"—

would break out from beneath the " *cinerem dolosum*" of smiles and courtesies, and the effect was sometimes amusing to the lookers-on.

E 2

Let me give an instance, of which I was a witness, and, partly, an actor in :

The third part I played at Covent Garden Theatre, was Mercutio, in " Romeo and Juliet," which was revived with great splendour and picturesqueness of effect, for the purpose of introducing Mrs. Nisbett's sister, Miss Jane Mordaunt, in the character of Juliet. J. R. ANDERSON was the Romeo, and the play was generally well acted, with this one flagrant exception, that the Juliet was a failure : and Miss E. MONTAGUE was, on after representations, substituted in the part.

This was, of course, deeply mortifying to Mrs. Nisbett, who,—for she was no judge of tragic excellence,—had built the loftiest hopes on her sister's success.

Now, it happened that Mrs. Nisbett had, at the same time, another cause of distress that weighed upon her. She was very closely *liée* by friendship with FEARGUS O'CONNOR, the Irish agitator (not Dan O'Connell, mind—he was " a mighty different" kind of an agitator !), and O'Connor, and a Chartist demagogue named Frost, had got themselves snugly confined in York Castle, with a Government prosecution hanging over their heads, for seditious and revolutionary speeches to a mob.

With these two causes for grief upon her spirits, she came down to the Green-Room the day after her sister's failure, looking very much depressed, and, even through her veil, her inflamed eyes showing traces of recent tears. Everybody was, of course, full of silent sympathy for her, showing itself rather in manner than in words. But Vestris could not resist the opportunity of having a fling at "a rival in distress !"

There were several persons in the Green-Room— Mrs. Orger, Mr. Farren, Mr. Cooper (I think), myself and others: Mrs. Nisbett sat a little apart, on my right hand, with veil down, and sadly silent. Vestris led the conversation to Frost, the Chartist riots, and the coming trials. She did not mention O'Connor by name, but she made it sufficiently clear that he was the principal object of her attack ; and it was through him that her shot at poor Nisbett was to be aimed. She let loose a torrent of invective against Chartists and Radicals generally ; winding up with this comprehensive condemnation.

" *I never*," said she, with pointed malice, "*knew any man on the Radical side who was really a gentleman !*"

Poor Nisbett winced in her corner ; I know not whether any look of sympathy, or any expression of face of mine, called Madame's attention to me ; but she added in the most marked manner (for I was known to have a decided leaning towards at least *liberal* opinions in politics),

" Did *you*, Mr. Vandenhoff?"

Now I felt the malicious impertinence of this appeal, and I resolved to rebuke it. To gain a moment's time to mature my thought, I asked, as if I had not heard her question,—" Did I what ?"

She repeated—" Did you ever know a man really a gentleman, on the Radical side in politics ?"

Now Vestris had let her desire to wound make her overlook, like a bad swordsman, her own vulnerable point : she had, for the moment, entirely forgotten (no wonder, perhaps, among so many !) a *liaison* of hers in former years, with a certain well-known T. D., a decided Radical member of the House of Commons, and, consequently, she was put entirely *hors de combat*, when I repeated her question,

" Did I ever know a Radical and a gentleman?" and then added,

" O yes ; and you too."

" Who, who?" she said, "name one."

" Tom Duncombe !" I coolly replied, looking quite unconscious of intention.

It was a bombshell in the enemy's camp. The effect was *foudroyant !* No one spoke—scarcely seemed to breathe—Farren alone gave his, Hм ! the rest were silent. Vestris fumbled with the keys of the wardrobe, that always hung by her girdle, and, very shortly, left the Green-Room.

Then Nisbett threw back her veil, started up, put her arms round my neck, exclaiming, " God bless you !" and burst into tears.

From that time we were good friends.

She kept a handsome close-carriage and pair, living in good style at Denham Cottage, Hammersmith, anticipating, probably, the amount which she expected, and afterwards did receive, in right of her widowhood. She was a good creature, supported mother and sisters, and educated her brothers, one of whom was called to the bar, and is now in practice in London. She was indeed devoted to her family, having no children of her own, and was lavish in her generosity to them. In goodness of heart, gaiety, and liberality of disposition, as well as in the peculiarity of her temper and the bent of her talents, she seems to have much resembled the celebrated

Peg Woffington, of Garrick's day: in respectability of character and social position she was vastly superior to her kind-hearted but reckless predecessor.

By her marriage with Sir WILLIAM BOOTHBY, a baronet, very much her senior in years, she became entitled to be addressed as " your ladyship ;" and she was, by her second husband, again withdrawn from the stage, to preside over his house. The enamoured old gentleman did not, however, enjoy his felicity more than about a twelvemonth ; and she was again a widow, in the maturity of her charms. The income she was entitled to by her marriage settlement with Sir William, was not, in her ideas, sufficient for her expenditure, with all the family claims that she felt called upon to answer ; and, after a decent period of mourning, she again returned to her profession, was again warmly received, and played at the Haymarket and Drury Lane Theatres, under the popular name by which she had won the affections of the London public, and by which she will be long remembered— Mrs. NISBETT.

I often endeavoured to persuade her to visit this country, which I assured her would prove an *El Dorado* to her ; she had a great desire to follow my counsel ; but family considerations prevented her, and so New York never saw her. I have always regretted that it was so ; she would have been the most popular favourite that ever visited the country ; and it would have been a great advantage to the public taste to have witnessed the performance of the greatest *comédienne* of the English stage. It would have shown, at least, that the extreme of frankness, gaiety, and the *abandon* of a mirthful nature, are quite com-

patible with grace and elegant manners; and that
an actress of taste and a true artist can give full
scope to her animal spirits, her sense of humour, and
her ambition to please, without descending to affectation on one hand, or vulgarity on the other ; and, let
me say, this would be a useful lesson to some of high
pretensions.

Ill health, at length, compelled her to retire,
temporarily as she thought, from the mimic scene ;
and she fixed her residence, as I have said, at St.
Leonard's, on the South Coast. A cottage—or rather
it should be called, from its handsome dimensions and
style, a country mansion—was built for her, which she
called Rougemont, from its elevated situation and
the profusion of red roses that grew about it. I used
to tell her that she wished to suggest Rosamond's
bower by the name. In this elegant retreat she died,
peacefully, at about forty-eight years of age, attended
to the last by her old mother, whom she had always loved so well, and to whom she had ever
shown more than a daughter's duty and protecting
care.

In person she was above the medium height, of
a graceful form, and brunette complexion, with a
nose slightly *retroussé*, gipsy-like, almost. She always
suggested to me the idea of Cleopatra, Egypt's black-
browed Queen.

Like Milton's nymph, *Euphrosyne*, in her train
came

> Jest and youthful jollity,
> Quips and cranks and wanton wiles,
> Nods and becks and wreathéd smiles,
> Such as hang on Hebe's cheek
> And love to live in dimples sleek !

Gone! passed away !—

Stilled is that thrilling voice, hushed that ringing laugh, never to wake an echo more !

MISS FOOTE (Countess of Harrington),

I have mentioned Miss Foote (Countess of Harrington), and I dwell on the recollection with pleasure. She had left the stage some years before I trod on it, to grace a more elevated sphere : I never, therefore, had the pleasure of playing with her. As a boy, I have seen her often at the Liverpool Theatre, in Rosalind,—and what a fascinating Rosalind she was ! —Annette, in the " Little Jockey," (how she drove *the fellows* wild with her archness, her playfulness, her vivacity, her breeches and top-boots—heaven save the mark !—and her singing of

" The boy in yellow wins the day !")

and in Letitia Hardy, in which she was a zephyr, a wave of the sea ! Perhaps one of the most bewitching things she did was Kate O'Brien, in " Perfection, or the Lady of Munster." My father used to play Charles Paragon to her. Ye gods, how I envied him ! How I wished myself a man, that *I* might be able to act with her ! How I watched at the stage-door, after the play was over, to see her step into her carriage (she had the prettiest little foot in the world ; and her leg !—oh !) how I longed to offer my hand to assist her, and dared not ! how I wrote to her for an order for the theatre, on purpose to get her autograph ! how delighted I was when she sent it to

E 5

me—an elegant, ladylike, tapering, graceful signature, (I have it yet !)—

Admit Two,

Maria Foote.

How I kissed it ! how I got one of the actresses to present me to her, and how I blushed and trembled (I was about thirteen) when she spoke to me and smiled ; and how insulted I felt when I heard her say, aside to my introducer, that I was " a fine boy !" All this I will not attempt to describe.   You must imagine it, reader ; and imagine, if you can, what a creature she was !   It was not that she was so beautiful—I have seen twenty more beautiful women ; —but she was lovely, she was lovable ; she was all grace, all fascination !   There was a hazy, dreamy tenderness about her blue eyes that entwined itself voluptuously about the heart, and

> " Took the reason prisoner."

When she spoke,

> " It was an alarum to love !"

She did not sing with great art or finish ; yet it was a delight to hear her.   Who that ever heard can forget her *Cuckoo-song* in Rosalind !   Her limbs were dainty as a fawn's, and her motion—by the bye, it was of her that this description was written :—

> With what a waving grace she goes
> Along the corridor. How like a fawn,
> Yet statelier. Hark ! no sound, however soft,
> (Nor gentlest echo) telleth where she treads ;

> But every motion of her shape doth seem
> Hallowed by silence. Thus did Hebe grow
> Amidst the gods a paragon !

And this, in the mouth of a monk,—

> " When joy is in her eye, 'tis like the light
> Of heaven; blue, deep, ethereal blue ;
> And, were she but a saint, I'd worship her ! "

And this,—

> " Her face as fair
> As tho' she had look'd on Paradise, and caught
> Its early beauty : then her smile was soft
> As Innocence before it learned to love !"

Unfortunately, she learned to love early ; and loved " not wisely, but too well."

Colonel Berkeley, eldest son—but by some flaw in the marriage-ceremony, not the *heir*—of his father, Earl Berkeley, was one of the most magnificent and fashionable men of his time : his was indeed the perfection of manly beauty. I saw him in his old age, when he had been ennobled by two several titles, bestowed on him by royal favour: first, Baron Lord Segrave ; second, Earl Fitzhardinge. I saw him when he had reached, if not passed his eightieth year ; and a finer specimen of octogenarian bloom I never set my eyes on,—considerably over six feet high, straight, broad-chested, and fresh-complexioned, No wonder that, in the bloom of manhood, assisted by those who should have guarded her innocence, he triumphed over a simple girl, dazzled by his personal accomplishments and superior rank.   Thus, the gentle Maria gave her heart to one who did not reward it with his hand ; and, yielding to the truthful tenderness of her nature, withheld no boon that love could ask or confiding affection could bestow. There were family reasons why Col. Berkeley should not marry; and Miss Foote had to bear the burthen of maternity, without the honours of a wife. Col. Berkeley always treated her with great care and respect, and her offspring with paternal care and affection; but she felt her position keenly: the consciousness of it tinged her life with a melancholy that lent an additional charm to her soft and delicate beauty.

Of course there were not wanting men, rich and unscrupulous, to offer her consolation, in a new attachment, to be cast off when it became irksome or inconvenient, after the example of her first lover. But her heart was not depraved, and she shrank from *liaisons* that would dishonour her in her own eyes. At length came one who made honourable proposals to her—a gentleman of fortune, a Mr. Hayne, commonly called *Pea-green* Hayne, from the rather remarkable colour of a frock-coat he wore. But those were the days of *loud* colours in dress; black did not then overspread all backs as with a pall. So, Pea-green Hayne proposed, and, after some hesitation, was accepted. But it appears he hardly knew his own mind, or, like some other braggarts, his courage failed him when he should have taken the field. He backed out, and repudiated his matrimonial liability. A jury, however, took a different view of the case, and awarded to the insulted Maria £7,000, by way of damages for the *Pea-green's* breach of promise.

It was fortunate she escaped from this matrimonial cage, (though she carried some of the *gold bars* away), for a brighter destiny was in store for her, which was wrought out curiously enough.

Madame Vestris loved her, as rival actresses and rival beauties usually love each other—(the *odium theatricum* is not so virulent, but quite as active as the *odium theologium !*) In spite of this fond affection —resembling that which a certain cloven-footed personage is proverbially said to entertain for holy water —Madame engaged her for the little Olympic Theatre, at a large salary, and it was to Madame that she owed, most unintentionally on Vestris's part, you may rely on it, her accession to the rank and title of the Countess of Harrington. Green-Room gossip thus tells the story :

The EARL of HARRINGTON, who, as Lord Petersham, had been what we should call now the greatest *swell* of his day—a fast man, the fastest—a leader of fashion in dress, carriages, snuff, and *roué-ism*—(there was the Petersham coat, the Petersham hat, the Petersham mixture, &c. &c.)—had succeeded, in late years, to his father's title and fortune : he was probably ten or fifteen years younger than Col. Berkeley ; and at the time of which I speak (1836), might be about fifty-five years of age : Miss Foote was about thirty-five. The Earl was still a gay old boy, who, I fear, did not come under Dr. Johnson's category of those " whose follies had ceased with their youth ;" he still retained his hankering after the *dames des coulisses* and the piquant delights of a *petit souper*. Having a mind to pass an evening agreeably, he invited his old acquaintance, Madame Vestris (this was before her union with Mathews), to sup with him at his princely mansion, and requested her to bring an agreeable and lively companion with her. Vestris invited a young lady of the theatre, whose name I

will not mention, to accompany her.   She, having a
due regard for a reputation as yet untarnished, declined the equivocal honour.   I don't know what
suggested Miss Foote's name to Vestris's mind, as
a substitute; but Foote was invited, and went.   A
fortnight after that supper she was Countess of
Harrington, as the law directs!

I believe Vestris had a severe fit of illness, in consequence—*an attack of spleen.*

The Earl died: his brother succeeded to the earl-
dom; and Miss Foote, that was, became Dowager
Countess.   I believe she still lives.

Perhaps it may gratify the curiosity of some
readers to peruse the following list of actresses who
became, by marriage, allied to the nobility of
England :

ANASTASIA ROBINSON,	*Countess of Peterborough.*
Miss MELLON—married the banker Coutts; and after his death became by marriage—*Duchess of St. Albans.*	
(Miss Burdett Coutts, daughter of Sir Francis Burdett, inherited her vast wealth.)	
Miss FENTON (the original Polly, in the Beggars' Opera),	*Duchess of Bolton.*
Miss FARREN,	*Countess of Derby.*
Miss BRUNTON,	*Countess of Craven.*
Miss O'NEILL, by marriage with Mr. (after Sir Wm.) Beecher,	*Lady Beecher.*
Miss STEPHENS,	*Countess of Essex.*
Miss FOOTE,	*Countess of Harrington.*
Miss PATON, by marriage with a son of the Duke of Richmond, from whom she was divorced, *at her own suit,* and became the wife of Wood the singer, by whose name she is so well known in this country,	*Lady W. Lennox.*
Mrs. NISBETT,	*Lady Boothby.*

MR. HARLEY (J. P.)*

was another of the old school of comedians, since
passed away, belonging to our company, who had
been an associate and friend of Jack Banister, Joe
Munden, and the other actors of the preceding generation, and now preserved the traditions of the stage
in old comedies. Harley was immensely funny, sometimes by the mere force of grotesqueness of manner.
In such parts as Bob Acres, Mark Meddle, Nick
Bottom, there was a serio-comic earnestness about
him, that was highly humorous ; he had a glibness of
speech, too—I mean, in his best days—which served
him well in Touchstone, Autolycus, Trinculo, and
other Shaksperian clowns, in which he had the great
merit of a scrupulous adherence to the text, and said
no more, nor no less, than was set down for him ; his
singing of a comic song, too, was irresistibly ludicrous,
and never failed to set the house in a roar.   He had
a habit of fixing his eye, in his song, on some person
in the pit, just behind the orchestra, and singing at
him ; bobbing his head at him, and treating the butt
to all sorts of *mugs*, hammering the jokes of the song
into him, by iteration, till the individual attacked
began first to titter, then, as Harley's grimaces proceeded, to laugh out, and lastly, overcome by the
battery of nods, bobs, and queer faces that the actor
let fly at him, was fairly convulsed with laughter ;
which, of course, spread to his neighbours, so through
the pit, and thus through the whole house: or,
perhaps the *butt* was annoyed and embarrassed by
being thus singled out, as a *point d'appui*, to have

* Mr. Harley died August 22nd, 1858, and was buried at Kensal
Green, by the side of Feargus O'Connor.—ED.

fun poked at him ; his irritation, or confusion, amused his neighbours, and they laughed at his annoyance ; Harley continued his fire, the man's vexation increased ; those in the vicinity grew louder in their enjoyment of it, and the rest of the house joined in, ignorant of the real cause, but believing they were carried away by Harley's drolleries. The trick never failed, one way or the other.

" *That*, George," said Harley to me, " I learnt from *old Joey* (Munden). ' Always fix your eye,' said Joey, ' on some one man in the pit, sing at him, till he laughs, and then you have 'em—the rest are sure to follow.' "

Harley was a most valuable member of a company ; highly popular with the public ; always ready to serve the interests of the theatre ; pleasant and obliging to his brother actors ; never known to say a harsh word *to*, or express a harsh opinion *of*, any one ; he had every one's good will ; was always engaged at a leading theatre, on a good salary, and continued to perform at the Princess's up to a very short time before his death.   In private life he was very much respected ; and, from his economical habits, was thought to have accumulated a large fortune ; but it was, I believe, found, that over-confidence in the opinions and resources of friends had led him into money engagements which had considerably diminished his means.

He died in an advanced age—upwards of seventy— at his house in Harley-street, where he had lived, with his sisters, a bachelor's life, for many years. His great delight was the theatre—whether acting or not ; he was hardly easy out of it, even if he did not play.   He never missed being present at the first night of a new play, or a new performer; and his criticisms were always of the most encouraging kind. It must have been something hopelessly bad, indeed, of which Harley could have uttered a decided condemnation. His time was divided between the theatre and the Garrick Club, of which he was one of the oldest members. He was *my sponsor* on my admission to it.

He has had many imitators, in a more or less degree, who have become favourites of the public. Buckstone, Wright, Compton, and Widdicombe, are all of his school—they may be called the *Harleian Miscellany*.

The only sarcastic thing I ever heard him say was in reference to this very point. It was about five years ago, at the Garrick Club; he felt that he was gradually nearing his turn, and he saw his crack parts falling into other hands, and other favourites taking his place with the public.

" It is rather hard, George," said he, " to have people pick your brains, and take the bread out of your mouth, too."

He died very tranquilly; and his last words were a quotation from one of his favourite parts—Bottom, in the " Midsummer Night's Dream." He had been ailing and failing some weeks; and was seated, apparently more comfortable than usual, in his large easy chair, when, after a silence, he said, suddenly, (in Bottom's words,)

"I have an exposition of sleep,"

turned his head aside, closed his eyes, and never re-opened them.

"Alas poor Yorick !"

THE COLUMBINE.

Attached to the Covent Garden Company of that day was a fair lady, who figured annually in the Christmas pantomimes as Columbine, Miss F—— much admired for the classic contour of her face, and the elegance of her form. She has, for some years, been withdrawn from the stage, and lives under the protection of his Royal Highness the Duke of ——. She has, by her royal lover, several children, remark·able for their beauty—worthy of the beautiful race from which they spring. The lady's position is peculiar. A Royal Duke is under very binding restrictions as to marriage, and is expected to receive his wife at the State's hands; but the (quasi) Duchess is treated with every consideration and respect; has a handsome house, and elegant villa, carriages, retinue, and attendants. So that Miss F—— is probably as happy as ever she dreamed of being, as Columbine, in the impossible bliss of the last scene of a Christmas Pantomime, where the good fairy unites the faithful lovers, amidst a profusion of garlands and a general illumination.

VI.

IN addition to the characters of Leon, Lovewell, and
Mercutio, which I have mentioned, the other parts
I played during my first season at Covent Garden,
were Modus (Hunchback), Ctesiphon (Ion), Colonna
(in Leigh Hunt's new play, the Legend of Florence,
which ran fourteen nights), Careless (in the Double
Gallant, a revival of an old comedy of Cibber's),
Laertes (Hamlet), Claudio, to Mr. Charles Kemble's
Benedick, before the Queen, on his brief return to the
stage, by her Majesty's command ; and Marc Antony
at the Victoria Theatre, for the benefit of the
dramatic fund.

During the season I had diligently studied and
rehearsed at home, Hamlet, Othello, Rolla, Claude
Melnotte, Virginius, Benedick ; for these, with Leon,
Julian St. Pierre, Duke Aranza, and Faulconbridge,
I had procured, at considerable expense, an appropriate wardrobe ; and these formed my present *reper-
toire*, with which, on the close of the Covent Garden
season, I started on a provincial tour.

Except the five nights I played at Liverpool, Preston, a manufacturing town in Lancashire, gave me my first starring engagement, and the opportunity of testing my powers before an audience, in Hamlet, Othello, and other parts which I had never yet played. During my week in Preston I tried my wing in them, before venturing on a larger field, and was fortunate enough to win both applause and money; of the first, abundance; of the second, much more than I expected from so small a town. I played six nights, and received for my share £50, not bad for a novice in a little country theatre.

I began to think myself on the high road to fame and fortune! This was in June, 1840. My next engagement was for a fortnight, at the Theatre Royal, Liverpool; where I opened, in July, to a fine house, in Hamlet; was greatly received in it, and highly complimented,—much more highly than I deserved, I am sure—both by press and public.

Mr. J. R. ANDERSON was, after the first night, associated with me in this engagement, and we played Romeo and Juliet, Othello (alternating parts), Julius Cæsar, and other plays in which we could appear together. For my benefit I relied on my own attraction alone, and played Claude Melnotte, with Harriet Faucit as the Pauline. I had a very good house, and did well by my ten nights.

On Saturday, 1st August, I played at the Theatre Royal, Manchester, for the first time; Mercutio (Romeo, Anderson), and Petruchio in the afterpiece; receiving £10 for my night's work.

I had now not been quite ten months on the stage, and had the gratification to find myself received in the largest provincial theatres as an acknowledged star in the leading characters of the drama. I therefore diligently pursued the study of my profession, adding new parts by degrees to my list, and playing, during the next twelve months, in several provincial towns, besides second and third engagements at Liverpool and Manchester, increasing my experience of the stage, attaining ease in my new parts, and establishing a reputation in the country. During this year I first played Macbeth, Charles Surface, Marcus Brutus, Octavian, Master Walter, and Richard III.

As I returned to Covent Garden Theatre the season after, this is all I need say of this part of my dramatic career, except to record a few incidents that occurred to me, and which may be perhaps amusing.

A One-Armed Actor.—Can any one imagine an actor playing Icilius, Iago, Pizarro, Banquo, with only one arm? Such a mutilated hero did I encounter at Leicester, near where the battle of Bosworth field was fought. He had lost his arm,—not in that bloody fight; but it had been accidentally shot off. In Icilius, the deficit was concealed by his toga, in Pizarro by his mantle, in Banquo by his plaid; and thus I had really not noticed the poor fellow's mutilation, though I had observed that he seemed rather one-sided in his action, till I played Othello; and then, what was my horror, on seizing him, in the third act, to find that I had got hold of an armless sleeve, stuffed out in mockery of flesh,—for he did not wear a cork arm! I was almost struck dumb; and it was only by a strong effort that I recovered myself sufficiently to go on with the text. Poor fellow ! he was a remarkably sensible actor and good reader ; but, of course, he could never rise in his profession with only one arm !

" Misery acquaints man with strange bedfellows," says Trinculo ; and country theatres acquaint one with strange readings, I say. I have met with many strange perversions of text and meaning ; but nothing, perhaps, so outrageously wide of the mark, and so ingeniously absurd, as one that a Polonius gave me, at a small theatre in Lancashire. He came in, at rehearsal, in the second act, to tell me that the actors were arrived ; and proceeded to describe them in this manner :

"The best actors in the world, my lord ; for tragedy, comedy, history, pastoral, pastorical comical, historical pastoral, scene individable, or poem unlimited. *Plautus is too heavy, and Senna is too light !*"

" I beg your pardon," I said, not wishing to wound his vanity, " but are you quite right in the text there?"

" Right in the text !" said he, rather indignantly ; " I should think I am. I ought to be : I've played Polonius twenty-odd years ; I played before you were born, sir !"

" Very possibly," I replied, "and yet you may not be right, after all. Oblige me by looking at the book, for certainty." (The prompter was, as usual, making out a cast, or a list of properties, or doing anything rather than attend to the prompt-book.)

" Look at the book !" said he, " I shall do no such thing. What for, I should like to know ? I've played Polonius with your father, sir, and it's strange if I don't know the text."

" It is strange," I replied ; " and yet I think you will find that you are at fault in this passage. I have always read, and heard it given—

' Seneca cannot be too heavy, nor Plautus too light,'

Seneca being a tragedian, and Plautus a—"

" O fudge !" said he, " I know what Senna is, as well as you ; as for Plautus, I don't know what that is, nor I don't care ; but I've spoke it so for twenty-five years, and I ain't agoing to change it now !"

" O, very well," I said, " if you are resolved to talk nonsense, do so."

Accordingly, at night, when he came to the passage, he walked deliberately up to me, looked me full in the face, and in a very emphatic tone, said,

" Plautus *is* too heavy, and Senna *is* too light !"

I could only wish him a good dose of it, by way of clearing his thick head ; but it passed with the audience ; apparently no one noticed. Perhaps he had read it so to them for twenty-odd years, and they were used to it : who knows ?

———

A PRACTICAL JOKER.—There was a low-comedian, familiarly called Dick Hoskins, whom I occasionally encountered at several of the small country theatres in the North of England, and who was an inveterate and practical joker on the stage. He was always very well behaved with me ; but when he came in contact with a tragedian for whose talents he entertained a contempt, or whose person or manners displeased him, woe to the unhappy subject of his fun !

All his tragedy was turned into farce, when Dick was in the humorous vein. Thus, he played the Grave-digger, one night, at, I think, the Rochdale Theatre, in Lancashire, to the Hamlet of a Mr. C——, a most solemn and mysterious tragedian, of the cloak-and-dagger school. This gentleman's tragedy was in Dick's eyes much more intensely comic than his own broadest strokes of farce; accordingly, Dick held no terms with it, and showed the unfortunate object of his merriment no quarter on the stage. When, therefore, Hamlet approached the grave to hold his dialogue with Dick in it, the latter began his antics, and extemporised all sorts of absurd interpolations in the text—which he spoke in his own broad Lancashire dialect. There was not a great house, and Dick allowed himself full license. Mr. C—— scowled fearfully; but Dick was unabashed. At length he put a climax on his audacity, that " topp'd the infinite of insult."

The theatre was built on the site of an old dissenting chapel, which had formerly stood there, in which a preacher named Banks had held forth, and in the small graveyard attached to which the Doctor —for he was popularly dubbed Doctor Banks—had been buried some twenty years ago; and his name was familiar yet. So, after answering Hamlet's question—

" How long will a man lie in the earth ere he rot ?"

Dick proceeded in due course to illustrate his answer by Yorick's skull ; and taking it up, he said, in the words of the text—

" Now here's a skull that hath lain you in the earth three-and-twenty years. Whose do you think it was ?"

" Nay, I know not," replied Hamlet, in his sepulchral, tragedy-tone.

" This skull, sir," said Dick, pursuing the text thus far, and then making a sudden and most unlooked for alteration—

" This was DOCTOR BANKS's skull !"

And the word skull he pronounced like bull.

Of course the house was in an uproar of laughter and confusion. The victimised tragedian stamped and fumed about the stage, as well he might, exclaiming, " Yorick's, sir, Yorick's !"

" No," said Dick, coolly, when the tumult had subsided, taking up another skull, and resuming the text—

" *This* is Yorick's skull, the king's jester; but " (going off again) " t'other's Doctor Banks's, as I *told* you."

This was too much; this was the last straw on the tragedian's back ! He jumped into the grave, seized the (very) low-comedian by the throat, and a most fearful contest, never before—or since, I hope —introduced into the play, ensued, in which Dick held his own bravely, and succeeded at length in overpowering, in a double sense, the worsted tragedian, whom he held down in the grave with one hand, while he flourished " DOCTOR BANKS's skull " in triumph above his head !

The curtain was dropped, amidst roars and shrieks of laughter, in which King, Queen, monk, and courtiers—who, in the vain hope of arresting the row, had been sent on with Ophelia's empty coffin—were compelled to join, forming a tableau, which finished the play for that night.

F

A QUEER VISITOR.—I had just finished breakfast
at the hotel at Bolton, a small town in Lancashire,
where I was playing a short engagement, when the
waiter told me that a gentleman wanted to speak
with me.

" Who is it ?" I asked.

" I don't know," said the waiter ; " he's rather a
strange-looking gentleman, sir."

" How, strange ?"

" Well, sir, I can't exactly say ; he looks queer,
somehow ; I think, sir, he must be one of the actor-
chaps, or else a gipsy."

" Oh," said I—a highly complimentary alterna-
tive, I thought to myself !

" Well," I added, " let me see this strange gentleman."

" Yes, sir ;" and the queer-looking chap was
brought into my room.

A queer-looking chap he was indeed ! A tall, gaunt,
high-shouldered, raw-boned, bossy-faced, hook-nosed,
sun-burnt, and hollow-cheeked individual, with a pair
of keen, restless, black eyes, deep set, under shaggy
overhanging eye-brows ; dressed in a faded frock-coat
which had once been brown, but was now of no positive colour, and which—having formed part of the
wardrobe of a smaller man than its present wearer, to
whom by some freak of fortune it had lapsed—being
too short for him in every way, showed his bare, bony
wrists, innocent of wristbands ; a dark double-breasted
waistcoat, buttoned close across his chest, to conceal,
perhaps, his bosom's secret—(a scarcity of linen)—a
pair of trowsers that, having probably been derived
from the same source as the coat, presented the same

exiguousness of length, and displayed the tops of a
pair of very seedy and travel-worn high-lows,—a fuzzy
head of hair, so promiscuous and so indistinct of tint,
from dryness, age, and the dust of the roads, that it
was impossible to guess at its original shade,—such
were the principal features of the strange-looking gentleman, who now, with a rusty, battered hat in his
large, muscular hands, presented himself, bowing, to
my notice.

His name was Hall, or Hill (I forget which), he
said, in a husky, hoarse, foggy voice ; such as one
hears so often on a London cab-stand, indicative of ·
Old-Tom propensities, or a weakness for Geneva—
perhaps in this case, poor fellow, of a consumption.

" You seem tired," I said ; " pray sit down."

He did so, thanking me ; and, after a preliminary
cough, by way of clearing his throat, he began, in a
somewhat less thick utterance—and in a style semi-
oratorical, semi-theatrical : the style, in fact, adopted
usually by the presenters of snuff-boxes, pieces of
plate, gold watches, and testimonials generally, to the
happy *recipient* (to use the set phraseology) who has
paid the day before, through his agent, the full price
of the article to be presented to him—

" I am commissioned, sir," he said, "by Mr.
Parish, the manager of the Blackburn Theatre, to ask
if your engagements will allow you to give us the
aid of your splendid talents for a few, say three or
more, nights ; and if so, on what terms you would
consent to visit us."

Now, there was nothing in this address particularly *outre* in itself: it was the grandiloquent *ambas-
sadorial* style of the man, coupled with his mean and

F 2

wild appearance, that made it ludicrous. He had all the burlesque dignity and self-importance of a ragged plenipotentiary from Otaheite!

" I have not the pleasure," I said, " Mr. Hall, of being acquainted with Mr. Parish."

" A highly respectable and responsible man, I assure you, sir : the soul of honour, sir," quickly replied the ambassador, laying his hand on his breast.

" What plays are your company capable of performing, Mr. Hall ?"

" Any, sir, and all," he answered, with a flourish : " We are *up* in all the stock tragedies, and have an efficient company."

"A good leading actress, Mr. Hall ?"

" An angel, sir ? young, perfect, talented and *amenable*." He laid particular stress on the last epithet.

" A rare assemblage of qualities," I said ; " but let me order you some breakfast, Mr. Hall ; you seem fatigued. How did you come ?"

" Walked, sir !"

" Walked !" I repeated ; " why it's twelve miles."

" I know it, sir, he replied ; " but exercise is good for me, and I preferred it to the coach ; it will do me good."

A good breakfast, thought I, would do you more good ; and, the waiter just then coming into the room with a letter for me,

" Order a beefsteak for this gentleman," I said. " Tea or coffee, Mr. Hall ?"

" Why," said that gentleman, " you're very good, sir ; but if you'll allow me, I'll take a little ale."

" Bring some ale, waiter," I said.

" Ale, sir ? yes sir ;" and with a look of ill-concealed wonder, the waiter left the room.

As soon as he had closed the door, my new friend wished to resume the subject of his mission ; but I stopped him by saying,

" Wait till you've had something to eat, Mr. Hall, and then we'll attend to that little matter. Meanwhile," I said, " there's the *Times;* excuse my reading and answering a letter."

In a few minutes the steak and ale were brought in. The strange gentleman fell to without ceremony, despatched them in a few minutes more, and gave me notice, as I continued my writing, that he had finished, with a satisfied explosion of breath, something between a yawn, and a " paviour's sigh."·

I turned towards him, as he rubbed his hands together, in token of the refreshment of his inner man ; and he said, in a theatrical way, quoting from the Merchant of Venice—

. " Well, sir, shall I have your answer ? Will you pleasure us ?"

" Well, Mr. Hall," I replied, " I am in your neighbourhood. I have three vacant nights next week, and I will come to you Monday, Wednesday, and Friday, for a clear half of the receipts, each night."

" Those are very high terms, sir," he replied, raising his eyebrows and screwing up his mouth. " I am commissioned to offer you a clear third, and half a benefit. My power extends no further."

" The value of a thing," I answered, " is that which it will bring, you know, Mr. Hall. Allow me to ask how much money you play to ordinarily. What

were the receipts of the house last night, for example ?
I trust to your honour."

" Well, sir, last night was a bad night. We had
not a great house last night."

" Come, now ; had you thirty shillings ?"

" O yes, sir ; we had thirty shillings."

"Not much more, eh ?"

" No, not much more," said he, with a comic
smile.

" Well, suppose I play to an average of twenty
pounds nightly, and you pay me half of it, if your ordinary business does not produce' more than two
pounds, you'll be a considerable gainer by the trans-
action."

" Yes," said he ? " if that were certain—"

" Nothing is certain," I replied, " in theatrical
matters ; but I have every right to expect it ; and it
is only on the terms I have mentioned that I can consent to visit you."

" Well, sir," said he, " my instructions are to secure your services, and therefore I must accept your
terms."

A scratch of a pen on a sheet of paper settled the
agreement ; and Mr. Hall, with a profusion of bows
and thanks for what he was pleased to call my " hospitable treatment," took up his hat to depart. There
was a farmer's light taxed-cart at the door, and finding its owner was going as far as Blackburn, I gave
him half-a-crown to take my strange-looking friend "
to his destination.

The next week, on Monday, I reached Blackburn
early in the morning, and about half-past ten o'clock,
my strange negotiator was ushered into my room,

accompanied by " another spirit" almost as strange as himself; a very swarthy, powerful man, considerably over six feet high, with jet-black glossy hair, that hung on the sides of his cheeks in short ringlets. He was dressed in a velveteen suit, and had altogether a regular gipsy look and air. (*Par nobile fratrum!* thought I.) The last stranger was duly presented to me, as " Mr. Gould; our stage-manager, sir !"

They had called to show me to the theatre; and I got up and followed them, to the rather dingy back-street in which it was situated. The company was assembled, and we commenced the rehearsal of " Othello." The tall Gould was the Iago, and my Desdemona was the " angel" aforesaid, a well-looking young woman, who, without seeming particularly to understand them, was very perfect in the words of the text. My new friend, the stage-manager, barring occasional extraordinary, and hitherto undreamt of readings, was pretty safe; and though there was a general air of *seediness* about the *corps dramatique*, they were all evidently desirous of doing their best, and we got through the rehearsal tolerably satisfactorily. The Emilia, it is true, did not seem to have any innate reverence for Shakspere, or any intimate acquaintance with her share of the dialogue, or her connection with the plot; and Roderigo, a very melancholy-looking youth, with a very tallowy complexion, and very thin legs, and a squeaky voice, seemed particularly innocent of every thing connected with the play, especially as to who he was, what he was, and where he was, and *why* he was what he was, who he was, and where he was. However, as I had little to do with these individuals, their malfeasances did not much trouble me.

In the evening I went rather early to the theatre, and was agreeably surprised by finding that a very good-sized room had been fitted up as my dressing-room, cleaned, carpeted, sofa'd, well lit, with extra lights, and in every way made snug. This attention to my private comfort gave me better hopes of the appointments for the stage, about which I confess I had my doubts. But, when we came to the Senate-scene, I was pleased to find a respectable array of properties, with a Duke, who, though he had the snuffles in his utterance, was well-dressed, and correct in the text. Barring a few little *contretemps*, which did not seem to affect the enjoyment of the audience, if they did not even increase it (certainly they gave uproarious tokens of delight at the burlesque and *Bombastes-Furioso* death of Roderigo, who, in his agony, kept his leg quivering and shaking in the air as if he were galvanized,—while Iago kept sticking his sword into him, and at every stick, a fresh kick) —except this, and one or two other rather striking effects, the play went off with immense applause, and the actors were evidently highly satisfied with their own efforts in the Shaksperian Drama.

The house, as I had prophesied, was well filled; and after the performance I had my first interview and settlement with the manager: and a strange settlement it was.

He walked into my room as I had just finished my change of dress, and washed off the last tint of Othello's swarthy hue; and said, with a strong Lancashire accent—

"Moy name's Parish, sir; A 'm th' manager o' this cuncearn, and aw've coomb to settle."

" Good evening, Mr. Parish; I hope you're pleased with the house to-night."

" It's a foine (fine) house, sir ; yaw've doon well: and every neet (night) I expect yaw'll do better. Yaw've got th' stoof in yaw, and th' chaps loike you."

I bowed—he went on.

" A don't know haw much is in th' ouse; A haven't counted th' brass (money) ; but I took it all mysen', and so there's no cheating here."

With that he turned his back to my dressing-table, and emptied out of his coat-pockets as I looked on with wonder, a large quantity of silver and copper. Having turned his coat-pockets thoroughly out, he next put his hand into his waistcoat-pocket, and fished out a £5 note, which he laid down on the table ; and lastly, he pulled from the pockets of his pants a couple of sovereigns; those also he deposited with the rest of the current coin of the realm, saying—

" Theere ! theere it awe is, just as A tuk it. Now th' bargain is auf and afe (half and half) ; pretty stiff terms, maister, but yaw've airn't it (earned it); so count away; and yaw take and A'll tak afe ; and then all 'll be straight 'twixt you and me."

So down we sat " to count the brass ;" the £5 note, with the two sovereigns upon it, were placed in isolated dignity, as became their aristocratic denomination and value, at one side ; the copper we piled into shilling heaps of twelve pennies, and the silver into heaps of twenty shillings, or more frequently of forty sixpences (the price of the gallery being sixpence), representing the £1 sterling.

During this interesting " financial operation," not a word was spoken on either side ; the piles being duly made up, it appeared on counting them, that there were twenty pounds ten shillings in silver, and two pounds and sixpence in copper; which, with the £5 note and the £2 in gold, amounted to twenty-nine pounds, ten shillings and sixpence; large receipts for a small country theatre, I can tell you!—(I have seen less in a very large one, with a good company, and two or three London actors in the cast.)

Well, Mr. Parish was evidently no Michael Cassio —no great arithmetician; but after some little difficulty, he gradually, after a good deal of puzzling and scratching of his head (there was no pen, pencil, or paper in the room), satisfied himself that the half of £29 10s. 6d. was £14 15s. 3d.; whereupon, making an exact division, he said—

"Theere! theere's thy share, and here's moine; A 've given thee th' gowd (gold) and th' flimsy (bank-note, 'cause A s'spose yaw won't be wanting to carry the copper; and A can pay it away to moy fowks (folks) at onest. So that's settled!" said he.

"And a very simple and straightforward settlement, too, Mr. Parish!"

"Whoy, yaw see, sir" (he replied), "A 'm not much i' th' littery loine (literary line); moine's mostly headwork; A don't do mooch wi' pen an' ink. A 'm a scaffolder, Oi am!"

"A scaffolder! Mr. Parish?"

"Aye; we're open-air chaps, we are; we play under canvas i' th summer, and i' th' winter A 'm forced to go into th' regular business, in walls; and it welly ruins me. But yaw see, I mun keep my people together agin th' summer time, or A should lose 'em. However, yaw'll find me aw reet (right), upreet and downreet. And now, sir, we mun hae a glass togither, if yaw please, just to wet th' first neet, and for luck for th' others."

With that he pulled a bottle of brandy out of a capacious side-pocket (I had observed the neck of it sticking out, and guessed its purpose), poured me out a rather stiff allowance, in the one glass which was in the room, assuring me that it was the " *reet sort.*" I added some water, which he declared would " spile (spoil) it," and drank to his health.

He then poured himself out about half a tumbler, and without running the risk of spoiling it by any elemental addition, shook hands with me in the most cordial manner, wished me "luck," and drank it off.

This was the system of settlement he followed every night; and, looking back on the many theatres I have played in since, and the many managers that have settled with me, I am inclined to think, that though it was not the most formal, or "high-Roman fashion" of settlement, it was, perhaps, the fairest and honestest that I have ever been favoured with.

The company was, in fact, a *Show*-company—scaffolders—that played in booths in summer, and in winter, betook themselves to small theatres, doing the best they could, and sharing the profits—if there were any.

My two other nights (Rolla and Hamlet) produced two excellent houses, and I took away from this petty place, as my share, about £40.

I went thence to Liverpool, for twelve nights, and did not do better in that large city, though Mr. ELTON (a London actor of fair standing) played with me. I received £15 per week, and a clear half-benefit ; my benefit was about £90; so that the two weeks gave me about £75.

Poor Elton was lost in a steamer going to Glasgow, a week or two after. He was a good actor, diligent, conscientious, intelligent ; and an estimable man.

VII.

AFTER a year's absence in the provinces, during which I had played a great variety of parts, in tragedy and comedy, I was invited to rejoin the Covent Garden Company, still under the Vestris management. Anderson had gone to Mr. Macready, at Drury Lane, and I was engaged to take his place at "the Garden." Knowles had written a new play for the theatre, entitled, "Old Maids," in which I made my reappearance, on the 12th October, 1841, and was honoured with a very flattering reception.

Mrs. Nisbett and Madame Vestris were the Old Maids; Charles Mathews, Harley, Walter Lacy, Frank Matthews, and Mrs. Humby, were in the cast. My part was the serious character in the comedy : a young Claude Melnotte-y kind of London apprentice, who falls in love with Lady Blanche (Vestris), fights a duel with Sir Philip Brilliant (Mathews), who takes him with him to the army, and brings him back " a colonel and a hero," to wed, of course, the lady of his love.

The point most applauded was the duel, between
Charles Mathews and myself, in the first act,—a
regular fencing match, with rapiers, distinguished by
great impetuosity on the part of the young *cit*, met
by great coolness and courtesy on the part of the
baronet.   It never missed fire.   ANGELO, the great
maitre d'armes, was present at our last rehearsal of
it, and we had the advantage of his suggestions and
approval.   Of course, therefore, it was

> " A hit, a very palpable hit !"

The comedy was not, however, attractive ; -and,
after a (hard) run of thirteen nights, it was withdrawn.
It was the last but one of Knowles's dramatic efforts;
this one, and his tragedy of the " Bridals of Messina,"
produced last season, proved that his imagination and
energy were on the wane : it was time for him to
make the *Partridge-cry* of " *Non sum qualis eram.*"
I suppose he felt this, for he *wrote only once more for*
the theatre—the "Rose of Aragon," which was almost
a failure—and very shortly after took to preaching
against acting and the drama !   O strange !

> " The food that was once as sweet to him as locusts, is now as
> bitter to him as coloquintida !"

But he cannot unwrite what he has written ; and
"Virginius," " William Tell," and the " Hunchback,"

> "Shall plead, like angels, trumpet-tongued, against
> *His* deep *damnation*

of the stage, and its professors !   So, let him preach!
We will set his dramatic triumphs against his anti-

dramatic diatribes, his works against his sermons, his practice against his preaching.

The following metrical *jeu d'esprit*, by POOLE, published in the *Argus* newspaper, gives a tolerably lucid account of the plot and characters :

THE NEW COMEDY,

ADAPTED TO THE USE OF SCHOOLS AND YOUNG PERSONS.

Addressed to Master Timothy Hughes, for the Benefit of himself. and his Fellow Pupils, at the Establishment of Dr. Bangputtis Little Peddlington, by Poole.

There was once—" But when ?"—Heaven bless your souls,
To ask such a question of Sheridan Knowles !
There was once, as I tell you, on Ludgate-hill,
(And "if he's not gone he lives there still,")
A jeweller, worth near a plum or a lack,
Whom his friends called Blount, and his wife called Jack.
The sight of the shop always brought to their anchors
All dandies who kept an account at their bankers.
There were diamond buckles, and amber canes,
And golden pins, and invisible chains,
And emerald brooches, and ruby rings,
And, in fact, no end of such sparkling things.
And the dandies they called him a regular *brick,*
For the jeweller gave unlimited tick ;
Nay, rather than out without buying you went,
He would do your paper at six per cent.
And besides all the other good things of his life,
He'd a couple of sons, and a capital wife.
And (whisper it not in the streets of Gath, Hughes,)
He finds a good double in clever F. Matthews.
Sons he had two, as I've said to you—*and* enough—
One's played by Harley and t'other by Vandenhoff—
(Not Vandenhoff *pere*, he's *frere* Jonathan's visitor,
But Vandenhoff *fils,* who was bred a solicitor ;
And for reasons the writer's unable to guess
Changed Q. B. and C. P. for O. P. and P. S.)

Harley's a son who attached to his trade is,
V. *au contraire* is attached to the ladies.
Harley, it's true, thinks the *counter* good sport,
But fencing in general is Vandenhoff's forte.
H. sticks to the shop, and he likes nothing *but* it;
V. fights with his stick, and he threatens to cut it.
In maidenly hatred and scorn of poor man
Two ladies are living—as well as they can.
The one is called Blanche and the other's called Anne,
But to give them those names seems to me a dull plan;
I've got a much better—you'll think so—it is but
To call B. Madame Vestris and A. Mrs. Nisbett.
I've left out my hero, Sir Philip—my valet,
My footman, my coachman, my cook, and my Sally,
They ⊢hall enter all melodramatic and mystical,
So here goes for the play in a style most artistical.

ACT THE FIRST.

Two servants talk twaddle; then enter Sir P.,
In such a fine dress as you never see.
It's spangled, its ruffled, it's slashed, and it's tied,
There's glitter all out and Charles Mathews inside.
His valet comes with him—examines his dress,
Which deserves all his praises, I'm free to confess;
He gives him two crowns (for he's no ways close-fisted)
For smoothing a wrinkle that never existed;
Then, changing his smile for a visage much crueller,
Walks out—for he's going to blow up his jeweller.
He enters the shop (much like Rundell and Bridge it's,)
And finds Master Blount in particular fidgets.
For just as occurred in—I think it was—*Amilie*,
There had been a slight row 'twixt the heads of the family.
For F. Matthews was vexed at G. Vandenhoff's conduct,
And felt he should like to have V. in a pond ducked;
While mamma (Mrs West) took the part of her son,
And talked—a true woman—ten words to his one;
And all parties felt sulky as heart could desire,
When in came Sir P. to add fuel to fire.
Sir P.—that's Charles Mathews—is all in a heat
About a fine gem which he'd lost in the street—
"The fault was your own, Mr. B., for you set it;
Will you give me another?"   "I wish you may get it."

High words are exchanged, and a row they'd have had,
But Vandenhoff pops to the aid of his dad;
And by way of at once setting matters all right,
The knight and the shop-boy go out for a fight.
Now, this exquisite shop-boy, you'll please understand,
Had been taking six lessons of Mr. Roland,
And proving by no means a dolt or a loon,
Was exceedingly strong in his feint in segoon.
So they fell upon guard—the juvenile's skill
Is no match for the cool and the practised Sir Phil.
V. is hit, and he faints—and—to come to an end,
Sir Philip determines to make him his friend;
So, telling V.'s father to cease from his clavers,
He gets all his wounds healed and plastered by Travers.
Then the fiddlers all into the orchestra scamper,
And down comes the drop scene, and up they strike Zampa.

ACT THE SECOND.

In the act above mentioned (and eke in the next),
To say what they do I am rather perplexed.
Mr. Harley, released from his shop, takes high airs,
And is hocussed, see, *passim,* " High Life below Stairs ;"
The maid-servants hoax him with malice infernal,
And the footmen salute him as lord and as colonel:
Pretty speeches are passed 'twixt the Anne and the Blanche,
Whose heart-snow they'd pass for a small avalanche;
But the private flirtations and loves they can't smother,
In neatest blank verse they detail to each other ;
And Sir Philip's in love with fair Blanche, and Miss Anne
Pretends to assist him, and does all she can,
By flirting and teaching him Greek words and Latin,
To win him from fair Blanche's silk to *her* satin.

ACT THE FOURTH.

There's something important now happens here—which *is,*
Madame Vestris from petticoats jumps into breeches,
Calls on Anne in disguise—kisses maid-servant Jane,
When she squalls, Madame threatens to kiss her again.
And by this time young Vandenhoff's grown quite a hero,
With valour at "boiling," and love down at "Zero ;'
And Blanche, who emboldened by twenty per cent. is,
Calls, dressed as a page, on the *ci-devant* 'prentice,

And really behaves most uncommonly rude,
And rings all the changes on jilt and on prude ;
Till Blount, who I really forgot, Hughes, to mention,
Had paid her some little plebeian attention,
Which, like that of most men who young ladies pursue,
Had warmed into love when he found 'twouldn't *do*,
When she libels his mistress, gets plaguily raw,
And on the *incognita* threatens to draw,
And only keeps quiet his nature revolting,
By making his bow, and then instantly bolting.

ACT THE LAST.

Le commencement du fin, as folks call the last act,
Has a great deal of business, of course, to transact :
Sir Philip finds out with Lady Anne's book
She has rather judiciously baited her hook ;
And finding that Blanche has her own fish to fry,
He takes Lady Anne—no bad choice by the bye.
Then Vestris and Vandenhoff make up their match,
And John Blount's wife cries off when it comes to the scratch ;
And each lady the other in epilogue aids—
And downs comes the curtain at last on *Old Maids.*

On the withdrawal of Old Maids, a maid of a very
different order, and superlative in attraction, succeeded: I mean Miss ADELAIDE KEMBLE, second
daughter of Charles Kemble, and sister of Fanny.
She made her début at Covent Garden Theatre, in
Norma (English version), on the 2nd November,
1841, with such decided success, that the opera was
repeated three times a week, to overflowing houses,
up to the early part of February following ; in all
about forty nights ! She had previously sung, with
some success, at *La Scala,* and other houses in Italy,
where she had received the highest possible musical
education ; but in her native England, and in the
theatre which had been the scene of the Kemble-and-
Siddons triumphs, and which might be considered as
her

" assign'd and native dwelling-place,"

the *furore* she created was unbounded. The aristocracy and fashion of the metropolis filled the private boxes nightly, and the public vied with each other for seats in the general boxes and body of the house.

It is a pleasure to say that she fully merited the enthusiasm she excited, which is not always the case; for the good public just as often allows itself to be lashed into ecstacies for well-trumpeted humbug, as it bestows its favour on real genius. In the former case the factitious fervour soon dies out; in the other it grows into a permanent and lasting flame. So it was with Miss Adelaide Kemble. She was a thorough artist, with a fine voice, under admirable control, and with perfect purity of intonation. Add to this, that she possessed considerable dramatic power, and played, as well as sang Norma, with great *abandon* and natural passion. Her triumph was complete; and carried her through not only this season, but through part of the next. She was shortly after married to M. Sartoris, an Italian gentleman, has retired from the stage, and has since, I believe, resided with her husband at Rome.

The next new character in which I appeared was Stanmore, in Bourcicault's " Irish Heiress,"—a long, disagreeable, but highly important part, which I undertook at the particular request of author and management; because, though it was not such a one as, of right, belonged to me—there was no other person in the theatre, disengaged, to whom it was considered safe to intrust it. It was about thirty lengths (1,200 lines long)—a villain, without a good point or a redeeming situation. I did the best I could with it: endeavouring to lighten its features somewhat, by an easy, gentlemanly, *insouciant* style, instead of making him the old, accepted, conventional stage-villain, with black hair, and a scowling face.

Bartley, the acting manager, rather chuckling at the up-hill part I had had, said to my father, who was present the first night,—

" Well, what do you think of your son?"

But he took nothing by his motion; for, said the governor, " My son *saved* your play;—that's what I think."

Mr. Plausible grinned, and was silent.

The play, however, only survived two nights, in spite of a cast including Mr. Farren, Mr. Harley, C. Mathews, Mrs. Nisbett, Madame Vestris, and Mrs. Orger.   In this country it had, I have understood, considerable success at the Park Theatre.

I give the following list of the COVENT GARDEN COMPANY in 1841-2, as a specimen of what strength was deemed necessary in a metropolitan theatre, in those days:—

GENTLEMEN.

Acting and Stage Manager:
Mr. Geo. Bartley, acting and stage manager, with a great variety of business; the bluff, hearty old man, *peres nobles,* Falstaff, &c.

Light Comedy and Eccentrics:
Charles Mathews (Lessee.)   Walter Lacy.   F. Vining.

Leading Business:
Geo. Vandenhoff.   John Cooper.

Old Men:
Wm. Farren.   F. Matthews.   C. W. Granby.

Low Comedy :

J. P. Harley.   D. Meadows.

Irish Characters :

John Brougham.

Heavy Business :

C. Diddear.   J. Bland.

Walking Gentlemen :

C. Selby.   A. Wigan.   H. Bland.

Pantomime and General Business :

Messrs. Payne.   Messrs. Morelli.
   „   Honner.   „   J. Ridgway.
   „   T. Ridway.

LADIES.

Mrs. Nisbett.   .   Madame Vestris.   Mrs. Glover.
Mrs. W. Lacy.   Mrs. H. Bland.   Mrs. Brougham.
Miss Cooper.   Miss Lea.   Mrs. S. C. Jones.
Mrs. Selby.   Mrs. W. West.

Columbine :

Miss Fairbrother.
Two Misses Kendall, with a large *Corps de Ballét.*

Opera.

In addition to the above we had regularly engaged to support

Miss A. Kemble,

Messrs. Harrison, Binge, and Horncastle, *tenors.*
Mr. Stretton, *baritone.*
Messrs. Borrani and Leffler, *bass ;* and a fine Chorus.

The above list will give the reader some idea of a full company ; and of the expense of conducting a great London theatre, such as Covent Garden *was.*

There is nothing else, noteworthy, that occurred
this season, except the fact that, in spite of the large
houses drawn by Miss A. Kemble, three nights during
the week—out of which she, I understood, received
£20 a night—*half salaries* only were paid at the latter
portion of the season. The fact is, we had such a
full company, especially with the additions that were
necessarily made to it for the production of opera, and
such a lavish expenditure was incurred in the getting
up of every new play, that it would have required
more than extraordinarily good houses nightly, to meet
the immense outlay in salaries and decorations. The
consequence was, that the season closed earlier than
usual ; and the reins of management fell from the
hands of Vestris and Mathews, and were transferred,
for the coming season, into those of Mr. Charles
Kemble.

He very politely offered me a renewal of my engagement, which I declined, with thanks, having
made up my mind to try my fortune in the United
States, from which my father and sister had just returned ; they were engaged by Mr. Kemble as his
principal supports.

I therefore put myself in correspondence with Mr.
Simpson, of the Park Theatre, and arranged with
him for a fortnight's engagement there, in September, 1842.

During this year I played with my father and
sister at Liverpool—the first and only time that we
ever appeared together. The plays selected were
" Romeo and Juliet," " As you like it," " Ion," " The
Wife," " Love," " The Hunchback," and " The
Bridals of Messina : " the latter we played four nights

in succession. Our joint engagement created considerable interest, and drew fine houses; but my
father, I was sorry to see, was very ill at ease in
playing with me, and I felt no less *gène* with him.
He could not get over his feeling of disappointment
at my having adopted the stage as a profession: this
affected his acting, and I saw that it did: it was continually betraying itself, and destroying his abstraction, and his self-identification with his character, for
the night. My sister was aware of this, too; and, of
course, she was unpleasantly acted on by her consciousness of it. In fact, it threw us all off our
balance; and we were very uncomfortable all round.
The audience, of course, knew nothing of these " secret stings:" to them, the affair was a delight, and
to us, in their eyes, a triumph. They applauded,
and called us, night after night, regarding us as the
happiest, most united, mutually-contented family
party ever seen upon any stage! How true is my
motto—

Decipit

Frons prima multos, rara mens intelligit
Quod interiore condidit cura angulo.

The tinsel glitter, and the specious mien
Delude the most; few pry behind the scene.

Previous to my departure for the United States I
played a farewell engagement in Liverpool, appearing
in Macbeth, Lord Townley, The Stranger, Faulconbridge (Mrs. WARNER was the Lady Macbeth,
&c.), Virginius, Jacques; and, for my farewell appearance, on the 1st August, 1842, Hamlet: Miss
JULIA BENNETT (Mrs. Barrow) was the Virginia and
Ophelia—at that time in the fresh bloom of youthful

beauty, almost girlish in appearance (she could not have been more than twenty), and the *beau ideal* of feminine softness and delicacy.

G. V. BROOKE was the leading actor there, in the full possession of his voice, which he afterwards lost to a great extent ; that is, its tone became enfeebled and impaired ; under that disadvantage he was afterwards seen in this country; when, from that very defect, people were puzzled to know how he had acquired his English reputation. At the time I speak of he had a noble organ, and great natural qualifications : had his study and culture been equal to his personal gifts he would have been, *really*, a fine actor.

W. J. HAMMOND, who afterwards died in New York (in 1848, I think), was then the lessee and manager of the Liverpool Theatre Royal, and in his hands it lost its high prestige, as the school in which artists were formed for the London arena, to which, "in its high and palmy days," it was the stepping-stone. But its glories were past ; it had fallen from its high estate. From being next in rank to the metropolis, and where, "as I have heard my father tell," John Kemble was wont to say, a tragedy was as well done as in London, it had, in 1842, sunk to the level of a mere country-theatre. And this fact of the decay of the Liverpool Theatre Royal was most significant of the general decline of the drama in England, which has been going on with a

"*facilis descensus Averni*,"

ever since! So I turned my face to the United States. "Meliora speramus !"

VIII.

CORALIE WALTON, THE COUNTRY ACTRESS.

An Episode from Real Life.

No more her sorrows I bewail,
Yet this will be a mournful tale,
And they who listen may believe.—THE GIAOUR.

CHAPTER I.—MYSTERY.

O Desdemona! dead! dead! dead!—*Othello.*

" VIRTUE," writes the accomplished Mrs. Jamieson—
one well qualified to speak authoritatively, philo-
sophically, yet kindly, on all that concerns her own
sex,—" Virtue is scarcely virtue till it has stood the
test."

How many proud virtues are there that walk with
stately step, arched neck, and curved lip, through
the admiring world, that have won the lily-crown
without the martyr-struggle—that have held their
unruffled course, without trial or temptation to turn
them from their flower-strewn path. *They* are happy,
and should be charitable; nor think too harshly of
those whose steps have been through whirlwind and
through flame : no wonder if sometimes the poor head

G

grow dizzy, the foot trip, the brain throb, and the
victim fall! Have pity on her! Let it not still be
true that

> "Loveliest things have mercy shown
> To every failing but their own,
> And every woe a tear can claim,
> Except an erring sister's shame!"

There are, too, examples of humble, heroic, mar-
tyr-virtue, struggling against temptation, in obscurity
and secret; loving goodness for goodness' sake, and
uncheered by men's approval, unseen and unregarded;
yet, like the diamond, preserving the heaven-born
brightness of its unsullied purity in the depths of
darkness and of gloom.

Of such a one am I now to tell the simple, yet
touching story. Poor Coralie Walton! May the earth
lie lightly on thee, now thou sleepest beneath it, for
whilst thou wast upon it, it was hard and bitter to
thee!

She was an actress in a small country theatre, in
England, scarce more than seventeen years of age;
her form light as an antelope's, graceful as a fawn's;
her features of classic outline, yet soft as Hebe's; her
auburn hair fell in waves, not curls, upon a neck of
transparent whiteness; and her clear blue eye, when
it met yours, looked out—with the frankness of maiden
truth—from beneath long, dark lashes, veiling its
depths, and lending an additional softness to the melancholy which cast a gentle shadow over a face too
young for sorrow, and yet too serious for happiness.

My first of five performances at the S—— Theatre
was to be Virginius. I learned by the bill, which the
call-boy handed to me in the morning, that the Virgi-

nia was to be a Miss Coralie Walton; and I met her
at rehearsal. She was dressed in remarkably good
taste; very plainly, but very neatly. Her *toilette* was
the simplest possible; evidently of no very expensive
materials, yet so harmonious in its simplicity, and so
exquisitely adapted to the person of the wearer, so
well fitting her shape, so scrupulously clean, so trim,
that it never entered one's head to remark the materials, satisfied with the completeness of the general
effect. She was a little—the least in the world—above
the middle size; and she looked like a young lady
in her morning dress—I speak of course of countries
where a lady is never seen at breakfast in brocade and
diamonds! The manager introduced her, and her
salutation was perfectly easy, and *comme il faut;* distant, as to a stranger—yet not stiff or over-formal—
that stranger being a brother-artist.

In rehearsing, she was literally exact in the text;
appeared familiar with the accustomed business* of
the scene; and she received any little suggestion that
I made to her with politeness and a silent bend of
acknowledgment. She wore a veil at first, but when
she commenced the scene, she raised it for the convenience of our set-dialogue; so that I had a fair opportunity of remarking the delicacy and nobleness of
her features. At the conclusion of her share in the
rehearsal, she bowed and left the theatre.

We had not exchanged twenty words, and yet I
felt myself strangely interested in her. I inquired

---

* It may be necessary to explain to the general reader, that what
the actor calls the business of a scene is the movement, the doings,
and the changes of relative positions, by which it is accompanied.

of the manager who she was : he knew nothing of
her history, he said ; she had come amongst them
about twelve months ago ; had presented herself to
him, an utter stranger, without recommendation or
introduction, soliciting employment in his theatre.
Struck by the modesty, and what he called the gentility of her appearance, he had given her an engagement to play the "walking ladies," at a very moderate
weekly remuneration, for which she expressed herself
extremely grateful.   Her attention to her duties had
been so exemplary, he said, her general conduct so
winning, and her improvement so rapid, that, on his
leading-lady suddenly leaving him, six months since,
in a huff, for some fancied slight to her dignity, he
had put Miss Walton into her place, at first as an
experiment merely ; but, finding that she acquitted
herself in her new position with satisfaction to the
audience and to himself, he had retained her in it.
" And never," he added, " was there a more obliging
or ready creature : she has a remarkably quick study,
and will sit up all night to get up in a new part, if I
ask her."

" You don't ask her, often, I hope?" said I, feeling
how likely such a disposition was to be taken advantage of.

" Why," said he, " in a country theatre, we are
sometimes obliged to get ready in pieces in a great
hurry ; and we can't be very nice about calling on
our people ; and you stars, you know, require your
plays to be perfect: so all have to stir themselves."

" Yes," I said, " I suppose it is so. But she seems
sad, melancholy. Has she no friends ? Is she an
orphan ?"

" I don't know," said the manager ; " there's some mystery about her. She never mentions her family. I once hinted at her connections—her home. 'Home !' she exclaimed, with a dark, lowering look, such as I had never seen on her face before, and with a sort of a shudder, I thought. Then, after a pause, she added, ' Never mention that word to me again. I will faithfully perform all my duties, and I thank you for the employment you have given me ; but never, never, talk to me of home again, if you desire me to remain with you !' Since then, I have, of course, been silent on the subject. My wife is very much attached to her ; but she rather avoids society, and nothing can draw her into confidence."

" She is very beautiful," I said ; " and if her talents be at all equal to her personal attractions, she must soon be transplanted to a London theatre."

" O, she has already had a very good offer from London, which she has declined ; this much she confided to my wife, one day," said the manager.

" She is biding her time, perhaps," I said ; " and waits till she can go to London in a more assured position, by practice and experience. If so, I commend her ; she is right."

" No," replied the manager ; " she told my wife, who pressed her with a woman's curiosity, that she never would set foot in London again."

" Again ? then she came from thence ?" I suggested.

" I don't know," answered the manager ; " that's what she said, however. Excuse me, I see there's the printer's devil ; I must make out to-morrow's bill : Othello, eh ?"

" Yés," I said, " if it's agreeable to you."

" Perfectly," and we parted; the manager to make out his bill, I to my hotel, and my early dinner.

During my solitary meal—the inevitable sole and mutton chop, and half-pint of sherry—I confess my thoughts would run on the lovely Coralie Walton, and the seeming mystery that overhung her. I longed feverishly for seven o'clock, that I might see her act, and observe how she would acquit herself on the stage; for a rehearsal gives little insight into an actor or actress's capabilities. Virginia is not a great part; but it would be sufficient to call forth her sensibilities and pathos, if she possessed them; so I waited for six o'clock; then went down to the theatre rather earlier than usual, found some boys already flattening their noses at the gallery door, and some eager *pit-ites* gathering by degrees.

There was a good house. I got through my first scene, and came to the second one, in which Virginia enters. I was nervously anxious to see how she would look, in the simple Roman drapery of the character. When I gave the *cue* for her entrance, I declare I felt my heart beat quickly—and why? I knew not !

With my back to her place of entrance, I did not hear her light foot, which, encased in its little sandal, made (in the language of the text of this very play)

"a sound so fine
That nothing lives 'twixt it and silence;"

but a positive thrill through the house, and a burst of admiring applause, told me that she was on; the next moment she was at my side.

So sweet a vision I had never seen ! She was the perfection of girlish beauty, the type of classic grace, the *ideal* of feminine softness, all tinged and shaded by a pervading sadness. Having very slightly, and I thought, rather contemptuously, acknowledged the reception given her by the audience, she commenced the dialogue, in the most sadly musical voice that ever fell upon my ear.

I paused a moment—gazing upon her with what might at least pass for a father's pride in his lovely child, but which I fear had a deeper admiration in it— before I answered her ; and when I did, I found my own voice unwittingly subdued almost to the quality of hers ; she filled me with respect, with tender interest ; and the scene that followed was listened to with breathless attention, and straining eyes ; you might have heard a pin drop, so silent was the house. When, with the words,

"Kiss me, my girl,"

I printed a paternal kiss upon her clear white fore-head, I felt a thrill run through me, that told me how thin was the partition that divides sympathy from love.

She played Virginia sweetly ; delivering the text with remarkable intelligence and sensibility ; her gestures and attitudes were marked by that grace which is

"beyond the reach of art."

and which nature alone can give.

One thing, in her scenes with Icilius, struck me strangely ; she seemed almost to shrink from her lover, not merely with a woman's natural timidity,

but as if she shunned his touch as hateful to her;
and when, in that solemn betrothment, in the second
act, I placed her hand in his, with the adjuration to
him,

" You will be all her father has been,
Added to all a lover should be,"—

when with these solemn words I placed her hand in
his, I am sure I observed a shudder, a *frisson*, pass
through her frame. Strange! Could it be a
woman's affectation,—mere *coquetterie?* May be;
women are hard to fathom. May I say of myself,
that I never played Virginius with such *élan*, such
truthfulness of feeling, before or since. As I advanced into the part, this young, beautiful creature,
became really to me

" my cherish'd
And most deservedly beloved child :"

she clung to me with a gentle, confiding tenderness,
as if she would fain throw herself, with all her fears,
her griefs, her sufferings, upon a father's love. Tears
streamed from her uplifted eyes; I caught the infec-
tion; and the audience wept, and women sobbed in
sympathy.

At the close of the fourth act, which ends with
Virginius sacrificing his daughter's life to save her
honour, as the curtain fell, there was a simultaneous
outburst of enthusiasm, and a prolonged call for our
re-appearance. I went towards the place where I
had laid her down as I stabbed her, and found her
surrounded by the ladies of the theatre, who were
applying restoratives to her nostrils and temples.
When they had come to raise her from the stage,

they found her insensible; she had fainted, and I
suppose remained in that state till the curtain fell.
She was now gradually recovering; a little eau de
cologne, brought from my dressing-room and poured
into her lips, awakened her to consciousness; she
gazed wildly around, and on recognizing her situation,
burst into an hysteric passion of tears. These she restrained by a strong effort of her will. The "call" continued loudly in front of the house; and on the manager asking her if she was now able to go on, she
placed her hand calmly and silently in mine, walked
on with me before the curtain, like one in her sleep,
passed across the stage, mechanically saluting the
audience, and the moment she was out of their sight
disengaged her hand from mine, and without a word,
hurried away. I saw her no more that night.

The next day's rehearsal was Othello, for the night.
She was on the stage in due time, looking paler and
more subdued than ever. To my inquiries after her
health, she replied that she was much better now;
the heat of the theatre had been too much for her,
she said, that was all.

But I observed her frequently apply her handker-
chief to her lips, and I fancied I perceived the stain
of blood on it, when she withdrew it. "Poor child!"
I thought, "is it so?"

She rehearsed Desdemona in a very low voice, as
if speaking were painful to her. We scarcely exchanged a word together, out of the set dialogue, in
which she was scrupulously perfect; and I could only
endeavour to express a silent sympathy.

When the rehearsal was over, I spoke to the manager, representing what I had observed, and ventur-

G 5

ing to say to him, that I really thought Miss Walton was too ill to continue playing thus, night after night.

"But what am I to do?" he said; "she's in every piece you play; I don't know how to supply her place. To-morrow 'Wild Oats,' you know; and she's up for Lady Amaranth."

"Can't we change the play, I said; "do Macbeth; let your wife play Lady Macbeth, which of course she has often done; and give Miss Walton at least a night's rest."

"Very good," said the kindly manager, "be it so! I shall be glad to spare her a night."

"The night after we can do Pizarro; you can get on without her for Cora, I dare say."

"Well, we'll try," said the manager.

So there were two nights' respite for the poor girl.

As Desdemona, she looked charmingly; but in her acting there was this remarkable peculiarity, that, as she shrank from Icilius's love last night, this night she 'shrank from Othello's, and really seemed to shudder at my embrace! What could it mean?

The last scene, in the chamber, she played with terrible earnestness: her asseverations of innocence, her prayers for mercy, her agonized supplications, her heart-rending shrieks, and her convulsive death-struggle, tore my heart, and made me really

> "call that a murder which
> I thought a sacrifice."

The death-calm into which she fell, when the deed was completed, was no less terrible to me. I could not help fearing that she *was* dead; a chill came over me; for if so, 'twas I that had killed her! When I put my hand on her heart, in the action of the scene, as she lay there more white than snow,

"and smooth as monumental alabaster,"

there was no throbbing; her pulse seemed motionless; her breath would not have stirred a feather! Oh, how I longed for the scene to end!

The knocking at the door came; Emilia entered, and, at the proper time, approached the bed where Desdemona lay; how eagerly I listened for the dying words—

"A guiltless death I die. Commend me to my kind lord!"—

but they came not. To Emilia's question,

"Who hath done this?"

she returned no answer; all was silent, still as the grave!

Good God! *could she be really dead?* There was no time for thought; I hurried through the scene. Emilia, the manager's wife, was evidently as anxious as I. I thought every one who had to speak drawled out their words with maddening deliberation. I raced through *mine* like one bewildered! At last, Iago has left the stage; one more speech; Othello strikes the poniard to his heart, and, thank God! the curtain is down.

I sprang up from the stage; rushed to the bed; but she, she moved not, stirred not; there she lay pale as her sheets, unconscious as the grave!

" Water, for Heaven's sake, water! " I shrieked.

Water was brought, and her hands and temples were bathed with it. The kind wife of the manager held smelling-salts to her nostrils, and endeavoured to force *sal volatile* and water through her teeth. At length, she slowly opened her eyes, gave a sigh, and a burst of hysterics followed.

"Thank God!" I exclaimed, for I knew then she was safe. In this state she was carried, wrapt up, to the Green-Room; her corset was cut; a physician was sent for, and she was sufficiently recovered to be sent to her lodgings in a carriage, under the care of the manager's wife, who, in her stage clothes, just as she was, attended her; carrying out the service of Emilia to her mistress beyond the limits of the mimic scene. Ah! there is much kind feeling behind the scenes of a theatre, when it is really called for, whatever jealousies, envies, and heart-burnings may have scope there at ordinary times. But *where do these not have play?*

As for me, all night long, that calm, impassable face—

"So coldly sweet, so deadly fair,
As if the soul were wanting there"—

haunted me, and banished sleep from my eyelids.

IX.

CORALIE WALTON.

———◆———

CHAPTER II.—LOVE—THE AMATEUR.

Why, what were life—what were it worth? though rich
In all that makes its worth, unless made rich
By her dear love, the riches paramount,
And crown of all!—*MS. Play.*

I was glad to learn the next day that Miss Walton
was quite composed. Rest, the surgeon said, was all
she needed; a few days would restore her. The two
next nights she would not be called on to appear,
fortunately; but the *third* was my " benefit and last
night." ·The play fixed on was " Hamlet," and she
was to be the Ophelia. I besought the manager to
change it, but he was inexorable; " for," said he, " it
is the strongest play we could put up with your
name, and there will be a great house."

" But," I said, " what are a few pounds' difference
in the receipts, compared to the risk of the health,
perhaps the life, of this poor child?"

" I am just as sorry for her," he replied, " as you
are; but, you see, I know all about it. Half of it is
mere nervousness, the result of a little love-affair, in
which she was disappointed; and *love scenes* awaken
the recollection of it."

" Ha !" I said, "that then explains"—

" To be sure it does," he said, interrupting me ; " did not you see she could not stand them ?   Now, there is no love scene in ' Hamlet ;' she'll get on well enough in Ophelia—you'll see."

" Pray," I said, " may I ask"—

" Ha !" he interrupted, " I see you are interested. Well, step into my room, sit down, and I'll tell you as much as I know of it ; which is not much, after all."

I eagerly assented.   We seated ourselves, and the manager began :

" Of course, a girl like this, with her attractions, has had hosts of followers ; half the young fellows of the place have gone crazy about her.   At L———, the town where we play in the winter, the son of the richest landed proprietor in the neighbourhood wrote letter after letter to her, sending her the most costly presents, and making her the most extravagant offers, if she would accept his protection."

" And how did she accept these proposals ?"

" Very calmly, but very decidedly.   She did not get up any scene, nor make any explosion. She came to me one day, with two letters, and a casket containing a necklace, brooch, and ear-rings, in magnificent pearls,—' Mr. Henderson,' said she, ' I am here utterly friendless and unprotected, unless I can rely upon your kindness.'   I assured her I should be happy to serve her.   ' Then,' said she, ' do me the favour to return these letters, and this casket to Mr. ———, and request him to desist from troubling me with any further notice.   I presume,' she added, ' as an actress, I am exposed to these importunities ; but I wish you to tell him that I consider them insults, nevertheless, and that, if he is a gentleman really, he will at once desist from them. You may add,' she continued, ' that I have left word at the door, that no message from him shall be received ; and the servant-girl has liberty to keep any presents that he may send to me in future ; therefore, beg him not to waste his time and money on one who is so utterly insensible as I am.' All this she said without any display of indignation, but with a contemptuous coolness, by no means flattering to its object."

" And how did you proceed," I inquired.

" I executed her commission," he replied, "to the letter. ' And who the —— are you, sir,' said the young *swell*, ' to interfere in this matter? You're only the manager of a twopenny theatre.' ' Yes,' I replied ; ' one thing more.' ' What's that ?' said he. ' A man,' I replied, ' that will not stand by and see a good girl insulted, merely because her position exposes her.' ' Well, we shall see,' he said. ' We shall,' I replied, and left him. For a time his persecution seemed to have ceased, and he stayed away entirely from the theatre. One night he came, somewhat excited with wine, raved about the lobbies in a frantic manner; and, the next day, commenced the siege more pertinaciously than ever. Letters and presents rained in upon her, sometimes left at her lodgings, and sometimes at the theatre. She never opened them, but they were handed at once to me. Meantime, he made a hundred ineffectual attempts to introduce himself to her, all of which were defeated by the wit of an Irish servant-girl, who barred his entrance with a thousand excuses, and, I verily believe, would have broken his head with her flat-

iron, rather than have let him cross the threshold.
" Arrah ! what would he be botherin' the darlint for?'
said Biddy ; 'bad cess to him ! if it's wanting a
sweetheart she was, it's not such a spalpane as that
she'd be takin' !'

At last my young *furioso* comes to me, and
demands to know the meaning of it all: ' She has
received my presents,' says he, ' and now she puts on
airs, and pretends she won't see me.' ' Your presents,' said I, 'she has never even seen; both they
and your letters have been placed unopened in my
hands ; and, as they now amount to a large parcel, I
purpose sending them back this evening.' ' Bah ! '
said he, ' I don't believe a word of it ; it's a deep game
you're all playing ; I see what you're at; you're in
league with her to hook me in ; but it won't do, I tell
you.' ' You will have proof,' I said, ' before the
evening is over, of what my game is, and, I believe,
it will rather surprise you.' He left me, with threats
of vengeance on me and my theatre ; his father
was a magistrate, he said, and he would have me
drummed out of the town. ' I am glad,' I replied,
' you have mentioned your father, because it is to
him I intend to appeal.' ' Appeal, and be d——d,'
he said, and broke out of the room.

" I had already made up my mind as to my course :
I packed up all his letters and presents into one parcel, and sent them that very evening to his father,
with a note, explaining his son's folly, and requesting
him to use his authority to put an end to the persecution."

" That, of course, was effectual ?" I said.

" Yes," he continued : " the young *inamorato* was

seen here no more ; and we learnt that he had been
sent by his father, at an hour's notice, on business to
Germany.   The old gentleman wrote me a note of
thanks, and sent a gold watch for Miss Walton, which,
at her request, I immediately returned to him.   Bah !
these rich people think a jewel or a trinket is like
Hotspur's fop's ' parmeceti,' ' the sovereign'st remedy
for an inward bruise !' "

" But this," I asked, " is not the love affair that
Miss Walton's nerves are suffering from ?"

" O, no," replied Mr. Henderson ; "that's quite a
different matter.   That happened here.   But it's din-
ner-time now : I'll finish the story to-night, after the
play."

Macbeth never seemed so long and so tedious to me
as on that evening.   From Mrs. Henderson, who played
Lady Macbeth, I learned, with delight, between the
acts, that Miss Walton had slept through the greater
part of the day, and was much refreshed by it and
tolerably tranquil.   At length I was slain by Macduff, after the usual " terrific " cut and thrust fight :
never was death more welcome !   I hurried to my
dressing-room, undressed, re-dressed in an incredibly
short space of time, hastened to the manager, dragged
him to the hotel, and having snatched a hasty supper,
ordered the " materials" and cigars, and begged him
to finish his story.

" What I have related to you so far took place,"
he said, " at L——, the other town where we play in
the winter.   We left there for this place shortly after ;
and here Miss Walton's admirers were numerous.   I
really believe she might have married well, if she had
chosen ; but she positively forbade me to introduce

any of them to her, and acquired, at length, the *sobri-quet*, among the young fellows, of the *man-hater*.

" Among the most ardent and most respectful of her worshippers was a handsome youth, named Lionel Ransom. He was the son of a deceased officer in the army, residing with his mother. By her death, shortly after my first acquaintance with him, he came into possession of ready money to the amount of about two thousand pounds. He was an elegant young fellow, only just of age, without any profession or occupation : he had always been intended for the army ; but, from want of means or influence, his mother had failed to procure a commission for him. He had obtained a small income from his pen, by contributions to local papers, and sometimes to a second-rate magazine ; and was altogether a very accomplished, taking, young chap. His admiration of Miss Walton approached to worship ; but she repelled every attempt at an introduction. He was in despair ; and sat at the theatre every night, devouring Coralie with his eyes. I placed him on the free list, as the only compliment I could make to his devotion ; but he more frequently paid than took advantage of the privilege. At length, one day, he came to me at the theatre, and told me he had resolved to go upon the stage, and wished to commence with me. It was in vain that I endeavoured to dissuade him. He had made up his mind, he said ; he thought he had talents for the stage, and no other profession was open to him. He had some money at present, and would play at first without any pecuniary compensation, if I would give him some instructions in the details of the business. Of course I saw through the inspiring motive of his re-

solution : it was to be near the object of his adoration.
Finding him immovably determined, I agreed that he
should have an appearance ; and that, if successful,
he should continue to play with me, occasionally,
such parts as he might select, with ample time and
opportunity for their study, under my superintendence.

"Romeo was the part he chose for his *début :*
well I understood the reason why.   It would give
him an opportunity of pouring out his passion, unre-
proved, in the most beautiful of language, in the ear
of her who was the *Juliet* of his soul.   I enquired
under what *name* he would be announced.   'Under
my own, he replied ; I am doing nothing to dishonour it ; and I will show *her*—that is —I will show
everybody, that I am not ashamed of the profession I
adopt.'   'You are wrong, Mr. Ransom,' I said ; but
you must have your own way.'

"He was already perfect in the words of Romeo :
I instructed him in the business and action : he
fenced well, and his carriage was that of a soldier
and a gentleman.   He had a fine dark eye, an almost olive complexion, with a tinge of red in his
cheek ; and long, black, wavy hair.   All that he
wanted to complete his appearance for Romeo was a
befitting costume ;—*that* he procured from a first-rate
costumier in London ; and then he announced to me
that he was ready.

"It had been, somehow, tacitly understood between us, that not a word was to be said to Miss Walton about his intention until he should meet her at
rehearsal.   Then, for the first time, he was introduced
to her.   He turned very pale as he spoke to her.   She

was perfectly cool, collected, and indifferent; for I
don't really suppose she had ever spent a thought on
him.   The rehearsal passed off very well; he was
perfect, steady, and certain in the *business* in which I
had instructed him; and his reading of the text was
full of intelligence and feeling; though he evidently,
to my eye, restrained himself in its expression.   I
gave him three more rehearsals, and announced him
for the Monday following, under his own name, as he
had required.

" Public curiosity and wonder were excited to an
extraordinary pitch : for he was well known in the
town ; and the house was crowded in every part long
before seven o'clock.   I went to his dressing-room, and
shook him by the hand ; he was apparently calm ; yet
I saw there was a high excitement within.   ' Don't
speak to me, Henderson,' he said, ' and I shall be all
right.'   I left him without another word.   Ten
minutes afterwards the curtain drew up.   I played
Mercutio ; and I believe I was the more nervous of
the two.

" His entrance, as he crossed the stage at the back,
was the signal for universal applause ; but when, re-
entering at the first wing, he appeared, with the footlights full upon him, lighting up his face, and dis-
playing the perfection of his faultless figure and elegant costume, the applause rose into deafening cheers,
which lasted several minutes.   I did not wonder at
it ; for I assure you—no disparagement to present
company, sir"—(said the manager, smiling), " I never
saw such a Romeo to look at !   There he stood, without a touch of *rouge*, or the least aid from art, Romeo
himself, perfect in youthful grace and beauty.   Then,

when you think how she must have looked as Juliet !
I do believe the stage never before saw, together, such
a pair as that night played in my little theatre !

"He acted remarkably well ; there was very little
of the novice in his manner, and that little only made
his acting appear the more natural and less *stage-y* ;
for, after all, sir, you know we do a great many things
on the stage that nobody ever dreamt of doing any
where else, Mr. Vandenhoff."

" I admit it ; but we'll reform that one day," I
replied.

" Well," he continued, " their love-scenes went admirably. He was all fire, all fervour, all passion ; and
she, though she played Juliet with less *abandon*, as it
is the fashion to call it, than he displayed, yet she
acted with great truth and feeling. She had not then
begun to shrink from her stage-lovers, as she does
now : that feeling has arisen since. They were called
for three times during the play ; and, at the close,
bouquets were showered upon the stage, which he
picked up and handed to her, bowing respectfully,
and showing, before the curtain, by the attention and
empressement of his manner, the high consideration in
which he wished her to be held. Having brought her
off the stage he bowed to her, and wished her good-
night ; *that*, I believe, was all that passed between
them during the evening, apart from the business of
the play.

" I could not help asking her : ' Well, Miss Walton, how do you like your Romeo ? ' He is a gentleman,' was her brief and comprehensive reply, as
she walked hastily away.

" We repeated ' Romeo and Juliet ' three alternate nights. The next week they appeared together in the ' Lady of Lyons,' which was a still greater success. It took us through two weeks, three nights each; and the week after he played Jaffier to her Belvidera. The romantic motive of his coming on to the stage had got wind in the town, and the popular excitement knew no bounds; the houses were crowded; and, as Miss Walton's great propriety of behaviour was generally known, every one seemed interested in the young and handsome couple."

"And how," I asked, " did his suit thrive with her?"

"O," said the manager, " he had evidently gained ground. They shook hands now when they met, talked together pleasantly, and she had allowed him once to see her to her lodgings, wishing him good-night at the door; but he had never yet crossed her threshold. One night, Miss Walton had passed out of the stage-door to go home, after the play, attended only by the faithful Biddy, when a gentleman accosted her, evidently with the intention of intruding his company upon her. Biddy's quick eye at once detected in the stranger her former persecutor of L——— ; and opened on him with a storm of feminine invective, heightened by a strong Tipperary brogue. The intruder was, however, obstinate; he even attempted to take Miss Walton's hand: she turned and fled back towards the stage-door, pursued by her persecutor. Just as she had reached it, it was opened from the inside, and out walked Lionel Ransom : a glance told him the state of affairs. ' O, Mr. Ransom !' she exclaimed, ' you will protect me !' ' With my life !' he replied ; and I suppose it was the proudest moment *of* his life. ' Allow me, Miss Walton, to accompany you home; may I offer you my arm?' She placed her arm in his, and they were walking away, when the other—VERNON, we will call him—exclaimed in a loud, angry voice, and in his usual style of interrogation—' Who the——are *you*, sir?' Ransom paused for a moment, and said very quietly, ' In ten minutes I shall be happy to answer your question; at present, I am otherwise engaged.' ' You'll find me at the Queen's Arms Hotel,' said the other. ' I *will* find you there,' was Ransom's reply. He conducted Miss Walton home; this time she invited him to come in; with a view, I suppose, of preventing an encounter between himself and Vernon; but he declined the long-desired privilege, said he would have the honour of calling in the morning, wished her good-night, and hastened to the Queen's Arms.

" Biddy had not failed to inform him of the stranger's name; so he inquired at once, on entering, for Mr. Vernon. ' Who shall I say wants him,' asked the waiter. ' There is my card,' said Ransom; ' give it to him;' and he slowly followed the waiter into the coffee-room. There, Vernon was seated moodily, at a table, alone, with a glass of brandy before him; there were several persons at the other tables in the room. He had just got the card when Ransom entered. He walked quietly up to the table where Vernon was seated, bowed to him politely, and said, ' Mr. Vernon, you wished to know who I am; I have now called to tell you.' ' O,' said Vernon, brutally, tossing the card into the fire; ' I know d——d well who you are, now; you are the fellow that acted Jaffier to-night; I saw you strutting and swaggering in your

stage-clothes; but it won't do here, I can tell you.'
'Nor will your insolent bullying pass here either,' replied Ransom, calmly; 'I am the son of a British
officer, and I insist on your apologising this moment
for the insult you have just offered me.' 'Pshaw!'
said Vernon; 'do you know who you're talking to?
do you think I'll degrade myself by apologising to a
pitiful play-actor?' 'I think,' said Ransom, very deliberately, 'that he who insults a woman is usually a
coward when he encounters a man.'

"Vernon answered not a word, but sprang up,
seized the riding-whip at his side (he had ridden in
from L——, which was only twenty miles distant), and
aimed a cut at Ransom's face. Ransom, quick as lightning, parried the cut, and the next instant a blow with
the full force of his arm sent Vernon reeling to the
floor; the whip flew from his hand; Ransom seized it,
grasped the other by the collar, and, in spite of his struggles, inflicted on him a chastisement that left severe
marks on his face, and which it was likely he would
remember for the rest of his life. The whole affair was
so sudden, that the spectators had scarcely time to interfere, had they been disposed to do so; and landlord
and waiters came rushing in, just as Ransom, having
inflicted the last finishing cut, flung Vernon violently
to the other end of the room, exclaiming,—'Now,
sir, you know who I am; and if you desire any further knowledge of me, you can have it, when and
where you please.' With that, he strode out of the
room. Vernon, humiliated and disgraced, ordered
his horse ten minutes after, gallopped off in the darkness of the night, and has never made his appearance
here since."

"Well, now," I interposed, "surely Ransom's course was clear. Miss Walton could not be insensible to such ardent devotion."

"She was *not*," said the manager. "Of course, the affair was related with embellishments in the papers; some ill-natured comments were made; but sympathy was entirely in favour of the lovers—for lovers they now evidently were; in fact, the general belief was that they were engaged, and would shortly be married."

"And did it happen so?" I asked.

"No!—One day, about three months ago, Ransom went suddenly up to London; I happened to see him on his way to the station; he shook hands with me, said he should be back in a day or two; started by the next train, and I never saw him again."

"Dead?" I exclaimed.

"No; sailed for America a week after: he wrote me a hurried note from Liverpool; said he could explain nothing; he was a wretched man; almost out of his senses; begged me to accept his stage wardrobe, as he should never use it again, and said farewell for ever. I wrote to him at Liverpool, and as he had obstinately refused all remuneration for the nights he had played, I enclosed a post-office order for fifty pounds, which I requested him to accept as some compensation for the services he had done me; for he had drawn several good houses. I heard from him no more."

"Good heavens! and Miss Walton—?"

"Was obstinately silent; all I could get her to admit was, that she had had a letter from him, and

H

written to him in reply; she added that he would
never return!   After struggling with her feelings for
a night or two, she fell sick; had an attack of brain
fever; my wife attended her night and day; all her
ravings were of '*Lionel! cruel, faithless Lionel!*'
but nothing definite could be gathered from her disjointed exclamations.   Her illness lasted over six
weeks: I allowed her two more weeks to get strong
again, and paid her salary all the time.   Poor girl!
it was needed for medicine and little luxuries.   I got
on as well as I could in her absence, with the aid of a
pantomime which I produced; and last Monday was
the first night she has played since she acted Belvidera with Lionel Ransom.   And now I have told you
all about it."

"And this," said I, " explains her aversion to love-
scenes, and the peculiar shuddering she exhibits at the
approach of a stage-lover."

"Just so," said the manager; "but she'll get over
it by degrees.   The stage don't allow people to indulge their private feelings too much; there's no time
for it; and it's a good thing, too, that it helps to dis-
tract one from brooding on sorrow."

"That's true, Mr. Henderson; there's compensation in all things."

"Well, sir," said he; "it's late, and I'll wish you
good-night; and don't let Miss Walton's troubles
spoil your night's rest: she'll be all right in Ophelia
to-morrow, depend upon it."

"I hope so, for her own sake, poor girl!" I replied; "good-night!"

X.

CORALIE WALTON.

CHAPTER III.—Madness.

"There's rosemary; that's for remembrance! Pray love, remember!"
"And will he not come again?"—Hamlet.

The next morning ushered in a beautiful balmy summer's day, and before rehearsal I strolled down to the
meadows by the river's bank, that were clothed in a
bright emerald green, through which the winding
river glided like a silver snake. There were light
boats dancing and skimming over it; merry boys were
laughing and frolicking in them ; some were diving
into the clear water, and ever and anon at a shady
nook you would come upon a stalwart figure in cords
and hip-boots, up to the knees in water, rod in hand,
whipping the stream for salmon-trout. I strolled
leisurely along, glancing at the water as it sparkled
beneath the morning beam, and thinking of that wide
space of water I was soon to traverse, and of the new
world on whose theatre I was to appear. At an
angle, where the river turned rather sharply, in a lit-
le retired nook, wrapped up in shawls, and leaning
on the arm of the faithful Biddy, stood Miss Walton,
her eyes fixed on the passing river, and *her* thoughts,
too, probably, *across the sea.*

H 2

She started at my footstep, and her pale face slightly flushed at the surprise, as I raised my hat and advanced to her. She received me without effort or affectation; and I was delighted to find that she spoke quite composedly, and professed herself able and willing to play Ophelia that night. Still, I doubted and trembled for her, when I heard the frequent, half-subdued hacking cough, which interrupted her speech too often. As we walked together, Biddy fell behind; and I offered Miss Walton my arm. Somewhat to my surprise, she accepted it at once. After a pause, she looked up into my face, and said, " I think you have a kindly disposition."

" I should be happy," I answered, " to have the opportunity of proving that I merit the compliment."

" I thank you," she said; then, after a pause— " This is your last night here ?"

" Yes."

" You are going to—to America ?" she added, falteringly.

" Yes."

" Soon ?"

" In three weeks."

" Indeed ! Perhaps you would oblige me by being the bearer of a packet for me ?"

" For you ? Willingly."

" Thank you. It is not quite ready yet, but— when do you leave this place ?"

" To-morrow ; but I am to play three nights at L——— (the other town under Mr. Henderson's management), and you will, perhaps, accompany us ; at all events I shall be in the neighbourhood for nearly a week."

"Very well; then I'll get the packet ready this afternoon."

She was silent for some time ; and I did not interrupt the current of her thoughts by a word, till we drew near the theatre ; then I ventured to say to her,

" Miss Walton, I dare say you have played Ophelia before ? "

" Three times," she answered.

" Then," I said, " I beg you will not trouble yourself to attend the rehearsal on my account. I will make your excuses to Mr. Henderson, and we shall get on very well at night, I'm sure."

" She replied : " You are truly kind ; it will be a great relief to me to be excused from rehearsal ; I shall be the better for it, at night. Thank you very much."

She shook my hand quite warmly, and we parted. Of course, I duly excused her absence from rehearsal, which was to give additional assurance of her being equal to the labour of the night.

Night came, and Miss Walton made her appearance in Ophelia, a perfect impersonation of that sweet creation of Shakspere—involved in a destiny too harsh for her gentle spirit, her heart entangled in a love for one " out of her sphere," and *forsaken by him, on the motive of some terrible duty which she cannot comprehend.*

There was a very large audience ; the theatre was so crowded, that seats were placed in the orchestra, from which the musicians were excluded. All went on admirably, till Hamlet's violent and mocking scene with Ophelia, in the third act, commencing,

" Nymph ! in thy orisons be all my sins remembered !"

The moment I took her hand, saying, in the words of the text,

"I did love you once,"

I observed her mouth quiver with a spasmodic contraction; and the tone in which she answered,

"Indeed, my lord, you made me believe so,"

was mournfully touching. But when, continuing the dialogue, I went on—

"You should not have believed me; for virtue cannot so innoculate our old stock, but we shall relish of it: I loved you not!"

When I uttered these words she started from me as if she had trodden upon an adder, and her face expressed pain, anguish, terror, and so she continued to tremble and to shrink and to shudder, till my parting words to her, which I gave in a mingled tone of subdued love, compassion, and yet of irrevocable doom,—

"To a nunnery! go, go, go!"

Then she burst into a passion of tears, which seemed to shake her very frame, for, at least, two minutes. It was the perfection of acting—*if it was acting*—and as I stood at the wing watching her, during the applause which followed my *exit*, and which was taken up again on her passionate emotion, I thought I had never before known how deep Ophelia's love for Hamlet was, nor ever seen it so touchingly represented. Her closing speech, ending with,

"Ah, woe is me! seeing what I have seen, to see what I see!"

was the disjointed music of a breaking heart—

"like sweet bells jangled out of tune and harsh."

I was obliged to clear my eyes from a thick mist,

before I could go on again, for my " Instructions to the Players."

In the play scene which followed she had little to do ; but I could not help remarking, as I lay at her footstool, that there was a wild wandering of her eye, and a hysteric catch in her speech, most painful and alarming to notice. With that ended my " business" with her on the stage for the evening.

During the fourth act, according to my custom, after the severe and continued exertions of the three preceding acts of Hamlet, I remained quietly in my dressing-room. The principal features of the fourth act are Ophelia's madness, and the *return* of her brother Laertes, *from across the sea* ; in this, Hamlet is not engaged. I was half-dozing in my dressing-room, when my attention was suddenly aroused by the most piercing cries and hysterical shrieks ; I opened my door and listened ; it was evidently the voice of Miss Walton. I rushed down stairs ; they were carrying her, shrieking, and tossing her arms wildly, to the Green-Room. Poor girl ! the mimic madness of Ophelia had been fatal to her ; it had become a fearful reality ! The circumstances of Ophelia's story, Hamlet's abandonment, and her despair, she had made her own ; they had, in the earnestness of her acting, by a mysterious operation of the brain, been wrought up into a confused union with her own identity ; and though she repeated the text of her part correctly, and sang the touching snatches of song that rise up in Ophelia's love-lorn memory, she had lost all distinction between herself and the character she was playing. It was no longer Ophelia, it was she herself who was forsaken ; whose

lover had fled beyond the sea ; whose hopes were
buried in the grave ; whose heart was blighted ; whose
brain was maddened, and to whom nothing was left
but to despair and die !   Thus she rushed shrieking
from the stage, and was borne home a hopeless lunatic ; henceforth,

"The queen of a fantastic realm."

Imagine with what feelings I went through the fifth
act, and what a relief it was to see the curtain fall !

As I was sadly leaving the theatre the faithful
Biddy encountered me, with streaming eyes, holding
a small packet in her hands.

"Shure, your honour," said she, sobbing at every
word, "here's a parcel the darlint's after layving on
her dressin' table this night : she tould me if anythin'
happened her this night, to deliver it to your honour,
sir ; and the divel a bit o' me would trust it out o' my
hands till yourself got it.   O, murther ! murther !
what'll we do to save the cratur !   O, bad luck to
these theayters !   they'll be the death of her, they
will !"

I took the packet ; said all I could to console
poor Biddy, but in vain ; she left me sobbing almost
hysterically, swaying from side to side, and wringing
her hands, as she hastened home.

The first thing I did on arriving at the hotel was
to open the packet.   I found that the outside wrapper
enclosed another, tied with white ribbon, and sealed
with a seal on which was simply—CORALIE.

That second wrapper was addressed to " LIONEL
RANSOM, *United States of America.*"

Between the two was a note for me ; I opened it.

Written in a very pretty, ladylike, but unsteady hand, I read—

" You seem to have a good heart: I trust to your honour to deliver these to *him*, if you should ever meet him in America.   I feel
that after to-night neither you and I, nor he and I, shall ever meet
more in this world.

" Tell him I forgive him and bless him, and shall do so with my
last sigh.   Farewell!   My brain burns!   " C. W."

I placed the package in my writing-case ; and went to bed with a heavy heart.

The next morning I learnt that she had raved all night long, occasionally singing snatches of Ophelia's songs, and often, again, lying silent or muttering confused sounds, in which could be distinguished sometimes, " O mother! mother !"

That afternoon we left for ——, the other town under Mr. Henderson's theatrical purveyance ; and all the company,—except Coralie !   I played my three nights listlessly, and with a sad, dead weight upon my spirits.   On the afternoon of the fourth day, Thursday, the manager came to me, with tears in his eyes, and said in an agitated voice :—

" It's all over.   Poor girl !"

" Good God !" I exclaimed, " she's not dead ?"

" Read that," he said, handing me a letter blotted with tears ; " it's from my wife ; she was not wanted in the play last night, so I let her go back to see if she could do anything for that poor girl.   Read it, read it ; it concerns you."

I read these words :

" Poor Coralie Walton died at midnight, utterly exhausted, but
quite calm.   The last words she uttered, slowly but distinctly,
were—*Tell Hamlet not to forget.*"

H 5

XI.

CORALIE WALTON.

CHAPTER IV.—Despair.

One whose hand,
Like the base Judean, threw a pearl away
Richer than all his tribe!—Othello.

Three weeks after, in August, 1842, I stepped on board the good ship "Garrick" for New York. Coralie's package, of course, went with me, religiously concealed in a secret drawer of my writing-desk. One of my first thoughts, on arriving in New York, was to examine the play-bills of every theatre for the name of Lionel Ransom; but none such appeared. I next employed a theatrical agent to forward me bills of every large theatre in the Union, but in vain; none of them contained the name I searched for; nor were any of my personal inquiries more successful. I carried the little package with me wherever I went, to Philadelphia, Boston, Charleston, Baltimore, New Orleans, but in vain; he for whom it was destined was nowhere known in theatrical circles. He might have changed his name; but I met no one who answered his description.

In the early part of 1847 I was in St. Louis; and waiting in the office of the hotel, a few minutes before dinner, I heard a voice cry out aloud,—

"Halloa! Lionel, where have you been? we've been looking for you everywhere."

The name Lionel caught my ear instantly. I looked at the new-comer, to whom it was addressed, and felt assured, at one glance, that I had found my man. "To make assurance double sure," I examined the register, and there I found, under a date two days back, the name Lionel Ransom, U. S. Army.

The dinner-bell sounded, and I followed the party with which he was, and took my place opposite to them at table. I examined him with interest, but with caution, for fear of attracting his observation. Yes; 'twas he. There was the olive complexion, but pale, very pale; the thick, clustering, black hair, the dark lustrous eye, the elegant form that Henderson had described. Yes, my search was over; there sat Coralie Walton's Lionel, the lover who had abandoned her, and to whom I bore those sad remembrances, and her parting forgiveness.

How should I accost him? His companions seemed to look up to him, and treated him with more than ordinary consideration; he was polite and affable to them, but spoke little, and that, with a serious, grave, and earnest air. I did not observe him smile once. The wine that was poured out for him he put to his lips only, but did not drink. Dinner over, I heard him tell his friends, in answer to some invitation of theirs, that he was going to his room to write letters. I saw him go up stairs; and a few minutes afterwards I sent my card up to him, with a request to see him in private. The waiter returned, and showed me to his room. On my way thither, I stopped in my own room, took the package from its hiding-place, and put it in my breast-pocket.

He bowed on my entrance, and pointed to a chair. " Mr. Ransom," I said, seating myself, " I have desired to meet you for some years; have searched for you in vain; and have carried about with me a sacred deposit which I have never till now had an opportunity of placing in your hands."

" In mine?" he asked; " are you not mistaken in the person? Your name is of course familiar to me, though I never enter a theatre " (and a dark shade passed over his face); " but I am at a loss to conceive—"

" This will explain," I said, placing in his hand the package which I had drawn from my breast.

" This?" said he, taking it with an air of indifference; but the moment his eye rested on the seal, he exclaimed with a half-cry, as if a dart had pierced him—

" Good God! Coralie!"

I thought he would have fainted. He recovered himself, however; again looked at the package; kissed the seal passsionately several times, then bent forward to the table, hiding his face in his hands, and wept. I sat by, in silence.

When he raised his head his face had undergone a great change; his look was haggard, wild, almost savage; such a look as Romeo might have worn just before he drank the fatal draught at Juliet's tomb.

" Why do you come hither to raise the dead?" he asked, almost fiercely.

" In obedience to the command of the dead," I answered.

" What do you mean ?"

" That package," I replied, " was placed in my hands in August, 1842 "—

" The very month she died in," he exclaimed.

" You know it, then ?—With an injunction to deliver it to you, should I ever meet you in this country. I have now fulfilled her dying request. She bade me, further, to say to you, that she forgave and blessed you with her last sigh !"

During this he gazed on me like one spell-bound ; or like a man whose eyes are fixed on a spectre whose reality he doubts, yet dreads. I paused; but his gaze remained fixed upon me, steadfast, unchanging.

" Having fulfilled the duty imposed on me, I will now intrude no longer."

" No, no; pray remain," he said, raising himself from his abstraction. "I—I thank you—I may have more to say to you presently."

He then, with trembling hands, proceeded to open the package. From it fell a withered rose, whose leaves, as it dropped, were scattered like dust on the table. He gazed at them for a moment, then—

" The first little token she ever received from me ! —withered, withered, withered !"

Then appeared a watch, with a hair guard-chain.

" *My* watch," he said, " which I left on her table, when I went to London, to see her no more ; and this chain was of her hair !"—He kissed it, and again wept.

Then fell out a ring—an opal set in diamonds.

" This," he said, " is the only present she would

ever receive from me, as a pledge of that other plainer
ring which she never wore! O God!" he cried, " I
shall go mad !" and he started up, and tore his hair,
and gnashed his teeth !

"Pray calm yourself," I said, endeavouring to
soothe him; " it must be some comfort to you, that
her last remembrance was of you."

" Calm ! comfort !" he exclaimed.   " There is none
for me but in death—an honourable death, which I
am now seeking, and shall surely find !   Am I not the
greatest wretch that ever breathed?   Was ever a
villain black as me?   Have I not 'killed the sweetest
innocent that e'er did lift up eye?'"   (He quoted unconsciously: Shakspere supplying—as he never fails
to do those who love him—the very fittest language
for his impassioned thoughts.)

"Listen, sir," he said; " you are a man; you have
a man's heart, or she would not have trusted you with
these" (pointing to the scattered contents of the
package).   " To you I will reveal what I have never
yet confided to human being, though the secret has
racked and torn my bosom like an imprisoned wolf,
struggling to gnaw its passage through my heart.   It
will be a relief to me to set it free : it will be a justice
to her memory to let you know that it was by no
fault of hers that she did not bear my worthless name.
It may be some palliation of my cowardly abandonment of her, in your eyes, to hear what was the
dreadful secret that maddened me, blinded me, drove
me an exile from my country and my love !   Will
you hear me?"

" With the most fixed attention," I answered.

" Let me first tell you that, from the moment the

terrible blow struck me in London, that stunned my sense, and set my heart on fire, to the time that I found myself on board a ship, cleaving the Atlantic waves, I never had one instant's power of calm thought—one cessation of the dreadful rushing and roaring of the tide of blood that seemed to flow upon my brain—one lull of the surging billows of frenzy that seemed bearing me to destruction—one brief respite from the mocking fiend that goaded me to flight. When on board ship, I woke one morning from a feverish sleep to the full consciousness of all I had suffered, and all I had lost, no one can paint, no one can imagine my agony. I tore my hair, I beat my head, I rent my flesh with my teeth, in impotent rage at myself and my rash folly. I would have given all the rest of my life for but a minute's sight of Coralie, that I might have flung myself at her knees and besought her pardon. But it was impossible! Here I was, within my floating prison: the winds and surging waters without; no escape, no hope! no Coralie! In my despair I rushed, half naked, upon deck, and would have thrown myself into the deep, as if it would bear my body to her feet; but strong hands seized me, forced me down below, and lashed me to my bed. Three weeks' delirium was the result.

" The first thing that I remember, after that, was the words, ' a pilot has come aboard,' pronounced by some one near me. I turned my head, and tried to speak, but failed in the effort, from weakness; and the unformed words died upon my lips. A woman's voice (the stewardess, as I knew afterwards) then said : ' You must keep very quiet ; you are better now ; but you must not speak ; take this, and try to sleep.' She poured something into my mouth, which

I swallowed mechanically; and, in a few minutes, dropped into forgetfulness.

" When we reached the port of New York the doctor declared I was too ill to be removed immediately; and I remained three days on board the ship before they ventured to lift and carry me, bed and all, ashore. In a week after that I was able to sit up. The first use I made of my partially-recovered strength was to write an agonised letter to Coralie, beseeching her to forget the past, to look on it as a hideous dream, to forgive me, and, for God's love, to come to me; for that I had not strength to go to her, or that she would have seen me now, and not a letter. I could only just write these lines very slowly and unsteadily, enclose a Bank of England note to pay her passage out, and direct the letter, when I fell back exhausted. I did not recover from the effects of the excitement for several days. When I did, I found the letter had not been sent. I despatched it to the post-office instantly for the first steamer; and lived as patiently as I could the dreary interval that must expire before I could get an answer. At length it came—not from her—the superscription was in Henderson's hand-writing; and I knew, at once, that she was dead!

" Then my reason reeled again; and, for two months, as I afterwards learned, I was the inmate of a lunatic asylum. I fell into good hands. The captain of the ship in which I came had taken possession of my money and effects; and they were put into the care of the British Consul: so that, on my recovery, I found myself, after payment of all the expenses of my illness, in possession of about £500 in Bank of England notes. Procuring a draft for this, I immediately set out for the West; and, for some time, lived there the life of a hunter, roaming the pathless prairies, alone, or with wild and rude companions, with whom I held little converse, and had no sympathy."

" But, for God's sake," I exclaimed, " What could have been the motive of your abandonment ?"

" I am coming to it," he replied : " give me a moment to collect my thoughts."—He placed his hand on his forehead for a few moments, then resumed—

" As soon as I found myself, as I believed, in possession of the treasure of Coralie's love, patiently and proudly won, I pressed her to be my wife. Strangely enough, she always evaded my request, and seemed even troubled when I urged it. At last I grew almost angry at what seemed to me to be an excess of affectation. One day I reproached her that she was trifling with my love, and implored her, if she was really sincere, as I was, to name the day when I might call her mine.

" She looked me very seriously, even sadly, in the face, as she said : ' Are you sure, Lionel, that you love me well enough to make me your wife?' ' It is the eager desire of my heart," I exclaimed: ' the passionate wish of my soul !' ' Let passion be silent,' she said, almost sternly, ' while you ask yourself calmly and *dis*passionately, whether you will give your name to a poor, penniless girl, of whom you know no more than that she *is* that, and that she loves you.' ' If I know *that*, Coralie, I know enough.' 'Enough,' she said, 'you think it now; I must take care that you never think it too little. Suppose, Lionel,' she continued, after a pause of what seemed painful thought,—'suppose there were some circumstances connected with me, with my history, that might make you blush hereafter for your wife?' 'What *can* you mean, Coralie?' I said; 'I know you to be pure, virtuous, honest, true; what *can* there be that should make me ever blush hereafter for you?' 'You know nothing of my family,' she said: 'ought you *not* to ask of it?' 'Why?' I replied, 'you have never mentioned your family, and I have not either, because I concluded you were an orphan, and the subject might be painful.' 'I am not so,' she said; 'and, before I can consent to accept your hand, you must see my mother.' 'With all my heart,' I said: 'I will see her immediately, and ask her consent to our union:—where shall I find her?' 'In London,' she replied: 'I will give you her address before you go.' 'Give it me now, then,' I said, looking at my watch; 'for I shall go by the next train, and that starts in half an hour.' She sat down and wrote on a card, which she gave me; I put it into my waistcoat pocket without looking at it. 'There,' I said, 'is my watch,' laying it down on the table; 'I will wind it up before I go; and, by this hour to-morrow, I hope to be with you again, and to kiss you as my wife.' 'God grant it may be so,' she said, raising her eyes fervently to heaven; 'but I have an ill-divining soul! I feel, Lionel, as if this were our last parting.' 'Pshaw, Coralie, you are foolish;' I said. 'If it should be so, Lionel; if you should see cause to change your present feelings, do

me justice in your secret heart; remember you
sought the love of , the poor, unfriended girl, who
shunned all notice save that which gave her bread;
and, if you cast me off, at least remember that it is
my love to you alone that sends you on an errand that
may be fatal to my peace.' 'You are so mysterious,
Coralie, that I declare I can't at all understand you,'
I replied. 'What on earth should make you talk of
my desertion of you, my sweet love ? What on earth
could induce me to do it? And weeping, too ! Why,
this is foolish ! If your mother object to me, we
must endeavour to win her over, dear, that's all; but,
as for any wish of mine dividing us, nothing but
death, or *dishonour*, can ever part us.' I thought she
shuddered ; and I said, 'There, there, you're low-
spirited : now, *au revoir!* To-morrow, I shall be
back, and all will be well !' 'God bless you, Lionel,'
she said, as I printed a kiss on her pale cheek ;
'God bless you, and lead you back to me.' With a
final kiss on her lips, and a whispered farewell, I
hurried away to my lodgings, crammed a few things
into a travelling bag, hastened to the station, and was
just in time for the up-town train.

"Six hours brought me to London ; it was eight
o'clock. I took a cab to Charing Cross, snatched a
hasty meal, and, having finished it, I looked for the
first time at the card which Coralie had given me,
containing her mother's address. Mrs. WILTON, 14,
—— Place, was written upon it. So! I thought,
Coralie's real name is Wilton, eh ? She changed a
vowel only for her *nom de theatre*. I daresay her
mother is some very strict old lady, with very strong
prejudices against the theatre. Well, I must endea-

vour to overcome them ; or, after all, I thought, if
the old lady object on the score of my profession, I
am not bound to the stage ; it was my love for
Coralie that led me to it; the same love can take
me off it again; and we can be happy in some less
uncertain calling.

"With these thoughts I sallied cheerfully out,
called a cab from the stand, and desired the driver
to take me to 14, ——— Place. 'Mrs. Wilton's,
sir !' he asked. 'Yes,' I replied, 'Mrs. Wilton's.'
'All right, sir," he said, and I fancied the fellow
smiled. Strange, I thought, that he should know
the name when I gave him the number ! It was
now about half-past nine o'clock. I had an idea of
deferring my visit till the next day, but I resolved to
apologise to the old lady for my late call, get it over,
take the eight o'clock train back in the morning, and
be with Coralie at two p.m. On the cab rattled, till
we turned into a quiet street in the neighbourhood of
Portland-place, at the back of it, and the driver pulled
up his horse at a corner house. There was a Hansom
cab already at the door, out of which, as I alighted,
jumped two very over-dressed young women, and ran
laughing and talking very loudly, up the steps. 'Is
this Mrs. Wilton's?' I asked, as I paid my fare.
'Yes, sir,' said the cabman, 'this is the house. Take
the side door, sir, it's the privatest !' and the fellow
winked at me, as he drove away.

"By this time the two women had entered. I
walked up to the door, and found on it No. 14, in
brass figures, and underneath, on a brass plate, Mrs.
WILTON. Assuredly, it *was* the house. I knocked
and rang. Presently, a slatternly-looking servant

opened the door, when I asked if Mrs. Wilton was at home. 'She's at home, but she's very busy just now,' said the girl; 'what lady do you wish to see?' 'Mrs. Wilton,' I replied. 'O, very well; walk in; I'll tell her,' the girl answered. I was shown into a parlour—*salon*, I should call it—only half-lighted, but magnificently furnished, I observed, with large pier-glasses and elegant chandeliers. 'Well,' I thought, to myself, 'this is a degree of splendour I certainly did not expect." Presently, a loud burst of laughter, in which men's and women's voices blended, startled my ear from up stairs, and which was continued with increasing noise, and a sound as of glasses struck together, for some minutes. While I was wondering at this uproarious mirth, which I explained to myself by supposing there must be an evening party upstairs, the servant girl returned, to tell me that Mrs. Wilton was engaged at present; but 'wouldn't some one else do?' 'Some one else?' I said; 'no; my call is to Mrs. Wilton alone.' 'Well, then, said the girl, saucily, 'you'll have to wait: for she has company, and won't be at liberty for some time,' 'Very well,' I said, 'I'll return in half an hour, if that will not be too late.' 'Late!' she said: 'lord, no! nothing's late in this house!' and as she opened the door the burst of laughter from above rang upon my ears, more uproariously than before. A vague feeling of fear began to steal over me. I dreaded I knew not what.

" As I descended the steps a policeman stood under the lamp: probably, I glanced at him as I passed: for he touched his hat, and said, 'Good evening, sir; pretty merry up stairs to-night.' (He had heard the

laughter through the open window.) ' Unusually so,
I should hope,' I replied. ' O, no, sir, they generally
keep it up here—pretty fast chaps visit this house,
sir !' ' Why, in heaven's name,' I said, ' what house
is it ?' ' Well, sir, you surely ought to know,' he answered, ' you've just come out of it.' ' I went to see
Mrs. Wilton on particular business ; but I am an entire stranger to her and the house.' ' Well,' replied
the policeman, ' there's very few young men in town
that can say as much : why, it's as notorious an
ASSIGNATION-HOUSE as any in London !' ' Good God!'
I exclaimed, and fell as if I had been shot.

" ' Helho !' said the policeman, raising me : ' what's
the matter ? you're not well, sir ; take a drop o'
something at the tavern, here ; they've excellent
brandy, and it'll set you straight, sir.' I understood
the fellow's hint, slipped a shilling into his hand, and
bade him leave me. He touched his hat and walked
away to the public-house, turning, however, once or
twice, to cast a glance at me.

" Gracious heaven !—

" I was paralysed, stunned ; my knees knocked
together. I felt sick at heart. I pulled my cravat
from my throat, and sought to rouse myself by rapid
walking.

" For what must have been about half an hour,
though it seemed to me an age, I walked up and
down Langham-place, into which I had turned,
utterly unable to collect my thoughts, incapable of
fixing them on any point, only overpowered by a dull,
leaden consciousness of a terrible calamity having
fallen on me.

" By degrees it became clear to me again, in its

shocking reality.   Yet I could not believe it : it must
be a dreadful dream ; or I was labouring under some
fearful delusion.   I rushed back to the house with a
dreadful resolution ; knocked and rang loud enough
to wake the dead ; again the slatternly servant
appeared ; I pushed her aside, and rushed into the
house, exclaiming, ' Mrs. Wilton ! I must see Mrs.
Wilton, instantly.'

" ' Who wants me ?' a loud, coarse voice·asked,
from the stair head ; and a large, bold-looking
woman, about forty years of age, descended, excessively over-dressed, with bare neck and bosom, her
cheeks evidently made up with white and red paint,
but with a fine, and even classic contour of features,
in which, as she stood in the light, I was horror-
struck to trace a resemblance to Coralie's sweet and
innocent face !

" She motioned me into the *salon* I have mentioned, which was now brilliantly lighted ; and, seating herself, said with perfect ease, ' I don't think I
have ever had the pleasure of seeing you before, sir ?'
' No, madam,' I said ; ' and would to God I had
never seen you.'   ' How !' she laughed, contemptuously ; ' you surely did not come here, at this time
of night, to tell me that ?'   ' I came here,' I said,
' to see the mother of Coralie Walton, or Wilton,
whichever name she is to be called by : I *have* seen
her, and hope is at an end !   Good God ! the mother
of Coralie a —— !'

" ' Coralie !' she said, in quite a different voice ;
and, rising to shut the door, ' Can you tell me anything of her ?   *Can* you tell me anything of my
child ?   She has fled from my house.'—' Thank God,'
exclaimed I, ' she has escaped from its pollution ; let

me, too, leave it, and cursed be the hour in which I ever crossed its threshold!' 'But, my child, sir! my child! I demand to know where you have concealed my child!' 'If you do not know,' I said, 'where she is, I will not inform you: be it your punishment to know that you have blighted her happiness, and ruined mine for ever. Farewell!'—but as I laid my hand on the door, she dashed across the room, seized me by the arm, and swore that I should not leave the house till I had told her where she could find her child. She clung to me with a powerful grasp; but, by a desperate effort, I threw her from me, rushed out into the street, fled into Langham-place, as if pursued by fiends, jumped into the first cab I saw, drove to the Euston-square station, and was in Liverpool by the night train the next morning.

"Thence, I wrote to Coralie, in what words I know not—but a wild, a passionate, eternal farewell: yet, in a postscript I added that if she called on me to fulfil my promise, I would do so; but, that the day that wived her must widow her. Her answer came by return-mail—how I passed the interval I know not, except that I wandered about among the docks and the shipping, like an outcast or a robber.

"Her answer was like herself; I have it yet; I will read it to you."

He pulled from his breast a little silken pouch, out of which he took a worn and discoloured letter, and read, with faltering voice, these words:

"'Lionel, farewell! I make you no reproaches; I claim no promise; I release you from every tie; my sense of honour is as strong as yours; but my heart is crushed! Why did you ever wake it to a hope of happiness? May you be happy, and forget the wretched   CORALIE."

" How could I resist such a letter? Why did I not fly to her feet, and carry her across the sea, where her name and her history could never have been guessed at?"

" Ah! why indeed did you not?" said I; " that would have been the manly, the wise course."

" Alas! I know it now," he said; " but then I was blinded by that false spirit of honour which leads men to infamy; and, to maintain which, they barter their happiness and sell their souls to perdition. For this phantom I sacrificed my own peace, and blighted her hopes; was, in short, the murderer of her I loved: forgot her beauty, her innocence, her noble, truthful nature, and, like a coward, fled!—I made such hasty arrangements as I still retained sense enough to make, realized what money I could command, and in three days was on the Atlantic Ocean:—the rest you know!"

The next day the wretched man had departed to join General Taylor's army in Mexico, as a volunteer; and shortly after, in the list of killed at the battle of *Buena Vista*, I read the name of LIONEL RANSOM.

XII.

THE United States, her institutions, people, government, and wonderful progress, had been the subject of my eager inquiry and increasing interest, ever since I had been capable of understanding the philosophy of history, or of speculating on the theories of government. As secretary and solicitor to the Liverpool Reform Association—the first position in life which made me known in public—it had naturally fallen within the scope of my inquiries and speculations to examine the rise and advancement of that Greatest of Modern Republics; if, indeed, any ancient elective government may be compared with it. And it was therefore not merely with the ambition of an artist,

but also with the ardent curiosity and interest of a
theoretical republican in principle, that I walked the
deck of the fine ship THE GARRICK, which, under the
guidance of

"Him who has the steerage of my course,"—

was to bear me to the land where the great experiment of self-government by the people was in full
blast and full blow. It was my first long acquaintance with the sea, and I enjoyed it. I chose a sailing
vessel in preference to steam, that I might see the
ocean in its full swing and natural action, without
any Watt's-bit or Fulton-curb upon it; but curvet-
ing, caracolling, rearing and plunging like a war-
horse, with the ship for its rider. We had a delightful passage of thirty days; thirty days of calm, dreamy
enjoyment. I have made the passage by steam many
—about fifteen—times since; but for pleasure, for the
free rollicking, out-and-out sensation of being at sea (I
don't mean sea-sickness; heaven forbid !), give me
sails and wind, in preference to steam and coal-smoke.
On a question of time merely, steam for ever, of course :
but let him who loves the sea, trust to the winged
bird that skims the wave lightly and easily like a swan,
and in smooth water floats with unruffled plume
upon its bosom. " But, how about calms and head
winds ?" some one will say. " Well, in calms lie la-
zily down on deck like a turtle in the sun, and dream
of far-off lands and spicy groves ; or loll under an
awning, on a coil of rope, with a cigar in your mouth,
and a good novel in your hand, and, " let the world
wag "—you can " take your ease (as) in your inn ! "
If it blow hard, and the wind be a-head, hold on to a

I 2

belaying pin or a shroud, and listen to the whistling
of the gale in the cordage, and watch

> " the labouring bark climb hills of seas
> Olympus high, and duck again as low
> As hell's from heaven ;"

enjoy the storm, revel in its impotent fury, and rejoice
to feel the good ship staunch and firm as a

> " tower'd citadel or pendant rock,"

beneath your feet.   If you have not nerve enough for
this, or if, as *Trinculo* says,

> " *your stomach be not constant,*"

why, e'en turn in, wrap yourself snugly up, and sleep
in peace ; with the happy consciousness that you are
" in Heaven's hand, brother," and that there is no
boiler to burst, no paddles to smash, no machinery to
give way.   When the storm has ceased, the wind is
lulled, and the sea smooth again, jump up, forget your
qualms and sorrows past, take a brisk, invigorating
walk on deck, and go down to breakfast with the
appetite of a shark : if it don't answer to the whip at
once, touch it up with a thimbleful of cognac (mind it
be the real), with not a drop of allaying croton in it,
and you'll be surprised what a fillip it will give nerves,
brain, and stomach.

   This all pre-supposes that you are not in a hurry,
and can afford the time : if time be an object, take a
Cunarder, and do the trip in ten days.

   I set foot ashore in New York on the 14th September, 1842, and engaged rooms at the Old Clinton
Hotel, in Beekman-street, in the immediate neighbourhood of the Park Theatre.   The two brothers
Leland, the present proprietors of the Metropolitan

Hotel, were clerks in the office, and were remarkable
for attention to the guests. Let me say, that the
table d'hôte, set at that house—by no means a large
one—far surpassed in excellence, and superabundance
of good things, the tables which we now find, even at
the best hotels; there was not so much attempt at
extravagant display, but there was

             " that which passeth *show* "—

a really good, ample, well-cooked dinner; and the
price of board was about two-thirds of what it is now.
I have lived, in turn, at nearly all the best hotels in
the Union,—the Carlton, the New York, the Clarendon, in New York; Jones's, in Philadelphia; Barnum's,
and the Eutaw House, in Baltimore; Pulaski, in
Savannah; the principal hotels in Charleston, St.
Louis, Cincinnati, and Louisville, and the old St.
Charles, in New Orleans; and I don't scruple to say,
that the *feeding* at the old hotels that have passed
away was better, more generous, and more satisfactory, than it now is at the splendid and fashionable
caravanseries that have succeeded.

Men *will* seek some stimulus for their parched
throats, and exhausted, jaded spirits; wisely, or un-
wisely, they will drink some liquor, fermented or
distilled. Temperance apostles cannot eradicate what
seems to be a natural craving of the human system.
I have no doubt they do a great deal of good in
diminishing the prevalence of intoxication, and its
attendant ills; but, to a greater or less extent, *men
will drink;* and neither, water, tea, nor coffee seems
to satisfy the desire. They must have stimulus; it
is that which seems to inspire, and to give zest to,

social converse, and the friendly interchange of hospitality, when the overtaxed mind unbends, and for-
gets its daily cares in the happy evening hour.   Mind,
I only state a fact; I do not advise or applaud the
custom.   But, as the fact is, as the custom exists, it
behoves us to see that " the social glass " does not
conceal "a rancorous and deadly poison ?" Else, Bacchus, instead of being represented as the *rosy god*,
will have to be depicted as a hideous demon, with
blear eyes and bloated cheeks, whose emblems shall
be, not clusters of delicious grapes, but a death's
head, and cross-bones, with a

> " baneful cup, whose poison
> The visage quite transforms of him who drinks,
> And the inglorious likeness of a beast
> Fixes instead, unmoulding reason's mintage
> Charàcter'd in the face."

These effects of *Comus's* magic cup, are the exact picture of the results of indulgence in the baneful con-
coctions of the present day; and, therefore, be all
encouragement given to the *native grape*, and to those
who express its sweet juice.   *They* are the practical
Apostles of Temperance ; they furnish the antidote to
the poisoned bowl.   Wine-growing countries, it is
well known, produce few drunkards; *delirium tremens*
is unknown amongst them.   In the recent public
demonstrations and exultations at the prospect of re-
generation from Austrian bondage which have lighted
up Italy, as with a general illumination, no fact is
more pleasing or more significant than that no
drunkenness has been seen in street or public place ;
and that, among excited and freedom-maddened
thousands, no other intoxication has been exhibited

but the heaven-born delirium of newly-acquired liberty !

Let *us* apply the lesson.

On the posting-bills on the walls, which were much more modest and less monstrous than they are now, I observed my name underlined, to appear shortly, at the Park Theatre. One of my first calls, therefore, was upon Mr. Simpson, the manager. I found him a plain-mannered, unpretending, rather reticent man, meaning well, but slow, irresolute, and with no remarkable business capacity. Theatrical affairs, he told me, were at a very low ebb, and the prospects for the season, which had just commenced, were any thing but brilliant. I could not have come over at a worse time, he told me; trade was generally dull, money scarce, and every one felt flat, so that the theatre, of course, suffered. This was mighty pleasing intelligence to start with; however, I had to make the best of it.

It was arranged that I should commence my engagement on that day week, and we proceeded to discuss the plays in which I should appear. "Hamlet" was fixed on for my opening part. I proposed "Benedick" for the second night, and "Macbeth" for my third.

"Where is your Beatrice, and your Lady Macbeth?" asked Simpson.

"Why," I answered, "I have certainly not brought them in my pocket; I expected to find them here. It cannot be that the Park Theatre is without a leading lady?"

"We have no one for those parts," curtly replied

Simpson; "I tried to get Miss Cushman to play with you; but she's at the Walnut, Philadelphia—stage manager there."

"Can we do 'Othello?'" I asked.

"Not well," he answered; "a difficulty about Emilia."

"Good heavens!" I said, in despair, "what *can* we do?"

"We can do 'Virginius,'" he replied.

"Very well," I said (glad to find there was one play that could be done), "Virginius be it."

So, "Virginius" was fixed for my second night; and the other nights' business was to be arranged hereafter.

The fact is, that the Park Company, though it contained some excellent names, was weak in parts that the public usually expect to be strong. There were Messrs. ABBOTT, PLACIDE, BARRY, OLD FISHER (as he was called), Mrs. VERNON, Mrs. WHEATLEY; but the leading lady, a very amiable young lady, was quite a novice, unstudied and inexperienced; there was no heavy lady, for the Emilias and Lady Macbeths; and there was a great want of a good juvenile actor. The difficulties, therefore, in the way of casting a Shaksperian play were considerable.

With the sole exception of General GEORGE P. MORRIS, the kind, the genial, the warm-hearted lyrist, —the *Beranger* of America—I did not call on a single dignity of the *Press*. I did not know any of them personally, and I have through life abstained from back-stairs courting of the *Press*, or from any side-winded influence being attempted upon their opinion, or the expression of it. General Morris had been

mentioned to me, by my father, as a valued friend ;
as such, I presented myself to him, not in his character
of the editor of the New York *Mirror :* I called on
the gentleman, not on the *redacteur.* No editor,
reporter, or city writer, was I introduced to previous
to my appearance.

Meanwhile, I amused myself in and about the
city, and on Long Island ; and of course made the
acquaintance of many good friends and of nearly all
the thirst-provoking and palate-pricking drinks, for
which the New York *Bar* is famous through the world.

How many hundred times was I greeted, immediately after the ceremony of an introduction had
taken place, with the never-failing question of " Well,
sir, how do you like our country?" and frequently the
addition of " What do you think of our city ?"—two
very comprehensive questions, opening so enlarged a
field as to render it amazingly difficult to epigram-
matize an answer. The thing did not lie in a nutshell ;
it was a theme for a lecture, a discourse of at least
half an hour, to answer it properly. However, one
was obliged to dispose of it with a "glittering gene-
rality,"—if such a thing were at hand, and would
answer to the call. New York was not then the
magnificent city which she has grown now to be ;
there was no Fifth Avenue, with its princely residences,
and adjacent streets filled with houses that in Europe
would be deservedly described as mansions. Broadway was a long, irregularly-built, straggling street,
with low wooden shanties occasionally intermixed
with the brick houses. None of the present splendid
piles of stone at the Bowling-green, and no Stewart's,
no Grace Church, no Union-square ; so that the

answer to the question, " How do you like our
city ?" was not then so spontaneously rapturous as
it might be now. But now, the question is little
asked; or if so, is asked with a conscious feeling
of pride, and an assured confidence as to the answer,
as a reigning *belle* might challenge a certain compliment to the set of her bonnet, the elegance of her
toilette, and the perfection of her *tout-ensemble*. In
those days it was different.

A little *reténue*, a little recollection of the demands
and practice of courtesy, in social life, would be of
great advantage in this international intercourse.
When a man visits a gentleman's house, the host
does not call on him to admire his dwelling, to praise
his furniture, to go into ecstasies about his dinner
or his wines ; he gives him the best he has, and makes
him welcome. The guest, on the other hand, does
not find fault either with his room or its appointments,
his fare, or his entertainment ; he sees that the host
has been anxious to please and make him comfortable, and he thanks him, and is content. Still
less, if he be a gentleman, does he go away and ridicule and abuse his host behind his back : if he do so,
he puts himself out of the pale of social courtesies.
" Wit," as Sir Peter Teazle well observes, " is more
nearly allied to good nature than your ladyship
imagines ;" and satire and epigram cease to tickle
when their aim is to wound ; still more are they to be
reprobated when their point is tipped with the venom
of malice, to corrode and fester where it strikes.

A man may surely express his opinion, if asked,
without making it an insult. I have heard of one
who, being asked, before a number of people in Phil-

adelphia—silly enough perhaps—" if the mutton in England was as good as in America," replied, with an assumption of mystery, and in a subdued whisper, to the interrogation—

" If you'll promise not to tar and feather me, I'll tell you !"

" Well ?"

" Why, then," said the Englishman, " it is much better."

Now the implication involved in the condition against being tarred and feathered for candid-speaking was clearly a volunteered impertinence ; and was doubtlessly felt and remembered as such in the account against the impertinent's countrymen.

For my part, I have always expressed my opinion, when invited, freely, but not in offensive terms ; and I have travelled the country from Maine to New Orleans and St. Louis, several times over, and have never yet stood in fear of pistol or bowie-knife.

———

Revenons à nos moutons.

I made my first appearance at the Park Theatre, on Wednesday, 21st September, 1842, in Hamlet : Mr. PLACIDE (the best Polonius, and the best actor in his varied line in the country) was the Polonius ; Mr. ABBOTT, the Ghost ; Mr. BARRY, Horatio ; Miss HILDRETH, Ophelia ; Mr. FISHER, the Grave-digger.

Theatricals, as I have said, were at a very low ebb, trade in a stagnant state, and money very scarce. I could not expect a great house : there were only about £80 ; but it was, I assure you, not a bad

house for those times.   The tragedy was, with one or
two exceptions, generally well acted ; not, I confess,
as well as I had expected from the Old Drury of
America ; because the cast was weak in two important parts; but it went off smoothly ; I was vehemently applauded; at some points the applause was
long and enthusiastic, and I had reason to be proud
of my reception by a New York audience. Of course
I was called for; but that supererogatory comple-
ment, now staled even to disgust, did not, in those
days, involve a speech; so I was not under the necessity of ringing the changes on "honour," "kindness," "liberal support," "gratitude," "heart," "last
moment of existence," and the other round of set
phrases that go to make up a before-the-curtain
speech.

The press all spoke in favourable terms of me ;
some of them, in those of the most encouraging and
warmest approval.   I was but a novice ; it was only
my third season on the stage, and I might naturally
be somewhat anxious about the verdict of New York.
I rose early the next morning, soon had every paper
in my room, and had no reason to be dissatisfied with
the general opinion.   It had this great value to me,
that it was spontaneous, unsolicited, and uninfluenced.
May I, without boring the reader, make an extract,
which I confess gratified me much, by its tone of
candour, and the happiness of its expression?   It is
from poor *Porter's Spirit of the Times*, 24 September,
1842.

"THINGS THEATRICAL.—The principal event discussed in theatrical circles during the past week has been the appearance of
GEORGE VANDENHOFF at the Park, on Wednesday evening, in

Hamlet. In person Mr. Vandenhoff is tall and well-formed, with an open and manly countenance; his voice is of a strong and pleasing quality, and he treads the stage with grace and dignity ; indeed, he is calculated, in all respects, to 'give the world assurance of a man.' His performance of this most difficult character—the test, so esteemed, of a tragedian's abilities, gave great satisfaction to the large audience assembled to welcome him. For ourselves we confess he far surpassed the expectations we had formed of him, both in power and style. His readings were not only remarkably correct, but in good taste ; and his manner of delivery, free and without effort, avoiding the affected and conceited style of the younger Kean, as well as the monotonous and tiresome one of . . . . . Taken as a whole, the character has not been more ably performed, in this city, for the last six years. Mr. V. has evidently been well educated, has deeply studied the character, and understands it, and aims to impress the conception and beauties of the author upon his audience, rather than by 'tearing a passion to tatters,' to display his own strength of muscle and lungs. It may, with truth, be urged against him that he is young and comparatively inexperienced— that time and study will much improve him ; but the greatest present drawback upon theatrical prosperity, both here and in Europe, is, that actors are generally too old, or comparatively broken down before they arrive to any great degree of excellence, thereby rendering their performances devoid of that truthfulness of appearance so necessary in keeping up the scenic effect. It must also be conceded that he lacks the genius that enabled the elder Kean to electrify his audience by startling effects, and hold them in breathless astonishment in admiration of his almost superhuman efforts to depict the stronger passions. To all who expect such a performance, and are determined to deny themselves the pleasure of seeing a tragedy, until they can see it as personified by a Kean or a Kemble, we prescribe patience, mixed with strong hope and faith, and we only wish we may live long enough to enjoy the treat with them. But to those who are fond of tragedy, and are duly grateful for 'the gift the gods provide,' or, in more common parlance, are satisfied with 'the best the market affords,' we strongly commend Mr. Vandenhoff's performances as possessing more merit and developing more good sense and judgment than that of any other man recently among us."

The next night I played Virginius, the night after

repeated Hamlet; Leon followed; a new play by
Knowles, the " Rose of Arragon" (his last rose of
the autumn of his dramatic fame), was produced the
next week; but it failed to attract; it was displaced
for Macbeth, and a repetition of Hamlet; for my
benefit I played Claude Melnotte and Benedick, to
about 400 dols.

> "The time was out of joint."

and the theatre seemed in a state of compound
fracture;

> " No med'cine i' the world could do it good."

Mr. and Mrs. Brougham followed me, with very indifferent success; and the season was a most
disastrous one. Full salaries were seldom, I believe,
paid; and the fortunes of Old Drury kicked the
beam.

PHILADELPHIA.—My next engagement was at the
Walnut Street Theatre, Philadelphia; Marshall,
manager, Miss Cushman, stage-manager. Among the
company were William Wheatley, Fredericks, Susan
Cushman, Mrs. Maeder. In some respects, therefore,
it was stronger than the Park Theatre at that time;
but it had no Placide (the best comedian of his day
and country); and no Fisher (that most quaint and
useful actor); nor Mrs. Wheatley; nor was there so
good an actor as Barry in the heavy business.

I played six nights there. In addition to the bad-
ness of the times, it was election week, in October,
which contributed to damage my business, I received
only £40 for my share of the six nights; but the
manager told me the houses had been better than he

expected from the times ; so you may guess what times they were. Mr. Forrest followed me the Monday after ; I was present at his first night's performance, Macbeth ; and his house was not, I think, at all better than my last. If *he* could not draw in Philadelphia, who could !

Charlotte Cushman, whom I met now, for the first time, was by no means, then, the actress which she afterwards became. She displayed at that day a rude, strong, uncultivated talent ; it was not till after she had seen and acted with Mr. Macready—which she did the next season—that she really brought artistic study and finish to her performances. At this time she was frequently careless in the text, and negligent of rehearsals. She played the Queen to me in Hamlet, and I recollect her shocking my ear, and very much disturbing my impression of the reality of the situation, by her saying to me in the closet-scene (Act III.),

" What wilt thou do ? thou wilt not *kill* me ?"

instead of

" What wilt thou do ? thou wilt not *murder* me ?"

thus substituting a weak word for a strong one, diluting the force, and destroying the rhythm of the verse. She was much annoyed at her error when I told her of it ; but confessed that she had always so read the line, unconscious of being wrong.

I played Rolla with her, and she was, even then, the best Elvira I ever saw. The power of her scorn, and the terrible earnestness of her revenge, were immense. Her greatest part, fearfully natural, dreadfully intense, horribly real, was Nancy Sykes, in the

dramatic version of Oliver Twist ; it was too true ;
it was painful, this actual presentation of Dickens's
poor abandoned, abused, murdered, outcast of the
streets ; a tigress with a touch, and but one, of
woman's almost deadened nature, blotted, and tram-
pled under foot by man's cruelty and sin.

It is in darkly-shadowed, lurid-tinged, characters
of a low order, like this and Meg Merrilies—half
human, half demon—with the savage, animal reality
of passion, and the weird fascination of crime, redeemed by fitful flashes of womanly feeling—that
she excels. I never admired her Lady Macbeth. It
is too animal ; it wants intellectual confidence, and
relies too much on physical energy. Besides, she
bullies Macbeth ; gets him into a corner of the stage,
and—as I heard a man with more force than elegance,
express it—she " pitches into him ;" in fact, as one
sees her large clenched hand and muscular arm
threatening him, in alarming proximity, one feels that
if other arguments fail with her husband, she will
have recourse to blows. Meg Merrilies has been her
great *fortune-teller* and fortune-*maker*.

Susan, her sister, was a pretty creature, but had
not a spark of Charlotte's genius ; she pleased " the
fellows," however, and was the best walking-lady on
the American stage. (Walking-ladies, madam, are
not pedestrians, necessarily ; it is the English term
for what they call on the French stage, *ingenues ;*
young ladies of no particular strength of character,
whose business is to look pretty, to dress prettily,
and to speak prettily ; charmingly innocent, and deli-
ciously insipid.)

When Charlotte took her leave of the New York

public, previous to sailing, or steaming rather, for England, where she had resolved to try her fortune, I appeared, at the request of Mr. Simpson, as Benedick to her Beatrice, on her farewell night, at the Park Theatre (25th Oct., 1844). The house was by no means full; and she played Beatrice, that night, carelessly or over-anxiously, I don't know which—the effect of either is much the same. I recollect particularly, that she ran part of one act into another in a scene with me, in a very perplexed and perplexing manner. When we came off, she exclaimed—

" For heaven's sake, what have I been doing ?"

" Knocking the fourth and fifth acts together, extemporaneously," I replied.

The fact is, she was disappointed with the house ; the result being then of some moment to her. That audience little dreamt with what an accession of reputation and fortune she would return amongst them!

Looking over my papers, I find a most characteristic note from her to me during the above engagement at Philadelphia, which—for it contains nothing confidential—I give my readers as a curiosity. It is written in a bold, masculine hand, something " like the hand that writ it." The italics mark the words which were underscored, heavily.

> Wednesday night,
> *Half-past* 2.
>
> Mon Ami ——
>
> After a late supper, prepared for you (but no one could get a sight of you all the evening), and studying a long part—I have to request a great favour of you—viz., to take the enclosed packet for me to Boston. I have to-day written some three or four letters, not of introduction (that might *offend* you), but calculated to do you some service—*to* Boston. I shall only be too proud if

they are of any service to you—for without nonsense, I have scarcely ever seen one I should be more sincerely happy to serve than yourself—*and no humbug!* It is a matter of indifference to *me* whether you believe this or not—*I feel it*—and so *God bless you!* till we meet again. You shall hear from me shortly, and believe me sincerely your friend,

CHARLOTTE CUSHMAN.

P.S. Half asleep—a bad pen, no ink, no paper, and as low-spirited as a *fiend!* All *excuses sufficient.*

The manner in which she obtained her first engagement in London, is so characteristic of the spirit and *pluck* of the woman, that I cannot resist telling it, as it was related to me by Maddox, the manager of the Princess's Theatre (1845).

On her first introduction to him, Miss Cushman's personal gifts did not strike him as exactly those which go to make up a stage heroine, and he declined engaging her. Charlotte had certainly no great pretensions to beauty; but she had perseverance and energy, and knew that there was the right metal in her: so she went to Paris, with a view to finding an engagement there, with an English company. She failed, too, in that, and returned to England, more resolutely than ever, bent on finding employment there; because it was now more than ever necessary to her. It was a matter of life and death almost. She armed herself, therefore, with letters (so Maddox told me) from persons who were likely to have weight with him, and again presented herself at the Princess's; but the little Hebrew was obdurate as Shylock, and still declined her proffered services. Repulsed, but not conquered, she rose to depart; but, as she reached the door, she turned and exclaimed:—"I know I have enemies in this country; but—(and here she cast

herself on her knees, raising her clenched hand aloft)
so help me ———— ! I'll defeat them !" She uttered
this with the energy of Lady Macbeth, and the pro-
phetic spirit of Meg Merrilies. "Helho !" said
Maddox to himself, " s'help me ! she's got de shtuff
in her !" and he gave her an appearance, and afterwards an engagement in his theatre.

She opened there with Mr. FORREST, in Macbeth;
and carried away the honours of the night. It was
on this occasion that those marks of disapprobation
were showered on the great American actor, which
so highly incensed him, and which were attributed
by him, with great injustice, I believe, to Mr.
Macready's influence, and were so fatally revenged
in 1849, at the Astor Place Opera House, when
Mr. Macready was driven from that stage, and compelled to fly, probably for his life. Innocent victims
fell outside the theatre on that dreadful night, who
had no hand or part in the quarrel, perhaps scarcely
a knowledge of its cause.

On his first visit to England (in 1835-6), Mr.
Forrest received the most flattering applause from
press and public ; and one thing is certain, that if the
disapprobation manifested towards him, justly or un-
justly, on his second visit was a *got-up* thing, it was
not done in an *anti-American* spirit ; for Charlotte
Cushman, on the same night, was vehemently applauded and loudly called for. And, further, she
afterwards played alone at the same theatre ; that is,
without Mr. Forrest, and was always received with
great favour. She never fails, I believe, to attribute
her great after-success, and the harvest of fame and
fortune which she afterwards reaped in her own

country, to the instantaneous recognition of her talents in England.

MADAME PISARONI, the greatest *prima donna* of her day (1790 about), had so unfortunate a countenance, that when any *impresario* proposed an engagement to her, she first sent him a miniature of herself, as she actually looked, painted to the life, without flattery. If this did not frighten him, she entered into the negotiation ; and when she sang, she kept her hands in motion before her face, to prevent the audience from dwelling on it, lest its disagreeable features might destroy the effect of her marvellous voice and execution.

BOWERY THEATRE.—Passing through New York, on my way from Philadelphia to Boston, I accepted an offer from THOS. HAMBLIN, and played six nights at the Bowery Theatre; Macbeth, Hamlet, Iago (twice), M. Antony, Faulconbridge ; the great Tom himself was the Othello, Brutus, and King John. The business was not good ; all the theatres in New York were at the lowest water-mark, and even Mr. Forrest, at the old Chatham Theatre, was playing a wretched engagement. I was taken there by one of his greatest admirers to see him in " Metamora," and was surprised to find the house more than three-fourths empty. He, however, acted with his accustomed vigour ; and I freely acknowledge that, for power of destructive energy, I never heard anything on the stage so tremendous in its sustained *crescendo* swell and crashing force of utterance as his defiance of the Council, in that play. His voice surged and roared like the angry sea, lashed into fury by a storm ; till, as it reached its boiling, seething climax, in which the serpent hiss of hate was heard, at intervals, amidst its louder, deeper, hoarser tones, it was like the Falls of Niagara, in its tremendous down-sweeping cadence : it was a whirlwind, a tornado, a cataract of illimitable rage !

Boston.—I made my first appearance at the Tremont Theatre—now the Tremont Temple, and the scene of the Rev. —— Kellog's spiritual ministrations and manifestations—on 16th Nov., 1842, in Hamlet; and, with an interval of two nights' absence at Providence, played there, on re-engagements, altogether five weeks, during which I repeated Hamlet and Macbeth three times each, and appeared in Coriolanus and Hotspur, each for the first time. Dr. Jones, a fair and easy-going, good-natured, but not very enterprising man, was manager; and, I think, with the exception of that excellent, solid, sterling actor, John Gilbert, and his wife, the company was about as poor a one, as a whole, as was ever assembled in the walls of a respectable theatre.

I have to congratulate myself, however, that, in spite of the bad times, and the frightful depression of theatricals in the modern Athens—as Edmund Kean, I believe, baptized Boston, transferring to it the *sobriquét* of Edinburgh—I had the good fortune to play to some good houses, and to establish myself in the favour of that emotional, capricious, and rather uncertain public—a favour which, I think I may venture to flatter myself, I have since rather increased than diminished, both in the lecture-room and the theatre :—I have played in every theatre in Boston : Tremont, National (the old one under Pelby, and the last but one, which was burnt down during my engagement), and the Howard Athenæum. I spoke the first word in it that was ever spoken from the stage—the address on the opening night, 5th Oct., 1846. It was written by a clergyman, and was a lamentable specimen of clerical versification. At the Museum I have played several highly advantageous engagements, as friend Moses will confess ; and, finally, three engagements at the present over-large and *mal-acoustic* Boston Theatre, under the veteran Barry.

It is, however, an unfortunate fact that, in spite of the proverbial literary taste of the City of Notions, the Drama, properly so called—I mean the Drama of Shakspere, Sheridan Knowles, Bulwer, &c.—does not generally attract the Bostonians. Show and spectacle, glitter, blue flame and pantomimic extravagance, have infinitely greater charms for them. Hamlet, Macbeth, the School for Scandal, have no chance against the Ravels and pantomime ; and, I have no doubt, that Mr. Barry cleared more money for the stockholders last season, by the revival of the carcase of the old (one) horse-piece of the " Cataract of the Ganges," without a line of poetry—scarcely of common sense— in it, than he ever made in Boston by the most careful production of the highest Shaksperian Drama, or of the most elegant Comedy.

XIII.

NEW ORLEANS.—I had always desired to visit New Orleans. Finding theatrical prospects for the winter very hazy, at the North, and having received overtures from Mr. Caldwell, the proprietor of the old St. Charles Theatre, I resolved to try my fortune in the South. As I did not intend to stop on the way, I made up my mind to go by sea, as the easiest as well as cheapest mode of travelling the distance through. I therefore engaged a state-room in the " Oswego," Captain Oliver Eldridge, a sailing packet of about 700 tons ; laid in a few extra stores ; and, with the addition of a case of most excellent sherry, sent on board for me by the kindness of a friend, I looked forward to getting through the passage, if it might be a fortnight, perhaps, with comfort, and even with pleasure. I found our captain as fine a fellow as ever walked a deck, our ship an excellent sailer, our fare plain, substantial, and good. We had only four or five passen-

gers, none of whom deserve particular mention, except,
perhaps, a temperance man, one, M——, of Philadelphia; who, at the outset, inveighed strongly
against the use of wine, spirits, or of any liquors
fermented or distilled ; but whom, after twenty-four
hours' sea sickness, I charitably persuaded to take a
little grog, for the comfort of his stomach. He found
the prescription so efficacious against *mal de mer*, that
he stuck pretty steadily to it for the remainder of
the passage : a fact to which the grievous diminution
of my stock fearfully bore witness. He grew particularly fond of a certain amalgamation of Jamaica
rum, hot water, lemon and sugar, in the chemical
admixture of which I flattered myself I was an adept ;
and he acquired a singular taste for the delicate, pale
sherry which I have before mentioned, as forming
part of

"my little, but my precious store.'

Whether good or bad, in general, these indulgences of
the spirit brought up his flesh amazingly. He was a
thin, lath-y, dyspeptic-looking fellow; but generous
living made a new man of him. I never saw a fellow
on whose conscience the total abandonment of his tee-
total principles and practice sat so lightly; I should
rather say, so heavily ; for he increased in flesh the
more he rejoiced in *spirit*. Whether or no, he thought
it for my health's sake, as being of rather a full habit
and sanguine temperament, to remove temptation out
of my reach, I know not : if so, his zeal in my cause
was most self-sacrificing ; for he attacked the enemy,
my bottle, with the most unflinching devotion to my
service ;—though I will do him the justice to say,

that he so far carried out his principles strictly on this point, that he never drank any wine or spirits *of his own*. The steward had no account against *him;* no awful score; no "trim reckoning" could be thrown in *his* face. And the very last circumstances under which I saw him, the day after our arrival in port, when I went down to the ship to give orders about my baggage, were—seated in the saloon, with crackers and cheese, and a *bottle of my sherry, fresh opened, before him;* for he had a sublime contempt for the refinements of proprietary distinctions in the article of liquor: he was quite *Proudhommeish* in his views on that head. He seemed to think that, in these cases (liquor-*cases*), "*la propricté c'ést le vol*"—and he acted accordingly.

We made the passage in a little over nine days; and I congratulated myself that I had chosen the sea, instead of the, then, dreadfully tiresome land conveyance.

On arriving in New Orleans, I found the old St. Charles Theatre—which is reported to have been one of the finest buildings, for dramatic purposes, in the world—burnt down; and the American Theatre—a new stand, opened by Mr. Caldwell, on the destruction of his property in Camp-street—just closed by him for want of support; he had been able to keep it going only about a month, and that at considerable loss. The theatrical prospect was evidently refreshing —highly encouraging to a new arrival! However, I took up my quarters at the old St. Charles Hotel— and "lay back to see what would turn up."

Messrs. Smith (*Old Sol*, as he was called) and Ludlow were already engaged in the erection of a new

K

St. Charles Theatre ; men were at work upon it night and day ; it was to be completed and opened immediately.

Meanwhile, one Dinneford appeared in the field, as the lessee of the American Theatre, and made proposals to me to appear on the night of its reopening; a proposition which I declined, preferring to wait ; and, in the meantime, enjoying the "varieties" of the multiform, multi-coloured, multi-lingual, multi-ludal city, which is *levée* on the banks of the Mississippi.

New Orleans life was a very different thing in 1842 from what it is now that the sober, calculating, Yankee element is so largely mingled with the glowing, impassioned Southern and Creole nature.

It then had a very mixed aspect ; full of contrasts of colour, language, manners, conditions ; abounding in contradictions, anomalies, discords, and strange blendings of antagonistic elements.

One phase of its parti-coloured life particularly struck me. It was what were called *Society-Balls.* They were got up by subscription among men of wealth and fashion, by whom invitations were issued, and arrangements made that brought together, on the evening of each ball, the most agreeable men, citizens, and strangers, a select party, and the most beautiful *quadroons* that New Orleans could boast.

By the kindness of an influential friend I received a card for one of these *re-unions,* and attended it with great curiosity and interest. On entering the *salle,* which was a large, handsome, well-lighted room, I found a company, consisting of about a hundred, or a hundred and twenty, male and female ; the dancing was at its height ; but as orderly, decent, and well-conducted as in the *salons* of Paris or New York. As far as propriety of behaviour and *reténue* went, it would have made *Mabille* blush for itself— if *Mabille* ever blushed! No liberties, no freedom of action or words. There was a perfect blaze of warm, voluptuous beauty; an assemblage of as finely-formed, bright-eyed *houris* as ever I looked on at one glance. None of them were strongly marked with the features or betraying signs of their race; most of them would pass, in the glare of artificial light, as I saw them, for *brunettes,—bien prononcées*, it is true. Some of them showed no tinge of their descent at all; but could boast complexions—not *blondes*, certainly, but—of Anglo-American whiteness. Yet all these girls had in their blood the fatal taint of Afric's sun; though, in some, it was diluted by admixture to an infinitesimal point, that required the nicest eye to detect it—if, indeed, it could be detected at all.

Vogue la galere!

ST. CHARLES THEATRE, 1843.—The new St. Charles Theatre was completed in an incredibly short time (sixty working days, I believe, altogether), and I was invited by Messrs. Ludlow and Smith to appear there in the second week of its opening. I accepted, and commenced in Hamlet, on 9th February, 1843, playing Macbeth, and my usual list, and winding up, to the best house of the season, so far, with Claude Melnotte and Rob Roy, for my benefit.

The following brief notice, from the " Picayune," may show what they thought of me in New Orleans :

VANDENHOFF.—*New St. Charles.*—Young Vandenhoff made his first appearance last evening, as Hamlet, before one of the fullest and most fashionable houses of the season, and was warmly received and enthusiastically applauded throughout the performance. His readings are exquisitely given, evincing much study as well as scholarship; his enunciation and gesticulation are good, and his general conception of the difficult character he sustained gave full evidence that he had bestowed upon it much careful study, and that he well understands the wild yet subtle humours of the Dane. If we can find fault at all, it is with an excess of method in his attitude and action, and the too violent rendering of a few passages where a subdued manner would have been more effective. These faults were trivial, however, when placed in opposition to the general beauties of his performance, and we cannot but predict for Mr. Vandenhoff a highly creditable, and even brilliant career upon our boards."

But here, as well as in the North, the " bad times" most injuriously affected the theatre. Mr. HACKETT played alternate nights with me, to indifferent houses; and as his comedies and farces did not draw, he betook himself to Tragedy and Richard III ! This, I need not say, did not mend the matter. Strange, that so excellent an actor in certain character-parts, eccentric and comic, should have deceived himself into the belief that he could shine in tragedy, for which he has not, nor ever had, any qualification, except good sense and intelligence. When I say that his Kentuckian never ceases to amuse me by its hearty, audacious oddities ; that I consider his Solomon Swap the most natural and unexaggerated Yankee I ever saw upon the stage ; that I have alternately smiled and wept at his Rip Van Winkle, one of the most artistic and finished performances that the American Theatre ever produced—he will, I know, not take it ill, that I could not discover the merit or the design, if it had any, of his Richard III. An actor may have great intelligence ; a perfect understanding, and even feeling of his author, and yet fall very far short in the execution, even of his own conception. The art and the power that can touch and delight us in the simple pathos of Rip Van Winkle and *Monsieur Mallet* may be feeble to cope with the frenzy of Lear, and will crack and fall to pieces in the vain attempt to master and to give expression to the complicated agony of his pride, his affection, and his rage, the ruin of down-trodden royalty, and the wreck of a confiding old father's heart. These are the highest triumphs of the tragic power: it is not wonderful that Mr. Hackett, excellent comedian as he is, should fail to achieve them.

———

I must mention an incident which interrupted the Lady of Lyons, for a few moments, on my benefit night. Mrs. FARREN, then the regular actress of the St. Charles Theatre, was the Pauline; and in the scene in the cottage where—on Beauseant's producing a pistol, she falls fainting into Claude's arms—as I carried the lady up the stage, to place her in a chair, a voice from the pit cried out, in a very excited tone,

"Kiss her ! by ——, kiss her !"

I felt my cheek tingle with indignation ; and an involuntary shrinking of Pauline, on my arm, told me that she felt the affront too. I placed her calmly on the chair ; turned, walked slowly down to the footlights, and stood there in silence, casting my eye round the foremost seats of the parquet, with a view to detect the offender. The audience was still as death, for about half a minute ; then, suddenly, like a flash of lightning, a thought seemed to strike them ; I beheld a man seized, raised off his feet, and literally passed through the air, from hand to hand, across the parquet, till he was outside the door, before he could

know whither he was going! The whole was the
work of about ten seconds; and, after a hearty cheer,
I went on with the text. The words which followed,

" There ! we are strangers now,"—

spoken by Claude with reference to his position
thenceforth with Pauline, the house immediately applied to the stranger whom they had ejected, and
greeted them with the most uproarious laughter and
another cheer !

Poor fellow, I dare say he meant no harm; his
feelings overcame him; but then, you know, we must
regulate our feelings; or at least the inopportune
expression of them !

I next played six nights at Mobile, of which I
need only remark that the company was shockingly
bad; and the manager having got into a snarl with
the public by discharging a popular favourite, Mrs.
Stuart, I had to suffer the penalty of his obstinacy,
there being a very general league of absence from the
theatre till she should be restored.

I then returned to New Orleans, and played a
very satisfactory engagement of five nights at the
New American Theatre, under a new management,
producing, for my benefit, for the first time, the play
of " Love's Sacrifice," which had recently been brought
out for my father and sister, at Covent Garden Theatre.

Previous to my appearance at this theatre a low
attempt was made to get up a *row* against me on my
opening night. It scarcely deserves to be mentioned;
for it was defeated by the coolness and contempt with
which I treated it in anticipation. An insolent carpenter of the theatre had refused me admittance at
the stage door, although my name was underlined in

the bills, and I had come for the purpose of speaking with the manager. I did not bandy words with him, as I saw his insolence was planned; but pushed him aside and walked in, desiring him to " keep his hands off me, or I would have him taught manners." He muttered some threat, to which I gave no heed, but passed on, had my interview with the manager, and left the theatre, and thought no more about the fellow.

The next day was Sunday ; and, after church-time, several friends came to me to offer their services against the row which was to take place on my appearance to-morrow night.

" Row !" I exclaimed : "what about ?"

" What about ?" was the reply ; " Don't you know ? haven't you seen ?"

With that, each produced a small mean-looking scrap of paper, three inches by four, on which was printed the following " elegant compilation." I give it, with all its *false spellings* and *Malaprop-isms*, exactly as it stood :

G. VANDENHOFF.

GEORGE VANDENHOFF ! ! ! This individual, who is subsisting on the generous disposition of the American people, has, in an unguarded moment, thrown off his disguise, and stands before them in all his naked deformity — denouncing them as "common people, and that it was impossible to learn them manners—contaminating him with their tuch, &c. &c.

The subject of a King, who, according to the laws of his own country, is a vagabond, a solicitor of charity; and like the reptile, would bite the hand that warmed him into existence. Can Americans sit quietly down and hear themselves stigmatized by a foreign adventurer, while feeding him with generous munificence ? No ; but show this famous aristocratical hypocrite, that we appreciate his *noble* feelings and will take occasion to show it the first opportunity.

Some thousands of this manifesto, it appears, had been distributed; and I was advised to prepare myself for a storm. I smiled, and said, " Then, let's take a drink." I knew this was the usual Southern preparation for everything.

The next day I received a call from the British Consul, with the offer of assistance, if I required it. I assured him it was needless, and that I had not the slightest apprehension of anything. In the afternoon a deputation of butchers, from Lafayette, was announced, as having called to see me at the hotel. I received them, like a Secretary of State; and, having first invited them to " take a drink all round" (*pour applanir la route*), requested to know their pleasure.

They had called on me to learn the truth of the matter between me and that proclamation-izing carpenter, with a view to their action in the matter, *pro* or *con.* I told it. They expressed themselves perfectly satisfied : " they should be thar, and they'd jest like to see the first feller move a finger."

Well, night came : " Othello" was the play ; the house was well filled—all men ; not a bonnet to be seen ; this looked ominous. My friends of the deputation and their party were *thar*, in omnibus loads. I had to go on in the first scene as Iago ; and I requested the gentleman who had to accompany me as Roderigo, if he perceived any eggs or harder missiles flying, not to wait, but to take the first shot for his *exit-cue.*

Up rose the curtain ; on we went. There was a silence. I walked forward to the footlights, took off my hat, looked round the house with an enquiring

eye, as much as to say—"If any one has anything
to say against your humble servant, now is his time."
Not a word, not a hiss, not a sound. I smiled, made
a bow to the audience, put on my hat, and motioned
with my hand to Roderigo to begin the scene. Then
out burst the public voice, in a hearty cheer, in which,
I fancy, my Lafayette volunteers were not slow. The
play went on without disturbance; I received my due
meed of applause; was called out, at the end, enthusiastically; and had a tremendous house for my benefit, four nights after. The manager wished to discharge the carpenter; but, at my earnest request
(the rascal had a family), he was retained.

Passing through Richmond, on my way to New
York, I encountered Mr. Hackett there; and we
played one night together there: our half share of the
gross proceeds amounted to £3 each; so that there
were £12 in the house. Hard times, those!

I have since played and read, too, in Richmond,
myself, to very fine houses, and have received there
the kindest attentions, which I am delighted to acknowledge.

BALTIMORE, *April*, 1843.—Played six nights at the
Holiday Street Theatre, with only tolerable receipts.
Theatricals were bad everywhere; but I passed an
agreeable week, made some delightful acquaintances,
and laid the foundation-stone of that favour and
popularity which I have ever since enjoyed in that
elegant and hospitable city. Being called on for an
autograph—it is singular the rage some people have

for autographs—(I estimated their value in a business view only, as they may be good or bad at the
foot of a *cheque*) I wrote :——

> I've lived here a week on the daintiest fare,
> In this loveliest city of Maryland ;
> Where the men are so frank, and the women so fair,
> That I vow I've been dwelling in *fairy land !*

————

Passing through Philadelphia, played my second engagement, five nights, at the Walnut Street Theatre,
and one night for Marshall's (manager) benefit ; on
which occasion Charlotte Cushman played Romeo, for
the first time, I believe : I was the Mercutio. I lent
her a hat, cloak, and sword, for the second dress, and
believe I may take credit for having given her some
useful fencing hints for the killing of Tybalt and
Paris, which she executes in such masculine and
effective style : the only good points in this *hybrid*
performance of hers. She looks neither man nor
woman in the character—or both ; and her passion is
equally epicene in form. Whatever her talents in
other parts, I never yet heard any human being, that
had seen her Romeo, who did not speak of it with a
painful expression of countenance, " more in sorrow
than in anger."

Romeo requires a *man*, to feel his passion, and to
express his despair. A woman, in attempting it,
" unsexes" herself to no purpose, except to destroy
all interest in the play, and all sympathy for the ill-
fated pair : she *denaturalizes* the situations ; and sets
up a monstrous anomaly, in place of a consistent picture of ill-starred passion and martyr-love, faithful to
death.   There should be a law against such perver-

sions; they are high crimes and misdemeanours against truth, taste, and æsthetic principles of art, as well as offences against propriety, and desecrations of Shakspere. In his time women did not appear on the stage at all; now they usurp men's parts, and " push us from our stools."

NEW YORK.—Early in May I played my second engagement at the Park Theatre, in a series of comedies, assisted by Mrs. Brougham : Benedick (twice), Charles Surface, Jacques, and Ranger, in the " Suspicious Husband." Theatricals were still down in New York, and the business was *shy*.

Immediately following this I accepted a five nights' engagement at Pelby's National Theatre, Boston, he paying me a certainty of £10 per night: and the engagement was renewed the week after, with the addition of the name of Mr. (*Count*) Tasistro to the bill, as Iago, Joseph Surface, Cassius, &c.

And with this ended my first season (1842-'3) in the United States; probably one of the worst theatrical seasons ever known. Certainly I have never seen the Drama at so low an ebb since, not even in the great crisis of '57. When I reviewed my accounts, I found that I had netted about the same amount as the salary offered me by Mr. Kemble, for Covent Garden Theatre, and the receipts of country engagements in England, during vacation, would have amounted to. Still, I had made friends on this side of the water, and I made up my mind to remain in this country for the coming season, perhaps to make it my permanent home—which, indeed, it now is.

For what is home, but where the heart is?

" Domus et placens uxor,"—

a house and pleasing wife are the duality of possession
that constitute the perfect idea of *home;* the two facts
that grapple one to a soil with surest anchorage.
Now, as I have not only acquired both these here,
but have a raised a young offshoot who drew his first
breath beneath the starry banner of the Republic, my
domicile is, I think, sufficiently well assured.

XIV.

MISCELLANEOUS LEAVES—United States, 1843 to 1852'-3—Preliminary—MR. MACREADY—My First Meeting with him—Performances
with Him—His Characteristics—L'état c'est moi !—The Stage,
that's I !—Incidents—Henry IV.—Werner—Argumentum ad
Hominem—Astor Place Opera House—Restorations—Shakspere
—Mutilation of School for Scandal—*Resumé*—His Retirement—
Valeat !—MR. BOOTH—Scene with Him in Julius Cæsar, at the
Park Theatre—MR. SIMPSON, the Manager—KING JOHN, with the
KEANS at the Park—Broadway Theatre—J. R. ANDERSON—
Sophocles' ANTIGONE, with Mendelssohn's Music, at Palma's Opera
House—Grotesque Appearance of the *Chorus* of Greek Sages—
MRS. C. N. SINCLAIR (Mrs. Forrest)—Her *Début*—Engagements
with her, and Accounts—Result.

IN the following *miscellaneous leaves* I preserve no
order of date or arrangement ; but merely give such
sketches and reminiscences as occur in my note-book,
from 1843 to 1852-'3 : during which period I resided
principally in New York, making frequent trips across
the Atlantic, without any professional object, and
playing only occasional engagements in the principal
cities of the United States.   During the intervals of
these engagements I devoted a portion of my time to
public Readings of Shakspere, Sheridan, and the
Poets.   Already perceiving that this style of literary
entertainment would take a great hold of the public
mind, I began to give it conscientious study and earnest
attention, as a means to enable me to quit the stage.
I have happily been enabled to carry out my inten-

tions; and, in the calmer and more congenial arena of
the Lecture-hall, I have reaped a success which entirely
satisfies my ambition, and leaves me leisure to gratify
my love of books and literary pursuits.

MR. MACREADY.

My first professional meeting with Mr. Macready
was in Philadelphia, in October, 1843. I had been
playing for three weeks at the Walnut Street Theatre;
and was then engaged to appear with "the eminent"
tragedian, at the Chestnut Street Theatre, which
was opened expressly for his performances. Othello,
Werner, Richelieu, with repetitions, carried us through
the fortnight. I played Othello, Ulric, De Mauprat.

The two points that struck me most, as characteristic of this leader of the English Stage, were his
intense devotion to the work of his profession, as a
business, and his equally intense *egotism*, which
imperiously subjected, as far as he was able, every thing
and every body, to the sole purpose of making himself
the one mark for all eyes to look at, the one voice for
all ears to listen to, the one name for all mouths to
repeat and eulogize. It was *l'art de se faire valoir,
sur la scéne*, pushed to its highest point.

To attain this sublime of self-magnifying, author
and actor were to be sacrificed ; or, at least, diluted
and let down, where their " effects "—a word he was
very fond of—could in any way pale his own lustre.
Authors were lopped and pared down in speeches that
did not belong to *him ;* and actors were expected, and,
as far as in them lay, by his directions, were compelled
to lose all thought of giving prominence to their own
parts when he was on the stage. They were, in the

sight of his tyrannical self-aggrandizement, mere scaf-
foldings to support his artistic designs ; mere machines
to aid the working out of his conceptions ; lay figures
for his pictures, his groupings, his *tableaux vivants*.
As for any thing they might have to say, as far as it
was necessary to be said, as a *cue* for his speech, or
for the carrying out or explaining the plot in which *he*
was concerned, let them say it ; and say it in such a
manner as will make best for his reply ; otherwise, he
would prefer them to be silent. He was a perfect
verification of that description given by a *spirituel*
French author of the present day, and applied by
him to a certain notorious character occupying public
attention at the time he wrote it :

"Semblable a ces grands acteurs, qui n'aiment pas les pieces
d'ensemble, et voudraient jouer un monologue en cinq actes,———
n'avait pas l'air de soupconner l'existence de ses complices, assis
a côté de lui ; il se tenait à distance ; il s'isolait ; il voulait être
le centre a tous les regards et ne partager sa gloire avec aucun
subalterne."

Whatever was his part for the night, whether he
was Othello or Iago, Brutus or Cassius, Posthumus
or Iachimo, that part must be *the* feature of the play ;
and this was to be effected not by his own towering
and surpassing excellence in the character, but by
such an arrangement of the scene, and such a position
of every other person on the stage, as must make all
others subordinate, and put him on a pedestal, as it
were, always the main figure in the group, the most
prominent object in the action.

Thus, when he played Othello, Iago was to be *nowhere !* Othello was to be the *sole* consideration: the
sole character to be evolved, the all-engrossing object

to the eye and heart of the audience.   Iago was a
mere *stoker*, whose business it was to supply Othello's
passion with fuel, and keep up his high-pressure.

The next night, perhaps, he took Iago; and lo !
presto ! every thing was changed.   Othello was to
become a mere puppet for Iago to play with ; a pipe
for Iago's master-skill to " sound from its lowest note
to the top of its compass."   Iago's intellect, his
fiendish subtlety, his specious, calculating malignity,
were to be the sole features of the play.   Othello was
to be a mere fly, a large *blue-bottle*, struggling in the
meshes of the Italian spider.   Even the writhings
and convulsions of the victim were controlled and
restrained with *arachnian* ingenuity, by invisible liga-
ments, lest some natural movement, or throb of
agony might rudely make a breach in the continuity,
or destroy the artistic harmony of the elaborately-
wrought web !

Thus, this great work, this terrible duel between
brain and heart, the conflict of intellectual subtlety
with all-triumphant love ; this Machiavellian victory
of the base over the noble, in which Shakspere has
divided his wonderful power of characterisation on
the emotional and passionate, yet confiding nature of
the Moor ; his tenderness, his magnanimity, his terrible revenge, roused like a tiger to glut itself with
carnage : and, on the other hand, the profound, the
devilish philosophy of Iago, a compound of self-love,
envy, and malice, tracking their victim with the
patient, steadfast, unwearied staunchness of a blood-
hound ; this great work of genius and of the highest
art combined was to be in either case a one-sided
picture, " but half made-up," the interest varying

and changing to that half in which Macready was
dominant for the night, and on which alone light was
to be thrown.   If the Othello-side was in the
ascendant, Iago stood all night with his back to the
audience, his face unseen, his expression lost, sometimes even his words unheard.   If the Iago-side was
at the top, he occupied the centre of the stage all the
evening, while Othello gave the audience a rear-view,
and played lacquey to his "ancient!"   This "effect
defective" was brought about in both cases by "the
eminent's" arbitrary direction of the stage.

As to his reverence for the author, Mr. Macready
did not scruple to cut out a speech, or portion of a
speech, however beautiful, in the part of another actor,
if the retaining it would give that actor—especially a
favourite actor—too much hold of the scene, too much
apparent importance, or would keep the "eminent"
in the attitude of a listener too long, in the view of
his own overweening egoism.   Macready, in fact,
parodied the expression of Louis XIV., put by Bulwer
into the mouth of Richelieu, *L'état c'est moi;* the
"autocratic" manager and actor thought, and said
in practice,

"The stage—that's I!"

He was to be the Alpha and Omega; the embodiment
and living impersonation of the Aristotelian theory of
epic perfection; he was to be the *beginning*, the
middle, and the *end* of every play.

Let me verify what I have said as to his loppings
and parings of an author, Shakspere not excepted, by
an example or two within my own experience.

He was very fond of playing the celebrated death-

scene of the king, in the second part of Henry IV.,
for his benefit. At New Orleans, in 1849, I played the
Prince for him in this scene, and was really desirous to
give him every assistance in my power, not involving
a positive surrender of my own common sense, and an
utter sacrifice of the part I was to fill. All went on
smoothly enough, till I came to the Prince's beautiful
justification of the act of taking the crown from—as
he thought—his dead father's head. I spoke the
text as Shakspere wrote it :—

> "Coming to look on you, thinking you dead,
> (And dead almost, my liege, to think you were,)
> I spake unto the crown as having sense,
> And thus upbraided it :—" Take care on thee depending
> Hath fed upon the body of my father ;
> Therefore, thou, best of gold, art worst of gold :
> [*Other, less fine in carat, is more precious*
> *Preserving life in med'cine potable :*
> *But thou, most fine, most honour'd, most renown'd,*
> *Hast eat thy bearer up.*] Thus, my most royal liege,
> Accusing it, I put it on my head," &c.

Now the four characteristic lines in italics between
brackets—illustrative of the virtues superstitiously
ascribed in an early age to the *aurum potabile* or
potable gold—Mr. Macready insisted on cutting out,
because they added to the length of the speech. I
insisted on retaining them, for three reasons : first,
because Shakspere wrote them, and intended them to
be delivered ; second, because they were appropriate
to the period and the speaker ; third, because they
were familiar to readers, and their omission might be
attributed either to my ignorance of or my want of
appreciation of the text. As I was not one of those
who felt it necessary to flatter the "'eminent" by

blind submission, the text was saved from mutilation for that night.

Again, at the Chesnut Street Theatre, Philadelphia, in Byron's Werner—a character which Macready played to perfection, leaving nothing to be desired—Werner, speaking of the favour shown to Ulric, by his enemy Stralenheim, says:

> "'Tis but a snare he winds about us both,
> To swoop the sire and son at once;"

to which Ulric, with the impetuous confidence of youth, replies,

> "I cannot
> Pause in each petty fear, and stumble at
> The doubts that rise like briars in our path,
> [*But must break through them, as an unarmed carle*
> *Would, though with naked limbs, were the wolf rustling*
> *In the same thicket where he hewed for bread*."]

Surely, the italicised lines in brackets, apt, nervous, presenting a happy figure, forcibly illustrating the onward determination of youth, deserved to be spoken. Mr. Macready thought otherwise.

" I've cut those lines out," he said, at rehearsal.

" But," I replied, as they occur in my part, I have restored them."

" No, no," he said, " omit them."

" Why?" I inquired.

" I feel they're useless; they burthen the text!"

" Pardon me," I said, " as it is *I* who have to speak them, if I disagree with you. I think them particularly apt, and characteristic."

" Besides," he continued, " they lengthen the scene, and I wish them out."

" Lewis," I said to the prompter, " will you be

good enough to *time* my speaking of those three lines."

" O," said he, hastily, " that's too much ! Speak them, speak them, if you will: but they're quite superfluous."

Of course I *did* speak them.

These are trifles, but they show the man and his mind; had these lines occurred in any part of his, they would not have been cut.

Thus, again, in this very rehearsal of Werner, after Gabor's relation of the murder by Ulric, when the Hungarian has retired into the turret, to await Werner's decision, and Ulric, after an angry scene with his father, says, before he leaves him :

> " Keep your own secret, keep a steady eye,
> Stir not, and speak not ;—leave the rest to me !
> We must have no third babblers thrust between us :"—

implying of course that Gabor's mouth must be stopped as Stralenheim's had been ; Mr. Macready requested me to go up the stage, and speak these words from the extreme back of it, to him, as he stood in the very front of the footlights, with a face of anguish,—*the picture for the eye to rest on.*

" O no," I said, " I must whisper those words in your ear, surely ; not call them out loud: that would be to defeat their very object, by risking their being overheard."

" But," he replied, " I have always had it done so, and I wish you to do it in that manner."

" But," I said, " it's an inconsistency! Shall I, in the great hall of the castle, outside of which are doubtless sentries, pages in waiting, courtiers, and attendants passing and repassing,—shall I cry out aloud to you ; ' *this is a terrible secret which this man has revealed ; it involves the honour and safety of our house ; but keep still ; leave it to me, and I'll silence the fellow's lips forever !*'—that seems to me not at all *vraisemblable.*"

" Then you refuse to do it ?" he asked.

" I *could* not do it," I said ; " it is too inconsistent."

" Then," said he, angrily, " you are the first Ulric who ever refused me on this point."

I was somewhat touched by this artful reproach, and I replied :

" Mr. Macready, if you will give me your honour that, if you were playing Ulric, you would act the scene in the way you direct me to dô, I'll yield at once."

" Oh ! said he, with a peculiar inflection of voice, " *that's quite a different thing !*"

I thought so.

On his second visit to this country, in 1848, I played with him at the Astor Place Opera House, New York (his first engagement), Othello, Edgar (K. Lear), and other parts. The following is the *Herald's* notice of our joint appearance in Julius Cæsar : the reader will perhaps pardon my quoting it.

NIBLO'S ASTOR PLACE THEATRE.—Mr. Macready appeared last night as Brutus, in " Julius Cæsar." It was a finished performance, elaborate, chaste, quiet, dignified, grand, and natural throughout. The great actor is apparent in Mr. Macready, by not only the occasional bursts of genius at particular passages, and the display of talent at certain special points, but more, still, by the tranquillity and quiet of his manner, and the almost careless ease of his speech, deportment, and bearing.   We might say of Mr. Macready that his very finest hits, which produce the greatest impression (especially upon those best able to judge), are precisely those where he appears to make no effort at all, and where no energy, force, or violence, are perceptible.   For this reason, he appears to vulgar minds not half so good an actor as a more tumultuous, riotous declaimer would seem to them to be.   There were several fine points in the performance last night, especially the quarrel and reconciliation with Cassius; also, at the moment when the ghost of Cæsar leaves him, his recovery and effort to address the apparition was very fine. Mr. G. Vandenhoff particularly distinguished himself last night; his performance of Mark Antony was such as only could have been displayed by a man of extraordinary genius and scholarship, both of which Mr. V. unquestionably possesses in a very high degree. When, in his speech to the rabble, he suddenly dropped some of the vehemence of his action, and said in a natural, easy, tranquil tone of voice—"I speak that you do know"—the effect was admirable. Mr. V. will yet succeed in acting in such a manner as not to betray the theatre or the school in his voice, action, and manner, and then he will be one of the greatest, if not the greatest actor on the stage.—*New York Herald*, 18*th October*, 1848.

The *Express* thus spoke of the same performance :

Mr. Macready performed "Brutus" in "Julius Cæsar," on Monday evening, at this establishment.

We do not think it one of the greatest personations of Mr. Macready.   But he does nothing unartistically, and there were parts of this performance which were in his best manner.   It was unequal, however.   Thus, the conclusion of the quarrel scene with Cassius was far better than the principal portion of it, which he gave too much in the vein of Cassius himself. It was too impetuous. But the reconciliation was beautifully done.   The scene with the ghost of Cæsar was as great as was that with the boy *Lucius*, asleep; but the farewell to Cassius was far less feeling than we had a right to expect, and we do not know that we ever heard the great address to the citizens, "Romans, countrymen, and lovers," less effectively given, by an actor of high pretensions.

Mr. Ryder's was a very good *Cassius;* impassioned, impetuous, well-conceived and well read.   Mr. Chippendale's *Casca* was all that could be made of the part, of course.

Mr. George Vandenhoff, as *Marcus Antonius*, in point of fact, carried off most of the laurels of the evening. Throughout, he looked, acted, and read the part with great care and effect. It was a very artist-like performance, and drew down well discriminated applause from the audience, from first to last. Through great difficulties of stage position, in the scene in the Capitol, he made it most telling and effective, and so great was the enthusiasm, at the fall of the curtain, after his grand scene in the Forum, that he was called before the curtain, at the end of the third act, an honour not accorded to the *star* of the occasion, the whole evening.

I also played with him, that same season, at the St. Charles Theatre, New Orleans, the same characters, with the addition of M. Brutus to his Cassius. The latter was a great piece of acting; it was Cassius himself:

Impiger, iracundus inexorabilis, acer.

His Brutus, on the contrary, was an entire mistake; there was none of the philosophy of the Portico about it; no contrast to the impetuosity of Cassius: in fact, it was Cassius with a different " make-up ;" the mental characteristics exhibited were the same. And thus the light and shade so marvellously preserved by Shakspere in this great play were destroyed.

For his benefit, at New Orleans, Mr. Macready produced (as an after-piece!) the " School for Scandal," in three acts! cutting out the great scandal scene, the picture scene, and several other scenes ; so as to confine it, as much as possible, to the development of the " Plots of Joseph Surface," which character he played (as far as he remembered the words, for he was very imperfect), and which consequently became, of course, the feature, and, as far as he could

make it so, the only feature of the comedy. He insisted, too (to save himself trouble in dressing, I suppose), on wearing his own modern clothes : black coat
and pantaloons! I played Charles Surface, but of course
did not follow his example in this gross anachronism
of costume.

The truth is, Mr. Macready valued an author as
far as the author served *him ;* and he respected the
text, as far as it answered his purpose; so that his
Shaksperian Revivals, which were got up with great
care and attention, might have been designated, as
far as integrity of text went, "Restorations of so
much of Shakspere as suits *Mr. Macready."*

To sum up his merits, fairly and impartially : as
an actor Mr. Macready excelled in executive power
and certainty of effect, rather than in imagination,
individualisation of character, or poetic feeling. There
was an angularity in his outlines, and a hardness in
his style, that were only redeemed by the intensity
with which he wrought out his design. His attitudes
were stiff, and frequently ungainly; his rolling gait,
with an alternate thrusting forward of each shoulder
—which has been copied by the silly imitators (*servile
pecus !*)—was anything but graceful or manly, and
gave to his Macbeth, on his first entrance, the air of a
Lowland dancing-master in a kilt, rather than of a
Highland chieftain in arms : and his over-distinct,
staccato, equi-accented syllabification of utterance,
was painful to the ear, and utterly destructive of the
rhythm of English verse. The fact is, beauty and
grace in art were not Macready's study so much as
exactitude ; he had less a view to symmetry of form,
than to proportion in measurement ; the formal just-

ness of a right angle would be more palpably satisfy-
ing to his eye, than the elegance of a curve ; and his
ear found more pleasure in accent than in melody.
Thus, he seized salient points of character, and gave
them strong emphasis, and relief ; he was less competent to make harmonious combinations of parts into
a consistent whole. His power lay in passionate out-
bursts, not in philosophical analysis ; hence, his soliloquies were generally faulty, strained, violent, not
toned down by the softening influence of thought.
His Hamlet, therefore, had little melancholy, but
much asperity in it ; and his Othello was less the
noble Moor,—

> "who loved,
> Not wisely, but too well ; not easily jealous,
> But, being wrought, perplexed in the extreme,"—

than an enraged and desperate African, lashed into
madness, and roused to thirst for blood by vindictive
wrath and implacable revenge.

On the other hand, he was, in every character he
played, earnest, intense, energetic, passionate ; had a
voice of extraordinary range of compass; and brought
to the study of his profession, scholarship, industry,
and, lastly, an unwearied perseverance, that carried
him to his high " eminence," and distanced all his
competitors in the dramatic arena.

As a manager he was the great *martinet* of histrionic drill-masters ; as strict a disciplinarian, and as
rigid a professional formalist, in *his* way, as Carlyle's
Friedrich Wilhelm himself: and though there were
wanting Potsdam, or other giants—no theatrical
recruiting system supplying such prodigies—yet

L

every one who recollects Macready's managerial cam-
paigns at Covent Garden and Drury Lane will admit
that he brought his forces into the field in the highest
state of equipment and general efficiency. He had,
besides, the assistance of Talfourd, Bulwer, and other
first-class writers, whose plays shed honour and rained
guineas on his theatre, and were permanent additions
to the literature of the Drama.

In his retirement on his well-earned fortune,
honoured by the honoured, he devotes himself to the
calm pursuits of literature, and to schemes of educa-
tional philanthropy in his own neighbourhood; reap-
ing, I sincerely trust, a full harvest of those delights
of old age, so well described by the Roman orator,
the friend of Roscius, and the advocate of the poet
Archias. May he long enjoy them!

MR. BOOTH (LUCIUS JUNIUS!)—I first met Booth
(*père*) on occasion of Mr. Simpson's benefit, at the Park
Theatre, in 1844, previous to his (S.'s) going to England in search of novelties; for which purpose it was
hoped that this benefit would put him in funds. Poor
Simpson! he was always at low-water mark; and
the fortunes of the Park Theatre annually grew more
desperate. On this occasion a sort of *olla podrida* of
acting and singing, &c., was got up. I was requested,
and assented to play the second act of the "Lady of
Lyons," and two scenes from "Julius Cæsar" with
Booth, including the great quarrel-scene, in which
he was to be Cassius and I Brutus. Knowing Booth's
irregularity in business I did not go to the theatre for
rehearsal, as it was pretty certain to be a lost labour.
At night he did not arrive till very late; some time
after the hour at which our scene ought to have com-

menced ; consequently, I did not see him till he rushed on to the stage to me, after the flourish of trumpets, which announces the arrival of Cassius. On he came, with a brusqueness quite in character, confronted me, stopped, gave his usual long sniff—a sort of drawing-in of the breath through his nostrils, which was a habit with him—made a dead halt, glared, and—said nothing! I supposed at first, never having encountered him professionally, that it was his usual mode of commencing this scene; and that the long pause was merely the herald of the coming storm—a lull before the thunder crash. I waited patiently ; but not a sound, not a word! Booth still glared on me mysteriously, with blood-shot eye. At last, when I thought this pause threatened to

"stretch out to the crack of doom,"

I began to suspect the cause of the mystery ; and as gently as possible suggested that we had waited long enough, by giving him " the word " in an under tone :

" Most noble brother, you have done me wrong !"

This recalled him to himself, and broke his abstraction ; he gave another of his *sniffs*—said, *sotto voce*, to me, " Thank you !"—and coolly enough proceeded with his part—

" Most noble brother, you have done me wrong !"—

and so the scene went on.

Poor Simpson had but an indifferent house on this occasion, and there appeared little prospect of the Park Theatre *reviving* under his management. His *vis inertiæ* was impregnable ; nothing could rouse him to enterprise or activity, he kept on from year's end to year's end in the same old, beaten, worn-out track that led to the swamp of final stagnation. He was a man of good intentions, and honourable in business; but in those wretched days of theatrical prostration, a man was wanted with readiness in emergencies, an enterprising, active, indomitable spirit, to fight against bad times, and to renovate the whole system of theatrical management. Simpson, poor fellow, succumbed under a weight that was too great for him and died, oppressed by its responsibilities. I played but two engagements more at the Park under Simpson's management: one of a long duration in 1846, during which, under Mr. BARRY'S *stage*-management, were revived for me " Alexander the Great," " Antony and Cleopatra," " The Inconstant," and Ben Jonson's "Every Man in his Humour ," in which, for the time, I played the arduous character of " Kitely." The Park Theatre could boast at that time a really good company, especially for comedy, which we played with such good effect that old DE BEGNIS, the well-known *basso-buffo*, meeting me in Broadway, declared that comedies were then so well cast and played at the Park, that *" to see them was like sitting in Drury-lane Theatre in old times."*

My last engagement at the Park Theatre was the season after this with the KEANS, in their really great Shaksperian production of " King John " in November, 1846. The play was magnificently put upon the stage, under the care of Mr. Charles Kean, at a very great expense—I know not how many thousand dollars—in scenery, dresses, armour, swords, battle-axes, properties and appointments, which were all new, and arranged with historic and pictorial fidelity.

Well, what was the result of all this preparation and outlay? The piece ran, with some difficulty, to moderate houses, the best of which did not reach £160, for three weeks; and then, to Mr. Kean's great mortification and disgust, was superseded by the VIENNOISE CHILDREN (*Enfans terribles!* in Kean's eyes), who crammed the house to suffocation for the following month!

So much for Great Shaksperian Revivals! WILLIS thus spoke of it in the *Home Journal*, after giving an elaborate sketch of the historical features of the play:—

The *mise en scene* is perfect; perfect in costume, in scenery, in decorations, in banners, in arms, in *tout ensemble:* and the actors are all perfect in their parts. Miss Denny's *Arthur* is a charming performance; Mrs. Kean's *Constance* is a magnificent conception; Mr. Kean's *John* is highly characteristic of the dark and gloomy tyrant; and G. Vandenhoff's *Faulconbridge* is as dashing, manly, and spirited a representation of the gallant bastard as we can conceive. We do not wish it, *in any thing,* other than it is; it is bold, humorous, intense, and, above all, *natural:* were he to do *less,* he would not be *up to the mark;* were he to do *more,* it would be *overdone:* "*omne tulit punctum,*" and he well deserved the hearty applause which he received. Dyott's *Hubert* was respectable; and Mr. Barry's *King was* a king. All did well; in fact, the play is the most perfect thing ever put on the Park stage.

This was my last engagement at the Park Theatre. In 1848, on Simpson's death, it fell into Hamblin's hands, who opened it with a Bowery Company (!); and after struggling through part of a very bad season—worse even, than poor Simpson ever had known—it was burnt on the night of 16th Dec., 1848. So fell the Park Theatre, the OLD DRURY of

America ; and with it fell the Legitimate Drama in
New York. When will it rise again ?

The BROADWAY THEATRE, erected in 1847, was
supposed to have succeeded to the honours of the Park;
and was opened with the express intention of putting
an end to the *starring system*. I was engaged, and
played there a portion of its first season ; but, finding
that the scheme on which it was avowedly to be carried
on was utterly abandoned, and that not only was the
starring system revived, but that *stars* were attempted
to be made out of *rushlights*, I took the first opportunity of emancipating myself from the fetters of my
engagement, the spirit of which had been violated.
In point of fact, the date for which I was engaged
had actually expired ; so that, though my *evasion*
from the theatre was sudden, it was perfectly legal—
my contract being at an end by lapse of time.

Mr. J. R. ANDERSON played a very successful—I
mean, profitable—engagement at this theatre, the first
season of its existence : he drew well. I played Iago
to his Othello, and Fulvius to his Gisippus ; and the
junction of our forces brought great houses.

Anderson and I were of old acquaintance. We had
played together at Covent Garden Theatre in the season of 1839. I took his place there in 1841-2, on his
joining Mr. Macready, at Drury Lane ; and we had
also played together as *stars* at the Liverpool and
Manchester Theatres Royal. He is a good, frank,
manly fellow, as a man, and an excellent dashing
actor. His style, it is true, was formed too exclusively in the Macready school, and bore sometimes
too evident traces of the "master ; " but he has a fine
voice, a gallant bearing, and great knowledge of, and

experience in all the practice and details of the stage: for he has been on it since he was a boy, has played and pushed his way up through all the gradations of his profession, and merits great credit for the position which his own exertions have attained.

Mr. Macready introduced him to the London Stage in 1837, I think at Covent Garden Theatre, in the part of Florizel, in Shakspere's " Winter's Tale." He at once made a favourable impression; every year improved his position. His performance of Huon (Love), at Covent Garden, in 1839, and of Fulvius (Gisippus), in 1842, at Drury Lane (original parts), did him great service with the public. He became lessee and manager of Drury Lane Theatre in 1849-50 : a perilous experiment ! in which, if he failed, it was perhaps more owing to the decline of the public taste for theatrical performances than to any want of tact or exertion of his own. During his management of that immense concern, ' Azael the Prodigal," and " Ingomar," were his most successful productions: he was the original hero in each In this city he was at one time a sure card. His first appearance at the Park Theatre did not attract great attention; but his second and subsequent engagements were greatly profitable, and for a time arrested the backward race of that falling house. He has visited the States many times ; but, latterly, he has not been peculiarly fortunate in this city, where he played in 1852, at the Metropolitan Theatre. A temporary injury to his voice, which he has now quite recovered, was, perhaps, one cause of this waning attraction; or, his style may have palled on the public ear by familiarity; for there is no accounting for the fickleness of popular taste ; the

idol of to-day may be the martyr of to-morrow ;—or
worse, even, as the glorious, the neglected and broken
toy.   Anderson is a dashing representative of some of
the heavier comedy parts, requiring an admixture of
tragic power,—the *mixed* drama, as it may be called :
his " King of the Commons," for example, is by far
the best personation of the part that has been seen in
this country.   He had, of course, had the advantage
of seeing Mr. Macready in the character, and of avail-
ing himself of that great tactician's arrangement of
the scene and business of the play ; but I am inclined
to believe that what Anderson's performances of this
agreeable and taking part may have lacked in finish,
as compared with his original, it gained in fire,
fervour, and gallant bearing.   These are the characteristics of Mr. Anderson's style ; and, my opinion is,
that if he had trusted to them, and to his natural
impulses, more than to his reverence for Macready's
fame, he would have attained a higher and more
assured rank among the artists of the day.   He will,
I trust, receive these remarks in the spirit in which
they are made—that of friendly candour and honest
good-will.

———

SOPHOCLES' ANTIGONE—(PALMO'S OPERA HOUSE), 1845.

Among these miscellaneous leaves, it may not be
out of place to state that I was engaged for a fortnight at Palmo's Opera House (afterwards Burton's),
in Chambers-street, to produce the English version of
Sophocles' ANTIGONE, with Mendelssohn's music, in
the spring of 1845. I did my best with the resources
that were at my command ; got a representation of

the Old Greek Stage, with its λυχειον and ϑυμελη, and Altar to Bacchus, built on the stage proper; as good a company, and as efficient a CHORUS were collected as could be found: Mr. GEO. LODER directed the orchestra and the musical arrangements, which were fair; Miss CLARENDON's youth and classic features harmonized well with the *personnel* of Antigone ; I did my best with the part of Creon ; and we had the gratification of getting through the first night's performance of this novel and difficult style of play — an upraising of " the buried majesty of" SOPHOCLES— without a single trip or *faux pas.*

Our efforts were rewarded by great applause, the approval and cordially-expressed thanks of artists and scholars, but with very indifferent houses ! We repeated this *classic disentombment* twelve successive nights, and then " quietly inurned" the mighty Greek to sleep in undisturbed and unprofaned repose. It was truly a beautiful and highly interesting tragedy, aided by grand music. In Berlin and London it drew crowded audiences ; in New York it never paid its expenses.

Our chorus, which amounted to about forty, representing sages of Creon's Court, presented a very grotesque appearance; and one that, at first sight, nearly disturbed my gravity on the first night. OLD ALLEN had made the wigs and beards for these Grecian sages out of long white and grey *goat's hair ;* and, as the whole set were, I presume, contracted for, no great artistic care had been expended upon them. Now, Mendelssohn's music was very difficult ; and, on the last rehearsal, Mr. Loder found that his chorus, principally German, could get very well through their

L 5

work, if they could have the *score* before them, not
otherwise. It was therefore arranged that the music
should stand open before them : they themselves were
to be ranged close to the footlights on the stage, between the second or *raised* stage (the stage of the
Greek theatre) and the actual orchestra. Now, some
of these gentlemen being short-sighted, had, in order
to be able to read their score distinctly, put on their
spectacles; and, I ask you to fancy my horror,
mingled with a dreadful *envie de rire*, when I entered,
at seeing a parcel of goat-headed, goat-bearded old
fellows, in Grecian robes, with spectacles on nose,
confronting me, within the proscenium, opening wide
their mouths, and baa-a-ing at me, as it were, with
all their might ! They looked like an assemblage of
the ghosts of defunct Welsh bards, summoned to
their goat-covered hills by the wand of Merlin ; and
the spectacles might have been mistaken by a heated
fancy for the glaring of their spectral eyes !

Luckily, their backs were to the audience; the
actors alone were fully conscious of the awful *travestie*.

Mrs. C. N. Sinclair. (late Mrs. Forrest.)—In
1852 I played at what was then called Brougham's
Lyceum, now Wallack's Theatre—(there is great
merit in calling things by their right names !)—with
Mrs. C. N. Sinclair, who had just resumed her
paternal name in consequence of her divorce from her
husband, the great American tragedian. Trial by
jury is a great *Alfred*-ian institution ; " the palladium
of our liberties," and all that ; but, as my Uncle
Toby says, " it is not till the great and general review

of us all, corporal, the day of judgment, that it will be known" *what verdicts will stand and what will not!*

I was an utter stranger to Mrs. Forrest till I received, some time in 1851, a message, through the late GRANBY CALCRAFT, requesting me to call on her with a view of advising her as to her capabilities for the stage. I did so. I gave her my candid opinion that it was late in life for her to take such a step ; although she had qualities which, had they been cultivated and improved in earlier youth, might and would have led her to distinction. She, however, represented that she would soon, in all probability, have to depend on her talents for the stage, whatever they might be, for her support ; and that she wished me to give her instructions in three or four parts, to enable her to appear with some success.

I did not decide that evening, but called on her, by appointment, the following day; heard her read some passages of poetry to me, and consented to act as her instructor. I advised her immediately to study Lady Teazle, Beatrice, Margaret Elmore, Pauline, and Mabel, in the " Patrician's Daughter ;" and it was understood that, as she had no present means of payment, I was, on condition of getting her " up " in these and other parts, and playing the opposite part to her on her enagements, to receive half of the profits on our joint performances. I state this candidly, because there has been a great deal of misconception and misrepresentation about the matter. It stood simply thus: Mrs. Forrest wished to go on the stage ; she needed preparation ; she could not pay for it ; but it was probable that public curiosity would render her

engagements highly profitable; and, in consideration
of my instructions, and also of my performing with
her, I was to be allowed an equal share of the profits
which her temporary and factitious attraction would
secure. I hope that is clearly stated.

Accordingly, I instructed her in the delivery, the
action, the business, and the whole details of these
several parts; to which Parthenia, in " Ignomar,"
was added, on my obtaining the manuscript copy—
the first that had come to this country—from the
translator, Mrs. Lovell, in England. In opening,
after her divorce, in January, 1852, in Lady Teazle,
she acted entirely under my advice, contrary to the
suggestions of other parties, and even to her own
vow; other characters were proposed for her *début*.
I was confined to my room, at the Clarendon Hotel,
by severe illness, at the time, and she came up to see
me before she made her final determination. I
strongly insisted on Lady Teazle as *the* one of all
others in which her appearance, style, and general
capabilities would make the best impression; and
exacted a promise from her, before leaving me, that
no representation or persuasion of other parties should
induce her to deviate from this choice. She adhered
to Lady Teazle; and her great success in it fully
justified my selection. It was the most *artistic* performance she ever achieved: the one in which her
personal requisites and her education stood her in the
best stead. She never played any other part as
easily, as unaffectedly, or with as much success with
the public.

During her first fortnight I was not sufficiently
recovered to perform with her; but, in her third

week, I joined her, commencing with the " Lady of Lyons."

I give the receipts of the first eight nights of our joint performance. The terms were to share, after £20 ; that is, to share with the manager, he first deducting for himself twenty pounds.

The receipts of eight nights were—

1852, Feb. 16 to 23 inclusive, " Lady of Lyons." } Nearly £180 each.
  „   Feb. 24   .   .   .   " Love's Sacrifice." }

Mrs. Sinclair was then taken ill, and did not resume her performances till the 1st of March.   .

On the 12th of March we were engaged to give a reading, jointly, at the Tripler Hall (now the Metropolitan Theatre), for the sum of £60, which we shared equally. At this reading I had the honour to be *encored* in the recitation of " Young Lochinvar."

The course I adopted was, to settle in full with her on every engagement ; stating the account of each night's receipts, paying her the amount, and taking her signature to the account and acknowledgment for her share of the proceeds, at the foot of such account, in my book. And I have her signature and discharge to every such account of every engagement which we ever played together. .

The summary of those engagements up to May 26, inclusive, produced the sum of £914 for each.

To enable her to go to England, for the purpose of visiting her father (since deceased), I advanced her—besides having paid her the above half share, in full—over £500 ; which, with other sums advanced to her on her return, left her in my debt, for money lent, to the amount of over £560, on her going to California.

From California she remitted me to London, in 1853, on account, a draft on Peabody for £200 sterling, which leaves a balance due to me, at this day, of nearly £360, exclusive of interest, for money lent to her.

And this was the result of my engagements with Mrs. Sinclair; that I lost my time and my money, both, instead of having " put money in my purse," as has been generally believed. My sole motive for publishing the above statement is to show the true state of an affair which has been much misrepresented. It is an additional confirmation of the old proverb—

" All that glitters is not gold."

XV.

ILL health compelled me, in January, 1853, to
desist from professional exertion ; and, as change of
air was recommended me, I quittted new York for
Europe by the steamer Arabia, and arrived at Liverpool on the 6th February, considerably benefited by
the sea voyage.

Almost immediately on my arrival, Mr. Copeland,
manager of the two theatres there, stated to me his
desire to produce Shakspere's historical play of Henry
V. He had, he said, already prepared scenery and
appointments for the piece, which he intended to produce with great care, and at a considerable expense ;
and he invited me to play the gallant Henry. Finding that he did not desire to bring it out for some
weeks to come, I consented to the terms he proposed
to me for five weeks, commencing on Easter Monday
following.

Mr. Copeland asked me " how I would like to
be announced" in the advertisements. Whether I

would wish to be styled the "*eminent* tragedian," or
the "*distinguished* tragedian," or the "*classical* tragedian," or the "*highly popular* tragedian," or
the "*Shaksperian* tragedian;" in fine, what terms
of addition and self-glorification *(more histritonum)*
I wished tacked on to my name. I said, "*None;*
simply announce that Mr. G. Vandenhoff will make
his first appearance in Hamlet ; and let the audience
find out what *degree* I am entitled to, in the *Dramatic
College.*" As old Tobias says, "he was pleased with
my answer."

This self-labelling is very absurd. In champagnes,
we find that the best wine has the plainest and most
unpretending label. A very highly-embellished de-
vice on the bottle always suggests the idea of a domestic article, with a strong suspicion of the Jersey-
apple about it—excellent for cider, but a swindle in
champagne !

Accordingly, having quite re-established my health
in the interval, I commenced at Liverpool with Hamlet, to a densely-crowded house, on Monday, 28th
March, 1853, being my first appearance there since
my departure for the United States, in '42. I played
during the week Shylock, for the first time ; Claude,
in the "Lady of Lyons," twice ; and repeated Hamlet, and played the Stranger, also, twice. The week's
business produced great receipts.

The Monday following (4th April) I appeared,
for the first time, as Henry V. ; which was put upon
the stage by Mr. Copeland with great care and attention to scenery, costume, and appointments. The
play ran twenty-three successive nights to excellent
houses : though, I believe, they scarcely paid for

the extraordinary expenses incurred by Mr. Copeland
in his production of the piece—another proof that
Shaksperian Revivals, when got up with new and appropriate scenery and appointments, never remunerate the management. It was so, I have shown in
these leaves, at the Park Theatre, in the case of King
John, in 1846 : and Mr. C. Kean, in his valedictory
address at the Princess's Theatre, London, has borne
strong testimony to the general truth of the fact, by
declaring that it was only *his own resources* that enabled him to gratify the pride and ambition he felt in
producing Shakspere's dramas with that remarkable
splendour and pictorial effect by which his administra-
tion has distinguished himself in theatrical annals. There
is another drawback to these Shaksperian spectacles,
and one very serious and prejudicial to the moral and
intellectual effect of the drama itself.   I mean this :
that the spirit and interest of the action is lost in the
pictorial display; the text becomes of secondary importance to the audience ; the eye of the spectator is
entirely engrossed with the scenic effect, and pays
little attention to the actor,

"thinking his prattle to be tedious,"

except as far as he serves as *cicerone* to the *raree show*,
and becomes, as it were, a mere train-bearer to the
glories of the scene-painter and costumier. This I take
to be a powerful objection to the overlaying Shakspere's
drama with spectacular colouring and profuseness of
pictorial illustration ; that it is fatal to the interest of
the play itself, and utterly distractive of the attention
from the actor and the text. I have always seen Hamlet, Othello, Macbeth, and other of the greatest trage-

dies, produce the most intense effect when the scenic illustrations and costumes have been appropriate and reasonably correct, without being elaborately minute or extravagantly gorgeous. It is ruinous to the poet to make him stand as the mere *letter-press* to the *tableaux*. If *spectacle* is to be the main feature of our theatres—if the public taste has become so pampered by indulgence, that it can only be tempted by show and glare, then, I say, give it *spectacle, pure et simple ;* let the action and the dialogue be mere canvas-lines and clothes-pegs, and let them be chosen and arranged as such; but do not let us degrade the verse of him to whom Nature gave the " golden keys"

> " That can unlock the gates of joy,
>   Of horror, woe, and thrilling fears,
>   Or ope the sacred source of sympathetic tears,"—

do not let us make a *pack-horse* of *his* verse, to carry the scene-painter, the costumier, and the carpenter in triumph to the *gods !*

Pardon this little diversion, reader ; the subject hurried me away.

A little incident happened to me during this engagement at Liverpool that amused and pleased me. Desiring to get an early dinner in a hurry, I walked into a well-known establishment, called the "Crooked-billet ;" and, finding the large dining-room full, I entered a little side-room, where I found a plainly-dressed country tradesman, as he appeared, waiting for his dinner. I ordered mine ; and, after a few minutes, he said to the girl who waited—in a tolerably strong Lancashire accent—" Come, come, lass ; make haste ! time's munney !" (money). Then, turning to me, he added, " Isn't it, sir ?" Now it was the breathing-time of day with me, and I answered, " To you it may be : I'm sorry to say it is not so with me."

" Ha !" said he, after taking my measure with his eye, " I dare say you don't *trubble* yourself wi' busi-ness mooch."

" Why ?" I answered ; "*what* would you take me to be ?"

" Oh," said he, " I should take you to be aboov all business ; not to need it, I mean."

To give him a surprise, and see how he would take it, I replied : " How wrong you are ! I am an actor !"

" Are you ?" said he ; " then" (slapping his hand on his thigh) " I can tell you *who* you are. You are George Vandenhoff."

" How do you know ?"

" By the voice. I saw you play Henry the Fifth t'other night, and mightily pleased I was."

" Well," said I, " are you surprised to find that I'm an actor, instead of a man of fortune, which you took me for ?"

" Not a bit," he answered ; " you might as well be one as t'other ; and," he added, " I don't know that any one can do more than *look* like a gentleman, and *behave* like one, whether he has a fortune or not."

Pretty good, I thought, for a country tradesman.

After taking my benefit at Liverpool, and remain-ing for a week, I engaged immediately at the Man-chester Theatre Royal for four weeks ; one of which I played alone, and three in conjunction with HELEN FAUCIT. I have elsewhere described this charming actress, and will only say here, that it was the first

occasion of my meeting her professionally. We played
the usual business, but not to great houses ; for Miss
Faucit's attraction had begun to decline. I had the good
fortune to please the public here mightily : of which
fact they gave me, nightly, the amplest demonstration,
particularly in Jacques, Charles Surface, Hamlet, and
Rover in " Wild Oats." In all of these parts the applause was of that hearty determined kind, by which
a Manchester audience testifies its perfect satisfaction.
The management of the theatre proposed to me, before the end of my first week, a long engagement for
the next season.

Of course, after being so long absent from the
English stage, it was gratifying to me to find myself
so well, I may say so enthusiastically, received on my
return.

At the close of this engagement, not having entirely recovered my strength, I deliberately gave myself a holiday, bought a sweet little chestnut mare,
and indulged myself with a delightful equestrian excursion into North Wales ; starting from Manchester
on the 15th June, and riding *viâ* Chester, Bangor,
Beaumaris, Conway, Rhyl, Denbigh, Ruthin, Llan-
gollen, Oswestry, Shrewsbury, Birmingham, Kenil-
worth, Warwick, Stratford-on-Avon, Leamington,
Woodstock, Oxford ; and hence through Henley-on-
Thames, and Maidenhead, to London ; where I
arrived 10th July, having ridden 450 odd miles—a
most agreeable excursion. My little mare, a perfect
beauty, Arabian in form and style, and not more than
fourteen hands high, did her work admirably ; some-

times I rode her forty, sometimes even fifty miles a day; she never refused a feed, and entered London brisk and well, stopping a day or two at agreeable places, and aways finding capital inns, good beds, and excellent fare on the road; and my expenses, not exceeding, horse-keep included, an average of fourteen shillings and sixpence sterling per day. Of course I did not feed on turtle-soup, or drink champagne; but contented myself with a good, plain dinner from one excellent joint, beef or mutton, and a glass of sound, well-brewed ale from malt and hops, which you can get anywhere and everywhere in England and Wales.

I have made similar excursions in America, but not with the same pleasure as in Europe. In summer the heat is too oppressive there, and horse and rider suffer too much from it: besides, at the small taverns on the road you are not always certain of a dinner, unless you arrive at or about the gong-hour; nor are the roads in such fine order as those of England, which is the country of all others for a horseback trip, from the temperance of the climate, the excellence of the beautiful high-roads, the comfort of the little inns, the goodness and cheapness of the fare for man and beast, and the continued succession of villages between the large towns and cities, so that the traveller can never be at a loss for a good stopping place and civil treatment. These are two things, mind you, which one does not always find here, especially when one lights on any of those sort of amateur hosts, " who don't keep tavern, but take folks in "— in more senses than one—who make it a favour to give you very poor fare, a horrid, collapsing, mockery of a feather bed in the middle of summer, a "drefful bad" breakfast, and charge you hotel prices into the bargain !

I came upon such a fellow once, a Capt. T—— (of course he was a captain !), in a little village about eleven miles from Hartford, Conn., who would only allow me just so much straw for my horse's bed— about enough to litter a good-sized dog—and would feed him just as he pleased ; a regular ignorant, insolent, old bully : I let him know, however, that when I stopped at a tavern, whether it was called so or no, I was in the habit of having my way in such matters; and, by dint of coolness, and a determined standing on my rights, I brought his captainship to reason, and the next morning extorted from him a kind of apology, on the plea that " he didn't know what sort of a person I was the night before" (didn't know whether I would stand his insolence or not), "if he'd 'a knowed as I was a gentleman," &c. But I gave the old fellow a lesson on civility to " folks " in general, and a few words on the duty of a tavern-keeper, amateur or other, that I rather think he remembers.

———

On my arrival in London I found at my father's a note from Mr. Buckstone, the manager of the Haymarket Theatre, proposing to me an engagement as leading actor of that theatre, for the season to commence on the following October : and, after an interview with him, the terms of our agreement were settled. In deciding on my opening part, Mr. Buckstone was very much opposed to " Hamlet," or any other Shaksperian character, "for," said he, "it's no matter if you could play it as well as John Kemble, a Shaksperian play keeps money out of the house!" Here was a prospect in a first-class metropolitan theatre! I, however, adhered to my point, and "Hamlet" was finally decided on for the 25th October following. The theatre was to re-open on the 24th, and on the second night I was to make my re-appearance on the London stage, after an absence of eleven years.

There was, at this time, performing at the St. James' Theatre, a company of German *spillers* (players), with the somewhat celebrated EMILE DEVRIENT at their head. Observing "Hamlet" announced one night, I went, with my father, to witness the performance. It was SCHILLER's version that was given; and it was so faithful to the Shaksperian text, line for line, that there was difficulty in following it. Devrient's rendering of "Hamlet" was not without merit; though in the first act he was unnecessarily violent, and even grotesque in attitude and gesture. In the subsequent acts he improved wonderfully, mellowing, and growing into the character, and touching the assumed madness of "Hamlet" with great nicety of discrimination. The great drawback to his performance was a lack of dignity and grace; there was nothing of the *Prince* about him; and one shocking absurdity that he allowed himself to be guilty of would have gone far to destroy the effect of a much greater performance. It is so ludicrous as to be worth mentioning; though it was only carrying out a ridiculous custom to the extreme of inconsistency.

When, in obedience to the silent summons of the *Ghost,* who

> " wafts him to a more removèd ground
> As if it some impartment did desire
> To him alone,"

Hamlet made his *exit* with the words, in German,

> " Go on, I ll follow thee,"

there was some applause from the audience ; not very enthusiastic, but *some* applause. On which the German actor, who had scarcely passed the *wing* (side scene), immediately returned, breaking off for the moment from his obedience to the Ghost : and, abandoning his identification with Hamlet, advanced to the foot-lights, and bowed three times to the audience, in acknowledgment of their favour ! Could any thing be more absurd ? more fatal to the gravity of the situation ! I expected the Ghost to " hark back," too, but he was a *discreet,* as well as

> " an *honest* ghost,"

and did not return to the glimpses of the *foot-lights* to express his sense of terrestrial and mundane compliments. This was, unintentionally, the greatest practical satire on the *calling* system that I ever witnessed ; and made me blush for the servility as well as laugh at the absurdity of the *spiller* who was guilty of it. Such a violation of propriety, in obsequious flattery of the public, is " villanous, and shows a pitiful ambition in the fool who uses it !"

The interval between this time and October, when I was to make my *éntree* at the Haymarket Theatre,

I filled up by an excursion, on horseback, to St. Leonards, a delightful watering-place on the south coast of England, which I recommend to any health-seekers from this country who desire fine air and the best of sea-bathing. There is, too, a capital hotel there, which has been patronised by royal personages (I know this is always a recommendation to my *republican* fellow-citizens), and by the aristocracy in general ; I mean the Royal Victoria Hotel, admirably situated and capitally conducted.

From St. Leonards I rode to Brighton, the fashionable watering-place, as crowded as London, in the season, and where there is, perhaps, the best hotel in the world, the Bedford ; thence to Arundel, a pretty little town, with Arundel Castle on its skirt ; thence to Portsmouth, the most strongly fortified place on the south coast ; and thence to Southampton. From Southampton I crossed over, with my horse, to Cowes (Isle of Wight); thence, passing the Queen's residence, Osborne, I rode to the Sandrock Hotel, fifteen miles distant, near Niton, five miles from Ventnor, on the south of the island, and arrived wet to the skin, having ridden the last ten miles in a drenching rain ; but a good bed, dry clothes (my portmanteau, which, in these equestrian trips, I always send on ahead by rail, had arrived before me), and a good dinner, with a bottle of nearly the best claret I ever tasted, soon set me to rights.

When I inquired of Mrs. Kent, the landlady of Sandrock Hotel, which, by the bye, is one of the most picturesque and, at the same time, most comfortable little country inns in England—a rustic, cottage-looking house, backed by the high cliff under which it seems

M

to shelter, with a woodbine-covered porch, and a
sloping lawn, green as an emerald, bordered with
flower-beds, and looking out on the English channel—
when I inquired of the landlady how she happened
to have so fine a bottle of claret (Lafitte, which must
have been at least fifteen or twenty years old), she
told me it was laid in by her late husband, on the
occasion of the Princess Victoria (the present Queen)
and her mother, the Duchess of Kent, and *suite*, stopping
at this house, on their *tour* through the Isle of Wight,
about fifteen or more years before ; which sufficiently
accounted for the exquisite flavour thereof. It was
charged in the bill the reasonable price of nine shillings sterling. It could not be bought in this country
under £1. 1s. a bottle, IF AT ALL.

This trip to the Isle of Wight is one that I also
recommend to my friends who visit England. Cross
over from Southampton to Cowes ; thence by a carriage to Newport, four or five miles ; visit Carrisbrook
Castle ; thence to Sandrock Hotel, stay there a day
rambling about ; visit Black Gang Chine, a wild and
picturesque ravine on the sea-side ; the next day go
in a carriage to the Needles ; return *via* Sandrock
Hotel, dine there, and go on in the evening to Ventnor,
on the south side of the island, where the climate is
as balmy as the south of France, and the sea bathing
excellent. The whole excursion need not occupy
more than four days, and is truly delightful.

It is a delicious drive from the Sandrock Hotel to
Ventnor ; the nearest resemblance to which in this
country is a ride I am very fond of taking, from the
Weehawken Ferry, on the Jersey side of the Hudson,
up to Fort Lee. But the Isle of Wight is wonder-

fully picturesque and highly cultivated ; the climate
is balmy, but temperate ; and it is the most attractive
spot in England to indulge in the *dolce far niente.*

At the Sandrock Hotel I met, I think, the finest
woman I ever saw in my life. Miss Anne Costello
was her name, by inheritance or adoption, I know
not which ; but at that particular time she was
travelling under the highly romantic name of Mrs.
Brown, her *compagnon de voyage* being a gentleman
who temporarily sported that distinguished and *un-
identifiable* cognomen. She was, I discovered, one of
that numerous class of *femmes entretenues* in England,
so remarkable for their magnificent and voluptuous
beauty. She was above the middle size, splendidly
proportioned, with brilliant dark eyes, a brunette
complexion, rose-tinged on the cheek, luxuriant dark
brown hair, superb shoulders and bust, with the
roundest and finest waist I ever saw. She was a
grand Venus! I found she was possessed with an
ardent ambition for the stage, and was desirous of
placing herself under my tuition. I, however, declined the dangerous honour, and the stage has one
bewitching sin the less upon it.

"Of such stuff our dreams are made ;"

from which the waking is so terrible. Her protector
was a young man not over twenty-five years of age ;
not a fellow of much mark or likelihood, but he was
evidently given up, body and soul, to the influence of
her all-conquering beauty, and the result would probably be his ruin ! It was a miniature edition of
Antony and Cleopatra—friends, family, reputation,

M 2

fortune, were nought to him ; her smile was worth
them all ; and

> " Her beck might from the bidding of the gods
>   Command him."

Old Damas says well :—

" O ! woman, woman, thou art the author of such a book of
follies in a man, that it would need the tears of all the angels to wash
the record out !"

XVI.

In my note-book of the 25th October, 1853, I find
this memorandum :—

" Going to reappear in London after eleven years' absence, without knowing a single person connected with the London *press*
except Douglas Jerrold. By ' not knowing,' I mean not knowing
so much as to say, ' How d'ye do ?' to, nor have I taken steps of
any kind to secure a favourable judgment. Let us see the result."

On the 24th October Mr. Buckstone reopened the
Haymarket Theatre, newly decorated and embellished,
with the comedy of " A Cure for Love," and " The
Beggar's Opera ;" and on the following night I made
my *entrée* in the character of Hamlet with only one
rehearsal, and with a company whose *forte* was decidedly not tragedy.   Indeed, I do not remember ever
to have seen, at any respectable theatre, so weak a

cast of the play as ours was in many respects. There was no efficient "heavy lady" in the company—a cheering circumstance to start with! The Queen was, consequently, undertaken—with great kindness and courage—by a young lady of fine figure, and considerable personal attractions, whose appropriate and accustomed province was genteel comedy, gay widows in farces, and sprightly *intrigantes* generally—not exactly the wood from which Queens in "Hamlet" are made! I might, indeed, have well exclaimed,

> "No more like my *mother*
> Than I to Hercules!"

Horatio was very weak; being confided to a gentleman who had never before acted in the play, nor, as he candidly confessed, had ever seen it acted! His regular business was foplings in comedy and farces; his general style was of the lightest and flimsiest substance; consequently, Horatio was a dead weight on him. The Ghost, fortunately, was steady, careful, and respectable; Mr. Howe (the Quaker, as he was called, from his family having, I believe, belonged to the Society of Friends; and he is the only instance that I know of, of a Quaker's having taken to the stage) was never anything less in the multiplicity of characters assigned to him. The strength of the cast lay in the Polonius of Mr. Chippendale—who was also stage-manager—the Grave Digger of Mr. Compton, and the Ophelia of Miss Louisa Howard. The Laertes was a novice, and more unskilful even than the Laertes-es usually are, which is saying much, in the use of the foil. This, considering that the fencing-match in the fifth act is a main feature, and that on its execution, well or ill, depends, in great measure, the successful or unsuccessful winding-up of the play, was a particularly encouraging prospect for me! Luckily, all, even the fencing-bout, passed off without any glaring mishap; and the Queen, however deficient in weight, was letter-perfect in text, and scrupulously exact in the business of the scene; as, indeed, Mrs. Buckingham always was. I was warmly received and liberally applauded, though it was my first appearance at the Haymarket Theatre, and that audience is, proverbially, very self-controlling in its outward display of approbation.

Mr. Buckstone, the manager, came and congratulated me on my success at the end of the third act, as did the performers generally; and, a friend, H. Holl —a kind, good-natured fellow as ever breathed, and whom every one likes—came round from the front, to confirm by his report, in detail, the verdict which the audience had rendered by their applause. My father, as Holl informed me, and, as I had myself observed, was one of the auditory; deeply attentive, Holl said, silent, abstracted, wholly *in* the play; he, too, was content with me, and earnest in his approbation—as Holl reported.

So, of course, I went on to my fifth act with renewed spirits. Even the fencing-bout went off tolerably well, and I received a thundering call at the fall of the curtain.

Mr. Buckstone was pleased to make the following announcement in the bills and advertisements of the day:—

"Mr. George Vandenhoff having, on his first appearance, created a sensation equal to that made by any tragedian of the day, will repeat the character of Hamlet on Thursday and Monday next;"

and the *Times*, and the press generally, upheld the manager's judgment.

The following is the London *Morning Post's* notice, 26th October, 1853 :—

HAYMARKET THEATRE.—DEBUT OF MR. GEORGE VANDENHOFF.— If Mr. Vandenhoff has not gained fame and money from our trans‑atlantic brethren, he has certainly acquired experience and improve‑ment in their land, and to such an extent as to make us doubt his identity with the gentleman who some years since performed at Covent Garden Theatre under the management of Madame Vestris.

We have no hesitation in declaring Mr. Vandenhoff's Hamlet to be not only by many degrees the best at present on the stage, but also better than any that has been seen since the days of John Kemble. What he may make of other Shaksperian characters, requiring greater energy, passion, physical power and melo‑dramatic excitement, we are not prepared to say ; but of this we are sure, that his picture of the contemplative, philosophical, ele‑gant Prince of Denmark, who is only goaded into action by a supernatural visitation, and the pressure of terrible and extraor‑dinary circumstances, could not possibly be surpassed. In this age of strong accents and exaggeration, especially in theatrical matters, it is truly refreshing to meet with an actor who never " o'ersteps the modesty of nature"—who moves with gentleman‑like ease and grace upon the stage, and speaks the language of Shakspere with just emphasis and purity. Such is Mr. George Vandenhoff; but his merits do not stop here, for he is not merely a correct performer, but a great one. He not only satisfies us, but he delights us. First, by his really beautiful level speaking, which is truly " nature to advantage dressed." This, at once, honourably distinguishes him from all contemporary tragedians, not one of whom can make any effect except in passages of great excitement, where the delineation of strong passions may justify a spasmodic style of expression. Secondly, he charms us by the exquisite delicacy he imparts to his dramatic picture, and the masterly finish of its details : thirdly, by the sympathetic glow of feeling emanating from the heart—the genial, steadily‑burning poetic fire which everywhere vivifies his conceptions, and warms by its electric power the coldest of his auditors into admiration. Add to these, the influence of a very agreeable voice, a commanding figure, most graceful gestures, and an expressive countenance, and a fair idea may be formed of the very remarkable qualities of Mr. Vandenhoff, as exhibited on this occasion. We have preferred giving a general sketch of the *débutant's* powers to selecting special portions of his performance for praise. Where all was so evenly good, where the Horation precept

"Denique sit quod vis simplex duntaxat et unum."

was so finely exemplified, such a course would be scarcely just.

Mr. Vandenhoff was warmly applauded throughout, and called for with enthusiasm at the fall of the curtain.

The following is the criticism of the *Sunday Times*, Oct. 30:—

MR. G. VANDENHOFF'S HAMLET.—Mr. George Vandenhoff, the son of the celebrated tragedian, who some years since made his metropolitan *début* at Covent Garden, during the Vestris management, in the character of Leon, in *Rule a Wife and Have a Wife*, appeared on the Haymarket boards, for the first time, on Tuesday evening, after a long absence in the United States, where he has gathered hisrionic laurels in abundance. The character selected for his second entrance to the English stage was Hamlet, for which nature seems to have especially fitted him by bestowing upon him a graceful and commanding figure, fine expressive features, an intellectual head, a penetrating eye, and a voice capable of being modulated according to the passion or emotion to be delineated. The great merit of Mr. Vandenhoff in the character is the skilful manner in which he unfolds it without destroying its delicate texture. All his care seems to be to render Hamlet such as Shakspere certainly intended—gentle, contemplative, and philosophic, with a disposition naturally warm and generous, stimulated by a solemn supernatural revelation to an act of cruel vengeance, from which his soul recoils. It is the mind, and not the passions of Hamlet, that is excited ; he can moralize and weigh to the minutest grain questions of a present and future state, and can speculate with philosophic exactness upon the justness and morality of his terrible mission. No man whose passions were highly wrought upon could so abstract his reasoning faculties. Taking this view of the character, we entirely agree with Mr. Vandenhoff in what may be termed the subdued and intellectual reading he gave of it. The total absence of all clap-trap or trickery, either in voice or action, and the

M 5

consummate art with which, by the judicious reading of the part, he developed all its beauties, cannot be too highly commended. We admit that to ears accustomed—we will not say attuned—to the violence of some performers, or to exaggerated and stagey points—as far removed from dramatic truth as they are from nature—the reflective and poetic style of Mr. George Vandenhoff may appear insipid. We should as soon expect a confirmed brandy-drinker to relish the mild but generous warmth of pure claret. That Mr. G. Vandenhoff possesses power, as well as tenderness and pathos, we need but refer to his scene with the Queen in the closet, the play-scene, and his delivery of the passionate soliloquy, "O, what a rogue and peasant slave am I !" His advice to the players was an admirable combination of the familiar with the didactic style. Altogether, we do not remember any Hamlet of late years with whom we were so well pleased.

The *Illustrated London News* thus wrote :—

HAYMARKET THEATRE.— On Tuesday *Hamlet* was performed for the purpose of testing the claims of Mr. George Vandenhoff to the tragic lead of the company, and the trial was perfectly satisfactory. During the Vestris management of Covent Garden, Mr. Vandenhoff gave promise of perhaps more power than he now evinces, but was crude in style ; when he left us altogether for America, where by practice he has become evidently a finished artist. His *Hamlet* is certainly an elegant, and, in some situations, a highly wrought piece of acting. His success was incontrovertible ; and an honourable future awaits his exertions.

Finally, the *Thunderer* pronounced its oracular sentence. The following extract is from *The Times* (Wednesday, Oct. 26, 1853) :—

HAYMARKET THEATRE.—Playgoers of a dozen years' standing may recollect Mr. George Vandenhoff (elder son of *the* Mr. Vanden-hoff), who made his *début* at Covent Garden, during the manage-ment of Madame Vestris, as Leon in *Rule a Wife and Have a Wife*. He remained at that house for a season or two, playing the principal parts in several new and revived pieces, and was generally deemed a serviceable actor.

So much has happened, and such changes have taken place since the management to which we have referred, that Mr. George Vandenhoff had left no distinct impression on the memory, and when he re-appeared last night at the Haymarket, after a long absence in America, he had the reception of a completely new actor, and he has certainly re-introduced himself to the London public in a very creditable manner. Hamlet—the character which, like so many young tragedians, he has chosen for his opening—does, not, indeed, receive any new light from his interpretation, which he has based on long-established precedents, but, nevertheless, it is marked by a combination of elegance and carefulness which is not often to be found. If he created no great astonishment by what he *did*, he is entitled to great praise for what he avoided; for while, as we have said, his acting was founded on the conventional routine, he shunned all the old conventional tricks. By saying that he gives a castigated edition of the established Hamlet, we should, perhaps, convey the most accurate impression of his performance.

Reading with the utmost correctness, elegant in his movements, accomplished in the externals of histrionic art, and endowed with considerable advantages of person and voice (the latter being clear though soft), Mr. George Vandenhoff's forte seems to lie rather in the colloquial and gently pathetic, than in the violently passionate, and his elocution is marked less by force than by refinement. At the same time some situations, particularly the play scene, were powerfully worked up, and may perhaps justify the friends of Mr. G. Vandenhoff in forming sanguine hopes of future greatness. His performance throughout was heard with evident approbation, and he was called with loud applause at the end of the play.

The reader will, I trust, pardon me for making these extracts. As my connection with the stage was now nearing its close, I am naturally ambitious to leave some record of what was the opinion of the critics on my mature efforts; so as, in some measure, to justify the sudden step I took in abandoning the glorious uncertainty of the law, for the still greater and perhaps more glorious uncertainty of the stage.

May I be allowed to add that any credit I may have obtained by my performance of Hamlet I owe simply to confidence in Shakspere—to a conviction that he was, and is, sufficient for himself. What I mean to express is, that Hamlet is able to act out himself if the actor will trust to Shakspere for doing it ; if he will not "over-do" the master's work, but "use all gently," and not overlay a perfect picture of imperfect humanity with stage-trick, strained effect, extravagant attitude, and what Lord Shaftesbury, in his criticism on the play, happily calls "blustering heroism." There is no room for any of this in Hamlet, as I conceive it ; except in the one scene with Laertes at Ophelia's grave—and for his violence there the philosophic prince expresses his sorrow, and excuses it to Horatio, on the ground that he was in

"a towering passion,—"

except in this instance violence and rant are entirely misplaced. The more simply the character is presented to the audience the more thoroughly will the actor's impersonation of this extraordinary metaphysical epitome of the weaknesses of humanity in one of its noblest types carry out the master's design, and win its way to the popular heart. I am far from intimating that I have succeeded in this, myself; but I have aimed at it. It is not because Hamlet is a *hero* that we love him, and sympathize with him so intimately in every situation and every scene ; it is, rather, because, with the highest motives, the most elevated aspirations, and the most accomplished intellect, he is *so little of a hero in action*, that we feel his approximation to ourselves; and our vanity and self-love are flattered by recognizing the reflection of our own imperfections and irresoluteness in so grand, so

pure, so refined a mirror. In sympathizing with
Hamlet, we are paying court to ourselves, and finding a splendid apology for our own short-comings.
Now nothing can be less in harmony with such a conception than "blustering heroism," in "the 'Ercles
vein" of inflated tragedy. This is to throw the robes
of a player-king over the shoulders of the Apollo
Belvidere; or to dress up the Venus de Medici in
modern flounces, berthas, Valenciennes lace, a blaze
of jewellery, and the expansive extravagance of crino-
line!

It was quite clear to me and to everybody, from
the specimen exhibited in "Hamlet," that tragedy
was not the *forte* of the Haymarket company. The
part of Evelyn, in Bulwer's admirable comedy of
Money, was therefore fixed upon for my second
appearance; and the comedy being well cast, was
repeated six times during the next fortnight, and
several times afterwards during the season. I received many compliments on my performance of
Evelyn, both from the actors and the public press.
The most valued of all was my father's expression of
satisfaction, communicated to me by my mother.
He had said, she told me, that "it was as good as
the Hamlet, and he could not say more." Conceive
my delight at hearing this, when I recollected how
dreadfully my father had been disappointed by my
change of profession, and how little hope he had
entertained of my attaining eminence in a pursuit
adopted as an after thought, without the advantage
of a regular apprenticeship in early life. His present
approbation was therefore doubly valued by me.

The following notice of Evelyn, in a London

literary weekly, gratified me, I think, as much as
any critical eulogium I received ; and I pray the
reader's indulgence for quoting it :—

HAYMARKET THEATRE.—Bulwer's comedy of *Money* was produced at this theatre on Wednesday last, Mr. George Vandenhoff
sustaining the character of Evelyn. Mr. Vandenhoff's performance
of this character is chiefly remarkable for ease and naturalness.
There is no straining after effect—none of those attempts to draw
down applause by loud tones and violent gestures, which are so
frequently indulged in where an opportunity permits. Mr. Vandenhoff appears to feel that he was acting a part in the drama of daily
life, and that the conventional shouts and starts of the stage
would be out of place. His manner, throughout the piece, was
that of a well-educated gentleman, and his most earnest bursts of
passion were tempered to suit the situation in which they were displayed, and the circumstances by which they were produced. In
the scene at the club, in which he plays with such seeming reckless-
ness with Dudley Smooth, there was just sufficient exaggeration to
show that his wild demeanour was assumed, and yet sufficient
reality to indicate that Evelyn was, to some extent, affected by the
very excitement he was simulating. Nothing could be more truthful than Mr. Vandenhoff's acting in this scene. It completely
carried the audience with it, and proved, beyond doubt, that his
performance was the result of great study—that, in fact, it was a
display of that art which conceals art. In his passionate appeal to
Georgina, in the last scene, he was equally effective. The faltering
voice, the agitated manner, the nervous, almost frenzied anxiety
with which he listened for her reply, his whole existence seeming
to depend upon the few words she might utter—were finely contrasted with the burst of sudden joy which followed her avowal of
affection for Sir Frederick Blount.

Mr. Vandenhoff's performance of Evelyn places him in the first
rank as a performer of refined comedy ; and we must congratulate
Mr. Buckstone upon such an acquisition to his company.

But what shall we say of Mr. Buckstone as Stout—that shadow
of a character ? Shall we say that he was the very embodiment of
parochial pomposity, refined by legislative experience ? We might
say this, and much more ; but we fear we should convey but a faint
idea of the talent and infinite humour which Mr. Buckstone displayed. Dress and manner were alike admirable, and whenever his

round, red, and good-humoured face appeared upon the stage, it was the signal for a burst of genuine applause. Mr. Compton, as Graves, was as droll as usual; but was badly dressed, and did not look sufficiently lugubrious for the melancholy widower. Mrs. Fitzwilliam was *not* Lady Franklin, but was, as she always is, exceedingly clever and artistic.

Up to this time the regular leading actress of the theatre had been incapacitated by illness from playing with me ; but Claude, in the " Lady of Lyons," being selected as my third part, I had the full benefit of the lady's assistance !

Imagine my recognizing in this woman of some eight-and-thirty years of age, with a harsh brassy voice, a person brought out originally in the United States, fifteen years previously, by a certain *Yankee Delineator*. The unenviable reputation which she enjoyed in this country, she had, on her return to her own, marvellously well kept up ; being now, notoriously, the mistress of a married man, who was nightly to be seen in the private stage-box to witness her performances. As an actress, her style was coarse, her voice dissonant, and her manners had all the affectation and effrontery combined, that usually distinguish ladies of her stamp. Such was the person whom I found myself doomed, during a whole season, to address on the stage in the most courteous and refined language of chaste and respectful love ; into whose hackneyed ear I was to breathe the most impassioned vows, and whose form I was to clasp in my arms, with the ardour of a knight, and the devotion of a pilgrim at the shrine of a *virgin*-saint ! It was the greatest trial I ever met with on the stage. It was a perpetual and complete *désillusionnement*, eternally meeting and striking down my enthusiasm for an abstract *ideal*, by the coarse, common, hard, unpoetical, unloveable reality !

It was impossible to imagine that metallic-voiced, bold-faced woman, the gentle Clara, or the betrayed, heart-broken, self-sacrificing Pauline ! The contradiction was too glaring, too shocking; and this was the penance I had to look forward to, during a season of about thirty weeks.

Talent, as an artist, unless costly dresses and impregnable assurance constitute talent, she had none ; none, I mean, for the line of business into which she was thrust ; she would have made a good *soubrette*, of the most audacious kind, nothing more. Yet, here I found her, in the Haymarket Theatre, London, by force of the pressure from without of peculiar influences, occupying the position that women of unblemished purity of character, as well as of high dramatic genius, had hitherto adorned !

The " high and palmy days" of the theatre must be gone indeed, when such a person occupied such a place. For—however other situations, in the theatrical profession, may have been filled by women of loose lives and sullied reputations—the position of leading actress, at a leading metropolitan theatre, had hitherto, in England, at least, preserved its moral eminence ; and the loves, sufferings, self-sacrifice, and heroism of Juliet, Belvidera, Mrs. Beverly, had grown to be associated with the virtues of daily life, by the exemplary conduct of their stage-representatives. There is something revolting to the feelings in seeing such characters filled by a woman of known licentious and immoral life ; especially, when she does not possess the veil of genius with which to cover, or, at least, to soften the features of her irregularities. Characters that have been hallowed by connection with the names of Mrs. Siddons, Miss O'Neil, Miss Ellen Tree, and others, whom to name is to honour, should never be degraded and defiled by the low and unsympathising personation, or rather *travestie*, of a common *intrigante*.

I do not hesitate to say, that I consider the fact I allude to as the most fatal evidence of the decay of the drama in England that struck my mind. Such outrages on public decency and taste merit the contempt and neglect which they incur; and it behoves a decent public to rebuke them by their continued absence.

My fourth character was Benedick.

CHARLOTTE CUSHMAN was with us for a portion of the season. She opened in Bianca; I declined playing Fazio; but appeared with her in " The Stranger" several times, and as the Cardinal, in " Henry the Eighth," twice. She produced a piece by CHORLEY (Mrs. Hemans' biographer, and the musical critic of the *Athenæum*), which had great literary merit, but was hissed on the second night, and so failed, to Charlotte's great mortification; for she had what she deemed a very fine part in it, and on which, I believe, she very much counted for great success. On the reading of the play in the Green-Room, I surprised her and the author, by selecting (as the terms of my engagement gave me a right of selection in all new pieces) the character of an old *roué*, gambler,

thief and assassin, her father ; instead of the part of
a noble count, her lover.   They were both villains,
one of about thirty, the other of about six " lengths ;"
for seeing the failure of the piece, I chose the *shorter*
of the two knaves.   The author had named him Bal-
thasar ; but, as that was a very undignified appellation,
associated, in dramatic nomenclature, with servants
and torch-bearers, *et hoc genus omne,* Mr. Chorley
very kindly, at my request, dubbed him l'Incognito ;
thus shrouding him in mystery.   As I said, " The
Duchess Eleanour" scarcely lived through the second
night ; a volley of hisses settled her fate in the fifth
act ; and threw Charlotte Cushman back on her old
fortune-teller, Meg Merrilies.

Morton's " Town and Country" was produced for
me shortly after, and I had the satisfaction of repeating Reuben Glenroy five nights.   Mr. Chippendale played Old Cosey, with good effect ; Buckstone
was the Hawbuck ; Compton, Bobby Trot ; Hon.
Mrs. Glenroy, Miss Featherstone, now Mrs. Howard
Paul.

" London Assurance" was also revived (in which
I played Dazzle), but was stopped on its fourth representation by Mr. Webster, of the Adelphi, who had
purchased from the author the sole right of representing that comedy in London.   It was very well cast
with us, with the exception of Lady Gay Spanker,
which was intrusted to a lady utterly incompetent to
represent it, even if she had been perfect in the words,
which she was not.   In the celebrated description of
the steeple-chase, she *baulkled, boggled, fell,* and *floun-
dered* in the ditch.   Nevertheless, she was upheld by
some of the Sunday *Press,* who, I suppose, received

their *cue* from the management ; but the good sense of the public prevailed, and the ambitious attempt was pronounced a failure. In other respects, the cast was good :

Sir Harcourt	Chippendale.
Max Harkaway	Rogers.
Charles Courtly	Howe.
Dazzle	G. Vandenhoff.
Dolly Spanker	Buckstone.
Meddle	Compton.
Cool	Clarke.
Grace	Miss L. Howard.
Pert	Mrs. E. Fitzwilliam.
Lady Gay	————

The next new piece, and the only one produced this season at the Haymarket with any just pretensions to the rank of a comedy, was PLANCHE's " Knights of the Round Table." It was founded on a French piece, entitled, " *Des Chevaliers de Lansquenêt ;*" but it was so skilfully remodelled, and adapted to the English stage, that it had all the racy and varied effect of one of Fielding's novels skilfully dramatized—if such a thing were possible.   It is full of intrigue, action, and complication : as the *Times,* in a long and elaborate article, observed of it :

"So full of adventure is the story, that an unskilful playwright might, very easily, have made of it an indissoluble tangle. As it is, the complexity with which the threads of the tale are tied together is only equalled by the clearness with which all is explained at last."

On the reading of the comedy in the Green-Room I used my privilege of selection, and chose, not the part (D'Arcy) which the author designed for me, but Captain Cozens, the leader of " The Knights of the

Round Table," who are simply a gang of sharpers, and whose field of action is the gaming-table. Manager and author were surprised, and the latter somewhat disappointed at my choice. I confess, one of the motives that guided me was, that I thus avoided the position of lover to the leading lady, which was a relief, at any time, worth some sacrifice; but I thought that I saw, besides, that Captain Cozens might be made the strong character of the drama : the result justified my judgment. The following is the *Times'* notice of the performance :

"The piece has the advantage of admirable acting, and while we extend our commendation to all parties, we would particularly pick out Mr. G. Vandenhoff and Mr. Buckstone, inasmuch as the excellence of these gentlemen lay beyond the limits of their usual departments. Mr. Vandenhoff, who had inauspiciously opened the evening by an apology for a cold, fought so valiantly against this physical impediment that he presented one of the most finished pictures of a cool, deliberate, well-bred villain that has been seen for many a long day. Firm in his evil purposes, and proud of his mental superiority, Captain Cozens always showed himself the ruling demon of the scene, and not an attitude or a gesture was without its value. In Tom Tittler, Mr. Buckstone gives us a specimen of some legitimate acting, in which the oddity of the poor, but valiant Tittler, by no means obscures the chivalric foundation of the character. We could dwell at some length on the excellent manner in which Mr. Compton, as Smith, cheats the landlord, but we purposely omit all description of that episode. It is an anecdote that would set a company in a roar after dinner, and which, told in a dramatic form, makes the house ring with laughter."

The piece was admirably put upon the stage ; and the final scene of the fifth act, a view of London from Hampstead Heath, a hundred years back, was an elaborate " set ;" and, as was universally admitted, was so admirably painted and arranged, and the light so skilfully disposed, as to form a most perfect land-scape, equal to one of Cooper's or Moreland's.

DOUGLAS JERROLD, in *Punch*, said, in his concen-trated, quintessential way:

" Mr. Vandenhoff, in Capt. Cozens, was cold, subtle, venomous; he seemed as though *he lived on snakes !* a swindler whose sylla-bles are drops of poison."

The *Athenæum* was pleased to write :

" The success of the play greatly depended on the manner in which Mr. Vandenhoff supported his character."

This comedy ran fifty-four successive nights at the Haymarket Theatre. The scene alluded to by the *Times*, in which SMITH cheats the landlord, is so good, that I give it here, as I am sure very few of my readers have seen the comedy, which, I presume, owing to want of care and outlay in its production, did not, I believe, meet with great success on this side of the Atlantic.

SCENE FROM THE KNIGHTS OF THE ROUND TABLE.

A C T III.

SCENE.—*Coffee-Room at Locket's. Gentlemen dining at various tables—Waiters in attendance.* CAPTAIN COZENS *seated at a table in front. A table on right unoccupied.*

CAPTAIN. (*looking at his watch.*) Quarter past five—they are late. Waiter !

WAITER. Coming, Sir.

CAPT. A pint of claret.

WAITER. Yes, Sir—pint of claret (*repeating the order*).

Enter SMITH.

SMITH. (*advancing to empty table.*) Waiter !

WAITER. Sir.

SMITH. This table engaged ?

WAITER. No, Sir.

SMITH. Then I may be permitted to sit here?

WAITER. Certainly, Sir. Dinner, Sir?

SMITH. If you please, I should feel obliged—as soon as possible.

WAITER Bill of fare, Sir. (*giving it to him.*)

SMITH. Thank you. I may have anything I see here?

WAITER. Certainly, Sir. (*aside.*) Some country gentleman.

SMITH. (*surprised.*) You're very good. Then I'll say some *turtle*, to begin with.

WAITER. Turtle—yes, Sir. (*aside.*) An alderman, or a banker.

SMITH. To be followed by *Filet de Turbot, à la Hollandaise—Hashed Venison*, and *Apricot Fritters.*

WAITER. (*bowing.*) Yes, Sir. (*aside.*) Oh, a very rich banker!

CAPT. (*who has been attracted by* SMITH'S *manner, aside.*) Humph! Not a bad judge of a dinner, whoever he is!

SMITH. Some *punch*, of course, with the turtle.

WAITER. Yes, Sir—what wine, Sir?

SMITH. Is your *Madeira* fine?

WAITER.—We have some very fine, Sir.

SMITH. I'll taste your Madeira. (*takes up newspaper, and reads.*)

CAPT. (*aside.*) A bon vivant—dressed plainly, but like a gentleman —a stranger here; at least, I never saw him before.

Enter D'ARCY.

D'ARCY. (*seeing* CAPTAIN.) Ah !—there you are !

CAPT. You're late. Where's Sir Ralph?

D'ARCY. Up stairs with the Baron and the Chevalier—we've a private room. I made an excuse to slip down whilst dinner is serving, to see if you were here. What news?

CAPT. The bird is found.

D'ARCY. Hah !—you are certain?

CAPT. Certain.

D'ARCY. And—can be—secured?

CAPT. Whenever I please—to night, if I knew a safe cage for her till I could find a mate.

D'ARCY. The lodgings of one of our friends?

CAPT. No—I had rather not trust them in this matter.

SMITH. (*whose dinner has been served during the above conversation.*) Waiter !

WAITER. Sir?

SMITH. Champagne.

WAITER. Yes, Sir. (*serves champagne.*)

CAPT. (*to* D'ARCY.) Do you know that man?

D'ARCY. (*looking at* SMITH.) No.

CAPT. He knows how to live.

WAITER. (*to* D'ARCY.) Your dinner is served, Sir—the gentlemen only wait for you.

D'ARCY. I am coming. (*aside.*) I trust all to you.

CAPT. You may safely. What of your scheme?

D'ARCY. Come to night to Madame Boulanger's, in Golden-square —there is a dance there—

CAPT. Where you have lodged—*your sister?*

D'ARCY. Aye, aye! of course—you know—ask for me—I shall be there till twelve, and may want you.

CAPT. Good! [*Exit* D'ARCY.

SMITH. Waiter!

WAITER. Sir.

SMITH. A pint of Burgundy—and some peaches.

CAPT. (*aside.*) Peaches in May! half-a-crown a-piece, at least!

SMITH. (*to* WAITER, *who brings Burgundy and peaches.*) A tooth-pick (WAITER *hands him one in a glass*); and in about ten minutes you may send for—

WAITER. A coach, sir?

SMITH. No; an officer.

CAPT. (*aside.*) An officer!

WAITER. An officer—of the Guards, Sir?

SMITH. No; a peace officer—a constable.

CAPT. (*aside.*)
      and   } A constable!
WAITER. (*aloud.*)

SMITH. A constable.

WAITER. Lord, Sir! what for, Sir?

CAPT. (*aside, and rising uneasily.*) Aye, what for, indeed?

SMITH. To take me up!

CAPT. Take *him* up!

WAITER. Take *you* up, Sir?

CAPT. He's a madman!

SMITH. Well, I don't insist upon it, only take notice, I shall go as soon as I have finished this Burgundy.

WAITER. Well, Sir, your bill will be made out in a minute.

SMITH. Perhaps so; but it won't be paid in a minute—I've no money!

WAITER. No money. Here Master!

SMITH. I told you to send for a constable.

CAPT. (*aside.*) If the fellow is not mad, he's an artist.

Enter LANDLORD.

LANDLORD. What's the matter here?

WAITER. This gentleman, Sir.

SMITH. The landlord, I presume. Sir, the matter is exceedingly simple—I have eaten an excellent dinner, and have no money to pay for it.

LAND. Lost your purse, Sir—not in my house, I hope?

SMITH. Oh, dear, no, Sir! I had no money when I entered it.

LAND. And you ordered a dinner that comes to (*holding out bill*) one pound, eighteen and sixpence!

SMITH. No more! your charges are very moderate; I should have guessed two guineas at least.

LAND. And you can't pay it?

SMITH. It's a melancholy fact.

LAND. Then what the devil, Sir—

SMITH. My friend, my dear friend! pray don't make a disturbance; I have desired your waiter to send for a constable; what would you have me do more?

CAPT. (*aside.*) He is a great artist—a very great artist!

LAND. Sir, you—you're a rogue—you're a swindler!

SMITH. Sir, you are abusive—you are offensive! If you do not choose to send for a constable, I am your most obedient—

LAND. But I will. Here, Dick, run for a constable.

CAPT. Nay, nay; stop! don't be hasty! the gentleman is, perhaps, only a little eccentric. Allow me to say one word to him. Sir—(*to* SMITH.)

SMITH. Sir. (*bowing.*)

CAPT. (*aside to him.*) A little difficulty of this description may happen to any gentleman. If you will pardon the liberty I take, as an utter stranger, in offering you the trifling loan of two guineas. (*slipping them into his hand.*)

SMITH. My dear Sir, no apology, I beg. I am your debtor!

CAPT. Hush!

SMITH. Certainly. (*aloud to* LANDLORD.) Harkye, my friend. It is just possible I may be a rogue, but it is also possible I may be an Ambassador—a Minister of State—or an East India Director. I, therefore, only request you to decide whether you will send for a constable or not.

LAND. (*hesitatingly.*) Well, I should be sorry to do an uncivil thing by a gentleman for a guinea or two; and if you are a gentleman, I suppose, some other day, you might pay me.

SMITH. I *might* undoubtedly, but mind—I *don't say I will.*

LAND. Well, you are an odd gentleman, certainly, but I'll trust you sooner than have a disturbance, and a mob round my door— so I leave it to your honour (*throws bill on table, and exit*).

SMITH. (*aside.*) In that case—here go the two guineas! (*putting the two guineas which he has held in his hand into his pocket, and taking up his hat and cane.*) Your humble servant, Sir. (*makes a gracious bow to* CAPTAIN COZENS, *and putting on his hat, walks out, picking his teeth and humming an Italian air!*)

This season was marked by the sudden death of Mrs. FITZWILLIAM, Buckstone's faithful partner and ally. She died suddenly, of cholera. She was a good-natured soul, and a hearty, clever, versatile actress. One of the pieces in which she was best known in this country, was called " Foreign Airs and Native Graces." Of this little piece I have the following incident to relate. While finishing my studies for the law, in early life, I wrote a one-act interlude, entitled " The English Belle," and sent it to the Haymarket Theatre, during Mr. Webster's management, for acceptance. Nearly a year after the piece was returned to me, rejected ; and, a few weeks after that, this piece of " Foreign Airs and Native Graces"—this title being taken from a line of my rejected piece, " The English Belle "—was produced at that theatre, containing my incidents and a great part of the dialogue, with some additions : in fact, my piece, with a change of title and names of the characters.

In 1846 I played my own piece for my benefit, at the Howard Athenæum, Boston, under the title of the " American Belle,"—with MARY TAYLOR for the heroine, and WARREN for the Old Man. It went off with great laughter and applause ; but, of course, the press, in noticing it, discovered, naturally enough,

N

that it was almost a verbatim copy of "Foreign Airs and Native Graces." Amusing, very !

MEM : It is not always safe to trust a MS. farce to the reader of a theatre, when that reader is a farce-writer himself ! Mr. Moncrieff was, I believe, Mr. Webster's reader.

The SPANISH DANCERS, headed by the agile little Andalusian *Perea Nèna*, were the next novelty at the Haymarket Theatre; and such was their, or rather *her* attraction—for her *corps de ballét* were shocking contrasts to her rapid, flashing, *coquettish* movements, now like the curvettings of an Arab barb, fretting on the bit, anon like the bound of the antelope, and now again like the whirl and whiz of a steam engine —such was her attraction, that acting and actors became of quite secondary importance. Mr. Buckstone took advantage of the opportunity to rid himself of all salaries that it was inconvenient to pay, and of all services he could now dispense with, by the expedient of a notice in the Green-Room, closing the season on a Saturday night, and re-opening it on the Monday following, as a summer-season ! Ingenious and ingenuous !

During the season at the Haymarket Theatre I played the following parts in tragedy and comedy :

Hamlet, 3 times; Evelyn (Money), 12 times; Claude (Lady of Lyons), 9 times; Benedick twice; Rovely (in a three-act piece, called Ranelagh), 19 times; Cardinal Wolsey, twice; Stranger 4 times; Incognito (Duchess Eleanor), twice; Duke Aranza, once; Bob Handy, 5 times; Reuben Glenroy, 6 times; Dazzle, 4 times; Captain Cozens, 54 times :—an average of more than three nights per week, for a season of thirty-eight weeks.

The result of my experience was, that I made up

my mind to quit the profession of the stage as soon as
I could see my way clearly out of it: for I had now,
as the leading actor of the leading metropolitan theatre, with acknowledged success in a great variety of
characters, in tragedy and comedy, made this discovery—that, in the present condition of theatricals,
there was no prize worthy a rational ambition, or the
efforts of any man capable of other things. It was
evident to me, that the London Stage, as an arena for
the display of intellectual culture, or the cultivation
of artistic excellence, was near its end: it had become
a vehicle for spectacle and illegitimate attraction of
various kinds. I felt, at all events, that what little
talent God had given me was misplaced on the stage,
and I resolved, as soon as possible, to say farewell to
it—I hoped, for ever!

Meantime, I played a three-weeks' engagement at
the Liverpool Theatre: and next, an engagement of
two months at the St. James' Theatre, London, under
the direction of Mrs. SEYMOUR.

This theatre opened with a drama by TOM TAYLOR
and CHARLES READE, " the King's Rival," which did
not meet with the success which was anticipated for
it by the management. Charles Reade, in his preface
to the printed play, seemed to attribute this to the
deficiency of the representative of one of the principal
characters. After a forced run of the piece for a
month, to losing houses, we had to fall back on the
regular drama; and I found myself again playing
Evelyn, in " Money," and Charles Surface, on alternate nights, followed by Claude, Lord Townley,
Don Felix, and the never-dying, but much-abused
Stranger.

N 2

Illness compelled me to break off my engagement at the St. James' Theatre, which closed shortly afterwards, after a losing season of about three months—another proof that that theatre will never answer, except for French plays. Fashion supports them; but even they have not, I believe, always been profitable to Mr. Mitchell. It was the theatre that ruined BRAHAM, by his attempt to keep it open with English opera: and it will always be disastrous to any *entrepreneur*.

Let me do Mrs. Seymour and Captain Curling the justice to say, that they fulfilled their obligations to me, and, I believe, to every one whom they engaged, faithfully and honourably. Mrs. Seymour's playing of Nell Gwynne, in " the King's Rival," was an admirable piece of comedy, worthy of the best days of the drama; and, if the play had been equally well acted in more pretentious parts, I have no doubt that it would have been a great success; but, in the serious scenes, it was allowed to flag horribly. Both Tom Taylor and Charles Reade will bear me out in this, I am sure, from what fell from them immediately after the play on the first night. I played the King to oblige Charles Reade, although I had the choice of characters; but he considered it easier to find a Richmond than a King Charles, and I accepted the less interesting, but more difficult part, at his request. I received his and Tom Taylor's thanks after the first performance. The play itself is an excellent one, and ought to have succeeded. It would have done so, too, had there been a competent stage director. Had Mr. WALLACK, for example, put it on the stage, it would have been a certain success.

This short season at the St. James' Theatre was another proof to me that it was time to quit the stage. So powerfully had this feeling grown on me, that I continually had a fancy that I heard ringing in my ears, the Witch's ominous words in Macbeth :

" Harper cries 'tis time ! 'tis time !"

So, I ran down to St. Leonards aforesaid for a few weeks, and there shook off a violent attack of cold that had seized me. I was summoned back to town by an invitation from Sir JAMES MOON, the Lord Mayor, to a special dinner at the Mansion House, to be given by him, on the 27th February, to the members of the GARRICK CLUB, to which his lordship belonged. I mention this dinner, because the present President, Mr. BUCHANAN, then Minister at St. James', was among the invited guests, and made a happy *hit* in his speech. The Earl of Carlisle was there, too, in his Lord Lieutenant's uniform, with the Ribbon of the Bath, the night before he quitted town to assume the Vice-royalty of Ireland. The Chief Baron POLLOCK, also, and other notables sat at the *dais*.

The occasion of the dinner was this :

Many of my readers are, perhaps, personally acquainted with the little Garrick Club ("the little G," as Thackeray calls it,) in King-street, Covent-garden ; and those who are not so acquainted, yet know of it through the *éclât* of the recent difficulty between Mr. E. Yates and the author of " Vanity Fair," which created a sort of division in the Club—one party taking Yates' side, the other espousing that of Thackeray.

The merits of this " pretty little quarrel" I will

not discuss. It seems, however, strikingly to illustrate the trite moral, that " they who live in glass-houses should not throw stones." I regret the falling-out of the affair : for such " quarrels of authors" cannot be classed among the " amenities of literature ;" and " the little G" itself suffers damage, in public opinion, by the agitation of so puerile a matter.

My American friends may be interested to know that the Garrick Club was originated something less than half a century ago, by about a dozen gentlemen, chiefly members of the theatrical profession, who met together, formed themselves into a society by that name, gradually increasing their number, which at this day amounts to about three hundred. The Dukes of Beaufort and Devonshire were successively its presidents. Its list of members comprises the names of some of the most distinguished ornaments of literature and art; and it enjoys, or did enjoy—I trust the little family quarrel has not permanently disturbed its harmony—the enviable reputation of being the least formal and most *cosily*-agreeable club in London.

Of this club Sir James Moon is a member ; and, in the smoking-room one evening, being then an alderman, some one said to him :—

" Moon, *you* will be Lord Mayor before long; then you'll have to give us *all* a dinner at the Mansion House."

" I *will*," replied Sir James, " with pleasure."

Thus it happened that, being elected to the chief magistracy of the city of London the year after the pledge, he redeemed it by the invitation I have mentioned for the 27th Feb., 1855.

I find in my note-book on that night the following memorandum :—

"Dinner capital; speechifying *shy !*"

And so it was. Douglas Jerrold was there, and on coming out we agreed together on that verdict at the door.

It really was surprising that, among so many men of talent in so many different lines, there was not one really good, smart, telling speech made for the whole evening ! The Lord Mayor himself, the best of hosts, was decidedly " no orator ;" the Earl of Carlisle was not particularly felicitous on the occasion ; the Chief Baron ran somehow off the track on to *education ;* Thackeray was not (he never is) happy in his after-dinner out-pouring ; he requires pen, ink, and paper to make his thoughts and language flow easily ; and no one stood up to sustain the credit of the Garrick Club for *post-prandial* wit and extemporaneous fluency. Dickens was not present, or he would have redeemed its honour, and " sent his hearers *smiling* to their beds !" In vain the Lord Mayor's " loving cup " was handed round ; in vain delicious wines, of the most exquisite flavour and the most costly price, circulated in the extravagant profusion of a princely hospitality : they drew no responsive fervour from the lips that engulphed them down, and revelled in their lusciousness.

The solitary flash that lit up the tables—the solitary stroke that *told*—came from the forge of Mr. J. Buchanan, the American Minister. In reply to some toast of the Lord Mayor's, complimentary to the United States, Mr. Buchanan rose, put his hand, I think, into his broad white waistcoat pocket, and began :—

" My Lord Mayor, my lords and gentlemen, Republican as I am,"—he paused for a moment, and there was a solemn silence at his formal and rather ominous beginning—*Conticuere omnes intentique ora tenebant!*

" Republican as I am, there is one institution of Great Britain for which I feel the deepest respect and the most affectionate admiration.   I fervently pray that, whatever changes may take place—whatever reforms may be carried out, whatever alterations may be wrought by public sentiment and opinion—whatever revolutions, even (which heaven avert)! may take place in this country—I fervently pray that *one* institution, at least, may be spared—that *it* may continue to flourish, to grow, to increase, and be strengthened and confirmed! I allude, my lords and gentlemen, to THE PUBLIC DINNERS OF GREAT BRITAIN !"

Imagine the surprise, the shouts of laughter, and the cheers that followed this unexpectedly humorous turn to the solemn and imposing opening of his republican exordium! The American Minister had made a *hit:* he clenched it by courteously acknowledging the hospitalities he had received in England ; and, proposing the health of Lady Moon, sat down, amidst general applause.

It was to recount this little incident that I mentioned the dinner; which, " barring the spayches," as SAM LOVER, who sat next to me, said was, I think, the best I ever *ate ;*—or, " drank aither," Lover added. It took place in the beautiful Egyptian Hall of the

Mansion House, amidst its classic forms of sculptured marble; the fragrancy of the viands and the deliciousness of the wines, commended to our lips by strains of most exquisite music.

———

The morning after this great civic entertainment I mounted my horse and rode down towards Bath—arrived the day after—remained there a few weeks, drinking and bathing in the *eaux* of that once celebrated and fashionable watering place, where Sheridan found his wife, Miss Linley, eloped with her, and fought the duel with Mathews: from which circumstances it was supposed he took the idea of his first and best comedy—" The Rivals, or a Trip to Bath."

Having set myself on my legs again by the Bath waters, I rode up to London, sold both my horses—as good horses as ever were crossed; one, a little chesnut, about fourteen hands, the other, a light bay, about fifteen-and-a-half—put myself in the train for Folkestone, and ran over to Paris to take a peep at the great exhibition there, to see how nearly it came up to ours (which it did not), remained there a few weeks, *wrote an important letter, with an all-important proposition, to a certain lady in America,* came back to town, settled my affairs, declined an engagement which Charles Kean had offered me, at the Princess's, ran down to Liverpool, played there five nights, took a berth on board the " America" steamer, and arrived at Boston, after a stormy passage, on the 17th August, 1855.

Three days after (on the 20th—*dies memorabilis !*)· I was married, at Trinity Church, Boston, to the lady

N 5

to whom I wrote the letter aforesaid.   There was a
small crowd assembled, though we had endeavoured to
avoid publicity; and the late Hon. RUFUS CHOATE was
one of the first persons who came forward to congratulate us.   He was always a kind and sympathizing
friend; and his recent death was painful news to myself and to my wife.   We used to meet him frequently
at the house of valued friends in Boston; and it was
always a great joy to find Mr. Choate seated there, of
an evening, delighting the circle with the play of his
conversation, his happy facility of graphic, concen-
trated expression—with an occasional *Carlyle-ism* in
it—and that readiness of apt quotation which shed such
a light on his serious, and even his sportive sayings:
for he could call in classical authority, Greek, Latin,
or English, for each.   He had a quickness and aptness
in this that I never knew excelled.   None, who had
only seen him dark, mysterious, grand, and self-ab-
stracted as he

" thunder'd in the tribune ;"

or who had only heard him shaking, and at the same
time moulding to his will, the hearts of a jury by his
daring hypotheses and his impassioned eloquence;
while ever and anon, with lowering brow and weird
look of warning, he pointed at them that terrible in-
dex finger, as if threatening them with immediate retribution for a false or even a mistaken verdict—
none who knew him only in those severer hours,
could guess how simple and particularly unassuming
he was in private—how affably indulgent to inferior
minds—how considerate of their want of knowledge—
how calm, how gentle, how courteous to all.   He was

a man that all who knew loved : those who knew him
best, the most.   His great delight was his books :

"His library was dukedom large enough."

There would he sit for hours, engaged with his
favourite classics—of which he had ample store and a
great variety of copies—the delight of his youth, the
solace of his mature age ; always a refreshment of his
mental strength, and a rekindling of its energies,
jaded and exhausted in the close and wearying Court-
room.

I recollect a remark of his that struck me as peculiarly worthy of attention, coming from a mind of such
experience and sound judgment on the particular
subject as his ; and noting a fact, too, worthy of all
praise and imitation.   We were speaking of the conviction for fraud of the great bankers and defaulters,
Sir John Dean Paul, Strachan, and Bates, in England,
who were brought to trial without delay ; and, on
sentence being passed on them, it was carried into
effect at once, just as it would have been on the
humblest clerk convicted of embezzlement.   Mr.
Choate expressed his approbation of the strict course
of justice in this case, and added—

"Of all things that struck me as worthy of admiration on my visit to England, and that which im-
pressed me most, was the certainty with which crime
is punished there ; there is no escape for it."

"Why," I asked, "do you think, Mr. Choate,
those men would have escaped here ?"

"I am afraid so," he answered.

"You are supposing," I suggested, "that they
would have had you for their advocate."

" No," he replied, " I am supposing that they
would have got off through some loop-hole; by dint
of new trials, delay, and the default of witnesses,
wearied out or tampered with. Here the punishment
would be problematical; in England, it is certain."

I made a note of his remark.

A striking instance of the universal confidence
in Mr. Choate's well-established power over a jury,
was told me in Greenfield, Mass., where I had a
country-house last summer. Mr. Choate had been
down there on a special retainer, and had succeeded in obtaining the acquittal of a prisoner
charged with murder, against whom the circum-
stantial evidence was very strong. A day or two
after this unexpected result, two coloured children
—the eldest not over ten years of age—playing
together, got into a quarrel. One of them struck
the other, who, enraged at the insult, exclaimed—

" Look-a-here ! if you do dat again, I'll kill you."

" Den if you kill me you'll be hung," said young
Sambo.

" No," replied the infant contemplator of homicide,
with a precocious eye to the uncertainty of the law
—" No, I shan't neider; Mr. Choate 'll get me off:"
—a singular comment on the great advocate's remark
which I have quoted above.

Mr. Choate carried out in its full sense, Lord
Brougham's saying, that " in his duty as an advocate,
a counsel knows no one but his client;" and he
pleaded the cause of his client, whoever he or she
might be, as if his own life depended on the issue.
He argued, he wept, he warned, he threatened, he
implored ; he was at times Demosthenic in impulsive,

fiery outburst; bitterly sarcastic, and "terribly in earnest;" anon, he was Ciceronic in the graceful flow and polished cadence of his style. He neglected no effort, and despised no trick of oratory that could help his client and his cause; he put his whole soul into the action; and there can be little doubt that his unwearied and anxious labours in his profession wore out his life. His was

> The fiery soul, that, working out its way,
> Fretted the feeble body to decay,
> And o'er informed its tenement of clay.

XVII.

OUR honeymoon we passed chiefly in New York, at the comfortable Clarendon Hotel ; with the variation of a country excursion or two.

At a town in Massachussetts, where we passed a week of retreat and starvation, by no means congenial with our taste, or our constitutions, we met with a painfully amusing and original tavern-keeper. His "faculty" was to give the most niggardly possible dinners, and to arrogate to himself the merit of keeping an elegant and *recherché* table ; so that, after a lenten meal, from which one arose with appetite and temper both provoked, one had to endure the insult-added-to-injury of his self-glorification. This was too much for mortal patience to stomach. So, one day, all smarting with my wrongs, I encountered him wearing his usual smile of self-complacency, and rubbing his hands as if with the consciousness of being a model host and a pattern landlord.

"Well, sir," he addressed me, "how do you do, sir? how do you feel, sir?"

It is a point of courtesy with a certain class of people to repeat this question with slight variations, at least four times, as—

"How d' ye do, sir? how have you been, sir? how d' ye feel, sir? how d' ye do, sir?"

"Why, I feel very hungry, Mr. F——," I replied.

"Hungry, sir? ha'n't you dined, sir?"

"I have been in to dinner," I said; "but really can't say I have dined."

"Not dined, sir? Excellent dinner, sir; oysters, sir, stewed and fried—"

"Oysters in August!" I exclaimed, with a shudder.

"Well, sir, our people like oysters, sir, at any time."

"I'm sorry I can't sympathize with their taste."

"Well, sir," he answered, rather piqued, "we calhulate to set a first-rate table."

"Excuse me saying, then," I interrupted, "that your sum total is very wide of your calculations."

Well," he resumed, "we don't want no complaints; we calhulate to set a first-rate table, the best of everything; an' them as complains is outside barbarians to me."

"I'm afraid I must confess myself to be in that barbaric category; and to complete my outsidedness, I propose to take the afternoon train to New York."

I paid his bill, whch was not far short of what I should be charged at the New York or Clarendon hotels; happy to escape, without an attack of cholera, from his vegetable and bivalvine diet.

Before taking my wife to England I played five nights and one afternoon, at the Boston Theatre, under Mr. Barry's management, producing the sum of £582 net.

My wife (Miss Makean), who last season commenced a theatrical career at the Metropolitan Theatre, New York, and had played with success short engagements at the Broadway Theatre, N. Y., the Walnut Street Theatre, Philadelphia, and at some Western theatres, acted Pauline, and a part in the afterpiece, for my benefit ; and surprised me very much by her ease and ability, remarkable for one who had not played altogether more than forty times, and had had no early associations with the stage. It was no part of my intention that she should pursue a profession which I was eagerly desirous of abandoning myself; but I proposed to wean her from her *penchant* for the footlights by degrees.

It is a peculiarity of managers that they are never satisfied. Out of the above receipts, which Mr. Barry declared to be by no means satisfactory, although it was about the worst month of the theatrical year, my share was £105 ; leaving to the theatre £477.

The £105, my share, was convenient for the payment of my passage from England, and our joint passage per " America," back again ; we arrived in Liverpool in the middle of October.

On our way to London we ran down to Stratford-on-Avon ; my wife's first visit, and probably my last, to the Mecca and Medina of Shaksperian pilgrims.

Mine hostess of the Shakspere Hotel—young, blooming, gossipy and humorous—on learning my name, enquired if a Mr. Vandenhoff, who had delivered a speech there once, at a banquet in celebration of Shakspere's birth-day, was related to me; and, to my answer that he was my father, she rejoined—" I thought so, because you *feature* him so much."

Quite a Shaksperian phrase, I thought, for mine hostess; and I recalled the line in the sonnets:

> " *Featur'd* like him, like him with friends possessed."

That night I heard a watchman cry the hour—a custom which I had thought was exploded in England. It took me back, at once, to the sapient Dogberry and his instructions to the watch :—

> *Dogberry.* You shall comprehend all vagrom men; you are to bid any man stand, in the Prince's name.
>
> *Watch.* How if he will not stand?
>
> *Dogberry.* Why then take no note of him, but let him go; and presently call the rest of the watch together, and thank God you are rid of a knave. You shall also make no noise in the streets; for the watch to babble and talk, is most intolerable and not to be endured;—

and the rest of that admirable picture of the inept pomposity of a parochial dignitary, probably taken from life in Shakspere's day; but true now, as then, and good " for all time."

Next day we visited the tomb and monument, and afterwards the house and relics; paid the customary fees—thinking of Mercutio's

> "Fee simple? Oh simple !"—

and did not apostrophize, or exclaim, or wax enthusiastic, or write our names on wall or in book. I felt somewhat ashamed at my own apathy; but, with me, enthusiasm is always deadened by the hackneyed exhibition of any relic of the mighty dead which has been *maudlined-over* by thousands of frothy devotees. The shrine of a saint is desecrated and turned into ridicule by the legends of monks who reap a harvest from the credulity of miracle-swallowers. The showman at these hallowed spots of the world's worship is " a very beadle to " enthusiasm ; his set phraseology is a wet-blanket to imagination ; and the speculation of his fee-prospecting eye chases away all association of ideas congenial to the place.

By the tomb of Shakspere I should choose to sit alone, and

———" to the sessions of sweet silent thought
To summon up remembrance"

of his great creations; conjuring before my mind's eye the images of Romeo and his buried love; of Desdemona, Imogene, Ophelia, Viola ; Prospero, Caliban, Ariel, Miranda ; the Weird Sisters, the Thane of Cawdor and his fiend-like wife : and, as they passed in shadowy majesty, or airy grace, along the aisles of the silent church, I would glance up with reverence at the calm, placid brow in monumental stillness above me ; quoting now and then, perhaps, a passage from Hamlet, recalling some one of his subtle niceties of thought, mournful reflections, sarcastic truths, philosophic comments, or bursts of noble enthusiasm ; and thus—holding, as it were, a spiritual intercourse with the mighty master who " knew all qualities with a learned spirit"—who could sound man " from his lowest note to the top of his compass,"—in exalted enthusiasm of homage to that glorious mind which has

shed a light and lustre on human nature, I might exclaim :

"What a piece of work is man! how noble in reason, how infinite
in faculty ! in form and moving, how express and admirable ! in
action how like an angel, in apprehension how like a God !"

But to go deliberately, and in premeditated enthusiasm, to the church; to send the little lame boy,
waiting for a chance visitor, for the sexton ; to await
that functionary's methodical arrival; to see him
approach with his keys in his hand, and his official
smirk on his face ; to be by him *monkey-led* up the
aisle to the sacred corner ; to hear him dole out his
prescribed formula, and then to be called on to write
your name in the book, and pay the usual fee ;—all
this is so like the monotonous accompaniments of
baptism, marriage, or funeral, with which one naturally associates the sexton, that one feels it an escape
to get out of his clutches, and to gather together, in
solitude, our old ideas that clustered round Shakspere's
tomb, and which this scarecrow has scattered and
driven away.

The book of visitors, I observed, contained a long
list of Americans ; crowds of whom annually inscribe
their names as pilgrims to the shrine.

Apropos of reverence for relics :

Every reader of the Sketch Book recollects Washington Irving's charming paper on Stratford-on-Avon
—clothing the graceful enthusiasm of the poet in the
style of Addison. In its opening occurs this sentence :

" ' Shall I not take mine ease in mine inn ?' thought I, as *I gave
the fire a stir,* and cast a complacent look about the little parlour of
the Red Horse."

Now, mine hostess of the Shakspere Hotel had been (not, of course, at Washington Irving's visit) bar-maid of the Red Horse Inn; and she tells me that a considerable amount of " *entusymusy*" is occasionally expended at that hostelrie, by Washington Irving's countrymen, on the *poker with which he stirred the fire!* This was a species of Fetish-worship that mine hostess could not at all understand. " She couldn't abide," she said, " to see a parcel of men a-kissing Washington Irving's poker! Particularly (she added) as there a'nt no such thing in the house."

" As a poker?" I asked.

" A poker, of course, there is," she replied; " any quantity of 'em; but la, sir, it's no more Washington Irving's poker than it's the Pope of Rome's."

" Why," said I, " do you fix on the Pope of Rome rather than any other potentate?"

" Well, sir," she replied, " I've heard tell of people kissing the Pope's *toe;* but I can't say as I ever quite believed *that:* but *I've seen with my own eyes* half-a-dozen grown men a-kissing Washington Irving's poker —leastwise, a poker that passed for his."

" Very late in the evening, I should think, that must have been!" I suggested.

I don't at all wonder at this association of Irving's name with that of Shakspere in the recollections of Americans; for I have no doubt that the sketch of Stratford-on-Avon, by Geoffrey Crayon, has first excited many youthful imaginations to a thirst to drink at the Shaksperian fountain. I freely confess that my own love for him who sleeps on Avon's banks owes its first germ to that sketch, which I read when quite a boy. It at once awakened my curiosity and interest. All dramatic works were forbidden lore to me, at that age, at school; but I surreptitiously procured a " Dodd's Beauties of Shakspere," and eagerly devoured this concentrated essence of the poet. I kept it under my pillow at night; and, by day, stole into corners and secret places to enjoy it. It opened to me a new revelation; a new gospel of thought, language, sentiment, emotion; and I never parted with the scattered leaves—the *disjecta membra poetæ* —till I was enabled, at a later age, to study and explore the master's mind in the massive and harmonious fulness of his entire works, of which the *Beauties* were but a patch-work sample. All honour, then, to Washington Irving, and to Geoffrey Crayon's poker, which has stirred up so good a fire in a thousand hearts!

After a sojourn of some months in London, where I had the pleasure of making my wife known to my father and mother, who received her as a beloved daughter, we took a trip into Ireland and Scotland; and, by way of paying our expenses, while we gratified our love of the picturesque, I indulged my wife's inclinations, by making joint engagements at Dublin, Edinburgh, Glasgow, Liverpool, and other places. This answered a double purpose: first, that of paying travelling charges as aforesaid; and second, of cooling my partner's fancy for theatrical life, by showing her, without letting her suffer from the continual *désagrémens* that attend it.

One of the most ancient cities in England is

Rochester, in Kent. Its royal castle is celebrated in history for many important and bloody scenes, and there are curious legends attached to its ancient walls. My readers will recollect it from Dickens' story of the " Seven Poor Travellers." Thither we ran down from London, being invited to play a few nights, and spent a delightful week there; barring only the usual discomfort and annoyances of a small English provincial theatre. But we had a fine large, comfortable dressing-room, tolerable houses, immense applause. My wife enjoyed this old city much; it was so different from anything she had ever seen, or could see in her own country. I extract from her note-book a few *mems.*, which show her impressions:

" Here got the first sight of the chalky cliffs of Albion; and got plenty of the chalky soil *on my boots*, walking about. Crossing the bridge to Stroud, shall never forget the beautiful picture we saw from its centre. Below us, the Medway, bearing on its quiet bosom a fleet of little vessels, that seemed built like the boats—*feluccas*, I suppose, they are called—which I have seen in Oriental pictures. On one side, the grand old castle; roofless, uninhabited, desolate, yet grand and majestic in its ruins; its broken arches, draped with the overgrowing ivy, clinging to the crumbling walls; itself, ever fresh, green, and strong, like a firm friend, steadfast to fallen fortunes; and, here and there, bits of the old city wall, peeping out from beneath the same living canopy; with the quaint, old stone houses and the age-darkened towers of the cathedral frowning above. In the distance, the military *dépôts* of Chatham and Strood. On the other side, the sun, without a cloud, sinking slowly,

majestically, and, it appeared, almost reluctantly, in
a flood of gold and crimson, behind the white cliffs ;
like a Knight Templar of old, enveloping his burnished
armour in his snow-white mantle. It was a Sunday,
and crowds of people, in holiday attire, were passing
and repassing the bridge, chatting and laughing gaily ;
officers, in their bright scarlet regimentals ; soldiers,
of different corps, in different uniforms ; and labouring
men, with their wives and little ones—the contrasted
types of peace and war—all enjoying the day of rest ;
no drunkenness, no disorder. While, at the railway
station, hard by, the fuming and snorting engine alone
gave sign of unquiet and impatient eagerness—a type
of the energetic, sleepless, progressive will of man,
ever-restless and impatient for action, in the midst of
tranquillity and repose. Proudly, calmly, and it
seemed to me, almost sadly, the sun disappeared, as
if loth to leave the varied scene he gazed upon.
Never, in a city, have I seen so gorgeous a sunset, or
so varied a picture of animated, contented life. The
calm twilight that succeeded was equally charming
in its thoughtful aspect of gay serenity. The contrast
was wonderful !

" But the contrasts of the theatre were stronger
and stranger still ! Shall I ever forget Romeo and
Juliet at the Rochester Theatre ? That balcony
scene, especially ! The platform I stood on" (it is my
wife who speaks) " was a narrow door, lifted off its
hinges to uphold Juliet's feet ; resting very insecurely,
and scarcely wide enough to admit of a chair ; there
was one, but I dared not sit on it, for fear of a
mishap. The railing to the balcony was formed by a
carpenter's ladder, supported, at arm's length, by two

men : one behind the scenes, at one end, out of sight; and the other, on the stage, and masked by a piece of the scene ' representing *wall*.' Thus, I had a most frail and ricketty standing-place : I could not lean on the rail (the ladder), or the men would be unable to support it, at the full length of their raised hands ; and the platform was so narrow, so scanty, and so insecure, that I dared not move, for fear of falling backwards, or bringing the whole ' set ' down with me, in sight of the audience.   Talk of *love-scenes* on such a *platform !*

"I mounted to it by a crazy step-ladder ; and what passed between George, myself, and the carpenters behind, was something like this :—

[MYSELF. *Nervously, feeling the platform tremble under me.*   " Ah me !"

[*Then aside.* " Oh dear, I'm sure I shall fall.]

Oh, Romeo ! Romeo ! wherefore art thou Romeo ?

[*Carpenter below.*   " Its's quite safe, ma'am, if you don't move."]

Deny thy father and refuse thy name,

[*Carpenter, to the other man.*   " Bill, keep your side steady ! "]

Or, if thou wilt not, be but sworn my love,
And I'll no longer be a Capulet !

[*Then, aside.*   " O, how I wish the scene was over !"]

[*Carpenter below.*   " It's all right, ma'am, if you don't move !"]   .

'Tis but thy name that is my enemy !

(*Crack below !*)

[*Aside.* " O dear, dear ! I know it'll all come down ! "]

[*Carpenter.* " Bless you, ma'am, it's as safe as the church !"]

What's in a name ?

[*Carpenter,* " Steady with that ladder, Tom."]

That which we call a rose
By any other name would smell as sweet !

[GEORGE. *Aside to me, from behind his hat.* " Cut the scene short, Mary ; " and I made a great cut.]

Romeo, quit thy name ;
And for that name, which is no part of thee,
Take all myself !

[GEORGE, as ROMEO—I take thee at thy word ! *Juliet starts !*]

[Crack ! crack ! went the platform. I trembled.]

[GEORGE. *Aside.* " Keep still, Mary, for Heaven's sake !"]

Call me but love, I will forswear my name,

[" Curse those carpenters !"]

And never more be Romeo.
MYSELF. What man art thou,

[*Carpenter, below.* " Don't you turn, ma'am, or you'll be off?"]

—that thus bescreen'd in night
So stumblest on my counsel ?

[*Aside.* " O dear, its all giving way."]

GEORGE.—I know not how to tell thee who I am ;

O

[*Aside.* "Don't try to move, Mary, keep quite still "—]

My name, dear saint, is hateful to myself,

[*Aside.* " And cut the long speeches !"]

Because it is an enemy to thee !

[MYSELF. *Aside.* "O George, I'm sure it's going !"]

Mine ears have not yet drunk a hundred words—

[GEORGE. *Aside, to the men outside.* " Mind those props are safe."]

[*Man's voice.* " All right, sir."]

MYSELF.   Of that tongue's uttering, yet I know the sound.
          Art thou not Romeo, and a Montague ?
GEORGE.   Lady, by yonder blessed moon I swear—

[MYSELF.   *Aside.*   "You've   cut   four   long speeches !"]

[GEORGE. " Never mind ; get through as quick as you can !"]

[*Actress's voice below.* " Mrs. Vandenhoff, you've caught your dress in a nail ; mind it don't trip you."]

A hiss from the audience !

" And so on, till the end of the scene ; when, just as, with fear and trembling, I had descended, and put my foot on *terra firma*, the whole *side-front* of Capulet's house, balcony, terrace, platform, and all, came clattering to the ground, in sight of the audience. George rushed off to

                 his ghostly father's cell
His help to crave, and—

the rest of the line was drowned in the roars of the audience."

N.B. — *Never to play Juliet in future without seeing and trying the balcony in the morning.*"

In Dublin we found continual sources of amusement in the drollery and humour of the people, and the singular and shifting traits of character which they present. The Dublin audience is in itself a study. Some of their extemporised interludes and episodiacal dialogues, and even interruptions of the play, annoying as they are to the persons on the stage, are frequently highly amusing to a mere spectator. Their sense of the ludicrous is intense; and when any peculiarity of an actor's manner strikes them comically, no matter how serious the occasion may be, their fun is sure to find vent.

Thus, Mr. ————, a very dignified and rather over-solemn tragedian, playing Virginius at the Dublin Theatre, in the scene where he betroths his daughter to Icilius, in the touching and beautiful words of Knowles—

> " Didst thou but know, young man,
> How fondly I have watched her since the day
> Her mother died, and left me to a charge
> Of double duty bound—how she has been
> My cherish'd thought by day, my dream by night,
> My sweet companion, pupil, tutor, child—
> Thou would'st not wonder that my drowning voice
> And choking utterance, upbraids my tongue
> That tells thee she is thine,"—

the actor, who had given this passage with an almost clerical solemnity of manner, that smacked little of the Roman soldier and father, had just got to the

o 2

words, "that tells thee," and was about to join the
lovers' hands with the final, "she is thine," when
a voice from the gallery broke the spell, and, at the
same time, woke up the audience with this exclamation, uttered in a loud and threatening voice—"*I
forbid the bans!*" Shouts of laughter, hurrahs, and
yells, succeeded the joke; and the actor did not recover himself for the night.

I recollect once visiting the Dublin Theatre, before
I was an actor myself, when the play was Hamlet;
that character being sustained by a gentleman named
Butler, and the part of Horatio by Mr. H. Cooke.
The "boys" in the gallery were full of their fun
during the whole play, being especially facetious upon
the Player-King, and any of the subordinates whose
tenuity of leg, or peculiarity of voice or action, gave
a handle for a satirical jest or a rude witticism. Of
course, this gallery by-play was by no means advantageous to the legitimate effect of the tragedy, which
was continually interrupted by a cross-fire of jocose
dialogue. Thus, in the play-scene, where the King
lies asleep in the garden; as Ludovico advanced with
stealthy step and timorous action to pour the poison
in his ears, a fellow cried out to him, "Aha! ye
poisoning blackgyard! I'm watchin' you!" On
which he was reproved by another, from the opposite
side of the house, exclaiming, with assumed gravity,
"Whisht, Tim, wid ye! or ye'll wake up the ould
gintleman aslape in the cheer!" With such absurd
commentary did the play drag through the five acts.
On the fall of the curtain there arose a general shout-
ing and hurrahing, in which the name "Butler,
Butler," was frequently heard. After some minutes

of increased and increasing uproar, the actor so called presented himself, and acknowledged the doubtful compliment. But this was not enough to satisfy the imperious *gods*. A voice from above gave them a fresh hint, by calling out, " We've had the *Butler*, boys, now, let's have the *Cook!*" The idea was snatched at instantly ; and nothing could quell the riotous vociferations for " Cooke, Cooke !" that succeeded, but the re-appearance before the curtain of that actor, who had played Horatio !

The presence of the Lord-Lieutenant himself, with his *suite*—to do honour to whom on what is called a *Command-night* (because the performances are supposed to be *commanded* by the representatives of her Majesty) the lord-mayor and civic authorities, in their " robes and furr'd gowns," attend, with their wives and families, and the theatre is usually crowded— even the ceremonial and state of such an occasion as this is not always sufficient to quell Paddy's inherent love of fun, and the assertion of his free liberty of speech from the gallery. Sometimes, on these nights, the Lord-Lieutenant, and the audience generally, are made acquainted with little circumstances of the family history, or antecedents, of some of the spectators in the boxes, male or female—no matter which — whose *consate* Pat wishes to take down, by revelations from the gallery of incidents or facts (or even inventions) that throw the house into convulsions of laughter, and the unfortunate subject of the attack into the most painful confusion.

But the external show of reverence of the Irish for rank and title is, generally, very marked : I am speaking particularly of the lower orders, who, when

they can restrain their native turn for satire and sly
humour, from which no one is secure, look with a
sort of awe, not perhaps unmingled with bitterness,
on the Lord-Lieutenant and his state.   The Earl of
Carlisle held the vice-regal office in 1856, when we
were in Dublin ; and, in connection with this fact, I
must relate an incident that amused us excessively,
illustrating, as it did, Pat's veneration for rank, and
his half real, half ironical respect for the gentry, or
what he calls the *quality*.

My wife and I had engaged a jaunting-car—as the
Irish call those strange, awkward-looking, but particularly easy, two-wheeled carriages, in which you sit
side-ways, two on a seat, back to back to two others
on the other side, with your feet on a ledge over the
wheel ; and we were driving along the quay towards
the Phœnix Park, when, at some distance a-head, I
observed an open carriage and four, with postillions,
approaching at a rapid rate.   I perceived that it was
the Lord-Lieutenant's equipage ; and our driver, who
had, for an Irish boy, been up to this time unusually
taciturn, presently made the same discovery, which
he announced to us in almost a whisper.   The carriage came on, and in it I recognised Lord Carlisle
and an *Aide*.   Having had the honour, some years
before, of being presented to the Earl of Carlisle,
when he was Lord Morpeth, as the carriage passed
I raised my hat ; a courtesy to which the Lord-
Lieutenant was entitled from the meanest stranger.
Of course, the salutation was courteously acknowledged and returned by his lordship, as the carriage
whirled by.   What was the surprise, and at the
same time the amusement of my wife and myself,

when our taciturn, many-caped driver, glancing round
at us, exclaimed in a tone of wonder,—

"O, murther! Sure there's the Lord-Liften'nt
after bowing to 'em!"

Then, applying the whip to his horse, which, up
to this moment had maintained a very leisurely, not
to say lazy pace, he cried out "Get up, ye blackgyard!
Sure you've *qualaty* behind ye! (*whip*.) Isn't the
Lord-Liften'nt after bowin' to 'em! Go long, you
divil! (*whip*.) Sure you've *qualaty* behind ye! Would
ye disgrace yourself, ye lazy vagabone!"

And with these exhortations, repeated and varied
at intervals, he continued to stir up his lank, lazy,
broken-kneed steed, till we arrived at the park-gate.
There descending from his perch, with an air of profound respect, he spread a small piece of carpet for
my wife to put her feet on as she alighted, muttering
all the time some words in which "Lord-Liften'nt"
and "qualaty" were alone audible. Desiring to walk
about the grounds, we left him engaged in polishing up
his harness with the greatest diligence, with the same
under-toned accompaniment of *Lord-Liften'nt* and
qualaty, kept up all the time. After strolling through
the beautiful park, one of the finest promenades in any
city in the world, we returned to our jaunting-car
and our driver, who by this time had polished the
plate-work of his harness into a wonderful state of
brightness, and had wrought such an improvement in
the general appearance of his machine, that we hardly
recognised it. He again spread the piece of carpet
for my wife's feet (as if, after walking nearly an hour,
there was any danger of her boots being soiled now,
but this was an Irishman's gallantry), mounted to his

perch, touched up his steed with his whip, and again exhorting him not to disgrace *qualaty* that the Lord Liften'nt was after bowin' to, and reviling him, whenever he relaxed his speed, as a vagaboue and a blackgyard, drove us home in much better time than he ever dreamt of making when he first took us up. When we alighted, there was the same Sir Walter-Raleigh-ceremony of the carpet, the same mutterings about the Lord Liften'nt and the qualaty; and, of course (which after all, I very much suspect was the end and aim of all his delicate *attintions*)—on receiving the fare, a leering request for " a trifle to drink your honour's health ; which *pour-boire* could not, of course, be refused by *qualaty* to whom the Lord Liften'nt was after bowin' to !

We spent a very happy time in Dublin, with delightful country jaunts, on the never-failing *car*, among the romantic scenery of the Wicklow mountains.   Mr. Harris, the manager, I found a man of honour and a courteous gentleman ; and my wife established herself, at once, in the favour of the rather uncertain audience.   She made an especial impression in " Evadne," which she repeated several times in her fortnight's engagement, and was always enthusiastically cheered in her last scene.   The play, it will be remembered, is the production of the celebrated Irish author—a college-mate of my father, by the bye—RICHARD SHIEL, the highly-polished and yet impassioned orator, and sometime associate of DANIEL O'CONNELL in the great agitation that was crowned by the grant of Catholic Emancipation in England, and opened the doors of the House of Commons to Shiel and others of his countrymen.

In Edinburgh, too, we spent an agreeable month, never weary of its picturesque Old Town, its Calton, its Arthur's seat, its Holyrood, its Castle, its Scott's monument, and the thousand recollections that they awaken and recall. Edinburgh, at night, is I think, one of the most striking pictures that can be conceived—a great effect of light and shade, blending in the mind the past and present. Standing in Prince's-street, in the new town, you look up across the gorge of the railroad and the intervening gardens, and, some hundreds of feet above your head, you see another town, of ancient aspect, the thousand lights of which look down, like watchful eyes upon the modern street and its "fire-new" improvements; while, on your right at a distance, darkly frowns the massive old Castle, in which the unfortunate Mary was a prisoner, and from a window of which she let down her infant son, afterwards James I. of England, in a wicker-basket, to the arms of friends below. This night-effect is very extraordinary, and impresses you, both in itself and by association; conjuring up to your imagination stately processions of the feudal age, with its " bonnetted chieftains,"

" All plaided and plumed in their tartan array,"

with their rude manners, savage feuds, boisterous revels, and bloody raids, brought into unexpected contact and contrast with the regular forms, manners, and habits of modern civilization and order.

Every one that has an opportunity should run over from Liverpool to Edinburgh, visit Roslin Castle and Hawthornden, in the neighbourhood, make a run

to Glasgow, thence up the Clyde, and take a peep at
the Trosachs and Loch Lomond.

At the Edinburgh Theatre we met with particular
favour from the public, and received some unusual
marks of their approbation.

I was delighted to find that in Dublin, Edinburgh,
Liverpool, and indeed in every large city where my
wife appeared, her claims were at once admitted, without any allowance, or disparagement, on the plea of
her novice-ship.   She was judged simply on her own
merits ; and I have frequently had the pleasure of
seeing her triumphantly recalled before the curtain
at the Dublin and Liverpool Theatres, in Mrs. Haller,
Evadne, Margaret Elmore, and other parts.

Much as I deprecate this practice, as too frequently
a hackneyed and unmeaning compliment, I must except one occasion on which it gave me real pleasure,
from its being the spontaneous and free act of the
whole audience—an audience, too, to which we were
utter strangers.   The incident occurred at the Edinburgh Theatre Royal.   On the *exeunt* of myself and
wife, as Macbeth and Lady, in the murder-scene, in
the middle of the second act, the applause that followed was kept up for several minutes, long after I
had washed the blood from my hands behind the
scenes ; nor would the house allow the scene—which
should continue with the entrance of Macduff and
others—to proceed, until *we* had re-entered, and had
been greeted with loud cheers, the pit rising to us.

This burst of enthusiasm was particularly remarkable, as Mr. Windham, the manager, observed, because the Edinburgh audience is proverbial for its re-
serve, and for the severity of its judgment.   The

fact was, therefore, recorded as something especially worthy of note in the theatre of the Scottish metropolis; and I trust the reader will excuse my pardonable vanity in mentioning it here.

We had the satisfaction of playing *Hamlet* in Glasgow to the fullest house, as the manager declared, that had ever been known in the theatre. The " gods" were uncomfortably crowded, and, in consequence, unpleasantly obstroperous; so that the greater part of the play was " mere dumb show." I took the opportunity of being alone on the stage, to give them a lecture on good behaviour, objecting especially to their making *me* uncomfortable *on the stage*, because *they* were uncomfortable *up-stairs*. This had its effect while I was on; but the moment I made my *exit*, the uproar began with fresh vigour. Sir William Don, who played in the afterpiece, had a hard time of it. I confess I did not leave Glasgow with a very exalted idea of its audience: a ruder set and a ruder manager I never met with. His wife was a charming woman, but he ———! *Beauty and the Beast!* These are the kind of fellows that make one hate a theatre, and all connection with it.

Of Mr. and Mrs. Windham, on the contrary, of the Edinburgh Theatre, we retain very pleasant recollections; though it was really lamentable to see the utter decay of theatrical taste in a city which had formerly been so great a patron of the drama. When Sir WALTER SCOTT lived, he was a frequent visitor at the Edinburgh Theatre; and WILSON (CHRISTOPHER NORTH,) and JEFFREY might have often been seen there. But that day has entirely gone by. The Edinburgh Theatre, now-a-days, can seldom boast of a distinguished or educated audience : the boxes are usually deserted; and the pit is no longer tenanted by those sturdy critics whose opinion and applause were of value to the actor, and set the seal on his reputation :

" So runs the world away ?"

After a year pleasantly spent in England, Ireland, and Scotland, we took passage in the Canada from Liverpool, and arrived, in the middle of November, at Boston. Having played an engagement that was offered me immediately on my arrival, I set about carrying out my cherished desire of entirely quitting the stage, which had entirely lost its charms for me, and which appeared day by day, and night by night, to be sinking lower, as an acknowledged source of intellectual amusement. I have never, as some, I think, without reasonable grounds have done, claimed for the stage the position of a moral instructor; *that* I do not consider by any means a necessary part of its purpose. But, when it ceases to be regarded as affording amusement worthy of the attention and encouragement of cultivated minds, and only *pays* when it panders to vulgar taste or local prejudices, then, for my part, I desire to escape from a profession which, while attended with many heart-wearing annoyances, offers no high object of ambition, and neither elevates the mind nor fills the pocket.

Henceforth my appearances in public are confined to the lecture-room ; and my ambition is fully satisfied in being received as an Interpreter of Shakspere's inspired page, without the aid or drawback, whichever it may be considered (and there are strong arguments for either view), of stage accessories, costume, scenery, and a company of actors. I never stand at the reading-desk, in my plain, evening *toilette*, with the works of him who

" was not of an age, but for all time,"

open before me, that I do not congratulate myself on being freed from the pomp and circumstance of the theatre, its conventional trammels, and its inharmonious accompaniments.

" Aye, marry ! now my soul has elbow-room !"

There is nothing to contract its flight, to disturb or interrupt the current of my conceptions, or to break the consistency of my design. If my audience do not answer to my calls on their emotions by a sympathetic communion of heart and mind with mine, then the fault and the shame are mine alone. If they do, if they follow me, not only with eye and ear, but with quick and ready vibration of the chords of feeling, awakened by touch or tone of mine—if we are united for the moment, in a brotherhood of affectionate reverence for him who stood at Nature's altar as her high priest, to whom she committed the arcana of her mysteries, and gave the magic key that unlocks the fountain of the heart—if, through my ministration, a thought, a word, a precept of his shall take root in a single mind, and bear for fruit the study of his liberal philosophy, the love of his enlarged humanity, to which nothing that is of man is indifferent—then I shall feel that the tangled yarn of my life has at least some golden threads in it, though few and rare, and that I have cast at least a pebble on the great cairn raised by the world to Shakspere's name.

XVIII.

SUMMING-UP—Advice to the Stage-struck---A View of the present Condition of the Stage—The Theatre and its Purposes—Farewell.

In November, 1858, I had the honour to be admitted to practice at the Bar, in this country.

Perhaps my recent assumption of this character will be sufficient to authorise, and excuse, my final *summing-up* of the result of my experience of theatrical life, with a few words of *gratuitous advice* " to all whom these presents may concern."

To any ingenuous youth, then, who may be now meditating a plunge into that uncertain, or rather *certain*, " sea of troubles," that shines and glitters in the seductive dazzle of the footlights---to such a one I say: Go to sea, in reality; go to law, go to church, go to physic ; go to Italy and strike a blow for liberty (if cause and opportunity again offer) ; go to anything, or anywhere, that will give you an honest and decent livelihood, rather than go upon the stage!

To any young lady with a similar proclivity, I would say : Buy a sewing machine, and take in plain-work, first ! So shall you save yourself much sorrow, bitter disappointment, secret tears.

Unless he be eminent, an actor is nobody. His motto must be *aut Cæsar aut nullus,* or he will

always be a subaltern. He must have the Hotspur
feeling, that

"it were an easy leap
To pluck bright honour from the pale-faced moon,"

or he will make no spring at all.

Yet how few can, or do, attain to eminence. And
even eminence, now-a-days, when attained, does not
lead to great material results. The day for making
fortunes on the stage is past ; while the same, or a
less amount of persevering labour than is requisite to
raise a man to distinction in the theatrical profession,
would make him rich in any other.

A man may be a second or third-rate preacher,
lawyer, doctor, architect, engineer, and make a good
income, hold a respectable position, live in clover, die
in honour, be buried in state, and lie under ostentatious
marble with an adulatory epitaph, enumerating the
virtues which he *ought* to have possessed—a rather
doubtful certificate for Paradise !

An actor is great or nothing :

" Mediocribus esse poetis
Non Di, non hominess, non concessere columnæ,"

is as applicable, *mutato nomine,* to players (*histrioni-
bus*) as to poets ; for certes, a middling actor, neither
gods (in the gallery), men (in the pit), nor critics in
the columns of newspapers, can endure !

As for the idea that there is any thing degrading
in the practice of the actor's art, in itself, that I
imagine, is a worn-out prejudice. Can it degrade the
mind to devote one's powers to the vocal interpretation of the outpourings of a great poet's heart and
brain ; to identify oneself, by a subtle, metaphysical

transformation—of which a great actor only is capable
—with the lofty aspirations and the enthusiastic
hopes and feelings of the noblest heroes and patriots
—the high intelligences of past ages—that, by the
poet's "so potent art" are recalled to transient life
upon the mimic scene? And, in the exhibition of
the darker passions of our nature—as men have been
considered benefactors to science who have bequeathed
their bodies for dissection for the advancement of
physical knowledge—is he not a public benefactor
who devotes himself, living, body and mind, to the
animated illustration of the terrible workings of
passion, and lays bare his own trembling and quivering heart for our intellectual profit and example, and
the disclipline and correction of our minds?

This is what the great actor does, who stands
before us the fit representative of Macbeth, Othello,
Lear, and other characters of passionate excess, carrying with them the retribution of suffering and despair.
To do this worthily, the actor must devote himself
to the study of the human heart, its nicest shades
and subtleties; the various characters of men, the
springs and motives of their actions, their passions,
and the expressions of those passions, as modified by
age, character, or circumstances; and, fortified with
this study, and this knowledge, he must set himself
to present pictures of humanity in the strong colours
of truth, touched by the softening pencil of poetry,
and gilded with the light of imagination. If, to the
fulfilment of this task he should bring sensibility,
taste, fancy, mental culture; a noble and flexible
voice, a fine presence, a graceful bearing: and
should crown the whole by an education that should

have elevated his intellect, and attuned his soul to
the grand and the beautiful by communion with the
great poets and orators—then to be called the first
actor of the day would, indeed, be a noble title !
Such a one would be the living, breathing word of the
poet and the philosopher ; the voice of the oracles of
their wisdom ; the high-priest at the shrine of human
nature ; the interpreter of man to man himself !

And if such a man were wanted at the present
day ; if the public taste—or inclination rather, let us
call it—demanded so high a standard, doubtless such
a one would arise. Garrick and John Kemble were,
from traditional report, men of such minds and such
accomplishments.

But the fancy of the day runs in a much lower
direction, and seeks for much inferior sources of gratification ; so that eminence, now-a-days, does not im-
ply greatness. For it is not the grand, the lofty, the
noble, the pre-eminent, that pleases ; but the flashy,
the slight, the trivial, the transient, which delights.
It is in vain to cry out on the decline of theatrical
talent. It is the public taste that makes actors, and
elevates or depresses them, as it is itself high or low.
Authors write plays, dramas, farces, such as will
please ; the actors fulfil their task, and perform all
that can be required of them in being equal to what is
set down for them by the author, and what the public
requires. It is hardly probable that, henceforth, men
and women of education and talent will embrace the
stage as a profession ; for those qualities are daily less
called for in its practice. Petty pieces make petty
actors. A great theme demands a great poet ; a
rhymester is sufficient for a paltry subject. No great

artist was ever made by painting dwarfs and carica-
tures, though he may occasionally have indulged in
such triflings; nor were Garrick, Kemble, and others,
the great masters of the dramatic art, formed by
cramping their powers to the dimensions of local
dramas, occasional pieces, or the sweepings of the
French Theatre : and these are the staple commodity
of the modern stage, furnished in compliance with the
requirements of the taste of the day.

I am willing to confess that, in my experience of
the stage, I never recollect a period since I was a
boy when the legitimate drama, as it is called, in
its highest form—the tragedies of Shakspere, the
comedies of Sheridan and his compeers, or the plays
of Knowles and his contemporaries—were sufficient,
even when unexceptionably played, to keep a London
theatre open with good houses, unless aided by some
extraordinary combination of talent, or some extravagant outlay for spectacle and scenery, which rendered
it unprofitable, if not ruinous, to the manager.

We know full well that John Kemble, Charles
Kemble, and Mrs. Siddons, frequently played together
to bad houses at Covent Garden; and that the
manager of that day was compelled to have recourse
to mere spectacle, even to the introduction of horses
on the stage, to prop the falling fortunes of his house.

Garrick himself, we know, from his life, was
under the necessity of refreshing his waning popularity by an absence on the continent. Edmund
Kean's novelty wearing off in London, it was necessary to back him up by the junction of Mr. Young,
an actor of the Kemble school ; and their union, for
a time only, drew audiences which neither, alone,

though supported by the strongest companies, could
attract. I have myself seen Mr. Macready and Miss
Helen Faucit together, at the Haymarket Theatre,
more than once, play to considerably less than the
nightly expenses of the house.   At this moment I
do not believe that there is any living tragedian who
could, on his own attraction, half fill any first class
London theatre, even if supported by unimpeachable
company.   It is a fact that more money is now-
a-days spent in theatrical amusements nightly, than
was ever known in what are called the palmy days
of the drama ; and it is also a fact that the pieces that
find most favour are those of the lightest and flimsiest
texture.

As an art, therefore, acting is fast dying out ; for
there remains no school for its cultivation.   Drury
Lane and Covent Garden were formerly such schools,
in which the great actors of that day flourished for
the example of the younger ones who should succeed
them ; but these great English theatres are now both
converted into Italian opera houses.   Mr. Charles
Kean has terminated his connexion with the Princess's
Theatre, and so ends his series of Shaksperian Revivals, which, according to his own showing, did not
remunerate him, and which nothing but his own
private means enabled him to carry out.   The Haymarket Theatre alone remains for the production of
plays and dramas, chiefly taken from the French, the
main purpose of which is the exhibition of Mr. Buckstone, the manager's, drolleries, the annual Christmas
pantomime, and Easter burlesque.   Such is the state
of the drama in England.

In this country it is much the same.   Tragedy

and comedy, properly so-called, no longer attract or interest an audience ; they have become as wearisome as a thrice-told tale ; their place has been taken by drama, melodrama, interlude, and farce.

Mr. Forrest is the only tragedian who can fill, or even half fill a theatre in New York, by his own attraction ; and the other legitimate stars (heaven save the mark !) are compelled to confine their illusory brightness to the Western cities, with not very dazzling effect even there. A lower and less cultivated audience has succeeded to the critical and discriminating public, whose approval it was once an actor's ambition to merit and obtain ; and the style of the stage is lowered accordingly. Actor and auditor act and re-act on each other. Rant has taken the place of passion ; extravagance has banished simple nature and truth. That " smoothness and temperance " which Shakspere inculcated, and which was once considered the *acmé* of art — " even in the torrent, tempest, and whirlwind of passion " — is now regarded as " slow ; " and as the sign, not of a proper self-control and well-regulated taste, but of a want of energy and power : as if violence were not always a mark of self-distrust, and a want of self-command.

There was a time, too, when the stage was regarded as a school of refined pronunciation, elegant carriage, and distinguished manners. The great comedians were men of high cultivation, and accomplished in all the externals of a gentleman. They kept the best society, were formed in it, and by it ; and perpetuated and popularized its graces. Society

" lent them no grace they did not pay it back ; "

and to see them on the stage was like being admitted
to a most agreeable, high-bred party. It was a kind
of education, in the day of Elliston, Lewis, Charles
Kemble, and their immediate successors, to witness
a good comedy — we learn this from Lamb and
Hazlitt—and men, to a certain degree, copied the
bearing, gestures, pronunciation, style, and carriage
of these artists, who made grace, and elegance of
speech and action, the particular object of their study.

"How many fine gentlemen," exclaims Hazlitt,
" do we owe to the stage!" Mrs. Montfort and Mrs.
Abington were the models of fine ladies in their day,
and divided the town on the point of superiority in
elegance.   It was her lady-like air and refinement
of manner that set a coronet on the brow of Miss
Farren, and elevated the representative of Lady
Teazle to the state of the Countess of Derby.   It
was the same on the French Stage in the day of
Racine, Moliére, and Voltaire. A celebrated beauty
and wit of the Court of Louis XV. declared that
she was acquainted with but two men who knew how
to converse with ladies—Le Kain the actor and the
Marquis de Vaudreuil.

These qualities are, now-a-days, not looked for by
the public ; and are, consequently, not cultivated by
the actor. Vulgar familiarity passes for easy elegance ;
strut and swagger for dignity and grace.   Buffoonery
is more welcome to the general audience than humour ;
practical jokes than the most sparkling wit ; and
everything is sacrificed to the bringing down a round
of applause, or the raising a boisterous laugh.

Is this the fault of the actor ?   No ; it is the fault
of the public.   It is, of course, within the province

of the drama's patrons to choose the nature and
quality of their amusements ; but they cannot, with
any appearance of consistency, turn round upon the
actors, and blame them for the decline of the stage,
as an elegant, a refined and refining source of pleasure, when that decline is the result of the public's
own action, and of a compliance with its standard of
taste. The actor is not to be expected to be above
his audience ; and, though he may—as, no doubt, he
frequently does—despise them in his heart, yet, if
he continue to appear before them, he will assuredly
fall to the level of their tastes and desires, however
repugnant they may be to his own.

I have never claimed for the stage the dignity of a
moral teacher, though it does in practice frequently
fulfil that office, incidentally ; but *that* is supererogatory : something which it may do, and frequently
does, but which it cannot be required to do ; and
which, when it does, it puts forth an additional claim
to the support of the wise and the good. Art and
morals are distinct : it is only to be required that they
shall not be antagonistic.   The Laocoon—

> " The father's love and mortal's agony
>   With an immortal's patience blending ; "

and the Apollo Belvidere,—

> The God of life, and poesy, and light—
> The sun in human limbs array'd, and brow
> All radiant from his triumph in the fight,—

these great creations of the sculptor's chisel are preserved and cherished to delight the eye of taste, as
works of art, and as types of humanity in its most
elevated aspect.   Who expects them to point a moral

from their pedestals? Their purpose is to stand perpetual models of ideal beauty and grace—triumphs of the art which arrays the " poetic marble" in eternal glory.

, So, to claim for the stage, or to demand for it, the office or the dignity of a moral instructor, is absurd ; that is not its purpose or its province. We have no more right to expect the stage to be either a pulpit, or a school of morals, than we are entitled to demand of it theological discourses, or lessons in political science. The stage is simply a picture of human life in action, in which man may see himself " as in a glass;" both " his better and his worser part" fairly exhibited ; and, if the exhibition be a true one, it is the fault of the looker-on himself if he be not moved by self-contemplation to self-correction and improvement. The moral must be left to be in-ferred by the conscience of the audience.

> " Is there no play
> To ease the anguish of a torturing hour?"

exclaims Theseus, in the Midsummer-Night's Dream. If the stage furnish an intellectual relaxation for the mental drudgery of thought, a relief to the cares and business of the day, it fulfils its purpose, and deserves well of the commonwealth, as long as it avoids coarseness, vulgarity, and buffoonery. When it de-generates into these, when it no longer aims, by the elevation of the picture it presents,

> " To touch the soul with tender strokes of art,
>   To wake the genius, and to mend the heart,"—

then, it ceases to be worthy the pursuit of a self-respecting man, or of the support of a refined and self-respecting community.

It is, in fact, with the public and the press that the correction and regulation of the theatre must lie. Who are the natural censors of the stage, if not the public who patronise and the press whose duty it is to animadvert upon it?

" The theatre," says Sneer, in the ' Critic,' " in proper hands, *might* certainly be made the school of morality ; but now, I am sorry to say it, *people seem to go there principally for their entertainment.*"

This ironical sentence of the cynical Sneer contains the whole gist of the matter. People go to the theatre to be amused, to be entertained ; and all that it behoves the moralist or the legislator to see to is, that the entertainment shall be wholesome—that the popular mind, especially the youthful portion of it, be not corrupted by its amusements, nor drink from a treacherous, Circean cup, poison instead of refreshment.

Let press and public do its duty : the power is in their hands to sustain or to condemn. The amusements of a people take their tone from the people themselves ; and the theatre is, of all institutions for the people, the one most subject to, must under the control of, public opinion.

> " The drama's laws the drama's patrons give,
> And they who live to please, must please to live."

That is the kernel of the whole matter.

———

Perhaps it will not be deemed an inappropriate closing of these " Reminiscences," if I end with a

P

passage from a satirical poem of my own, entitled
"Common-Sense," which I have delivered on several
occasions in New York, Boston, Albany, Baltimore,
Cincinnati, and other cities. It expresses my view of
the stage, as a social institution, and an intellectual
relaxation, worthy the anxious attention of the philosopher, the moralist, and the statesman.

THE THEATRE.

Youth seeks amusement as for light of day
Pine flowers, and drink bright colours from its ray;
Who would condemn to shade the rose's bloom,
Or bid it waste on darkness its perfume?
As well Youth's fresh impulsive spring to cage,
And chill its summer with the frosts of age!
Those solemn Mentors who, with awful frown,
Would put each popular amusement down
Bar whist, the theatre, the lively dance,
Send waltz and polka skipping back to France,
May well take heed lest in their zeal to curse
Each favourite sport, they drive their flocks to worse!

There is a time for serious thought, for prayer,
An hour for pleasure and an hour for care;
The mind must have relief, relax, unbend,
Or stupor, gloom, will be its dismal end;
Mere idleness is the high road to sin,
The heart, all empty, lets the tempter in;
Debarr'd from wholesome spur, 'twill fly to evil,
And give itself to rum and to the devil,—
Well if the gallows-tree, or maniac's chain
Revenge not Nature and her outraged reign!

The point to aim at 's mental recreation,
The rock to shun is moral dissipation;
Plain COMMON SENSE may surely draw the line,
Without the aid of schoolman or divine.

The elephant that stands upon his head
And dances hornpipes, surely can't be said

With all his aptness for *insane tuition*,
To be an Intellectual Exhibition :
And none, I'm sure, but very silly gabies,
To woolly horses flock, or *bogus-babies*.

From Pan's rude reeds the solemn organ grew ;
A panting kettle first attention drew
To steam's vast power : e'en Fulton might have toil'd
And died unknown,—*had not the kettle boil'd !*
To Franklin's kite that drew from heav'n its fire
We trace the germ of telegraphic wire,
And two vast continents may owe the joy
Of close communion, to a paper toy !
From small beginnings vast conceptions rise :
If sound, the project lives, if hollow, dies :
So, from the humble plank of Thespis' cart,
First dawn'd the DRAMA, rose the actor's art ;
How vast a progress from the crude first thought
Have mellowing Time and conqu'ring Genius wrought !

Where Ganges rolls—ere Europe's stage began,
A native Drama rose in HINDOSTAN :
Yes, there, in that wild land, in earliest age
The Hindoo had his DRAMA and his stage :
In every age, in prose, blank verse, or rhyme
Some form of Drama lives in every clime.
Think you the stage plays an ignoble part,
That thus it stirs the Universal Heart ?—
The stage's purpose ask of COMMON SENSE ;
'Tis surely *to amuse, without offence*
To taste, to virtue, decency, or truth,
To virgin modesty, or candid youth ;
To " show the age and body of the time,"
Or stained with folly, or debased with crime ;
The world s great glass, wherein Humanity
May view, in action, Life's Epitome.

'Tis not the province of a social art
To lash at vice, and snatch the Pulpit's part.
The *painter's pencil* takes no *moral* view :
Good taste requires his drawing shall be true,
His colours fair, perspective just ; the scene,
Such as from *Nature's studio* he may glean :

                                              P 2

Tell *him* his works no moral maxim teach,
He'll say—his business is to *paint*, not *preach ;*
Sufficient if his canvas shall display
No vulgar detail, no offensive *trait.* *
Such, too, the Drama's plea and just defence,
Arraigned before the Bar of COMMON SENSE.

The TRAGIC MUSE Man's deepest passions shows :
Invests with life imaginary woes,
Or lays the wounded, writhing spirit bare,
In all the torture of a black despair :
But when for harlot guilt she claims our tears,
Then drive her from the scene with mocking jeers ;
A recreant, false, deceitful, whimp'ring jade
That sports with feeling, and makes tears a trade !†
Whose is the fault if *you* don't interfere ?
The players act what you delight to hear :
Did you but hiss, or, better, stay away,
You'd ostracise each false, licentious play :
No manager repeats what does not pay.

Yet nobly SHAKSPERE'S acted moral shows,
That straight from heart to head instruction goes ;
Not by dull rule or musty apothegm
Conceiv'd in spleen, begot in cynic phlegm ;
His is no fable with a *moral tail*
Tack'd on for clearness, if the text should fail :—
Hamlet, Macbeth, Othello, Shylock, Lear,
No shadowy forms from Fancy's realm appear,
But living, thinking, tortured flesh and blood,
As if before our eyes exact they stood :
We see them, know them, feel they acted so ;
Question their minds, wonder what next they'll do ;
And when, at length the closing curtain's down,
We grieve, as if the suffering were own,

---

* This is a good rhyme to English ears, a bad one to American ; in England, the word *trait* retains its French sound in pronunciation (like tray) ; in America it is anglicised to rhyme with *fate.*

† As in such plays as *La Dame aux Camélias ;* produced on the American stage under the title of *Camille*, in which a harlot is the heroine, and dies a martyr to *virtuous love, the hard-heartedness of Society* and *consumption !* Faugh !

   " An ounce of civet, good apothecary,
    To sweeten my imagination ! "

Take home the lesson to our silent bed,
And con the sermon by the poet read.
Thus Shakspere works; but you need not be told
When Nature made his mind she broke the mould;*
Her greatest triumph, and her sole despair;
He "had no brother" and he left no heir;
No second Shakspere shall the world e'er see,—
Abstract and voice of all humanity!

The COMIC MUSE trips lightly on the stage,
Holding her mirror to the fleeting Age:
With wit and humour harmless laughter moves;
Mocks Fashion's follies, and its fickle loves;
With diamond pencil polishes her phrase,
And many-coloured forms of life displays.
What if false sentiment, perhaps e'en worse,
Loose words, may stain the comic poet's verse?
Efface them,—hiss! they are its shame, not boast;
Shall useful service for a *word* be lost?
The skilful doctor does the best he can
To cure the fever, not to kill the man.

The Drama's now a great establish'd fact
That can't be blink'd, ignored; howe'er attack'd
By vain abuse or angry prejudice;
The time's gone by when *playing was a vice;*
When bigots mark'd the actor with a ban,
(Tho' saintly crowds to hear his accents ran),
Denied him sacred rite and hallowed grave,—
Filching from God the soul he made to save,—
And, for the pleasure which his life had giv'n
On earth, refused him, dead, a place in heav'n.
No! wiser days bring gentler feelings in,
And "Nature's touches make the whole world kin!" †

Then, since no power can "put the Drama down,"
Best try, by reason, to improve its tone:

* This idea I borrowed (unconsciously at the time—I discovered the source afterwards) from Byron's Monody to Sheridan; but it is, surely, much more applicable to Shakspere; brilliant as Sheridan was, his genius was not like Shakspere's, *universal.*

† The absurd bigotry that formerly *excommunicated* Actors, and denied them the rites of the Church, in Roman Catholic countries, is now mentioned to be smiled at. Fancy *Moliére* being denied burial in consecrated ground!

Don't cut it root and branch, with ruthless knife,
But wisely prune it to more healthful life;
So shall it thrive and bloom a goodly tree,—
Bearing rich fruit, from blight or canker free;
Ennobling thoughts shall twine around its stem,
It's leaves shall grace the poet's diadem,
Domestic virtues flourish in its shade,
Till moralists, disarm'd, shall own its aid
To warn, instruct, encourage, and persuade.

In taking leave of the theatrical profession in these pages,—for I have never taken any formal public " farewell " of it—let me express my kindest wishes for the well-doing of all those with whom I have sometime trod the mimic scene.   Most especially do I wish success and honour to such as conscientiously strive to maintain the dignity and grace of the stage, and aspire to merit a share in that noble eulogy, by which — through the person of John Kemble—the poet Campbell has shed a glory on the profession of the stage :—

His was the spell o'er hearts
    Which only ACTING lends,
The youngest of the sister arts
    Where all their beauty blends :
For ill can POETRY express
    Full many a tone of thought sublime,
And painting, mute and motionless,
    Steals but a glance of time :
But, by the mighty ACTOR brought
    Illusion's perfect triumphs come,—
Verse ceases to be airy thought,
    And SCULPTURE to be dumb !

On the annexed page is given a part of a New York play bill, showing the cast, &c., of Mr. Charles Kean's revival of King John.

TAYLOR AND GREENING, PRINTERS, GRAYSTOKE-PLACE, FETTER-LANE.

PARK THEATRE.

Boxes $1.   Pit 50 Cents.   Gallery 25 Cents.

THE GREAT SHAKSPERIAN REVIVAL!!!

MRS. CHARLES KEAN & MR. CHARLES KEAN

IN SHAKSPERE'S TRAGEDY OF

KING JOHN.

To give additional effect to this Play

MR. GEO. VANDENHOFF

Has been expressly engaged to represent the Character of FAULCONBRIDGE.

IN ANNOUNCING THIS

GREAT SHAKSPERIAN REVIVAL!

The Manager begs respectfully to state, that no labour or expense has been spared in endeavouring to attain the UTMOST FIDELITY OF HISTORIC ILLUSTRATION !

☞ *In consequence of the enormous expense attending this performance, THE FREE LIST, with the single exception of the Public Press, must be suspended, and no orders can on any account be admitted.*☜

Wednesday Evening, November 18, 1846, will be

Performed SHAKSPERE'S Historical Tragedy of

KING JOHN,

(Produced under the Immediate Direction and Superintendence of Mr. CHAS. KEAN, at a cost and with a degree of Correctness and Splendour, it is believed, hitherto not witnessed in any Theatre.)

THE SCENES painted on upwards of 15,000 square feet of Canvas, by Mr. HILLYARD, Mr. GRAIN, and Assistants.

THE COSTUMES, COSTLY ARMOURS, 176 in number, DECORATIONS and APPOINTMENTS, from the Authorities named hereafter, by Mr. DEJONGE.

THE MACHINERY, by Mr. SPEYERS.

☞ The indulgence of the audience is respectfully solicited between the first and second Acts, as the whole of the previous scene has to be removed for the purpose of exhibiting a Panoramic View of Angiers, the French Camp and Distant Country: the Stage thrown open to the Walls of the Theatre.

ENGLISH.

JOHN, KING OF ENGLAND .. .. **MR. CHARLES KEAN.**

Prince Henry, his son, afterwards King Henry III. .. .. Mrs. Sutherland
Arthur, Duke of Bretagne, son of Jeffrey, late Duke of Bre-
    tagne, the elder brother of King John .. .. Miss Denny
William Mareshall, Earl of Pembroke .. .. Mr. A. Andrews
Geffrey FitzPeter, Earl of Essex, Chief Justiciary of England .. .. Heath
William Longsword, Earl of Salisbury .. .. Chanfrau
Robert Bigot, Earl of Norfolk .. .. McDouall
Hubert De Burgh, Chamberlain to the King .. .. Dyott
Robert Faulconbridge, son of Sir Robert Faulconbridge .. .. .. Fisher

PHILIP FAULCONBRIDGE, his half Brother, Bastard Son
    to King Richard the First.. .. .. **MR. GEORGE VANDENHOFF**

James Gurney, servant to Lady Faulconbridge .. .. Povey
First English Knight .. .. Gallot
Sheriff of Northamptonshire.. .. .. Milot
Herald.. .. .. Anderson
Peter, of Pomfret, a Prophet .. .. Matthews
Pages to King John .. .. Mrs. Gallot and Miss Flynn

Green Knight with Buckler and Martel De Fer, De Warrene, Oxford, Hereford,
Arundel, FitzWalter, De Percey, De Clare, De Ros. Knights,
Esquires, Herald, Attendants on Herald, Trumpeters,
Banner Bearers, Bretagne Knights, Bretagne
Standard, &c., by Auxiliaries.

FRENCH.

Philip, King of France .. .. Mr. Barry
Lewis, the Dauphin.. .. .. Stark
Melun, a French Lord .. ..Bellamy
Chatillon, Ambassador from France to King John .. .. .. Sutherland
Herald .. ..Sprague
Citizen of Angiers .. .. G. Andrews

De Blois, D'Arras, St. Omer, De Bretel, De Roye, De Neuville, De Beaumont,
Barons, Knights, Herald, Attendants on Herald, Trumpeters, Banner
Bearers, Citizen of Angiers, Citizen Soldiers, &c.,
by Auxiliaries.

AUSTRIANS.

Leopold VII., Archduke of Austria. surnamed Lymoges .. Mr. S. Pearson
Austrian Knights and Standard Bearer of Austria, by Auxiliaries.

PRIESTS.

Cardinal Pandulph, Legate of the Pope .. .. Mr. Bass

Notarius Apostolicus, Grand Master of the Templars, Archbishop, six Bishops
two Mitred Abbots, Priests, Monks, Knights Templars, Knights
Hospitaller, Temple Banners, Host Banner, Trinity
Banner, Italian Gentleman Attendant on
Cardinal, &c., by Auxiliaries.

LADIES.

Elinor, the widow of King Henry II, and Mother of King John..Mrs. Abbott
CONSTANCE, Mother to Arthur .. .. **MRS. CHARLES KEAN**
Blanch, Daughter to Alphonso, King of Castile, and niece
    to King John.. .. .. Miss Kate Horn
Lady Faulconbridge, Mother to the Bastard and Robert
    Faulconbridge .. .. Miss Gordon
Attendant Ladies .. .. Mesdames Burrows, Milot, Misses Hall and Haydon

SCENE—sometimes in England, and sometimes in France.